KISSED
BY THE
ANGELS

ABOUT

Sophie Martin-Ca
Birmingham, England
her time between Ne
with her husband Ma
Na-Eireann Canning,

Sophie has travelled extensively, visiting – to date – 96
of the world's countries; travelling some of the remotest
regions of Asia, Africa, South America and Europe.

Sophie has contributed to a variety of British, American
and Australian magazines and travel guides. She studied
Irish History and Sports Science at and in association with
New York University and the University of New South
Wales, Sydney, Australia and has studied various academic
and craft-based courses at eminent educational facilities
worldwide: from Meditation in Nepal, to Thai Massage
and Buddhist philosophy in Thailand to Ceramic Art in
Zimbabwe and Costume Design in New York City.

Kissed By The Angels is her first novel.

SOPHIE MARTIN-CANNING

KISSED
BY THE
ANGELS

**TRANSCENDENCE
BOOKS**

A Transcendence Books Paperback
KISSED BY THE ANGELS

First published in 2002 by Transcendence Books,
244 Fifth Avenue, Suite A230, New York, New York 10001, USA

This edition published by Transcendence Books 2005.
Special overseas edition 2005.

www.transcendencebooks.com

9 8 7 6 5 4 3 2

Copyright © Sophie Martin-Canning 2002

ISBN: 0 9542676 0 5

**The author and publisher are grateful to the following corporations for the kind
permission to reproduce extracts from the following lyrics:**
Warner Chappell, IMP LTD, Griffin House, 161 Hammersmith Road, London,
W6 8BS. For – Moondance. Viva Espana. Holiday.
Carlin Music, Iron Bridge House, 3 Bridge Approach, Chalk Farm, London, NW1
8BD. For – Green Door. Be My Baby.
Music Sales, 89 Frith Street, London, W1D 3JB. For – Please Release Me (for
Acuff-Rose). She Was Just Seventeen (for Sony). Everybody's Free (for Peer
Music). Like A Virgin (for Sony). Bloody Sunday.
MCPS (Celtic Songs), Elgar House, 41 Stretham High Road, London, SW16 1ER.
For – Fields Of Athenry.
Carlin Music (address as before) & EMI, 127 Charing Cross Road, London,
WC2H 0QY. For – When Irish Eyes Are Smiling.
Warner Chappell & EMI & Music Sales (all addresses as before). For –
Back To Life.

While every effort has been made to contact copyright holders,
if an acknowledgement has been overlooked, please contact the publisher

Printed and bound in Great Britain by
Caric Press, Rickits Green, Lionheart Close,
Bearwood, Bournemouth, Dorset, BH11 9UB.

acknowledgements

To my sublime husband, Martin Canning, thank you for all your help, support, patience and infectious enthusiasm throughout the process of this book and in our lives in general. Thank you for having the unfailing ability of making me happy all day - every day. Thank you Marty, for simply being - you.

To my parents, Carmel and Paddy Martin - what can I say? I owe you both a greater debt than I could possibly express here. Thank you for instilling in me the desire to chase my dreams. Thank you for believing in me. Thank you for guiding me so precisely and lovingly on every step along the path of life. Thank you for laying solid foundations for my life to be built upon. Thank you for being the finest mom and dad anyone could wish to have.

Thank you Dean and Bomber Martin for being big brothers every little girl should have. Thank you not just for being extraordinary brothers but for being my cherished friends, too... I think that says it all!

When I was near to completing Kissed By The Angels and my frustrations were running high and inspirations low I felt guilty doing anything other than working on the novel - that was until my niece, Ava Martin came into the world on 21st August 2000. In Ava's presence she immediately had the ability to make me forget about everything except her. Thank you, Ava for making me smile when I think of your name, for all your kisses and for having that wonderful talent of chilling-me-out!

Thank you Ronnie Gibbons for so many things, but especially for teaching me: 'Wisest is she who knows what she does not know.' Wherever you are, I hope you know we all love and miss you. Ronnie, may God bless you and keep you safe.

Thank you Peter Nolan for being a truly wonderful friend. Thank you for being on the end of the phone at the ready with helpful advice or invaluable inspiration while the majority of the world slept. Thank you for all your help and encouragement in the process of getting this book into print. I look forward to a lifetime of friendship.

Sue and Tom McGhee, I am indebted to you both. Thank you for creating the most exquisite book cover imaginable. Thank you for all your professional wisdom, especially your 'Stay true to your art' advice. Thanks for being great friends.

Thank you Tim Ledgard for your proofreading and editing expertise.

Thank you Bryce Courtenay, who without knowing planted the first seed of the desire to write a novel, which grew into Kissed By The Angels.

This book is dedicated to my divinely beautiful husband, Martin Canning – you are my angel, my love, my life – we are and always will be... one.

And

To all the victims who lost their lives in the terrorist attacks on September 11th 2001. May you all be at peace flying through the paradise skies – with the angels.

The fear of the Lord is the beginning of knowledge:
But fools despise wisdom and instruction.
Proverbs (1:7).

kissed
by the
angels

every few decades a book is
published that changes the lives of
its readers forever.
kissed by the angels is such a book —
a magical story about learning to
listen to your heart, read the omens
strewn along life's path and, above
all, follow your dreams ...

kissed
by the
angels

BOOK ONE

INTRODUCTION

"Oh, it's here, I'm off to sunny Spain, y viiiii-va Espan-yaaa. Ohhh, I'm a takin' the Costa Brava plane, y viiii-va Espan-yaaaa."

Amid the scratched stainless steel, under the surgical spotlights, Daddy's beautiful blue eyes sparkled, like the hot midday sun glistening over a turquoise tropical sea which stretches its aquatic fingers to caress the shore with hypnotic, carefree rhythm, as he tickled my toes to the rhythm of his embarrassing ditty. It certainly wasn't a harmonious performance of vocal talent; rather, it was comparable to a severe case of tinnitus, where the ringing in one's inner ear won't stop. Absolutely nothing can terminate the constant resounding annoyance. Although that *was* Dad's motive for acquiring a Latino accent and honouring us with his Costa Brava rendition - to deflect my attention from the pain of the treatment which the doctor was about to commence.

I endeavoured without speech and with limited movement to remove him from sunny Spain and shut him up - but nothing seemed to work; his midday sun never set, and his dancing eyes reflected his love affair with life as he continued his song.

1

I closed my eyes, trying to convince myself I really wasn't there in a hospital theatre with Dad crushing my adolescent notion of my cool street credibility (because of course the doctor cared about such things), but the darkness my eyelids provided only gave life to the image of the nurse brandishing a lace fan, my Dad maracas, and the doctor trading his laser for a guitar, as they all danced the fandango.

The embarrassment Dad's singing produced eventually ceased and my body adapted to the tickling sensation in my feet as the invasion of burning hair into my sinuses struck the first chord in the melody of pain. The second, third and fourth chords soon followed, the pitch of agony falling and rising in perfect melodic contours, covering every note on the instrument of discomfort. The pain was akin to a sharp knife stabbing and a stainless-steel kettle, full of boiling water, hitting the area simultaneously. The pain didn't merely hit the affected area of my face; it travelled through each nerve and muscle, like an electric current through a circuit of multi-coloured wires, causing my hands to form a fist and my fingernails to dig deep into my palms, compelling my knuckles to turn the shade of a virgin bride's dress. My pelvis sporadically twitched as I clenched my buttocks together and pointed my toes as taut and straight as a prima ballerina preparing for a perfect pirouette.

Unfortunately there was no refined performance of *Swan Lake*, only a duckling enduring the pain in what could have been an emergency-room television drama - lying on the crisp white sheets, atop the aluminium-framed bed, with the white-clad doctor to my right, the wry-smiling, chubby nurse stroking my bare arm to my left, and my devoted father at my feet. His song would now sound euphonious - if only I could hear it. It was now merely a faraway echo in the valley of my mind.

The pain continued its expedition of agony. As it disembarked at my brain, an invading voice in one of

2

those faraway valleys of my mind squealed, "It's insane to put yourself through this. Why are you going through this torture?"

From some distant place in the darkest depths of my brain the answer to this question astoundingly appeared, like a jumping jack springing out of an ornately painted box.

There was no other voice, only realisation that there was most certainly a reason why I lay on this hospital bed with a laser burning my lower cheek - why I tolerated this pain.

'If I endure this,' I thought, as I gritted my teeth and held my breath, 'if I go through this pain, then maybe, just maybe Emmet O'Malley would consider looking at me.'

It wasn't the only reason, but this mantra built a strong pain barrier, making the treatment somewhat bearable. Dad's voice became perceptible once again. It appeared he had departed sunny Spain and had made his way to his homeland.

"When Irish eyes are smi-lllling, sure 'tis like the morn in Spring. In the lilt of Irish laughter you can hear the angels sing. When Irish hearts are hap-py, all the world seems bright and gay. And when Irrrrr-ish eyes are smiling, sure, they steal your heart away."

Attempting to shut him up, I caught his very own smiling Irish eyes, although they were not focused on me. They were looking into the distance, absorbed in some magnificence only he had the pleasure of witnessing.

For all Dad's witticisms and perpetual smiles, he would never directly look at the actual process of my treatment. I suspected he felt my pain himself, although he would never admit to that. That's why Mammy invariably sat alone outside the operating theatre. She would be in more of a nervous state than myself.

"I can feel every pulse, every flash of that laser. It makes me feel sick and faint. It hurts me more than it does you," she insisted, in her soft-spoken Irish accent. I could never comprehend that intuitive sense a mother has when I was younger.

Mammy was astounding though; she investigated the most recent and advanced medical treatments available world-wide, sending out her research letters as haphazardly as cross-pollination seeds in a gale - being prepared to harvest her crops wherever they grew in abundance.

Mam often appealed for help on the road to discovering the perfect treatment, although not from the medical world. Every Tuesday she would go to the grand gothic church, with its gigantic stained-glass windows. The natural sunlight shining through would cast a heaven-like splendour on the white-washed stone statues of the saints and the tilted beatific face of Our Lady. The rays of light were like the fingers of God touching His servants, adding a glow of devout appreciation. The spectacular ornate figure of Jesus suffering on His cross was suspended from the oak beam rafters, reminding each and every parishioner He died for their salvation.

Mammy would light a candle then kneel on the red leather-covered mat. Bowing her head, hands clasped tightly together, she mumbled the prayer to Saint Martha.

"Oh Saint Martha, I resort to thee and to thy petition and faith, I offer up to thee this light which I shall burn every Tuesday for nine Tuesdays. Comfort me in all my difficulties through the great favour thou didst enjoy when our Saviour lodged in thy house. I beseech thee to have definite pity in regard to the favour I ask." In silent prayer she begged for her favour. "Intercede for my family that we may always be provided for in all our necessities. I ask thee, Saint Martha, to overcome the dragon which thou did cast at thy feet." Hail Mary's and an Our Father ensued.

After nine consecutive weeks all the smoke from each of her scented candles would have risen into heaven, transporting her prayer via Miraculous Martha to the Almighty Lord, who would then in His Elysian kingdom contemplate the granting of her entreaty. She had done this regularly for as long as I could remember. When I was much younger I found the whole procedure terribly confusing.

4

"What do you pray for on your Novena, Mammy?" I would ask.

"To see light at the end of the tunnel, darling," was always her reply. I always imagined this dark, winding, concrete tunnel with a frosted ray of sunlight peeping through in the distance. At four years of age I thought praying for light in a dark tunnel a complete waste of time. The lighting of the candle was the most exciting feat for me. I was mesmerised by the orange flame which ecstatically leapt and cavorted in the consecrated breeze, causing the candle to weep with enchanted joy.

I only realised as I got older that she was praying for me. I was the dragon cast at her feet, and the light in her tunnel would be a significant noticeable result: a token reward for all the pain I went through.

What I've learnt over the years is that we all experience pain at some point in our lives: psychological or physical torture. We all have grievances in ourselves - misconceived or not. Whether it be unwanted freckles or moles. Maybe you think your bum is too big. It could be an uninvited beer belly making an appearance in the unforgiving mirror. Maybe you think you're too thin. Or your hair is too ginger, or even too grey. Or simply not there at all. Possibly you consider your boobs to be small or your thighs too fat, or even your nose too big. There could be family problems. Religious problems. Racial problems. Something - however big or small - tortures us all. The list of these gripes is as endless as tomorrows and yesterdays.

The grievance which caused the majority of *my* pain was the port-wine-coloured birthmark on my right cheek, chin and neck. Pain to remove it - pain to keep it.

It was on my first school day that I first experienced any pain or confusion regarding my facial markings. It was on that particular day I realised my birthmark *was* somewhat out of the ordinary.

It is on my first day at school that I will begin my whole extraordinary tale. The day I was to realise I wasn't just

5

different because I had a mark on my face, but different in an altogether special and unique way...

The truth is, I have a story to tell that is so unbelievable it almost sounds preposterous. Before you start, I can only reassure you - every word is true...

CHAPTER ONE

I was so excited at the idea of starting school. My brothers, Dominic and Patrick, had been going for as long as I could remember. How I envied them going through the cast-iron gates, in their green and gold uniforms. They looked so smart entering a world unknown to myself - but much sought after.

Mammy and I returned to school each lunch-time for the boys. Dominic usually appeared in the same state as he'd entered. Every chestnut hair perfectly in place, uniform unruffled and knees clean. But, Patrick, well - socks were crumpled at his ankles, the tie knot virtually at the back of his neck, shirt un-tucked, jumper slovenly tied around his waist, cap balancing on the side of his head with blond curls cascading around his cheeky, mischievously-masculine Shirley Temple-looking face. Each day I pondered long and hard over his appearance, wondering which kind of lessons got him into this dishevelled condition. It was all too exciting, I can tell you.

My day soon arrived to find out exactly what happened behind those gates. I didn't know what to do first on preparing my things. I had checked my Mickey Mouse pencil case a hundred and one times. I packed and unpacked my new white plimsolls, smelling their fresh rubber soles in the process. I kept looking at my green and gold uniform dangling like a deflated, abandoned rag doll, which Mammy had hung on the wardrobe door - name labels were neatly stitched on each garment - wishing the day would be over so I could wake up and go to school, just like my brothers.

Nothing of significant intrigue had really occurred in my young life so far, so school was top of the priority list. There was the weekly dig to Australia in Grandma Maggie's back-garden - to no triumphant avail. Walking down the upward-bound escalator in *Marks and Spencer* had caused quite a rousing to-do. I had sat and sulked as I watched the red imprint of Mammy's slender hand on my calf slowly disappear. Oh, and being kidnapped by gypsies in Ireland - now that was thoroughly exhilarating. Although I suppose it wasn't really kidnapping, more like me toddling off of my own free will. Away I went from my brothers chasing a baby bull around in circles. Down past my grandpa's dilapidated barn which smelt of manure and soggy, urine-drenched straw. Past Paddle, the one-legged duck - who had endured quite enough of my taunts - across to the sweet aroma of cooking food sizzling over the enchanting camp fires, where the gypsies had settled themselves quite nicely on Grandpa's land, with their brightly painted carts and penny good-luck trinkets.

After searching every nook, cranny and hay bale around for me, Dad resorted to climbing on the thatched roof of the old grey-stoned farmhouse. Shading his eyes from the afternoon sun, which was brighter than a mountain of mustard grass, he looked into yonder. Over the peat bogs, the grazing cattle, through the shadows cast by the ancient Celtic crosses which marked the resting place of my ancestors, past Paddle, the one-legged duck, and over into the gypsy field. All he could see were women with black hair trailing down to the tops of their legs and men with cabbage-shaped heads and unruly black curls springing out from under what could have been cabbage leaves. Amongst all the mayhem and black hair, there I was. My blonde curls stood out like a solitary diamond amid coal as

I ate a bowl of coddle and happily chatted away to a gypsy lady with golden earrings larger than a hula hoop and a paisley-patterned head-scarf that flapped away in the summer breeze.

Dad said they'd been worried sick, had been looking for me for hours. Mammy was apparently at the end of her nerves.

The excitement came to the same end as Mammy's nerves had, which had successfully been brought back to life by some cowslip tea. The earring-clad gypsy had informed Mam the tea would calm her fraught nerves. "Cowslip blossoms, boilin' war-ta and hon-ey, nerve tonic, me dear, nerve tonic."

The idea of starting school was the stimulation my young brain needed.

"Orlagh, it's only six-thirty. What on earth are ye doing up?" Dad groggily enquired, stretching and yawning in bed.

"I can't be late for school, Dad. I have to be org'nised this mornin'." I stood over their huge bed, caught on a finger of the dawn sunlight which peeped through a small crack in the curtains. I watched as the ray of light illuminated my long golden curls as they bounced up and down like a spiralled spring against my nylon 'I am four' nightdress.

"Yer've three hours 'til yer've to be at school. If ye don't get some more sleep, ye'll not last the day. Ye'll be napping and that'll not please your new teacher, Mrs O'Reilly, now will it? Yer don't want to be in her bad books on your first day now, do ye? Go on with ye now, I've a million and one bricks to lay in a few hours."

I dragged my feet back to my bedroom, first checking if either of the boys were up. Unfortunately they were sound asleep. I thought it best if I tried to sleep. I didn't want to be in trouble on my first day and I certainly didn't want to miss anything. I soon went into a deep sleep, dreaming of being Mrs O'Reilly's star pupil and making Mammy and Daddy so proud.

"Orlagh, come on now, darling. It's eight o'clock, time for school," Mam bellowed, as she opened my curtains to a beautiful warm September day. I could never understand why she had to shout to wake me. I was, after all, only in the bed next to where she was standing. It was as though she was shouting through a loudhailer, like a lifeguard calling reckless swimmers into land from the wild perilous waves of the ocean. It was no longer safe swimming in *my* land of dreams - the red danger flag was up. Imminently the caterwauling waves from Mammy's tongue were to be washing into the shores of my warm bed. Dad was my preferred waker-upper. He would be quietly spoken and everything would be calm, like the dawn silence. I wasn't usually one of those children who woke at the crack of dawn; I loved my bed. This morning was an exception; I didn't have to be told twice. No waves were going to trickle past my valance. Today I didn't even mind Mammy brushing my hair in the heavy-handed way that she did. Everything had to be just perfect.

Mealtimes were always such fun in our house and breakfast was no exception. Mam ceaselessly waited on us all hand and foot. She never seemed to sit down and eat. She was forever running, like a diner waitress, but without payment or tips, unless Dad proclaimed:

"Yer've worked hard today, Grania, so yer have, and I've got a little tip for yer."

"And what'll that be, Rory, love?"

"Don't get bettin' on them horses." He loved his joke, however many times he told it.

Dad always played some kind of game to occupy us as we waited for our meal. Spin The Spoon was a favourite. We all started with ten points. Dad or Dominic would spin the spoon and if the rounded end pointed at you, you lost a point. Whoever lost their points first - lost the game, and subsequently had to do a forfeit. Strangely, the majority of times it landed on me. I'm sure they had it fixed. I was endlessly doing forfeits. But today I won spin the spoon, which I considered a perfect start to this momentous day!

Dad went off to work first and gave me the usual million sloppy kisses before he left. He cupped my head into his huge hands, "mwar, mwar, mwar," he sounded, as his spittle transferred from his soft moist lips to my dry skin. "Mwar, mwar," over my eyelids. "Mwar, mwar," over my forehead. I burrowed my chin into my chest to evade any more loving torture. Undeterred, he placed tiny crystals of salivation on to my curls. Mam reckons I was the most kissed child ever.

The three of us got so much pleasure in seeing Dad drive away in Betsy, his old navy-blue van. It was like chitty-chitty-bang-bang! It made the strangest noises; coughing, spitting and farting, like a toothless old man in a fusty, urine-smelling chair. As he started the engine, a huge grey cloud of smoke appeared from the exhaust. We all disappeared momentarily, until the cloud evaporated into the atmosphere to add just a little more pollution to the air over the industrial city of Birmingham.

"Come on, you three rascals. You'll be filthy standing in those exhaust fumes, so ye will. What've I told you before? You'll get headaches and be sick. Don't come crying to me when you do. I don't know why yer father doesn't replace that old thing with something half-decent. Get ready now, we'll be leaving in five minutes."

Mammy went through the everyday locking-up routine, like a prison warden, checking and re-checking that all doors which should be locked, were. I was waiting with impatience, while the boys ran riot in the front garden.

We finally departed and made our way up the long what was once black, but now faded to grey, asphalt school driveway. It seemed to take an eternity, with Mammy and the boys telling me what I should and shouldn't do. I was too busy concentrating on not stepping on any cracks which crossed the tarmacked surface - I couldn't risk bad luck today.

We eventually arrived in the playground. The boys continued to their classes as I had watched them do a thousand times before. Today I had a different feeling as they waved goodbye. I was so excited because I would know what kind of things they got up to when they left me. As Mammy and I waited in the playground for the new entrants to be sorted into their specific classes I really couldn't believe what I was observing. There wasn't a group of excited new pupils as I had expected. No, all I saw were crying children. Girls crying I could understand. But the strangest sight of all were the boys - *crying*! How silly. I had never witnessed such a scene before. Boys didn't cry. Well, Dominic and Patrick certainly didn't. This was such a fantastic adventure - why on earth were any of them upset, boy or girl?

"This must be Orlagh Emmet. What a perfect name for a lovely and I must say brave little girl. My, you've grown an awful lot since Patrick left my class. It must be those extra inches which've made you so brave. " Mrs O'Reilly beamed. She seemed to smile with every feature on her wonderful, kind face. Through her inviting, rosy cheeks and with the same huge, happy, ocean-blue eyes Dad had. Not the tropical shore-line, ocean-blue, which crashes to the golden sand with carefree rhythm, but the colour of the deepest ocean only Captain Nemo could explore. I was a little unsure of the dress she was wearing. It was like my granny's curtains, with great swirling patterns meandering over her huge contours. I figured it must be hard to find clothes so big, as Mammy wore normal-looking clothes and she was always complaining nothing ever fitted her tiny figure.

The first sentence she had spoken to me, on the most important day of my life so far, totally confused me. I didn't know why I was brave. I had only got dressed, eaten breakfast, won spin the spoon and walked to school. I didn't see any bravery in that. Maybe there was a surprise in store for me. I figured all these children who were crying must have had it before I'd arrived.

I watched Mammy's unusually sad face as she waved goodbye. She must have had something in her eye, because she continually rubbed it with her knuckle, which made it quite red. I was quite glad she was leaving. I wanted to get on with this business of school.

We arrived in the classroom to find desks had been allocated boy-girl-boy, which produced more banshee wails and crocodile tears from the girls. Boys were fun to be with; I just couldn't see what the problem was. This day was getting more and more confusing as it continued and we hadn't even started any type of lesson.

As I was the only dry-eyed pupil in the class, Mrs O'Reilly chose me to dispense the new exercise books. They were the colour of a stormy sky, just like the classroom storm they would inevitably provoke.

Mammy had sat with me every day while the boys were at school, teaching me the alphabet and counting with a brightly coloured abacus. I soon caught on that when I showed Dad when he returned from work what I had learned that day, he would say I was the cleverest girl in the world and reward me with ten (or if I was really clever) even twenty pence. Thus, I was a diligent student with Mam so I could reap the benefits upon Dad's return.

It was now time to make use of all what I had learned with Mammy. I took it upon myself to fill in my name, which I was so very proud of. Dad always said not many little girls are named after golden princesses, which there wasn't - I was the only Orlagh I knew. I wrote my name quickly, I'd been doing it so long I didn't really have to think about it. I then set to daydreaming of the day when I could make the 'O' less of an egg shape, so it would appear like a perfectly round circle, where the beginning and end would meet without an overlap. After I'd mastered that, maybe I would be able to join it all up together in the beautiful way Dominic did. Mrs O'Reilly then interrupted my daydream:

"Come on now, everyone." Mrs O'Reilly clapped her

hands. "I want you all to line up at my desk with your new exercise books and I'll write your names on them, so then you can copy as best you can." When I heard this I thought I was to repeat the *Marks and Spencer* escalator 'to-do' and end up with an imprinted hand on the back of my calf.

As each child returned to their desk after Mrs O'Reilly wrote name after name on the new books and, as my turn got ever nearer, my nervousness increased. The adrenaline pumped through my veins, like a boxer about to enter the ring. I'd heard terrifying stories from Patrick about what teachers did if you misbehaved. Now I was really in for it, and on my very first morning too.

My hands were shaking as I handed over my filled-in book. My eyes were fixed on the scratched parquet flooring. On the verge of an explanation I raised my eyes to see Mrs O'Reilly's rubicund face was full of smiles. Relief swept through me - I wasn't in trouble.

"My goodness, class, we have a genius among us! Orlagh Emmet has already learnt how to write her name. She will be our first gold-star pupil. The pupil with the most gold stars by half term wins a prize."

This was incredible, I thought; I get rewarded for my knowledge from Dad, and if I keep pleasing Mrs O'Reilly I'll gain lots of these marvellous gold stars and win a mysterious prize at the end of term. I had come to the conclusion that being clever was the only way to go. I decided from then on to be extra attentive.

Then, unfortunately things got confusing again. A Scrabble hand of wonderful vowels and common consonants had been replaced by: Y, K, X, W, V and Z. A corpulent boy raised his hand.

"Yes, Robert, what would you like to know?" Mrs O'Reilly sounded a little shocked at the awakening of her class. Robert's eyes were virtually non-existent from the excess flesh of his cheeks pushing them closed, along with the long black fringe which touched his eyelashes. If he had been wearing a black-and-red-striped woollen jumper you would have thought he had jumped out of the pages of The Beano. A high-pitched squeak was uttered from a tiny hole lost in the same fat which hid his eyes.

"Do all clever people have horrible, red faces?"

Now I thought this was like one of Dad's mind-teasers he used to ask us to fathom out - I never did, it was always Dom or Patrick who got them, well usually Dom; Patrick's mind wandered along with his feet outside to the football.

Do all clever people have horrible, red faces? Well, Mrs O'Reilly had sort of a red face; it was blotchy with her pale snow-white complexion peeping through, but it wasn't horrible. My grandpa almost always had a red face, but Dad said this had something to do with the beautiful-shaped bottle full of a brown liquid he kept by the side of his armchair at all times. I knew Grandpa was clever, but his face wasn't horrible either.

"Now what do you mean by that, Robert?"

Oh great, I thought, Mrs O'Reilly doesn't have a clue either. Robert's chubby face lit up with delight as he realised he had baffled the teacher.

"Well," he replied. "You have a red face, all your cheeks are red and my mom said you're very clever and I must listen to you. And Orlagh, the girl you said was a genius, well, she has a horrible red cheek and chin and even her neck is red and really horrible - so she must be *really* clever." The tiny hole which released this high-pitched squeak closed and turned into a derisive smirk as he affirmatively nodded his head.

Orlagh, oh, wow... he was referring to me! I didn't think I had any part in this conundrum. Why did he think my face was horrible? Sure, I had a red cheek, chin and neck but I didn't think it was anything out of the ordinary. I began to get lost in a grey, winding maze of avenues in my own mind.

Today, my first day at school I was to learn that my birthmark *was* somewhat 'out of the ordinary', that I was different from the rest of the children in my class - in my school. Not one other child had what I had. I was the solitary black child in a bigoted southern state school. I was the leopard with no spots, or in my case, too many.

Mrs O'Reilly's already blotchy red face went redder, spreading down her neck like a contagious rash, to her gigantic cleavage which was being held in by my granny's curtains.

"Well, Robert, I'm glad to see you've been observant." His back straightened, his lips pursed together and his chin rose a notch or two at the praise he received. "But in my class we're all very compassionate to our fellow students and your first lesson will be that you must hold your tongue when you have such a serious and degrading comment to make. You'll apologise to Orlagh and myself immediately."

Robert once again sunk into his hunchbacked position and the formation of his three chins reappeared and wobbled like a jelly on a tea-party table as he shook with obvious anger and snarled, "Ssss-orr-rry."

The sound of the great brass bell, which indicated playtime, came as a great shock. It felt as though Mammy had only just left. With the confrontation between Robert Reeves and Mrs O'Reilly time had just flown by. Now it was playtime. Time to make new friends. Or so I thought.

In the playground I seemed to be the centre of almost everyone's attention. Mrs O'Reilly had brought about too much attention to myself, telling them I was a genius. They had taken the literal sense of the phrase and wanted all their hurtful, discomforting questions answered. 'Did the doctor make you bleed when you were born and couldn't stop it?' 'Did your mom spill beetroot juice on your face and couldn't get it off?' 'Did you smudge your jam sandwich and not have a wash?' 'Jam roly-poly.' 'Err, can you catch it?'.'Red-face.' 'Strawberry-face.' Juvenile jeers, accompanied with two-front-toothless sniggers. My perfect day was being spoilt by questions I couldn't answer. I was walking deeper and deeper into the maze in my mind, turning left and right, meeting incessant dead-ends, spinning around in circles. I wondered if I would ever find the right path and view the frosted ray of sunlight I imagined Mammy prayed for at the end of the concrete tunnel.

No attention had ever been paid to my birthmark before, only when I went into hospital for treatment. And then I was getting so much fuss I didn't really take any notice of the significance of what the whole procedure was about. It wasn't about removing the red mark on my face, but receiving sweeties like red, sugary cola cubes, multi-coloured jelly babies or soft melt-in-your-mouth flumps. Having a giant bottle of Lucozade was a bonus. Drinking it was okay, especially because it turned the inside of your mouth the colour of rust. But the orange cellophane paper which wrapped the bottle was the most significant asset. It kept me occupied for hours as I placed it over my eyes and turned everything in sight orange. My treatment meant acquiring new colouring books and maybe a doll. Not that I received too many dolls, having made it quite clear I didn't want them. Dollies were for sissy girls. Secretly, I did like them, but Dominic and Patrick had put this idea into my head so, if they thought that, then I had to also. I considered my treatment to be just a big adventure as we travelled all over the country and met many doctors and nurses who always seemed to look at me with their heads tilted sideways. The nurses always gave me nurses' paper hats and plastic aprons so I too could be a nurse when we returned home.

After playtime it was back to a short lesson and the bell sounded once again. We all said in unison, "Good evening, Mrs O'Reilly," as we pushed our tiny plastic chairs under our new desks. Robert Reeves, the boy who had prompted the entrance to my grey winding maze, elbowed me and squeaked with his almost non-existent mouth.

"You've had it tomorrow, Ribena-face."

Those were the final words of my first day of school.

17

I dragged my feet to meet Mammy, who waited excitedly at the school gates. She bombarded me with questions: "What did you learn? Who did you sit next to? Is Mrs O'Reilly nice?"

"Mammy, I can only answer one at a time," I replied sarcastically, repeating what she said to us if we blitzed her with too many questions at once. She smirked and told me to answer one at a time. I told her how Mrs O'Reilly thought I was so intelligent and about my gold star, but I didn't recount the incident with Robert Reeves. I thought she might be angry with me for causing so much trouble on my first day. I was subdued about the whole school subject.

I was a little bewildered with Rubbery Robert's (as I had since decided to name him) *'You've had it'* comment. When Mam or Dad said that it usually meant I was in big trouble. But what had I done to him? This preoccupied my mind for the rest of the day. I had to work out a solution to the 'You've had it' dilemma, draw up a map and make a trouble-free exit.

The appearance of Dominic and Patrick an hour later took my mind off my new-found predicament and playtime took over. It wasn't too much longer before Dad returned home from work in Betsy. As he emerged from the driving seat, he ran over to where we were playing on the front lawn and swept me up into his arms. His scent was a combination of sweat and dust, forming his distinctive bitter-sweet smell which he always possessed after a hard-working day. I watched the grass spin and my golden curls fly as he spun me around like I was a sharp blade on a roaring helicopter, making me so dizzy that when he put me down I staggered like a drunk departing a pub.

"How was me favourite girl's first day at school?"

"Okay," I replied, uninterested in my long-awaited independent inauguration into the real world. My usual garrulous manner was absent.

18

I could sense Dad's disappointment at my uninspired demeanour. The same barrage of questions I had received from Mammy followed from Dad, with the added, "Did someone upset you, baby doll?"

How is it that parents know everything? I didn't give any clue that Rubbery Robert had been nasty, so how did he find out? Maybe he'd met Mrs O'Reilly on the way home - but no, she didn't hear him say, 'You've had it'. My most perfect day had turned into a complete disaster, and the excitement of my second day of school was diminishing with the thought of more nasty comments and further confounding questions.

I won spin the spoon again at dinner, so the sun was peeping from behind the grey clouds. Twice in one day - an absolute miracle.

The boys and Dad proceeded to the boxing gym, another adventure I longed to experience. But tonight I was happy watching *Charlie Chan*, my absolute favourite programme. Charlie Chan himself never ceased to mystify me, with his number one son and number two son. I couldn't come to terms with why Mr Chan didn't give his children proper names. When it was over, rather than emulating Charlie Chan and pretend to type up case reports on my plastic *Petite* typewriter as I usually would, I was back to pondering over my school predicament. What was so wrong with me? Was this mark on my face some kind of nasty peculiarity which only naughty children possessed?

The boys and Dad returned, smelling of perspiration and the inside of sweat-filled leather boxing gloves. We had our supper snack and were all sent upstairs to wash the milk moustaches from our faces and to brush our teeth. The boys were consistently teasing me about my new status as a school child. I was usually pretty tolerant of their taunting, but tonight I found it annoying due to the Rubbery Robert situation. I made my way back downstairs to complain to Mam and Dad of the boys' jeers. On reaching the bottom step I could hear my parents whispering. The hushed tones immediately caught my attention. I tiptoed to the kitchen door which was ajar and held my breath so I could hear better and so they couldn't hear me.

"There's definitely something wrong with her," Mammy said. I detected agitation in her soft Irish accent.

"Ach no, it's her first day o' school for goodness sake. She'll be fine tomorrow," Dad replied, in his idiosyncratic, carefree manner.

"No, Rory, there's definitely something up. This morning when I took her she was as happy as Larry, the only child in the whole of the starting class not crying. She was even comforting some of the other children. I know it's all a little bewildering for her, the first day and all, but she hasn't uttered a word all night. She's pondering over something, I know it. She didn't even tell me the whole plot of *Charlie Chan* or ask me the million questions of what she didn't understand. Or type up her reports which I always have to look over as though I'm the number one son. No, no - there's definitely something up. Do you think someone has commented on her birthmark, Rory?"

I felt like running in and telling them the whole story - but no, I couldn't do that, I would break my cover and then I would be in even more trouble for ear-wigging.

"Maybe so, Grania, I didn't really think of that. Ye don't think that would upset her, do ye?" Dad now sounded a little more concerned. He had called her by her Christian name, so I knew he meant business.

"Oh Rory, when you tuck her in have a word with her, would ye? Find out what's happened and sort it out for her. If it's what we think - tell her *the* story."

"All right sugar, think it done! First, the continued adventures of 'The Friendly Farting Giant', then down to serious business."

Dad was over being anxious, back to love-some nicknames and thinking of his continued tale of our bedtime story hero. This meant a quick exit for me as quietly as possible back up the stairs and into the bathroom to Dom and Pat without so much as a complaint to Mam and Dad about their taunts. I just about made it before Dad began his ascent, clapping his hands and singing his theme tune to 'The Friendly Farting Giant'.

We had a superlative bedtime story serial. It wasn't *Black Beauty, Snow White, The Princess and the Pea* or even *Star Wars* science-fiction for the boys. No. We had this bizarre character from Dad's eccentric imagination, who lived in a land which was two-thirds smaller than what he should have been living in, who went around causing unintentional mass destruction from excess flatulence. I'm sure he enjoyed narrating it as much as we delighted in listening. It was told in Dominic and Patrick's room. I got into bed with Dominic. There was no way Patrick would have his four-year-old sister in bed with him; he was seven, much too cool for that kind of carry-on. But Dominic, who was nine, took me under his wing and my place was set for our hilarious bedtime story.

"Now where were we last, kids?" Dad always started by testing our attentiveness of the previous evening.

All three of us dived to answer first. Patrick was fastest and loudest tonight. "In Canada, he had come down from Toronto to the American border where he had farted and farted and caused a huge canyon in Lake Ontariac and caused a huge waterfall, the most beautiful in the land, called Niagara Falls." He didn't stop for breath for fear Dominic or I might interrupt.

"Correct, Pat, me boy, only it's Lake Ontario not Ontariac. Well, he continued on his journey to find his lost fartin' tribe. First he went back to New York City, his favourite of all cities as the skyscrapers were the perfect size for chairs. The World Trade Centres being his favourite as they are the tallest buildings in the whole wide world, so were the perfect height for Freddie to sit on. He also liked them because they're flat on top, not like that

21

Empire State Buildin' with its spiky top which used to stick in his bum. By the way, before the World Trade Centres were built the Empire State was once the tallest. Anyway, he headed on his journey after his little rest and a bite to eat. Well, in fact it was all the food from every Indian restaurant which covered a whole street on the east side of Manhattan, and we know what Indian food means for Freddie, don't we, kids?"

We all screamed in unison, "FARTING DESTRUCTION!" We obtained so much delight out of uttering the taboo word.

"Keep it quiet up there, you lot, you'll wake the whole neighbourhood," Mammy shouted, with a hint of humour in her voice.

"So he set off after his snack," Dad continued. "A little step took him over the Hudson river to the state of New Jersey, also known as the Garden State. He tried his best not to squash any people. We all know how much he likes people, don't we now? He'd decided to head west over the vast country of the United States of America. How many states are there now, I can't quite remember?" Dad placed his index finger over his lips.

Dominic was usually first to get these tricky questions.

"Fifty, isn't there, Dad? Hawaii was the fiftieth; that's why we have Hawaii Five-0, right?" Dominic answered enthusiastically, as Patrick leapt out of the covers, humming the TV series theme tune and pretending to paddle like the men at the start of the show.

"Sure, Fifty. Enough paddling now, Pat, we're all gettin' soaked here. Well, after all that Indian food Freddie's stomach was already a-rumblin' and when Freddie's tummy rumbles it sounds like an earthquake, so it does. By the time he got to Kansas, the Sunflower State, he was tryin' to hold in his farts but little ones kept escapin' and he caused a wee tornado. Nothing too serious but there were a few barns and ald bikes flyin' around as well as a few balls of tumbleweed."

"Is that what Dorothy out of the Wizard of Oz was caught in, Dad?" I asked, concerned for the star of my favourite movie.

"Yes, it was one and the same, but not a tornado that Freddie had caused. Anyway, he was headin' south, he wanted to get to Mexico for supper. He loved the spicy food they have there. Chilli and jalepeno peppers are his favourites. And what does spicy food mean to Freddie?"

"FARTING DESTRUCTION!" we all screamed. Dad had recaptured our full attention with our participation in the story.

"Freddie had no sooner got into Arizona when he could feel the biggest fart ever comin' on. It felt so big he had to sit down, crushin' hundreds of trees as he did. He couldn't keep it in any longer and heeeeee...................." An elongated 'heee' was our cue for the finest part of the tale.

We shouted using every breath of air from our lungs, along with controlling our laughter. "HE FARTED AND HE FARTED AND HE FARTED AND HE FARTED AND HE FARTED UNTIL...."

Dad concluded the story. "He farted until the biggest, hugest, most mammoth hole in the ground that you've ever seen had formed due to his fart, and it became known as the Grand Canyon. All in the day of Freddie The Friendly Farting Giant."

"More, Dad, more," we all pleaded.

"No, enough, it's time to sleep. Come on, Orlagh, darlin', another big day ahead for you tomorrow, so it is."

Oh no, my thoughts of tomorrow and my most probable confrontation with Rubbery Robert, about this thing that upset him so much on my face, was at the forefront of my mind once again. Dad carried me into my room feet first. My hair dragged along the floor and all the blood rushed to my head.

Dad placed me into my imitation patchwork quilt, which kept me occupied on nights I couldn't sleep. I would endlessly trace my index finger around the lines of the different-patterned hexagonal shapes. Things were getting serious, I could tell by the look on his face. His dazzling blue eyes were not smiling as much as usual. The crow's feet which were beginning to form were not as prominent.

"Mammy said you've been quiet since finishin' your first day of school. What's up, baby doll?"

I contemplated answering this question. All my concern, confusion and upset prompted me to tell him everything. I told him all about Rubbery Robert and my new dilemma of what was wrong with me.

Dad then proceeded with clarification and related the whole extraordinary story. The most important bedtime story I was to hear. On his magical spinning wheel he set the tension and speed, twisted and wound by his imaginary bobbin, to spin the most glorious yarn. A yarn which was to be passed to future generations. A story to be shared around cosy flaring fires as snow falls delicately outside. A bedtime story which was really, *really* true...

"We could never tell ye before, we promised, yer mammy and me. We said we would only tell yer when ye were a big girl. Now I think yer a big girl. After all yer've started school." Dad nodded, confirming to himself now was definitely the right time. "It all happened when ye were a wee baby, only a few hours after ye were born. There yer were lyin' in yer crib next to Mammy who was in bed and I was sittin' in the chair next to her. We had no lights on as ye were havin' yer very first wee sleep. It had been a tirin' day for yer, havin' to be born an' all. What happened next was a miracle. Like when our Lord rose from the dead. A miracle, to be sure. It doesn't happen to many people, not many at all. We had never known anyone it had happened to, we'd just heard the stories. So when a ray of golden light appeared from the ceilin' of the room we both thought we were dreamin' - but it was no dream.

"The ray of golden light was directly above yer crib and

it made yer light up in the dark room. Then out of this same golden light a figure appeared, then another and another until there were five of 'em. They were tiny little perfect people with wings. They were all beautiful with long golden hair and shimmering white dresses and above each of their heads was another circle of light, much brighter than what they had appeared from; they were their halos, of course. When those little rings of light appeared that's when we knew for sure. They all hovered above yer head, then each one kissed yer face and all said together this blessing;

> 'Never have we seen one so fair.
> Who will have bright green eyes and long
>   golden curly hair.
> A smile so bright with teeth so white, and her
>   mind full of facts to share.
> For she's the one.
> The Chosen One.
> Who we put a mark upon, her beautiful skin,
> So each shall know,
> That when she grows; She's one of us -
> A Chosen One'

"They then explained to yer mammy and me that God had chosen you as His special girl. Out of all the millions of little babies born that year you were the most special, and they'd each kissed you to send His powers, so you could teach everyone on earth to be good and clever. And there are other jobs you've to do that we can't know about. And because there're so many millions of people they had to put a little red mark on your face to distinguish you from the rest.

"Then the light got fainter and fainter and God's messengers went back into heaven to help God out with the rest of His important jobs, like lookin' after sick people and watchin' out for the good people in the world, and such like. So that's why yer have this little red mark on yer face and people like Rubbery Robert haven't got a clue. They're what are called the bigots of the world, princess. But names are not going to hurt ye now are they? Because you have to be strong and remember yer're one of the most special and beautiful people in the whole wide world. So tomorrow when Robert is nasty to you, be ready for him. Get the strength of yer angels behind yer and give him that, one-two-bang-bang which I showed yer and he won't be nasty again. Now go to sleep, my wee baby, and don't you worry, the angels are watchin' over you as well as me, yer mammy, Dominic and Patrick."

I had been listening in awe as Dad told this magical story, not about Freddie The Friendly Farting Giant or one of his other wonderful Irish folk tales we loved so much, but about me. The whole truth about me and my fate. There was my light in my metaphorical maze, shimmering as bright as the sun, as dazzling as the angels' halos. The key to my destiny had been revealed. Here I was, four years old, lying wrapped in my patchwork quilt, presuming I knew the meaning to my life. *This* was as I'd totally expected first thing this morning - the most important day of my life so far.

After the customary sloppy kisses Dad left me wholly contented in bed with my recently discovered knowledge that I was a Chosen One. Rubbery Robert had better watch out, for I had the greatest power of all - God's power. I'd been kissed by the angels.

chapter two

I awoke with a wondrous feeling of confidence. I was set to conquer the world or at least for now Saint Columb's Roman Catholic Infants' School!

It was the usual agenda in the Emmet household, except I was feeling considerably happier this morning. Dad winked as I joined them all for breakfast. I sat down in what was actually the worst chair to have in our kitchen, as it meant I had my back to the portable television which sat in the corner of one of the worktops; Dad was to my right, Patrick to my left and Dominic opposite me in the corner, all within perfect viewing range of the television. Mammy didn't have a chair at the table. If she did she probably wouldn't have sat in it anyway; she was always running and stuffing food into her mouth as she went along with her job of feeding us. Dad was always saying she would get indigestion, but that never seemed to stop her. But this morning, even the fact I was once again in the worst position at the table didn't perturb me. Not on this special morning. The first morning of knowing I was a Chosen One.

Dom, Pat and I momentarily disappeared into Betsy's exhaust smog as Dad left for work. The boys then departed to school, shrieking their farewells to Mammy and myself. I watched as they excitedly ran out of our long, cracked, concrete-covered driveway, past the clump of pink, red and yellow rose bushes. The ageing buds were enjoying their final weeks of life before they wilted and decayed into the ground, fertilising the soil for the next generation. My brothers vanished as they went behind the gigantic emerald hedge which surrounded our front garden, then reappeared stopping at the lollipop lady in her luminous coat with a lollipop which stated: 'STOP CHILDREN CROSSING'. She stood in the centre of the road stopping a Hillman Avenger, Morris Minor and a Triumph Spitfire, just like Mammy's, except it was red and hers was blue and the passenger door probably locked - unlike Mam's. I had recently fallen out of Mammy's Spitfire, avoiding major injury, escaping with grazes, bruises, lots of criss-cross plasters, numerous oohhs and aarhhs, and chocolate compensation. The boys skipped and jumped and met with a group of friends on the other side who had a football, which they proceeded to kick up the long driveway to the school ahead. Boys were so cool, I thought.

When Mammy left me at school I saw there were a few not so cool boys in the playground, again, to my astonishment - *crying*. I wondered if Rubbery Robert had been offensive to them too. I would have to sort him out once and for all.

"Good morning, Mrs O'Reilly," the whole class chanted, as we stood behind our miniature desks and chairs, awaiting our signal to be seated.

"Good morning, class. How are we all today, on your second day of school?" Nobody responded, just grunts and sniffles were heard. "Well, today first up we're going to have an assembly, so we won't be sitting down. All line up at the door and we shall walk down to the assembly hall together."

We were ushered to the door, one table at a time. I was the last person on my table and the first person on the next table was Rubbery Robert Reeves. My heart started to thump faster as he stood behind me. The first of many

28

confrontations was set to take place. My mind endeavoured to unravel what I had previously planned for this showdown.

Mrs O'Reilly was busy escorting the rest of the class, so her attention wasn't on us. I could smell Robert's stale, orange-squash breath and see the traces of orange lines transferred either side of his top lip. He was sneering at me, trying his hardest to look contemptuous, but to myself appearing absurd with his two front teeth missing. His eyes appeared totally non-existent today, as he was squinting, which made them entirely disappear into his chubby cheeks; a few black eyelashes made an appearance through the flesh, escaping suffocation.

"I told you yesterday, you've had it, *Ribena-face*, and today you *have*," Rubbery Robert disdainfully stated. I wanted to explain that I was a Chosen One and share my secret. But no, I couldn't do that. My well thought out plan was quickly wasting away as my temper took over. The anger amphetamine had been absorbed by each nerve. Adrenaline rushed around my body. It was obvious to me that words would not control this moron, so I recalled Dad's one-two-bang-bang instruction and put it into action. I clenched my fist and drove it as hard as I could into his stomach, my hand momentarily disappearing into his fat, like a baker kneading dough. There was a sharp intake of breath from Rubbery Robert then a tremendous squeal emerged from the hole lost in his cheeks. He dropped to his knees holding his stomach. In my estimation he was totally exaggerating, as when I had retaliated to my brothers in the same way it didn't affect them at all; or maybe my anger had given me extra strength, or even the enlightenment of my recently discovered divine status. Or had the driving force of my punch been gliding on the wings of an angel? I wasn't sure. But what I was sure of was the fact I was in big trouble with Mrs O'Reilly. Her immense stature wobbled to the location of the incident, where Rubbery Robert was now curled up in a ball on the floor.

"Orlagh Emmet, what have you done?" She grabbed my arm and dragged me into the cloakroom adjacent to the classroom. "You wait here, young lady, while I see to Robert!"

I stood alone amidst the coats and pump bags hanging on allocated Lilliputian coat hooks. Each child's name was written in beautiful neat handwriting in black felt pen on white sticky labels above each hook. I sat on the bench which ran underneath the coats. My head was hung low and my hands gripped the varnished wood as I contemplated how I was going to get out of this one. I had really thought today was going to be the start of something special. As I heard the echoing footsteps of Mrs O'Reilly entering the cloakroom, my grip tightened on the bench. My knuckles turned as white as the milk in the mini-bottles which sat in a green plastic crate beside me. I didn't know whether I would make it to morning break to drink my milk. She towered above me, today in yet another dress of a similar print to yesterday's. My mind momentarily thought the lady who makes my granny's curtains must surely make Mrs O'Reilly's clothes, as this was way too much of a coincidence; two consecutive days and today she's dressed in the parlour curtains. Her huge breasts protruded over her colossal stomach. There just seemed to be never-ending bumps. Her chest vibrated. I was sure her heart was going to explode through her flushed skin. Her chest and face were red and getting redder. Her smiling deep-sea eyes were wide apart, causing wrinkles on her smooth forehead. A trickle of sweat slowly ran down her brow. I followed it with my eyes as it continued down her cheek. It stopped shortly at her jawbone, dripped on to her chest and disappeared into the deepest darkest depths of her cleavage. She took a deep breath. Her diaphragm expanded, enlarging her breasts even more. I was waiting for her to bellow her annoyance at me. I closed my eyes tightly, endeavouring to think of my angels. Where were they? Couldn't they come to help me now? But Mrs

30

O'Reilly merely sighed an exasperated sigh. She seated herself next to me on the miniature bench. Her enormous backside hung over the varnished wood in every direction. She placed a dimpled arm around my shoulders, the excess flesh flapping like wrinkled clothes on a line. A slight aroma of perspiration emanated from her armpits.

"Orlagh, darling, I don't have to ask what all that was about, I was waiting for it to happen. But, I sure didn't think it would happen so soon and I certainly didn't think you would've acted in the way you did. But a secret between you and me, I'm glad you did. It'll stop him in his bullying tracks. You've certainly hurt his pride more than his stomach. But just watch your temper a little more in future. If anyone gives you any problems you come straight to me. Okay, sweetheart?" She tapped the end of my nose with her finger. Her calm manner and her words, spoken in her soft Irish brogue, were a complete shock to me. She wasn't angry, she was pleased with what I'd done - and another secret! This was fantastic, all these grown-ups wanting to share secrets with me. Dom or Pat never shared their secrets with me.

How did she know what had happened? I hadn't said a word to anyone about Rubbery Robert except Dad, and he wasn't here. She sure was clever. She stood up and took my tiny hand in hers and we went back to the classroom where everyone waited in anticipation of our return. Robert had made a miraculous recovery and was standing looking extremely embarrassed at being vanquished by a girl.

My first triumph over a bully was a divine feeling. I went to assembly with my head held high, accompanied by the exhilarating feeling of euphoria, *and*, I was sure a parade of pious beings marched like toy soldiers behind me with arms, legs and wings synchronised. My angels had been there all along - hovering, watching, protecting.

chapter three

As time progressed the puerile jeers, taunts and mockery ceased, or rather I had it under control. With each thoughtless, scornful comment from classmates, there came a thump from me. Mam and Dad were certainly right; it stopped them in their name-calling tracks. Putting them in their place would make me feel a little better, although I did wonder why they were all so callous. I just wanted to be everybody's friend. I didn't want to have to fight, day in, day out, protecting my pride. But as things went - I had to. One by one pretty much everyone had something to say, even the people I thought were my friends. As groups huddled in corners I heard whispers like a snake's hiss: scar-face, red-face, jam roly-poly or phantom of the opera. I heard what I needed to, what I required to sort the good from the bad, the friends from the foes. But after experiencing my one-two-bang-bang combination, taught by Dad, they *wanted* to be my friend. Those were certainly the companions I could do without. I wanted friends who truly liked me for who I was, whatever I looked like, not because I had conquered their contemptuous comments and taught them a lesson they were not going to forget in a hurry.

There was one outstanding exception - Siobhan Connor. Siobhan was my best friend. The best friend anyone could ever have, and what made it even better

32

was that I was her best friend too! Mutual respect, mutual love. We were a team.

Siobhan wasn't present on my first day of school, or even my first term. Her first day was in term two and Mrs O'Reilly chose myself as her guardian. This was a fantastic new job. I showed her all around our classroom, which by term two I was pretty accustomed to. Her drawer was allocated in the same block as mine. Her pump bag hung on the peg next to mine and her name was placed on the morning register, right there - next to mine. Surely it was destiny that we were to be best friends.

Sitting cross-legged on the large green mat placed on the floor for story-telling time, waiting for Mrs O'Reilly to get organised, with my newly-found friend at my side, I began to sing a song, a song I had heard a girl singing in a talent competition on holiday the previous sun-drenched summer in the sea-side town of Weymouth. I thought it was fantastic, especially when Mammy had told me it was a 'tongue twister'. Tongue twister, I loved this phrase more than the song. It was so much fun to say, though the significance of the phrase was senseless to me because, when I sang it, it didn't twist my tongue.

"Suzie, Suzie, sitting in a shoe-shine shop. Suzie, Suzie, sitting in a shoe-shine shop, she shines and sits and sits and shines." Before I could continue, Siobhan interrupted.

"How do you know that song?" she indignantly enquired. I was shocked by her comment, not so much at her abruptness, but because these were the first words she had uttered unprompted.

"Well, I just do," I replied, vaguely.

"Well that's my song. I didn't think anybody else knew it!" Her long dark eyelashes batted up and down as she waited anxiously for the explanation as to where I'd acquired this tongue twister. I suddenly felt guilty. Was it her song I was singing? No, I decided if it was anyone's song it belonged to the girl in Weymouth. I proceeded to justify my claim.

"Well, Siobhan, if you must know, there was this talent show I was watching when I was on holiday in Weymouth last summer and this girl got up and sang it. So there, it's not *your* song at all!"

She jumped from her seated position on the green carpet and shouted excitedly, "It was me! That was me! Honest it was! It was me!"

Now everyone was in on our discussion, even Mrs O'Reilly, who was busily rummaging through her story-books, looking for one we hadn't already heard. She wasn't really one for organisation.

"Slow down, Siobhan, what on earth's wrong with you, young lady?" The look on Mrs O'Reilly's face was that of pity. She was probably thinking I'd given her my one-two-bang-bang combination. But for a change this outburst had nothing at all to do with me.

"It was me, Mrs O'Reilly! Honest it was me! Oh my goodness, it was me!" Now Siobhan had everybody wondering what was her.

"Now, slow down, take a big deep breath and start from the very beginning," Mrs O'Reilly stated, with her hands placed on Siobhan's shoulders, acting as stabilisers. Siobhan was so excited it looked as though she would topple over, like a child learning to ride a bike.

"Well, me and Mommy, oh and Daddy was there then, too - that was before the gambling..."

In this first sentence Siobhan had completely baffled me. How on earth did this have anything to do with *Suzie, Suzie?* By the looks of things she had Mrs O'Reilly in the same mystified state. Her head was cocked to one side, her hand leaned on her chin with the index finger stretched over her lips. She nodded for clarification to continue.

"It was a fantastic holiday, our last one all together. Anyway, Mommy put me forward into this weekly talent contest. I got up and sang *Suzie, Suzie sitting in a shoe shine shop*. Then, just now while we were waiting for you, Mrs O'Reilly, Orlagh starting singing this song. Then she

34

told me where she'd heard it and she said a girl sang it in a talent contest in Weymouth last summer, and that's where we were, Mrs O'Reilly, in Weymouth. It was me, honest. I'm not fibbing."

"Now, don't get too excited," Mrs O'Reilly pronounced. "It may've been someone else Orlagh had heard. That's a very popular song, you know."

"No it isn't, it's my song, Daddy said so. I can tell you the date I was there, that will prove it." I considered Siobhan had come up with a perfect solution to this conundrum.

"Okay, that's a very good idea, but first Orlagh can come and whisper to me when she was there. Do you remember, Orlagh?"

I certainly did remember. At that time only a few dates were prominent in my memory: my birthday, Mammy, Daddy, Dominic and Patrick's birthdays. Oh, and the birth of Jesus, of course. "All I can remember, Mrs O'Reilly, is that we were there when it was Daddy's birthday, and that's August twenty-first." As I whispered in Mrs O'Reilly's ear the sweet smell of her lavender perfume invaded my nostrils.

"All right then, Siobhan, you can tell us now. When was it?" We all waited in excited expectation of the date. I was hoping that it would be the same, then we were obviously destined to be best friends.

"It was when Mommy had her birthday. We had a big party and a huge cake with happy birthday in pink icing on the top."

"Yes, yes, but when is Mommy's birthday?" Mrs O'Reilly interrogated, now intensely involved in our possible previous encounter.

"It's August twenty-first!"

That was that, our companionship was surely fated, and as the days and months and years passed it grew stronger: a fierce relationship that endured through the good times and bad, unhindered through periods and puppy fat, continuous in bad-hair days and boyfriend catastrophes.

From day one we were committed to each other, with love, devotion and support. We were surrogate sisters. Nothing or no one could break that Suzie-Suzie-sisterly-connection - not initially, anyway.

I was much too excited to continue with lessons. I wanted to tell Mam, Dad, Dom and Pat all about my new-found companion. It seemed an eternity until Mr Corrigan performed his daily tintinnabulation. Ding-aling-aling. I ran down the long, faded-to-grey, tarmacked driveway, stopping only at the lollipop lady to look right and left and right and left again. I sprinted into our driveway, past our pillars with the ferocious-looking, concrete moulded lions on top and straight past Mammy who was leaning against one of the pillars where she could observe my every move as I escaped the confines of the classroom.

"Whooooa, slow down. What's the rush today?" Her waist-length brown hair blew in the winter wind. Her arms crossed over her chest, and an amused expression crossed her face. She was so beautiful, with soft and smooth, almost sallow skin. Her big chestnut eyes were, as always, bright.

"Oh, Mammy, I've got so much to tell you. It's so exciting. I've got a new best friend!"

My tale was then totally interrupted as Dominic and Patrick made an equally erratic entrance, with a few of their friends in tow, kicking a football full-force across our large front lawn, which was an adopted soccer pitch for the neighbourhood kids. Mammy always said this was kind of silly when we had the immense school fields directly facing.

"Hey you lot, come in, get changed, eat your dinner, then you can play out for as long as you like."

At dinner there was a chance to continue with my amazing news.

"I have a new best friend!"

"Did you ever have an old best friend?"

"Leave her be, Patrick, let her continue," Mammy declared.

I proceeded to tell them the whole remarkable tale. "It was meant to be. We've been put together in everything: the register, the pump bags, even the morning milk line. Mrs O'Reilly said it was surely fate. I'm not quite sure of the meaning, but it sounds super bazooka to me anyway. It was fate."

Dominic balanced his knife and fork on the side of his dinner plate and placed his elbows on the edge of the table. Hands clasped together in front of him, like a director heading a board-room meeting, he began to speak. I admired my eldest brother so much. He was clever and caring so I listened intently.

"You're together in everything because it's in alphabetical order, Orlagh. She's Connor, you're Emmet. There must be no other name in-between," he stated, with director's practicality. "But it sure is strange that she's the girl who was in Weymouth."

"Yeah, stupid," was Patrick's contribution to the conversation. He was the carefree spirit in our household. Mam said he was just like Dad. Dominic panicked, Patrick didn't. Dominic was sensible, Patrick was far from it. Life was one big game of football in Patrick's eyes, and nothing was going to stop him having fun, especially his five-year-old little sister. He did keep a secret watchful eye over me, when he wasn't teasing me, that is. In fact Dominic teased me too. But when grown-ups were present, Dominic cared - Patrick didn't!

I was a tomboy and until now I had no intimate girlfriends. I was one of the lads, or at least tried to be. I had to show them I was as strong, if not stronger. Just as tough, if not tougher. Life was hard being a girl trying to be a boy. So, when Siobhan arrived, although I still maintained my tomboyish status, it was a breath of freshly-cut-grass summer air. Now I could do girlie things - if the boys were not around, that was. Now I had a confidante, someone I could share the most secret of secrets with. Suzie, Suzie secrets.

CHAPTER FOUR

"If you could choose to be anyone, anyone at all in the whole wide world - a prince or princess, a footballer or pop star, who would you be, and why?" Mrs O'Reilly asked. This was our project on the morning of the day of our first parents' evening. We had a whole hour until lunchtime to decide. Which was an extremely long time for what I at first regarded as such an easy question.

My very first choice was to be Siobhan. She was my best friend and she was clever. She had been to private school before she started Saint Columb's, but had to leave when her dad gambled all the money and even her house away in card games and horse races. Siobhan said she knew nothing about the whole situation until she saw her doll's house and her bed - which wouldn't usually leave her bedroom - being strapped to the roof-rack of the car on their way to her Grandma's house, which was in the next road to my house. She hadn't seen her dad since that day. The final thought was the turning point in my choice. Siobhan didn't have a dad any more and there was no way I was going to be without my dad.

Secondly, I chose to be the eldest sister of my second best friend, Kelly. Her sister, Megan, was thirteen and beautiful. She had blonde, straight hair, which was cut into defined, layered steps which disappeared completely into the nape of her long neck. She called it a wedge, just like the members in her favourite pop group, The Human League. She wore make-up and mini-skirts which showed off her long, thin legs. I was visualising her figure when I thought about her boobs. No, I couldn't be her either; she would have to wear a bra, and that would be much too embarrassing. I soon became agitated.

Cinderella was another option. She went to the ball, wore beautiful clothes, married the prince and lived happily ever after. But she had a wicked stepmother and not a beautiful caring mother like mine, who didn't make me scrub floors. Mammy didn't even make me wash up after dinner, like some of my friends' mams. She did everything! She would say, "It's my job. You'll have plenty of time to do the chores. Go play. Go do your school work." I couldn't do without Mammy.

I went through so many different candidates, but none of them had what I did. I had Mammy and Daddy and, although they teased me at times, even Dominic and Patrick. I also had Siobhan and I would never find a better friend.

I also had so many things to look forward to. Firstly I was going to a hospital in London to have some brand-new treatment done on my birthmark. Dad said we would visit the Queen in Buckingham Palace and see the guards who stand stern-faced and serious, not cracking a smile, however much you try to make them laugh. To the Tower Of London to view the Queen's most exquisite jewellery, and see the men in their red uniforms with fingerprint-free polished brass buttons, who were called Beefeaters. Beefeaters, this was such a peculiar name. I assumed they must eat more beef than normal people. Maybe they ate it every day, not just on Sundays, as we did. Secondly, we were all going to see Dad's brother, Uncle Seamus, and his wife, Auntie Josephine, and my cousins, Carmel and Tommy, who lived in Canada. We were all going to travel together by car to Disneyland and I would see Mickey Mouse, Goofy and Pluto. I was so excited at the thought of the trip that I couldn't contemplate swapping that for anything.

But the most important entity was the presence of my resplendent celestial spirits. Not so many were as fortunate as I, to have been chosen by God to be one of His special girls, and have beautiful angels with luminous halos, delicate, translucent wings and flowing undefiled white dresses eternally watching over them.

I was perfectly happy being myself, so that was my choice and those were all my reasons. Of course I didn't put any details down about my angels; I couldn't let Mrs O'Reilly in on my secret.

I was a little apprehensive as I lined up to hand in my completed answer. Mrs O'Reilly had stated '*who* would you be?' which I think meant I had to choose someone. I really didn't want to be anyone else and I didn't want to tell lies, so I would just have to face the consequences.

Mrs O'Reilly was seated a foot or so behind her huge wooden desk, which was covered in big blobs of spilt blue ink. Her large body filled the chair. The tops of her legs and backside protruded through the gaps beneath the arms and backrest.

"Don't look so worried, Orlagh, darling, there's no right or wrong answer. It's just who you feel you want to be. Not everyone is going to want to be the same person, now are they? If they did, my life would be very easy. I'd be able to deal with all of you in the same way," she confirmed, with one of her famous comforting smiles, which exposed her shining tombstone teeth.

The bell was rung, indicating our release for half an hour of playtime. Upon our return we had the pleasure of one and a half hours of Religious Instruction from the parish priest, Father Maguire.

Siobhan and I headed straight for the hopscotch squares, which were painted in yellow and orange on the grey, tarmacked playground. The game always seemed so easy at the beginning, throwing the smooth, speckled brown stone, which we dug out of the garden area, on to the number one square. I jumped over yellow one, landing with each foot simultaneously on orange numbers two and three. I hopped on my right leg to yellow number four and continued through to number ten. I reversed and repeated the whole procedure until I reached number one once more. Still not stepping on the number one square, I reached down and retrieved the stone for Siobhan's turn. As the game progressed and the numbers increased, it became much more difficult. The stone continually rolled out of the prominent orange and yellow boundaries.

Over the noise of the children playing around us I angrily shouted to Siobhan: "I wish it was as easy gettin' number nine as it was when we had to get number one or number two."

"Yeah, me too."

"But that would make the game pointless, wouldn't it?" a strange voice whispered.

"Who said that?" I looked around for the owner of this mysterious voice.

"Who said what?" Siobhan asked, mystified.

"Ssshhhh, Siobhan can't hear me, let her continue to throw the stone," the mesmerising voice said. There was no one around who the voice could have belonged to, but strangely I wasn't scared. "Just remember," the voice continued, "this hopscotch game is teaching you more than just how to jump over squares to retrieve a stone. This game is comparable to life. At the beginning things seem so easy, so directional, so clear. You see black as black and white as white. Everything has reason and explanation. But as the hands of time glide by with an uncompromising momentum propelling their motion, and life's hurdles are placed in front of you, Orlagh, reasoning and clarifications are fewer. Black is a shade of blue and white is a dull winter-sky shade of grey, and this nonchalant innocence of childhood is yearned for. For this you are still to learn. But don't worry, we're going to guide you through the hopscotch court of life..."

"But who are you?"

"I'm Siobhan, stupid. What're you on about?"

The soft voice stopped as the end-of-playtime bell was rung, leaving me mystified about to whom it belonged and what it was talking about.

chapter five

Father Maguire was a hilarious character. He transfixed you not only with the content of his fascinating, erudite stories, but also with their delivery. Striding around our tiny desks with elongated paces, or striding up and down the grand aisle of the church, he invigoratingly acted as well as preached his homily. He would stop suddenly mid-sentence and freeze his whole body. Whether he was crouched, standing, walking or reaching his hands up to heaven he would stop, having us anxiously waiting for the next word or amusing movement. When he did decide to continue, the pitch of his voice would be at a different level. When he went to a high note he stepped on his tiptoes. On a low note he walked with his knees bent and back hunched over. He impersonated the good and bad guys in the age-old stories of life, keeping us absorbed on his teachings.

I loved the intricately embroidered vestments he wore while celebrating Mass, which were made with the most beautiful fabrics. The embroidery was similar to that on my Irish-dancing dress; Celtic crosses and birds of peace. Some of his vestments subtly glimmered like mother of pearl. Others were bold, in colours of purple and gold, like those worn by medieval kings or roman emperors. The arms were huge and wing-like, smaller at the top of the arm, becoming larger as they reached the wrist. I imagined myself climbing into the arm-hole, it being almost large enough for me to fit into comfortably.

Each Sunday I watched him shine the chalice after Communion wine, with his sleeves draped wide, flowing back and forth as though he were about to take flight. I used to wonder why they were made so large. I'd recently decided it must surely be to make him appear like one of my angels.

Today he wore his out-of-Mass clothes, which always seemed to be the same: black trousers, black shirt, black V-neck jumper, a white crisp collar and a brown, tweed flat cap, which he said kept his smooth, shiny, bald head warm. He always felt the need to tell everyone the facts of his hat.

"I need my flat cap, so I do. My bald head's not used to this cold, damp English weather. No, it's been enjoying the rays of the hot Calcutta sun for the last four years. Do you know what, though?" Before anyone could answer he continued. "One day when Mother Teresa and myself were out helping and teaching the poor Indians, sure, didn't my bald head get sunburnt? Mother Teresa went out herself the very next day and bought me a cream, black-banded boater. On her death that woman should be canonised for this act of charity alone.

"Now I wonder if Saint Alphonsus Liguori realised in 1732 when he founded the Redemptorist order of missionary priests I belong to, that by deciding to send us priests to a different mission the world over every four years he was going to put my bald head through all kinds of hell? I can safely bet Saint Alphonsus didn't give my bald head a thought."

Father Martin Maguire and his bald head had taken over as rector of St Columb's Roman Catholic Church. While his bald head endured the damp English weather for the next four years, we his pupils were in receipt of his extremely enchanting and enlightening wisdom, which I for one cherished.

"NOW! What's the name of your school?" Father

44

Maguire first bellowed, then whispered, this elementary first question. The variable volume of his voice was strange, but his defined Irish accent was beautiful, each word and syllable rounded and perfect. If the Queen of England spoke with an Irish accent, then we would say he spoke the Queen's Irish.

"*SAINT COLUMB'S*," we retorted.

"*AND!* Who is Saint *COLUMB?*" He had acquired an 'I've-got-you-now' smirk at this much more complex question. He positively did have me. I was baffled. My classmates looked equally bewildered.

"*WELL*, can anyone answer *THIS? WHO* is Saint *PATRICK?*"

Quite a few hands along with my own shot up at this question. Index fingers attempted to touch the ceiling. Father Maguire pointed his finger and nodded his head at myself.

"He's the patron saint of Ireland, Father. We celebrate Saint Patrick's day tomorrow, March seventeenth," I answered, having full knowledge of our patron saint's celebration day, due to many parties being organised in our family.

"*AND* what *DID* Saint Patrick do so *WONDERFUL* to be made the saint of all *IRELAND?*" he asked, probing me for more information on this extraordinary man. I wished I'd never answered. Now he thought I knew everything.

"Well, Father, all I know is what Grandpa told me. He said that Saint Patrick chased all the snakes out of Ireland, near from where Grandpa's from in County Mayo." As I concluded I wondered to myself if it was Saint Patrick who had done that, as Grandpa, along with Mammy and Daddy, gave me so much information that it was extremely difficult to remember it all.

"*YES*, Orlagh, my angel, that fine Grandpa of yours, Mr Patrick O'Toole, is *CORRECT*. He's also one of many men named after this great saint. Now I'll tell you what Saint Patrick did that was even more important than chasing snakes... that *HAS*, with the assistance of Saint Columb,

45

helped in the creation of what you all are today...
CHRISTIANS," Father Maguire confirmed, standing on his
tiptoes and pausing momentarily.

Father Maguire's high-blood-pressured cheeks became
redder as he pranced around the room. "Saint Patrick
wasn't born in Ireland, no, no, *NO*... he was born in
Wales. But he was not a Welsh man, nor was he an
ENGLISH man. He was what they called a Romanised
Celt. Almost all of you in this classroom are *CELTS*."

I knew I was certainly a Celt, as Daddy called me his
'Celtic warrior princess'. He said I was brave and bold just
like the ancient tribe we originated from.

"Before Saint Patrick became a saint he was playing by
his comfortable, civilised and predictable home. A young
teenager he was, when he was *KIDNAPPED*. Yes,
kidnapped, by the rough barbaric servants of *MILIUCC*.
Miliucc was one of the many Chieftains of Ireland. Saint
Patrick was taken away from his *LOVELY* parents and
home-cooked dinners, taken across the wild, perilous
waves of the Irish Sea to the barren lands of *IRELAND*.
The only companions he was to have for the next six or so
years in the long lonely days and nights of tending to
Miliucc's sheep, would be hunger, nakedness and *GOD*."

Sitting in my grey plastic chair, I pondered over this
eloquent story, despite incomprehension of the majority of
it. I think Father Maguire had forgotten he was talking to
five- and six-year-olds as he proceeded to ramble in depth
about Saint Patrick's life in Ireland. It didn't matter if I
didn't understand all of it, because my own interpretation
of the story occupied me as much as the humorous priest
dancing his way around the classroom.

It amazed me that yet another important holy person
was a shepherd. But a naked shepherd? It got me thinking
whether all shepherds were actually naked. I thought
about the shepherds who were tending to their sheep
when Angel Gabriel appeared to them to tell of Jesus'
birth. I realised they definitely weren't naked because

when I'd watched a nativity play the actors wore robes tied with string. I figured it must have been only Irish shepherds that were naked. There again, my family in Ireland who had a farm wore clothes and they had hundreds of sheep - but they had cows, goats and lots of chickens too, so I determined they mustn't be counted merely as shepherds.

"Saint *PATRICK* had been raised to believe there was a *GOD* in heaven, but he hadn't taken much notice of his parents' Christian teachings. But when he was alone amongst the never-ending fields of Ireland he began to *PRAY* and pray and pray and *PRAY*. He prayed to his sheep. He prayed to the grass. He prayed to the trees. He even prayed to the fluffy white clouds in the sky. He never stopped praying because he knew there was a *GOD* above and beyond those clouds. After six tortured years as a hungry, naked shepherd slave *GOD* finally sent him a *MESSAGE:* 'Your hungers are to be rewarded. You are going home. Look, your ship is ready.' But Saint Patrick was in the middle of the land of Ireland. There was no sea for miles around. So where was he supposed to see his *SHIP? PATRICK*, after hearing this mysterious voice, then realised he was a Chosen One, and he must serve the Lord."

At the mention of a Chosen One, my wondering mind had been entranced, for I was one and the same. It was said so in the poem recited by the angels: *'For she's the one, the Chosen One, who we put a mark upon...'* I also heard mysterious voices, like the one at the hopscotch squares. My attention was now captivated by the continuing saga of Saint Patrick. I wondered if the mysterious voice which had spoken to Saint Patrick and to me belonged to one of my angels or to God Himself.

"*WELL*, he finally escaped captivity the night after he'd heard the message and he walked and walked and *WALKED*. He walked hundreds of miles until he reached the sea. There waiting, bobbing in the water... was his *SHIP!*

God had answered his prayers. Because *HE* does, you know. He answers the prayers of each and every one of *YOU*. If you are good and loyal to Him and all the people around you, He will reward you. His reward to Saint Patrick was escape back to his wonderful family and friends. *BUT*, Patrick could not settle back into normal life with his family because he had received a calling. He had to answer to his innermost desire and he once again left his comfortable home and family life - but this time, *BY CHOICE*.

"He went to become a priest, just like me. But in Saint Patrick's times it was harder... much, much *HARDER*. The priests had to teach people about *GOD* and *JESUS* for the very first time. Not many people were educated. They were what you call *ILLITERATE*. They couldn't read, nor write. Now I know that in this year of 1978 it'll come as a great shock to you that in the times of *SAINT PATRICK* there were no such things as books to read for the ordinary person, or any books at all really, only the Bible and this was written in the ancient language of Latin. It hadn't even been translated into *ENGLISH*, all those years ago."

Now this did come as a great shock to me. I loved my books and couldn't imagine life without the adventures of *The Famous Five, The Naughtiest Girl in The School, James and the Giant Peach,* or *Charlie and the Chocolate Factory.* If they had no books, then I figured they must have watched television all day and night, when they were not running around naked looking after sheep that is, because Mammy always said that only illiterate people sit in front of the television all day.

"What Saint *PATRICK* discovered after he had finished his studies was that he needed to be back in *IRELAND*. He needed to help the people who suffered like he had. And there were so many of them. He returned to Ireland to discover his job was going to be even harder than he had first anticipated, because they were all - *PAGANS*. Does anybody know what a *PAGAN* is?"

The fidgeting stopped and the eyes fixed on the view of

the green playing fields out of the window reverted back to Father Maguire. It appeared as though I had been the only person enraptured by this enchanting legend. But even I, who had taken in every word of this amazing story, found this Pagan question far too difficult.

Father Maguire proceeded to answer his own question in an extremely passionate way. He seemed perturbed at the thought of these pagans:

"*PAGANS*... They are *HEATHENS* - non-believers. They think the sun comes out all by itself and that the rain falling on their crops to put food in their stomachs is just some kind of coincidence. They don't know there is a *GOD* in heaven. OR they don't want to believe there is a *GOD* in heaven because they're *LAZY!*

"The word of the Lord had not yet reached this isolated island in the Atlantic and it was full to the brim of these *PAGANS*. No learned men had discovered this beautiful land until Saint *PATRICK*. Or, no learned man had dared enter this island full of barbaric, uncivilised people, let alone begin to teach them. *WHICH*, my beautiful children, he did. One by one, clan by clan, he taught them the word of the *LORD*. He interpreted the Trinity by the shamrock, which grew in abundance in this lush green land. The Father, *THE SON* and the Holy Spirit were the three leaves of the plant.

"He transformed his adopted country for, although Saint Patrick was not born an *IRISHMAN*, he became one. He built beautiful monasteries and gave the people a reason to live and, more importantly, no fear of *DEATH*, because they soon learnt that if they loved and served the Lord they would be seated with *GOD* and *JESUS* in the paradise of *HEAVEN*.

"*SO*, when it is said that Saint Patrick chased snakes out of Ireland, it doesn't literally mean snakes; it means the *DEVIL*, along with all evil spirits. In their place he gave the people of Ireland education and *RELIGION*."

I was overwhelmed at the magnitude of this fascinating

story. I sat open-mouthed, astonished at the similarities between Saint Patrick and myself. He was not born in Ireland but became Irish. I wasn't born in Ireland, but I'm told by my parents that I'm most certainly Irish. Saint Patrick had received a message from God, just like I had through my angels. I wondered if this meant I was going to be a saint.

"But, my children, it doesn't just finish with Saint *PATRICK*. Oh no, there had to be people to continue his good work in teaching the word of the *LORD*. There were lots of monks, but the most outstanding to follow Saint *PATRICK* was Saint *COLMCILLE*, also known as *COLUMBA*. Or as we know him here in England - *SAINT COLUMB*.

"The night before Saint COLUMB was born, his mother dreamt of an angel. That angel gave her a gift of a dazzling silk cloak. It was covered with every flower of the world. With each flower depicted on the cloak came a scent. She was surrounded by wonderful colours her eyes had never witnessed and a fragrance so divine her nose could not comprehend. Then, much to her disappointment, the cloak floated away from her and up into the sky. The cloak then started to spread. It went east and west, north and south, as far as the eye could see... and further. It covered all of Ireland and Scotland and began to spread into France and Spain. The angel then spoke: 'This cloak signifies your unborn child that is as beautiful, as soft and as bright as this cloak. His brightness will shed the light of Christianity all over Ireland and eventually the rest of Europe. For he has been chosen to serve the Lord.' The angel then disappeared, leaving Saint Columb's mother mystified."

Oh my goodness, I could hardly believe my ears. My head was exploding with excitement. Another saint, another Irishman and another Chosen One. God surely must have given them red birthmarks too. I couldn't wait for this story to be over so I could ask Father Maguire the exact location of where the angels had kissed these important saintly men.

"*COLUMB* was born a prince. He was a great-great-grandson of the famous King O'Neill. There are a couple of O'Neills in this classroom. Do you know you're descendants of this great man, Columb? But Columb gave up his title and comfortable life to live the life of a holy man. *HE* too, like Saint *PATRICK* before him, established monasteries. Many, many, many monasteries where he taught monks to create and copy exquisite books. The books they copied had been transported from faraway places such as *EGYPT* and *GREECE*. They copied them in order to teach *EVERYONE* about Christianity. They had no paper then and had to use the skin of lambs. It was copying books which would change Columb's life *FOREVER*. For Saint Columb copied a book... one of the psalms of the Bible in fact, which belonged to another holy man called Saint *FINNIAN*. But Columb copied it without Finnian's permission. They had a big battle to see who owned the rights to the copied book. Saint *COLUMB* won. Many men were killed in the fighting, which upset the holy man, Saint *COLUMB*.

"For all the death caused by this battle Saint Columb gave himself a punishment. That punishment was to leave his beloved *IRELAND* and live in isolation on the island of *IONA*, off the coast of *SCOTLAND*." Father Maguire stood on his tiptoes in the centre of the classroom, arms wide apart, pausing so we could all absorb this profound truth.

"On the cold, rocky, untamed island of Iona Saint Columb established yet another monastery, to where many men and women travelled in order to be taught by the holy man himself. There was only enough room for a few people on the land; so, once they had become educated men and women, many were sent by Saint Columb to countries all over Europe to teach the people the word of the Lord. In most countries in Europe fighting had broken out and people had forgotten about being good, kind and

51

CHRISTIAN. Saint Columb's followers were sent to remind them of their forgotten faith. And so the word of the Lord was spread around the world.

"In remembrance of Saint COLUMB we've named our divine church and school after him. And just like we do for Saint Patrick we have a day when we celebrate all he did for us. That day is June the ninth. We wear a sprig of shamrock on Saint Patrick's day and on Saint Columb's day we must wear a leaf from an oak tree. The oak tree signifies the county and city of DERRY in Ireland which was Columb's favourite place in the world. Derry means *oak tree* in the Irish language, because of all the grand oaks which grew there.

"So there you have it, Saint Patrick and Saint Columb, two of the most important holy people in the world," Father Maguire whispered. His breathless body took rest in Mrs O'Reilly's chair. His arms hung either side of the worn wooden armrests, exhausted from all the jigging and prancing which had accompanied his wonderful story.

My mind was filled with rapturous delight. I was dying to ascertain the location of Saint Patrick's and Saint Columb's birthmarks and know if and *when* I was going to become Saint Orlagh.

The once bright March day was now dull and blustery. The clouds had lowered, turning from the fluffy white clouds to which Saint Patrick had prayed, to shades of grey. The wind rustled through the towering fir trees, through the open window and caused the green curtains to soar to the classroom ceiling.

The lunch-time bell rang out and the rest of the class proceeded to eat their quartered sandwiches and mini-snack bars which had been sweating in their musty-smelling plastic lunch boxes. I couldn't contain my excitement any longer and ran to where Father Maguire was still reclining in Mrs O'Reilly's chair.

"Yes, Orlagh, my child, what is it?"

"Well, Father, I have some very important questions to ask you."

52

Father Maguire's mouth turned into a one-sided smile. His chin lowered to his chest as he folded his arms and prompted me to proceed.

"I need to know, Father, where Saint Patrick and Saint Columb had their birthmarks. Were they on their faces, just like mine? And does this mean that I too will become a saint?"

"Why do you ask, my child?"

I wondered about revealing the extraordinary details of the night of my birth, but quickly decided Father Maguire above anyone would understand.

"Well, Father - I am a Chosen One. The night I was born lots of tiny angels flew out of a bright light which had appeared from the ceiling. All together they sang a blessing which said I was a Chosen One. Then they all kissed me. Some kissed my cheek, some my chin and the rest kissed my neck. Their angel kisses left this red birthmark so they could tell who I was from all the other millions of people.

"I'm going to London to have some treatment tomorrow, Father, which will make my birthmark disappear. I was a little worried about this at first because I thought, well, how will the angels know who I am. But Mammy and Daddy said it won't mean I'm not a Chosen One any more because the angels will still be able to see it. It'll just disappear in the eyes of nasty people, so they can't call me names any more. I don't know if you know, Father, but those kind of people are called bigots. Daddy said so. You see they don't understand that I'm a Chosen One. I'm sure Saint Patrick and Saint Columb had the same problem."

Father Maguire nodded continuously throughout my story. I knew he'd understand. Placing his elbow on the armrest, balancing his bald head on his hand, his index finger over his top lip with his thumb propped under his high cheekbone, he took a deep breath through his nose. His shoulders rose and chest expanded. Slowly he released the air from his mouth as he considered my question. I patiently waited for the momentous clarification.

"That's very interesting indeed, Orlagh. I did have an idea you were a Chosen One. Now to your question. I'm afraid I don't know, my sweet child, if Saint Patrick or Saint Columb had birthmarks just like you. But I do know in God's eyes you *are* a saint and you *are* his angel. You are a strong-willed and clever girl and you must continue to be so. God has chosen you to have a birthmark for a very special reason, like he chose for Saint Patrick to be kidnapped and for Saint Columb to have a battle with Finnian.

"We all at some time in our lives suffer, like Saint Patrick did as a slave and Saint Columb did when he was banished from Ireland and like you may hurt when you have your new treatment tomorrow and in the future when those bigoted people call you nasty names. But those sufferings, my child, bring patience, and patience brings perseverance and perseverance brings hope. It's hope, dreams and aspirations that we all need to endure on the long road of life, until we reach our destiny and join God in His kingdom of heaven.

"For God, my child, has sent His angels to you. He has poured His love into your heart and now in appreciation you must show God how strong and loyal you can be. You mustn't waste your precious life, but make a difference with it. You must stand out from the rest and achieve that little bit more than everyone else. For you absolutely are a special, *special* child."

I hadn't ascertained the position of Saint Patrick or Saint Columb's birthmarks, but I left the classroom with a strong sense of self-being along with a notion of transcending the realms of my childhood domain and all the people in it. I was determined to surmount the world. How, was unknown.

Due to the forthcoming parents' evening we were not required to return after lunch, which was an additional bonus to an already fascinating day. All my friends had gone home or were eating in the school canteen which smelled of overdone vegetables, combined with burnt custard. Dominic, Patrick and I never stayed for school dinners as we lived close enough to school to return home for Mammy's tasty snacks. A favourite was baked beans on toast with a layer of melted cheddar cheese on top smothered in fruity brown sauce and masses of pepper. Or there was poached eggs on toast, cooked to perfection so when you pierced the yolk it flowed like a river of lambent yellow water to be absorbed in the bed of wholemeal toast.

I proceeded to walk home through the desolate playground, passing the hopscotch squares and zigzagging my way over the snakes and ladders painted haphazardly around the playground, pondering how I was going to stand out and make a difference. I wondered what was going to aid me to soar to the top. Possibly, just like the wind which had empowered the classroom curtains to touch the ceiling, it was going to be an invisible, unspoken source. I glanced back at the classroom to see Father Maguire watching over me. He tipped his tweed flat cap and waved me on my way. I stopped daydreaming and ran the long driveway home, making sure not to step on any cracks. That was bad luck - of course.

Mammy looked slightly worried at my late arrival. Dom and Pat were already halfway through their bowls of steaming tomato soup. A mountain of buttered bread sat in the centre of the table waiting to be devoured by my rapidly growing brothers. I supposed I'd be left the heel - as usual.

"Where do you think you've been, missy?"

"With Father Maguire, Mammy. I had some very important things to talk about with him, you see."

Dominic and Patrick sniggered into their soup.

"Oh!" Mam sucked her lips into her mouth, "I see, well that's all right then. What did you talk about?"

"About being a saint. It looks as though I'm going to be one too, just like Saint Patrick and Saint Columb."

This statement brought about fits of laughter from the boys and Mammy's lips broke into a smile.

"It's true, Father Maguire said so. I'll show you. I will. You'll see." I was frustrated with the amusement at my forthcoming virtuous position. I departed the kitchen, slamming the door behind me, which rocked the china ornaments sitting on the shelf in the long hallway. The bang caused the bell in the telephone to vibrate, as though a minor earthquake had erupted. Mam was not far behind me, looking as though she too might erupt.

"Well, that's not very *saintly* behaviour, young lady. You almost took that door off its hinges. Get in here, eat your lunch and think yourself lucky you're not going to bed for the rest of the day."

Vanquished, I dragged my feet with my head hung low back to the kitchen table, where the boys were still giggling.

"I hope you don't behave like this with Mrs O'Reilly.' Mammy slammed my bowl of tomato soup down on the mat in front of me. It had now acquired a thick skin and the steam was furiously rising, evaporating into my downturned face. My eyes fixed themselves on the red soup, wishing to myself I too could acquire another thick skin to wrap around me so I could hide from my radically riled mother, who I'm sure, like the soup, had steam rising from the top of her head. "I hope to God for your sake that you have a good report this evening, I really do. Now eat that soup before I get really angry."

I didn't think she could get any angrier. As she turned her back heading for the sink, Patrick had his mouth wide open, nodding his head and holding his stomach, laughing silently, for fear Mammy would tell him off too.

I silently hoped I *was* going to get a good report. It was the first thought I'd had regarding my inaugural parents' evening.

"C'mon, Orlagh, let's go and play footie," Dominic and Patrick insisted.

"No. You only want me to be in goal. I'm sick of being goalie and being hit really hard with the ball. You only want me 'cause no one else wants to do it."

"Don't be stu-pid, Orle. You're the best goalie we've got, honest. C'mon, Orle, please, the gang really miss ya when you're not there," Dom implored.

"Okay then."

The afternoon passed by as swiftly as the innumerable times the leather-cased, grass-smelling football had flown past my defence. I loved being the only girl in the gang. Especially today because it took my mind off the forthcoming school report.

"Let's call it a draw," Dom shouted. "I wanna finish 'cause I'm starving."

Everyone agreed, except me. I was having thoughts of a bad report and was apprehensive of going back. No one took any notice of what I had to say. They grabbed their rolled-up T-shirts and jackets which substituted as goalposts and sprinted their way across the hedge-lined school field. I reluctantly followed, trailing way behind. Running past the green-louvered doors of the small electricity sub-station, I looked up at a gang of older boys and girls who had bunked each other up to sit on its pebble-dashed roof. It looked very exciting up there. Through the navy-blue steel gates I went, coming to an abrupt halt where Dominic was waiting to cross me over the road. He looked like the lollipop lady without the luminous lollipop stick as he looked right and left and right and left again.

I was pleased to see Betsy parked over her oil-stained space on the driveway. If I was in *big* trouble my telling-off wouldn't be as harsh with the presence of Dad. He often said when Mammy was scolding me, 'Leave her be, doll, she knows her mistake now.'

Running past Betsy, through the gate, we entered the kitchen via the back door. Dad had bathed and was sitting with his wet black hair slicked back like a teddy boy, looking like someone who'd just stepped out of the cast of *West Side Story*. His muscular bare chest was perfectly defined as he sat reading the newspaper. His smooth forehead shone under the fluorescent lighting, but his usual shining smile was absent. He dipped his chin and looked at me under his eyebrows. There was no, 'Hey baby doll, how was your day?' Panic struck. It could only mean one thing - a bad report.

I glanced over to where Mammy was standing by the stove, preparing our meal, with one yellow rubber glove on. Always one, never two. Her face too, was apathetic.

I perceived an unusual, deafening silence. I knew it was directed at me, I could feel it. I had to ask, I could bear it no longer. "What did Mrs O'Reilly say, Mammy?"

"Well, what didn't she say is more to the point, young lady."

"Mmmmmm," Dad added, taking a deep breath and biting his bottom lip, engrossed in his paper.

"She told me all about the work you've done. In particular she pointed out the exercise she gave you today, 'If you could be anyone in the world'."

I felt my jaw drop and my eyes open to their extreme limitation. I knew telling the truth was the wrong road to take. I should have picked someone, anyone except myself. I was in trouble, *big* trouble. Now where were my angels when I needed them? I was convinced the steam which had made its first appearance at lunchtime was back, pumping out of the top of Mammy's head like a demented whistling kettle.

They must have sensed my anguished thoughts because suddenly they both smiled. Mammy marched over, grabbed my face between her hands, the water off her one-rubber-glove-covered-hand soaked my left cheek. She then kissed my forehead, my nose and completed her display of affection with a huge smacker on my lips.

Dad discarded his paper, slapped his knee with the palm of his hand and nudged his head backwards. His bright blue eyes were now smiling along with his lips. I sat on his knee listening intently while Mammy relayed my report, confused at the change in my parents' demeanour.

"Mrs O'Reilly said you're the best pupil she's ever had. You listen to everything and try to answer all the questions, so yer do. You read perfectly and write beautifully. But what impressed her the most out of everything that you've done since starting was the, 'If you could be anyone in the world' question. In her thirty years of teaching you're the first child who's ever wanted to be themself."

"But why's that so good, Mammy? I was only telling the truth."

"Because it shows you're filled with confidence and happiness and you're content being exactly who you are, and that is very, *very* unusual. And that's not all. You seem to have impressed Father Maguire too. He caught me on the way out of the classroom and told me you're a very special and clever girl. So maybe what you said earlier about becoming a saint seems very likely. As a treat for being our best girl, I've bought you a big bag of flumps. You can have them after your dinner."

I sat in the living room after dinner eating my pink and white marshmallow-like flumps, which Mammy bought in preference to hard-boiled sweets. She always seemed to be worrying about our teeth. I was totally content with the outcome of the day. I thought I was definitely on the road to making a difference and possibly even becoming a saint.

CHAPTER SIX

The potent stench of hospital disinfectant invaded my nose as I was wheeled down to the operating theatre. The presence of numerous white-clad doctors with smiling nurses in plastic aprons and paper hats and the fact that I was being rushed through scratched rubber doors to have a general anaesthetic could not divert my thoughts from what I had discovered when I had first arrived at the hospital.

As Mammy, Daddy and myself drove through the suburbs of London towards the hospital, Dad supplied light entertainment by singing Irish songs, more so than usual because it was Saint Patrick's day. I daydreamed the time away, gazing out of the window as the sights of London flew past. I expected to see Buckingham Palace, the Tower of London and of course Big Ben, but instead I saw ceaseless rows of shops. There was also lots of litter swirling around in their own private miniature tornadoes. And people - there were hundreds of them milling around like groups of confused rats. Every so often we passed a huge opening with a blue sign above, stating a name, followed by a circle with a line through it. There were so many of them: Kilburn, West Hampstead, Finchley Road, Swiss Cottage. Many of the bewildered people seemed to be heading into these great openings, like rats heading for the drains. What could be the attraction in all these places, I mused. I decided to break Dad's merriment and enquire.

"What do all those shops sell, Dad? The ones with the big blue signs with the red circle and all different names on them?"

"Sure, that's the tube, baby."

"What's the tube?"

"Well, it's an underground train system which takes people all over the city, like buses or trains do above ground, except this is underground and extremely fast. Each name on the sign is the name of the area in which you are. We just passed Kilburn a little while ago, a big Irish area incidentally. Did you see all the Happy St Patrick's Day banners? Anyway, Kilburn's station was called Kilburn so people know exactly when and where to get off, so it was.'

"Do we have an underground in Birmingham?"

"No we don't, but for a very good reason. Do ye know what that is, doll?" He glanced quickly from the road to Mammy.

"Of course I do. You thought you had me there, didn't ya?"

"Well, go on then, clever clogs. What is it then?" Dad winked at me in the rear-view mirror.

"Because we have too many canals and there just wouldn't be enough room to build an underground system," Mammy concluded, assertively.

"I taught ye well, so I did, taught ye well." Dad slapped Mammy's leg. "Too many canals. In fact we have more mileage of canals than Venice itself. Not as many little canals of course, but we have miles and miles of long ones. At one time it was the premier system for getting goods from A to B and then from B all the way back to A."

I knew the hospital was in a place called Islington, but that's all I knew. I didn't know the hospital's name but I guessed the tube station by it would be called Islington. With Mammy navigating through the busy London streets we found our way to Upper Street, Islington quite smoothly.

"This is it. This is the road the hospital's on, Rory. The letter said there's a car park pretty much opposite." Mammy sounded exceptionally nervous. Her intuitive pain reactor must have been cranking into action.

"There it is." Dad pointed over to the hospital.

I couldn't believe my eyes. I was momentarily dumbfounded. Surely this must mean something. This was positively of major significance, I thought. There stood the tube station in Islington, adjacent to the hospital. But it wasn't called Islington. No, no, no. It was truly amazing - it was called... *Angel*.

"Are yer all right back there, princess? Yer've gone very quiet all of a sudden."

"It's called Angel, Dad."

"Yes, the station is the Angel Islington. Well spotted. Yer getting good at this, so ye're."

"No, but it's called *Angel*. Why aren't any of the others called Angel?" I was a little perturbed that my parents had missed the significance of the name.

"The whole area is named Angel and the hospital is called the Angel Hospital," Mammy replied.

That was it - it was surely fate. Of all the hospitals in the country I was going to one called The Angel.

Upon entry I was given a tiny gold cherub to place on my jacket. The lady at reception told me it was an angel to look after me while I was in hospital.

"I already have angels looking after me, thank you."

"Oh! Really? Well, another one won't hurt now, will it?"

"Let's put it on your lapel next to your sprig of shamrock," Mammy quickly interrupted. I suspected she didn't want me telling this woman all about my Chosen-One secret.

As I was pushed on my bed with wheels through the endless bare corridors which were only separated by scratched rubber doors (which fascinated me how everyone continued running into them at full force as if not aware of their presence), I watched the strips of fluorescent light merge into one long continual line. Mam and Dad were having their consultation with the doctor on the way to the theatre.

"We have no time to spare in the National Health Service, I'm afraid, so we'll have to talk along the way," the doctor stated candidly. "Has erm, errr." He glanced at his notes. "Orlagh here had any treatment previously? Did she have the radiotherapy by any chance?"

"Yes, she's had treatment," Mam began. "But not radiotherapy. She was going to have it but then we were told it would remove the red mark and replace it with a white one so we decided against it. We also discovered there were possibilities of cancer in later life too. Obviously not wanting to cause additional problems, we declined the proposal of that particular treatment.

"So she had the thorium X treatment. There were no side-effects and we were promised wonderful results. The thorium X was applied to the birthmark with a small brush similar to that of nail-polish, and was supposed to take effect immediately."

"Yes, yes, I know how it works."

Mammy raised her eyebrows at Dad. "She had three applications of thorium X before the supply came to an abrupt end. Manufacturers stated there wasn't enough demand and there was also considerable impracticality importing it from France. It didn't really cause great disappointment as the treatment didn't make any change to the birthmark anyway. So it was back to research, letters and consultations when I discovered cryotherapy."

"Yes, yes, cryotherapy. I'll explain the procedure in layman's terms - I mean, I don't want to blind you with science now, do I?" Mammy raised her eyebrows to Daddy again. "Cryotherapy, or cryosurgery, whatever you choose to call it, is the procedure of injecting liquid nitrogen, or dry ice if you like, into the affected area."

As I lay listening, I imagined large ice cubes being placed

into a syringe and being pushed through until the ice cubes came out of the needle all crushed up and were then injected into my birthmark.

"The liquid nitrogen will disperse around the hemangioma - sorry, birthmark, killing the dilated over-active blood capillaries which cause the discoloration, thus destroying the colour. When new blood vessels grow, they will hopefully be of the normal kind, therefore no red mark will be present. As simple as that. But I must stress ..." He lowered his voice. I strained my ears to listen to what he didn't want me to hear, trying desperately to ignore the squeaky wheel of the moving bed. "This is going to be very traumatic for a child of Orlagh's age and if she doesn't co-operate in the manner I wish then we'll have to cease treatment until she's of the age when she can both mentally and physically cope." His perfect white teeth appeared as he gave a dismissive smile. I imagined a star appearing in the corner of his tooth, like those in the toothpaste commercials.

Now I was determined not to cry or complain about any pain I experienced. Orlagh Emmet was going to be the bravest patient this doctor had ever treated. I'd show him, I thought.

As we arrived in the theatre I was lifted by the nurses and Daddy off the transportable bed to a permanent one. Mammy had kissed me goodbye outside and said she would see me when I woke up. She looked ashen and dreadfully nervous. Poor Mammy. I could almost hear the cogs turning on the wheels of her intuitive pain reactor as it cranked into action.

The whole of the room was either white or stainless steel. Numerous sizes and colours of long plastic tubes hung on the wall. I was beginning to feel a little apprehensive, but was soon comforted by the sight of Dad's face and the familiar touch of his soft hands stroking my bare arm as I lay bewildered in the starched hospital gown.

"They're going to put ye into a nice deep sleep now, baby doll. I'll be right here next to ye all the way through. When ye wake-up yer mammy'll be here too and it'll all be over, and we'll go to visit the Queen."

"How will they put me to sleep, Daddy? What will they do?" I had momentarily forgotten my brave disposition.

"See these tubes on the wall? These are what they call magic elephants' trunks. All yer have to do is put the end over yer mouth and nose, and breathe, just like normal and the magic elephant who's behind the wall sends magic air down his trunk which'll put ye to sleep. Simple - just like that!" That sounded exciting. Magic elephants and magic trunks.

The nurse unhooked the bright green trunk I'd chosen. I thought everything should be green on Saint Patrick's Day. She placed it over my face and a distinct-tasting air began to emerge through it. Dad leaned over and whispered in my ear:

"Remember, princess, this is the Angel hospital. It's full to the brim of your angels and they're all watching over yer."

I tried to stay awake, but there was just no way. Dad and the nurses all slowly faded away. An intense white light suddenly appeared from the ceiling. It was so bright and resplendent I almost closed my eyes. But I fought to resist. Out of the light flew six angels. They were just as Dad had described them with a golden circle of light above their heads and translucent wings which fluttered delicately. They hovered above me momentarily before each one flew down and kissed my eyelids shut.

chapter seven

I woke disorientated. Slowly, one by one, my senses again began to function correctly. First, my nose. The stench of disinfectant reminded me I was in hospital. I then felt a pain, not in my face where I expected it to be, but a numb throbbing in my left hand. My eyes gradually focused on a hazy figure at the end of my arm. Was it one of my angels about to make another appearance? As the image became clearer I realised it wasn't a heavenly angel, but my anxious mammy fiercely clutching my hand with both of hers. That explained the pain. If she squeezed any tighter I considered the possibility of it dropping off. Although, however much I tried, I couldn't complain. Only grunts and growls broke through my dry lips. Finally, my ears awakened to the soft sound of Dad crooning a slow, sad Irish ballad; "Low lie the fields of Athenry where once we watched the small free birds fly. Our love was on their wings, we had dreams and songs to sing. It's so lonely round the fields of Athenry."

I felt exhausted, with a throbbing pain in my right cheek (and left hand) but I didn't care. I didn't care because I knew that that little pain and lethargy would mean attention, and lots of it. Attention exclusively for me from doctors, nurses, Mammy, Daddy, even Dominic and Patrick. Taunts and teasing would cease and be replaced by sympathy and compassion. Everyone would inform me how very brave I was and I soon learned that the braver I acted the more consolation and praise I received. If I complained, I perceived people losing interest sooner. I knew that my bravado act would work and I thought I'd better do a performance worthy of an Oscar nomination for my present audience.

The doctor stood at the foot of the bed, clipboard in hand and his idiosyncratic, dismissive smirk plastered on his face. Numerous interns looked on with complete admiration as he began his analysis of my first cryotherapy treatment.

"How are we then, Orlagh, dear? Feeling poorly are we?" I recollected his comments from earlier: *'If she does not co-operate in the manner I wish, then we shall have to cease treatment.'*

"No. I'm actually *very well*, thank you."

"Oh, very well are we? You don't feel just a little bit sore?" On each word his chin lowered to his chest.

"Now tell the doctor the truth, Orlagh, darling. He won't mind how you feel. He needs to know so he can update all his records," Mammy remarked, sounding concerned.

"I really feel fine. My face feels like bruises I get every week on my arms or legs, that's all." Only I was going to know how sore it really was. "When can I come back for more? I want the red elephant's trunk next time,"

"Oh my, you've certainly proved me wrong, young lady. Which isn't very often, I must say." Turning to face his students, he widened his eyes and raised his brows. They all nodded in silent agreement. "Well, you can *positively* come back for more treatment, but it won't be for a few months, I'm afraid. You can't have too many anaesthetics. It'll be about four months. You'll have to come back in two months though, so we can see how the treatment has taken."

"What's an anaesthetic?"

"It's magic elephant's breath," Dad interjected rather fast. "A posh word for magic elephant's breath."

The doctors all looked as confused as I had been at the mention of anaesthetic. I didn't really care what they called it as long as I could have some more and see my angels again.

chapter eight

After I'd inhaled the first breath of the magic elephant at the Angel Hospital, and I'd encountered my beautiful, pious beings for the very first time, I yearned for our next assignation. I had so many questions to ask and secrets I needed to share with them. Secrets I couldn't even share with Siobhan. I longed to stroke their long golden hair, watch their fluttering translucent wings and hear their angelic voices. But I couldn't wait until the next breath of the magic elephant had been administered. That was much too far away. Four months, the doctor said. *Four whole months*. That was surely a lifetime.

"Jesus, these people don't listen to you, do they?" Taking a deep breath, Mammy lifted the letter which had just landed on the welcome mat and covered her mouth with it. She closed her eyes and tightly gripped the sides of the paper, causing it to crease and fold under her taut grip. I sat bewildered at the breakfast table as I ate my Sugar Puffs.

"Who don't, Mammy?"

"These hospital administrators, sweetheart. I categorically stated to them that we'd be in the States from the middle of June until the end of July. And when do they book you an appointment for? The beginning of July, that's when. Now there'll be more phone calls, more letters. Agh, Jesus, why?"

She slammed the letter down on the kitchen worktop, as if ridding herself of a deadly contaminating germ. The fruit bowl, which actually had more screws, odd nails and fuses in it than fruit, jumped, as I did, in shock at her uncharacteristically infuriated outburst.

My first thought was of my angels. I still hadn't had any further meetings since that in the hospital and I was convinced they'd return with the magic elephant's breath. I was now being told I had to wait longer to see my celestial spirits. I dropped my head and continued to eat breakfast quietly.

Mammy calmed down when she noticed my disappointment. "It's all right, baby, we'll get it sorted. Don't you worry." Placing her palm on the crown of my head, she pulled me towards her and kissed my forehead. "Just your luck," she mumbled, "just your bloody luck."

The holiday which had seemed a lifetime away was soon upon us. The brown leather cases were once again resurrected from the loft, dusted off and filled to the brim. I don't know how any of the numerous people who'd asked could have dreamed of fitting into our cases. There were certainly no stowaways in our luggage - although it appeared that way.

Luggage address tags had been provided by Air Canada. They had little belts attached to them which we could buckle around the handles. They were miniature versions of Dad's old cracked-leather work belt which was tied around our largest case. As far as Dad was concerned, these address tags would surely not suffice alone. He'd adapted his own labels which definitely made our luggage un-loseable - yellow tape. Heavy-duty, industrial yellow tape arranged all over our cases, stating our name, address and telephone number. There was one on the front, the back and one on each side. At whichever angle you viewed our cases, even if you were standing on your head, you could ascertain they belonged to the Emmet Clan of Birmingham, England.

"Agh Rory, is there need for all those stickers?"

"Now, sure there is, Grania. Ye can never be too careful. They won't be losing our bags now, will they? And sure, won't we be able to spot them quicker on the carousel? There're a lot of these brown cases around, but there'll be no missin' ours!"

"Yer can say that again."

It was my first flight and I thought it was fantastic. The whole travelling process had been an adventure. Even the drive with Dad's best friend, Uncle Tommy Two Saints, from Birmingham to London was fun. We were occupied with hilarious stories and sing-a-longs all the way to Heathrow.

Inside the airport everyone appeared excited, angry or confused. Smiling white-toothed women, with the reddest luscious lips I'd ever observed, who were wearing the oddest shaped hats imaginable, all endeavoured to be heard: 'Next please.' 'Can you move along?' 'Welcome!' 'What's your destination today?'

We always seemed to be late wherever we went - the airport was no exception. Dad just didn't agree with the 'check-in two hours before departure' rule. "Too many queues, too many eejits around. We'll get there when they've all checked in. Anyway, the kids'll just get restless if we're hangin' around too long."

Mammy just didn't agree with Dad's dilatory plan of action. She would love to queue like everyone else. Sit in the departure lounge reading a glossy magazine while waiting to be called to the plane by seat-number order. In fact, due to our late arrival we added to the demented hubbub, having to run to the check-in desk, were hurried through security checks, then heard:

"Would the final five passengers for Flight AC127 to Toronto please make their way to gate five. Would the Emmet family please make their way to gate five!"

I thought everyone was individually called to their flights by name.

"Never again, Rory. I'm tellin' you, never again," Mammy breathlessly chanted, as we jogged across the tarmac, dodging the luggage trucks and stair-tow trucks with their flashing orange lights. We avoided men with the largest red and green table-tennis bats I had ever seen. They waved them up and down, left and right. Everything and everyone seemed to be in a rush - except Dad.

Dad had been right again; there certainly wasn't a chance of us missing our suitcases. As we stood at the luggage carousel in Pearson International airport, confused and agitated people pushed their way to the front to fondle and pull at address labels as similar cases glided past. There was no fondling or quandary for us. Our cases emerged on the conveyor belt, which I had only previously seen on the *Generation Game;* although on this one no cuddly toys or coffee percolators came forth - just our extremely conspicuous cases which looked as though they'd caught a tropical disease and had acquired a luminous yellow spot.

We retrieved our diseased cases and proceeded through the gate which was marked 'Nothing To Declare'. I figured Dad had chosen this gate because it was green. Everything always seemed to be green with my parents - must be something to do with being Irish. Dad had his usual broad smile and nodded to each and every important-looking man in uniform. "How yers doin' there, boys?"

Maybe he should have just kept his mouth shut.

"May we have a word, sir, aye?" a towering, austere-looking man in a navy uniform with shimmering brass buttons asked. I didn't know why Dad continued to be nice to him; he looked so miserable.

"Oh, here we go again." Mammy sighed and rounded Dom, Pat and myself up, like a sheep-dog herding its lambs.

"What's your business here in Canada, sir, aye?"

"Well, I've brought me wife and kiddies to see this great land of yours, where in fact I lived meself for quite a while. Come to visit me brother, his wife and all me ald friends.

I've come to show-off me fabulous family." Dad presented us to him with the palm of his hand, like a game-show host revealing the wonderful prizes on offer.

I sensed something important was transpiring; Dad was much too serious. I thought I'd better help. I stood with my arms held tight to my sides, clutching my red vanity case, which was actually my nurse's case that I'd emptied of stethoscope and bandages and replaced with important travel commodities such as Mr Men books and sweeties. The case matched my red and white striped T-shirt and shorts perfectly, along with the red ribbons tied around my ringlet-filled pig-tails. I then gave the best smile I could, considering I'd lost my two front teeth. I must have impressed him because his face changed. He smiled as bright as his brass buttons, and winked. "I'm sorry to hold up you and your lovely family, sir. Have a wonderful stay in Canada, aye?"

As we emerged out of customs there were more strange faces standing behind steel barriers, being held back like a herd of wild animals. They all pushed to be near the front, grabbing their relatives as they appeared through the sliding glass doors.

"Why the eejits can't wait till they're out of everyone's way I'll never know." Dad looked like he was getting angry.

In the crowd I spotted a familiar face. A face which had visited us in England. A face which I ate ice-cream with at Stratford-upon-Avon and Parma-Violet sweets at Warwick Castle. A face which made the best home-made hamburgers in history (which we were not allowed to spoil with the dreaded ketchup). It was Dad's dearest friend, Teddy Bailey.

"Hey man boy, man boy, man, have you been to Chattanooga and a seen a biga da lika Rosa, with the biga da lika da watermelons?" Teddy's round face was evidently rapturous as he greeted Dad with this nonsensical salutation. They then became like numerous other rendezvous taking place in the airport, except they were in no one's way. They hugged for a long time, with tightly closed eyes and smiling mouths. Smiles full of love, friendship, and too much lost time.

"Come now, you two eejits. Where's the kiss for the lady?" Mammy pushed in-between their sentimental embrace.

Slapping Dad on the back Teddy directed his attention to Mammy. "Hey, sweetness, why you married this crazy guy I'll never know. If you'd have known me before, things would've been different, aye? Oh my, my, my, here's the most beautiful girl in the world, and the toughest little rascals in sight, aye?" He lifted me into his arms and spun me around like the propeller of a helicopter. He placed me down and simultaneously jabbed my two brothers light-heartedly in their stomachs.

"There you go, kids, a blueberry muffin each. That'll keep ya goin' till supper, aye?" He handed us the largest fairy cakes I'd ever laid eyes on. Upon tasting the succulent soft berries as they melted on my tongue, like butter in a hot pan, I came to the immediate conclusion that I liked Canada.

"Do you know, kids, Toronto means 'meeting place' in the language of the native Indians of the Huron tribe? That's what me and this fine example of a man, Teddy Bailey, did here twenty-three years ago - we met. It was when I moved over to Toronto as a boy of eighteen, so it was. I moved into Teddy's mammy and daddy's boardin' house. Teddy soon hooked up with Uncle Seamus and meself. Ach, Jaysus, we've never looked back. We sure had some craic, especially when Uncle Seamus got lumbered... I mean, erm, got engaged to Aunt Josephine. Teddy and meself travelled across America in a pink Caddy. Now that's a story. That's when we visited Chattanooga and met a biga da lika Rosa, with the biga da lika da watermelons."

"Okay, we get the picture. They know all about your escapades and your seven years over here, Rory," Mammy interrupted, laughing.

"But we don't know about biga da lika Rosa with the watermelons, Mammy."

Mammy raised her eyebrows at Dad. "Oh, you don't need to, Orlagh. Maybe another time. Let's concentrate on getting out of this airport for now."

"Now, Mau-reen and me figured that staying out at our weekend cottage would be the ideal option. As yers know, it's right on the banks of Lake Simcoe where the kids can play 'til their hearts' content. It's better than them being stuck in the house in Toronto with nothing to do," Teddy explained as we drove out to the cottage.

"That sounds great to us, Ted, doesn't it, Rory?"

"I'd go anywhere with this man... especially Chattanooga and see a biga da lika Rosa, with the biga da..."

"Okay, Rory." I could tell Mammy was only pretending to be angry. I wish she'd let Dad tell us about Rosa though.

"Is that the sea, Teddy?"

"No, Orlagh, sure that's Lake Simcoe, aye."

"But that's too big to be a lake, Teddy. The lake by us is only really small and you can see across to the other side. Daddy takes me and Dom and Pat there to feed the ducks on Sunday morning while Mammy cooks us our dinner. Are there any ducks on this lake, Teddy?"

"I don't think so, Orlagh, but we might find some Canadian geese. Will that do yer, aye?"

"Do they like bread?"

"Oh, I'm sure they do, aye."

"This lake looks really big to us, kids," Dad began. "Which it is, sure it's thirty miles long and has a holiday island in the centre. But do yers know that this lake's a teeny-weeny one compared to all the Great Lakes here in Canada?"

"Is Lake Ontario, where Freddie farted and farted and made Niagara Falls, a Great Lake, Dad?"

"Sure it is, Pat."

"Who's Freddie?"

"Freddie the Friendly Farting Giant, *Teddy*. You remember all his tales, *right?*"

"Oh sure I do, but I forgot this one. Remind me, aye?"

"When Freddie farted and farted he blew the great canyon known as Niagara Falls, so there was a place where all the water from all the Great Lakes could drain and then continue its journey up the Saint Lawrence River."

"Oh gee yeah, how could I forget that one? Rory Emmet, I always knew you were as crazy as a bedbug. Man boy, man boy, man, aye. Here's the cottage now, aye." Teddy manoeuvred on to the driveway as Maureen frantically waved on the doorstep.

"This is like Grizzly Adam's place. Are there any bears around here like Grizzly has, Teddy?"

"Oh, there's a few, Dom. Quite a few."

"It's gonna be great having you kiddies around the place. It's a shame it's only for five days though. I'd probably have a few kiddies of my own if it wasn't for your daddy, aye."

"What did Dad do then, Teddy?" Dom enquired.

"Well, Mau-reen and me we'd been childhood sweethearts. Back then Maureen had wanted to settle down, but I didn't. Your daddy appeared on the scene and things changed a little. That Rory Emmet said, 'Teddy, you're as crazy as a bedbug if you're gonna marry that Mau-reen. She's a great gal, but oh boy, man boy, you're way too young.' So what happens? I break it off with Maureen and hang-out with yer dad. Then he goes back to the old country telling me it was only a *vacation*. In the meantime Mau-reen married some jerk-off from Winnipeg and had the four boys. Jesus, man, Winnipeg of all places. The prairie land piece of shit. After yer dad didn't return from his vacation, I decided to go to England to re-live the good times of Canada and the States, aye? I arrived on his doorstep and what's he gone and done? Yeah... married yer mom. And what am I, aye? You've guessed it - up shit creek, man."

"So how come you're married to Maureen now, Teddy? What happened to the prairie land piece of shit?"

I was wondering the same as Pat.

"Patrick, watch yer mouth," Mammy shrieked.

"In all fairness to Patrick, Grania, that's the only description for that animal, aye. She had to escape from her not-so-idyllic little house on the prairie with her four boys, because that piece of shit had been beatin' her so bad. She made her way back home to Toronto. It was twenty-five years to the day after we'd broken up when we met by chance and she fell for my charms and good looks all over again. The rest as they say is history, aye."

"Arrhh, that's like a real fairy story."

"Ohh, don't you believe it, Orlagh," Maureen said, laughing.

"What have we got planned for today, guys, aye?" Teddy startled us out of our sleep. The sun was just about peeping its head over the earth like Dominic's, Patrick's and mine were over the sheets of the double bed we shared. "Water-skiing or dirt-biking? Niagara Falls or the CN Tower? Or shall Orlagh and me just go eat some coconut-creme pie? Urrr, erm, yum, yum, co-co-nut cre-am *pie!*" Teddy enthusiastically licked his lips with more vigour than one could imagine exerting at 6.00am. Teddy was the only person I knew who could think about consuming coconut-creme pie at the break-of-day. But with Teddy *everything* always seemed to revert to food.

His huge stature covered the length and breadth of the wooden door-frame. His podgy, smiling face urged us to get out of bed, rather like a lonely child wanting a playmate. We obliged and were led to a ready-made feast of chocolate chip and banana pancakes smothered in maple syrup. "Made in Canada, the best maple syrup in the world, aye," Teddy boasted. They were followed by bran and nut, cranberry and blueberry muffins to be washed down with hot-chocolate filled to the brim with melting marshmallows. Our taste buds encountered flavours never before experienced. Dom, Pat and I agreed this was surely worth rising for at 6.00am.

Mammy, Daddy and Maureen yawned their way out of bed a couple of hours later. After they'd consumed their own breakfast feast the adventure of the day proceeded. Over the five days we managed to take part in all the activities Teddy had suggested; from racing around Lake Simcoe on water skis, jet skis or in the speed boat, or flying through the forest on dirt-bikes. Our time in Canada was extensively exhilarating.

Clad in our new attire of Blue Jays baseball caps and mini-kits we did the tourist excursion to the CN Tower, which to me looked like a docked spaceship on a landing platform. On Teddy's request we ate sumptuous food in the tower's revolving restaurant. We made my first trip to the wondrous Niagara Falls, where we witnessed the calm Lake Ontario transform itself into a waterfall of immense proportion. Visiting a place where Freddie had actually farted was simply astounding.

The time came for our journey to continue like the water of Niagara, although we were not going east up the Saint Lawrence River. We left the serenity of Simcoe and headed out west to see Uncle Seamus and Aunt Josephine and experience more bizarre sights, sounds and tastes that are omni-present in a land filled with modernistic appliances, fairytale dreams and donut shops.

CHAPTER NINE

"Daddy, if you lived here you wouldn't have a job."

"Why's that then, Orlagh?"

"Because there's nothing built in bricks, everything's made from wood. Uncle Seamus's house is made of wood and it's not a log cabin like Teddy and Maureen's. Look, there's wooden shops, wooden pubs, even wooden postboxes. But there still seems to be millions of trees everywhere." I pointed to the gigantic trees which stood on their tiptoes to cavort with the clouds above.

"You may be right there, Orlagh, I never thought of that. But Uncle Seamus has certainly chosen a beautiful place to live, don't yer think, kids?"

"Yeah, Rory, Vancouver Island's a beaut' place an all, but if I see one more God-damn tree, I'll surely crack. They're everywhere. When I die I hope and pray you'll bury me as far away as possible from these trees. In Ireland... arrah, that'll be perfect. There's no fear of trees there, sure didn't the English chop them all down for their stately homes? Our beautiful oaks gone to build the abodes of the British aristocracy," Uncle Seamus proclaimed in his hilarious Irish-Canadian accent.

Mammy and Aunt Josephine re-bonded quickly. Women have so much to talk about, I thought. It was Aunt Josephine's ohhs, ahhrrs and tut-tut-tuts which first drew my attention to their conversations as I played nearby. I pretended to be engrossed in my game, but instead I was enthralled in the amazing new details I was hearing about my Nanna Bridie.

"So tell me the whole story on Bridie, Grania. Seamus doesn't tell me all the juicy details. Start from the beginning."

"Okay... Well, I think this will be beginning enough. Bridie's parents and family had emigrated to Birmingham from Dublin in pursuit of work when Bridie was a young teenager. Then when Bridie was about twenty she moved back to Dublin on her own."

"Why's that then?"

"No one knows, Josephine. Maybe someone does, but no one talks about it. Bridie certainly wouldn't tell yer. That one's got so many secrets up her sleeve. Anyway, in Dublin she met and married Dominic Emmet. He was twenty-five years older than her. They reckon she married him 'cause he had a little one-up-one-down. Apparently he was a good man. He'd have to be a saint to marry Bridie, I'll tell yer. He was a character too though, an old rebel he was, who'd recite Robert Emmet's epitaph speech every night."

"Who's Robert Emmet?"

"He was a leader of an uprising in Ireland in 1803. The uprising was intended to overthrow the English, but Robert Emmet got caught and hanged. Before they hung him he said in a famous speech that his grave shouldn't be marked until Ireland's free."

"Right, I remember now. Seamus is always going on about being related to him. Carry on anyway. They'd just got married."

"As you know, they went on to have Teresa, Seamus, Rory, Assumpta and Una. Apparently their life was happy until Bridie carried out the most inconceivable action imaginable. She left poor Dominic a note, her poor husband of twenty-five years, who was coughing and spitting his way closer to his death. The note told him to stick the Proclamation, Robert Emmet's epitaph and James Connolly's Starry Plough up his arse and she walked out

80

and left him, Rory, Assumpta and Una sleeping in their beds. They had no clue that their wife and mother was untying the thread of a family bond from around her wings and was taking flight into the night, never to return. Well, not for twenty years anyway. All those years later she turned up in Birmingham where Rory, Assumpta and Una had moved to after Dominic had died. He hadn't lasted long after Bridie left."

"How come they went to Birmingham? I don't like to ask Seamus 'cause he thinks she's a saint."

"Because Teresa lived in Birmingham with her husband, and Bridie's sisters were there too. When Orlagh was a wee baby, Bridie turned up in Birmingham as well. Twenty years she'd been gone. If it wasn't for Seamus, Rory would never have set eyes on Bridie again. I think because Seamus had left home before Bridie did a runner he didn't really turn against her. It was when Seamus visited England on his own that time that he persuaded Rory to meet up with Bridie. It took a while for him to come around - but he did, after lots of persuasion. That was six years ago, Josephine, and she's caused havoc in our lives almost every day since."

When Uncle Seamus and Dad were around the conversations on Nanna Bridie ceased and were usually replaced with Uncle Seamus ridiculing Aunt Josephine.

"French alone is enough. French-Canadian, Jesus, they're scary. But a French-goofy-newfy?... I must've been crazy. She tells me her grandfather was Irish... Hey, I know the Irish have a bit of a reputation for being a little dim, but give us a break here... we're all budding Einsteins compared to those Newfs."

"I'll give you goofy-newfy, Seamus Emmet, you thick Irish Mick," Josephine retorted, laughing.

"What's a goofy-newfy, Seamus?"

"Well, Orlagh, they're very hard to describe. But basically it's a person from Newfoundland. I can't believe my kids're half goofy-newfies."

I was so proud of my cousins Carmel and Tommy. They sounded like characters from *Charlie Chan* to me. Although I was continually told by Carmel that Americans and Canadians have very different accents, I couldn't detect a difference.

Carmel seemed to be angry a lot of the time. Mammy said it was okay though, because she was changing from a child to a woman and was confused. Everything in Carmel's words was 'garbage' and 'so *un-cool*'. I really wasn't looking forward to being thirteen if it meant boobs and boy problems. And if it meant playing with your brothers was 'un-cool' then I certainly didn't want to be at that temperamental age. Being a tomboy was fun: climbing trees, building log cabins, looking for snakes' nests and scorpions. The latter didn't appeal to me much, but I had to go along with their games. I didn't want to be excluded for being a sissy. I felt Carmel and her attitude problem missed out on all our adventures.

Each day before we departed on one of our intrepid escapades Dad shouted, "Who wants to see the donut queens?"

"Yeah, donut queens," we all yelled, excited at the thought of which luscious delights would fill our lunch box that day.

Dad took us to the donut store situated at the end of Seamus's road. A whole store full of donuts and only donuts: apple, cinnamon, chocolate, coconut, honey-nut - any kind of nut. Sticky toffee and even plain old jammy donuts. There were mini-ones and monstrous ones. There were trays upon trays of delectable indulgences which Dad let us choose from. Dom, Pat and myself selected only one. Tommy selected a box of six - all for himself.

"You'll end up like these donut queens if ye carry on like this, Tommy, me boy. I bet they eat more than they sell."

Dad had renamed the shop assistants the donut queens due to their large proportions. They must have eaten a lot of donuts to reach the size they were. The intended straight brown stripes on their uniforms were distorted and zigzagged around the contours of their huge backsides. They were always so friendly. "You have a nice day now, sir, aye?" was always their valediction as they tied the string around the box full of our delicious donuts.

We had so many wonder-filled days before we started our journey on to the mainland and down the west coast of the United States of America. Dad said there would be even more amazing days ahead. He always seemed to be right, so I wasn't going to begin to doubt him.

chapter ten

"Cal-i-fornia here I come. Right back where I started from," Mammy, Daddy, Seamus and Josephine sang as we were departing Oregon. Carmel sat in the back of the hired station wagon, her head was bowed and her hand covered her eyes. I didn't understand why she was embarrassed. It must have been her confusion again, as there were no strangers in the car. She had been enraged since the first of the Sambo's at the base of Mount Saint Helens. She didn't find it the least bit amusing. Well, neither did I - at the time.

We had visited Mount Saint Helens' volcano which resembled the surface of the moon. I was half-expecting men in space suits to bounce over the lunar-like surface, shouting: *'one small step for man, one giant step for mankind.'*

"It's been dormant since 1879," the smiling, white-toothed guide explained. He hadn't noticed an additional nine late listeners pretending to be absorbed in his history, but in hysterics at yet another successful deceptive free entry. Sneaking in made everything so much more fun, jumping gates and fences, like fugitives on the run. "Most of these peaks around us are relics of extinct volcanoes, including Mount Rainer which is the highest of our peaks here in this beautiful state of Washington. But Mount Saint Helens is a worry lately. It has a rumblin' in its tummy."

"So do I!" Tommy exclaimed, causing no end of embarrassment for Carmel.

There was added annoyance from Josephine. "Keep your God damn greedy mouth shut. What've I told you before?"

"But I'm hungry Mom, real hungry. Why can't we go eat now? This is borin' kinda stuff anyway. The most excitin' part was sneakin' in."

Josephine expressed as much anger as one can while still whispering. "There ya go again, motor mouth, tell everyone why don't ya? Do you just wanna get us arrested, aye?" Like Mount Saint Helens I'm sure she was simmering inside.

"Hey, why don't we all go'n eat now anyway? It's the best idea I've heard in a while. Enough about Mount Saint Helens, it's only a dormant ald piece of ancient rock. There'll be nothing excitin' goin' on here for a few centuries yet, I'll say." Dad saved Tommy from any further scolding.

"Sambo's, let's go to Sambo's!" Tommy hadn't learnt from his previous reprimand. He received a smack across the ear from Aunt Josephine as her lava rose to its pinnacle. Much like Mount Saint Helens did the following year when it erupted with a violent blast knocking the top off the mountain, killing fifty-seven people and destroying everything for miles around...

Dad had been wrong, for once.

We all descended the grey rock of the pre-historic volcano towards the gigantic effigy of a black man with smiling red lips which revealed his glowing white teeth. He wore red-and-blue-striped trousers and played a banjo. He was a huge version of Gollywog on the jam jars. The place looked thrilling.

Upon entering, Uncle Seamus had purchased a mini-Sambo doll for me. It was exactly like the giant outside and when you pressed his round stomach he sang, 'Oh those cotton fields back home'. Carmel said it was racist. I thought racist must be another American word for wonderful, because that's what I considered him to be and I planned on treasuring him.

We had a feast Teddy Bailey would have been proud of. Upon receiving the bill my dad's blue eyes were full of mischief. They shone and danced like fireflies in the night. "Seamus, why don't you and the girls take the kids and wait in the car. I'll settle the bill. Meet me out front."

"Can I stay with you, Dad?" I thought maybe I could choose some other piece of memorabilia from the cabinet of goodies if I stayed, like a Sambo's watch or moneybox to go with my new doll.

"No, Orlagh, hon, you go with Mammy and the boys and wait for me in the car."

"Oh, please, Daddy, let me pay with you." I pouted my eyes, feigning distress.

The others proceeded to the brown station wagon in the crammed car park while Dad and I headed for the check-out which had accumulated quite a queue. I enthused over the watches and games the Sambo's emporium had on display in the fingerprint-smeared glass case, while Dad whistled and tapped his feet to the sound of his own voice.

"Come on, Orlagh, let's go, princess."

"But we haven't paid, Dad."

He took a firm hold of my hand and led me to the door. "I *said*, lets *go*."

"Oh, Daaaa-d. I thought maybe I could have a watch to go with my new doll."

"Now, don't you think you've had enough for one night, young lady? Think yerself lucky Uncle Seamus bought ye Sambo. Now *hurry*," Dad said, with a perturbed urgency reverberating through his soft Irish brogue.

As we approached the door the kind man who had waited our table shouted, "Sir, excuse me, sir."

"Come on, Orlagh, *run*... Quickly."

I realised I'd left my new Sambo doll in the restaurant.

"But, Daddy."

"Sush now, keep it down and run."

86

I was getting distressed for real this time, but Dad wouldn't listen, he just wanted to run. I tried pulling away from his tight grip to run back to the restaurant to retrieve my cherished doll. I turned back to the door where there were now a few of the waiters trying to get our attention. Dad noticed this too and shouted, "Quick, Orlagh, run as fast as you can, big black Sambo the owner is coming and he's after us. God only knows what he'll do." At that I decided my life was more important than the doll. I imagined the giant effigy coming to life and battering us to death with his banjo. I ran as fast as my legs could carry me in the direction of the car.

Breathless, we reached where the car should have been parked. Had Dad in his haste become disorientated? The car was gone, nowhere to be seen. I was convinced Sambo would surely get us now. Maybe he'd captured and beaten the others already?

In the darkness of the car park I could just about observe the anguished look in Dad's eyes. We ducked down low and tiptoed quietly around the deserted cars. I attempted to snivel silently. I can tell you I was pretty petrified at the thought of Sambo coming. Dad squeezed my hand. He nodded his head in the direction of the restaurant. Our missing car was near the restaurant door. It seemed the others had evaded Sambo thus far.

"Okay, my brave princess, after three, run to the car. One, two... Oh, Jesus, there's Carmel. What the hell's she doin' over there?" Carmel was emerging from the restaurant which she had left five minutes before, passing the waiters who were looking for Dad and myself. If they knew she was with us maybe they'd keep her hostage, I thought. "Quick, run straight to the car now, Orlagh. No stoppin', de ya hear me?"

I ran faster than I'd ever run before. My only vision was that of Sambo chasing me with his banjo in hand to use at any time as a weapon. '*Oh, those cotton fields back home*' metamorphosed into a deep-South-sounding death threat. I was so scared I jumped straight through the opened window on the hatch-back door, landing directly on top of Patrick.

Dad was close behind. As he ran past Carmel he grabbed her by the waist and shouted, "Sambo's coming." She ran out of shock or maybe it was sheer embarrassment. The stunned waiters looked on as Dad and Carmel dived into the getaway car.

"Quick! Drive, Seamus, drive. Go, go, goooo!"

"What in God's name is going on, Rory?" Mammy exclaimed.

"Orlagh and me have just done a *SAMBOS!*" he shouted, slapping his knee and throwing his head back in hysterics. His teeth shone as bright as my lost Sambo's doll's had. Mammy took a deep breath, shook her head and smiled. She didn't look too worried about us having to escape from Sambo.

"Rory Emmet, you're a crazy God damn son of a gun, so ye are," Uncle Seamus proclaimed, slapping the steering wheel as he drove us over the boarder into Oregon state and most importantly away from Sambo.

Disneyland - the most important destination in our itinerary, was rapidly approaching and my thoughts of being killed by a giant black man with a banjo were eventually obliterated by visions of Mickey, Minnie, Goofy and Pluto dancing with Snow White and The Seven Dwarfs on a fairy-tale stage.

The exquisite views on the Oregon Trail were ignored due to my anticipation of arriving at the imminent destination. Fun and frolics with my brothers and Tommy in the back, on top of the luggage, gained more of my attention than the wondrous landscape.

Dad or Uncle Seamus drove with their hair blowing in the wind and their tanned arms leaning out of the window. Mammy and Josephine chatted continually with their Seventies perms and cut-off denim hotpants. Carmel's time was consumed with being embarrassed. The four of us in the very back secretly held socks or underwear out of the open window to see them fly in the wind. Some were lost in fits of laughter, sent flying down the highway like balls of tumbleweed from a hurricane.

The Redwoods National Park did succeed in diverting our attention and stimulated lots of excitement. I was captivated by the sight of the largest trees in the world. Trees so large we drove our car through their carved-out centres. Trees so tall tilting your neck back as far as was possible would still not enable us to view their tops. They were like the endless stalk in 'Jack and the Bean Stalk'. I imagined Freddie The Friendly Farting Giant mounted on top surrounded in gold while happily farting. But I soon learned if there was a giant of any form living in the Redwoods, it would be Paul Bunyan.

We proceeded down Highway 101 with its billboards covered in beautiful blondes promising cellulite loss or movie-stardom-status. We stopped off at the tallest tree, the widest tree and the oldest tree. We investigated many souvenir shops. They sold all kinds of Paul Bunyan memorabilia, like key chains, postcards and statuettes. There were pictures of Paul Bunyan standing by the Black Hills of Dakota which he'd apparently sculpted. Paul Bunyan standing knee-high in the waters of Puget Sounds holding an axe in his hand with his elbow resting on Seattle's six-hundred-foot Space Needle. Topping everything off was Paul Bunyan standing in the centre of the Grand Canyon, boasting creation. Patrick and I both agreed that was absurd. We tried telling one of the assistants with 'I Love California' askew over her gigantic breasts.

"Paul Bunyan didn't do all that, Freddie did." Patrick didn't want to shock the assistant too much, so he left out the friendly farting giant part.

"What, son? He didn't do what? Are you Aust-ralian?"

"No, I'm from Birmingham. He didn't make all those places, Freddie did."

"Alabama? My, my you certainly don't sound like you're from Alabama. Now I'll be damned. Freddie? You mean Fred Flint Stone? No kids I think it was Paul Bunyan. Why don't you go ask him about it yourselves. He's right down the highway. 'Bout two miles or so. But watch you don't stay in that sun too long, little girl. You're already quite sunburnt. Alabama? You sure had me there." She clicked her tongue and shook her head.

We met Paul Bunyan in an inlet off Highway 101. We sat on the large brown boot of the ancient giant who loomed one hundred feet above our heads. He talked and sang and talked some more. He knew all about giantdom and of the tales of the Irish giant Finn MacCool. He declared he'd met Freddie on a number of occasions. After much debate he eventually admitted the Grand Canyon was most certainly created by our farting giant.

CHAPTER ELEVEN

All the dreams I'd dared to dream about Disneyland had been granted. Snow White danced with Pinocchio and Pluto in an enchanting castle full of sparkle, fairies and elves. I witnessed flying carpets. I saw the lion, the witch and the wardrobe. I even met Alice in Wonderland. Disneyland certainly was heaven.

We were all being photographed next to Goofy when I spotted Mickey Mouse. I'd only seen him on stage dancing with Minnie so I didn't want to miss out on meeting him in person. No one would notice if I quickly slipped away. I'd be back by the time all the photographs had been taken.

Mickey was great. He even wanted to meet Mammy and Daddy. "Where're your parents, sweetheart?"

"Oh, they're over there with Goofy." I pointed to where they should have been. But there was no Mammy or Daddy. "Oh no, they're gone. My brothers and aunty and uncle have gone too. I'd better go'nd find them."

"Don't worry, you stay with me. Mickey'll look after you."

I couldn't wait with Mickey. I had to find them quickly. I ran through crowds of adults towering above me. Like the miniature ballerina in my musical jewellery box I spun around and around, desperately searching. They were nowhere to be seen. My whole family were gone - forever.

The anguish built up inside me. My nose began to

twitch and a lump as big as an orange had formed in my throat. I was well and truly lost. Lost in the abyss of this enchanting land.

The sound of trumpets and drums sounded as the daily procession of Disney characters commenced. Everyone rushed roadside to view the magical sight of Mickey and Donald dancing with Cinderella and Dorothy who wore her ruby-red shoes. I was left standing alone and quite frightened. I was terrified of my forlorn future in Disneyland. I wanted to run and steal Dorothy's shoes so I could tap my heels together and say, '*there's no place like home. There's no place like home.*' I was contemplating my theft when I heard a strange American voice say, "Hey little girl, what's wrong?"

Looking up, I saw the man who owned the voice. He looked fun, dressed all in red with a pair of Mickey Mouse ears on top of his head. I was sure I could trust him. I'd been warned not to talk to strangers, but this was a life-and-death situation.

"I've lost Mammy and Daddy and my brothers too. They were with Goofy and I was with Mickey and then they just disappeared into the crowd." I'd tried to fight back my tears, but the orange in my throat grew larger and the tears flowed as fast as the water on the log flume.

"It's okay, we'll find them. You just come along with me. My name's Reg." He took my hand, leading me away from where we'd been with Goofy.

"I think they're over that way, Reg." I was now beginning to feel a little apprehensive of this plastic-eared stranger.

"Yeah but sweetheart, I'm taking you to the lost children's office. That way they can come get you. We might be here all day looking for them." Reg smiled, appearing trustworthy. I figured bad strangers who were planning on kidnapping usually tempted you with sweeties or a look at their puppies. Reg had no alluring offers, so I guessed things would be fine. "Hey, look, here's the tram going in that very direction."

The brass bell on the back of the blue tram was rung by a black man dressed like Buttons. Ding, ding. "All aboard now, people. All aboard." Ding, ding.

Reg swept me off my feet and up on to the tram which travelled in the opposite direction to which I imagined my parents to be. This was a cool kind of an adventure. I sat on Reg's knee and we got to know each other. "I've told you my name, what's yours? And where're you from?"

"Orlagh, Orlagh Emmet. It means golden princess you know. And I'm from Birmingham."

"Birmingham! Really? I thought you were English or even Australian. I never would've thought you were from Alabama."

"Well, I'm actually Irish, but I live in Birmingham. Where's Alabama?"

"Oh, Irish, well that explains the ac-cent. Why, Alabama is where you live. Birmingham Alabama, right? Did you get sunburnt?"

Just like the lady in the souvenir shop, he was confusing. Alabama and sunburn? These Americans were a little crazy, I thought.

"Here we are, this is our stop. Come Orlie, lets go find your mommy and daddy."

"Orlagh. It's Orlagh."

"Sure, I know it is, Orlie. Come on let's go. There's the lost children's office, look."

An ominous-looking building stood alone and uninviting. I imagined I was going to be fed gruel and made to scrub floors with a wire brush which I had to dip into a tin bucket full of dirty water. Or maybe there was a Fagan-like character inside who'd make me steal handkerchiefs or sell red roses to tourists. I was convinced I was never going to escape.

Upon entering the portentous black doors we were greeted by an Hispanic Mary Poppins. "Olla. Oh, hello dharlings. What is it I cana be doing for you, dharlings?" She had the strangest accent I'd ever heard. Her white teeth shone, but her eyes were hidden by the peak of her black hat.

"Orlie here has lost her mommy and daddy."

"Oh dear, we shalla finda them for Orlie. Come, my dharlings."

With a black umbrella hooked over her left wrist she took my hand. She seemed kind, I liked her. I just wish they'd get my name right though. I said goodbye to Reg and thanked him for taking me there. Strangers weren't always so bad.

Mary Poppins led me into a room of crying children all clad in either red or green sun visors with 'I Love Disneyland' painted in white across the front. They all wore Mickey's upright ears or Pluto's floppy ones. None of them looked as though they loved Disneyland at all. They must have been consumed with the thoughts I'd had outside, of Oliver Twist and Orphan Annie.

I received my plastic sun visor. I chose green, of course. Mickey wasn't really in my good books; I figured he'd been to blame for me losing everyone, so I decided on Pluto's ears

"Just a spoonful of sugar helps the medicine go down, the medicine go down," bellowed out of the speakers as the real Mary Poppins danced and sang on a huge screen affixed to the wall. This wasn't bad at all. A free visor, Pluto ears and Mary Poppins.

"Come Orlie, we go shout for youra moder." I had visions of us standing on the roof of the lost children's building with soot-covered chimney sweeps and Dick Van Dyke, as the strange-sounding Mary Poppins and I made funnels with our opened palms and shouted, 'Mammm-meeee'.

I'm afraid it wasn't as exciting as that. Frustration ensued rather than exhilaration.

We proceeded to a white counter where another Hispanic lady dressed in her own clothes sat behind a large black microphone. She had a shining glow over her sallow skin. Looking at her perspiring skin, I became aware it was extremely hot. The air was stuffy and heavy and smelt like the inside of my brothers' boxing bags. Maybe it wasn't as great as I had first thought.

"Tella me youra full name, ah?"

"It's, Orlagh. Or-lagh Emm-it," I pronounced in my most comprehensible voice.

"Orlie Emmito. Hoe Key, Orlie. And livea, yeah... wherea?"

"Or-lagh," I repeated slowly. "Or-lagh Emm-it and I don't like liver thank you. Mammy tries to make me eat liver and onions, but I just don't like it." I was totally confused at this strange offer of liver. I hated liver.

"Liva? What do you talka? Onion? No onion. Wherea do you L-I-V-A?"

"Oh, I live in Birmingham, England."

"Hoe key, Orlie, I shouta for youra moder." She cleared her throat before making the announcement which was to be transmitted all over the amusement park so somehow my family and I could be reunited. I decided this was probably not going to be for a very long time - if at all. "Can de moder and farder of Orlie Emmito from a Birminghama Alabamo pleasa proceeda to the southa losta children. Orlie Emmito."

I tried again to correct them and ask where this Alabama place was. I'd heard it three times today and it was very disconcerting. "I know, my child, it'sa hoe key, dey come, dey come. His good for you toa stay outa de sun. You alreadya badly burnta." She rubbed her fingers across my face.

Sunburn? I had no sunburn. None at all. Exasperated and defeated, I left Mary Poppins to attend to another lost child.

I was distracted from watching the real Mary Poppins fly through the streets of London by the door being violently flung open. I thought bank robbers had mistakenly entered the wrong building. It wasn't bank robbers about to shout 'stick-em-up', but Mammy almost flying like Mary Poppins and screaming like the Banshee. She didn't screech the cry of death but, "Orlagh! Oh, Orlagh, my sweet child. What in God's name happened to you, darling? You silly billy you. We were all so worried. Come now, the others are waiting outside."

"Can I just watch the end of Mary Poppins, Mammy."

"No, baby. Daddy wants to see you."

"That's a grand cap ye have there, Orlagh, grand. Now don't be wanderin' off again, d'ye hear me?" Dad didn't allow me to answer. "Lets go ride the biggest roller coaster in the world."

"But I'm too small, Dad."

"That's a minor detail, Orlagh, me love. Come on gang, let's go. You stay close to me, missy."

I never left their side after that experience. I was amazed I'd been emancipated. Orlie, Alabama and non-existent sunburn. It had all been terribly confusing.

My height didn't restrict my chances of riding the most dangerous and highest roller coaster in the world. Not when Dad secretly lifted me up so my head was above the measure chart. The wind ripped through my curls and Dad squeezed my hand tight. I squealed and laughed as we did loop the loop, unaware of my idyllic childhood.

chapter twelve

The streetlights on Hollywood Boulevard merged into one swaying white line as I rubbed my watering, tired eyes. I longed for my bed in the motel room situated amidst the Hollywood hills. Views of the famous sign were visible from the insect-meshed window. My only view on Hollywood Boulevard as we waited for Dad to bring around the car were street girls, pimps and movie-star-wannabes animatedly chattering in flared trousers and tight tan-leather jackets.

I'd never been as eager to sleep. There was too much fantasy, too many accents and too many thrilling, death-defying rides for one day.

By the time I reached my bed I was delirious. All the thoughts, visions and memories of the day had merged into one long, deep sleep.

A resonant voice filled my room, like an echo in a mountain range. Was this extra-sensory perception? I didn't know. But I did know there was certainly a reverberating accented voice within my head. I shuffled my bum to where my head had been placed on the pillow. I tucked my knees under my nightdress, clutched the seam and pulled it over my toes in fright and anticipation. With my chin resting on my knees I awaited clarification as to where the voice originated.

The echoing voice was soft and amiable with a rhythmic flow. It was very similar to the lady's voice in the lost children's office.

The voice didn't startle or alarm me, but gave me an almost apathetic emotion: a strange feeling of non-existence. I could neither move nor talk - only listen.

Although it was dark, my eyes quickly became aware of the silhouetted outlines of the 'Sixties' furniture and the psychedelic pattern on the opened curtains. The darkness made the illuminated, undulating letters which spelt out HOLLYWOOD much more prominent from their distant position outside.

"Dis is de cidy of de angels. Wel-cum my child. You have cum homa. *Your angels* dey have message for you - de Chosen One." At that a gleaming funnel of yellow light appeared, descending from the nicotine-stained ceiling. It was so intense I squinted my eyes. They hurt so much from the beaming light I really needed to close them, but I couldn't risk missing this miraculous event. I was expecting the angels to appear out of this funnel, like they had at my birth and at the Angel Hospital. But no - there was only the dazzling light. I could hear my heart beating *loud*. Bum, bum, bum, bum. It sounded like the large drum at the head of the Disney procession. The beat didn't seem to be emanating from my chest, but echoing in my eardrums as I held my breath in expectation of the forthcoming events.

Out of the yellow ray appeared an opaque ball of light, like a huge smoke ring. Encased in that ball of frosted light was an angel, enclosed like a fairy in a round ornament-like snow scene. Perhaps I could shake it and make snow fall delicately around her ethereal body. But there was no snow - only an angel. Solitary, exquisite and delicate.

One at a time more angels appeared, all in their own transparent capsules. As each opaque ball emerged it began to float slowly and steadily towards me, like a single cloud on a summer's day. As the ball got closer it glowed brighter, making the encased angel more defined and precise.

I was filled with tranquillity as the first encased angel hovered in front of my face at eye level and began to speak. "We are the auguries of your life, the pedagogues, the mentors and the protectors. We are each others' secret." The angel and the ball of light speedily moved upwards. Upon ascent the angel disappeared and only the frosted ball of light remained. My eyes followed the ball as it flew and hovered above my head. Although there was a mirror hanging on the wall above the bed, there was inexplicably no reflection of this magical sight, only the reflection of the distant Hollywood sign. The letters of the sign were faint and obscure, like the bottom line on an optician's sight-test board. The ball of light then entered the mirror, causing the faint reflection of 'Hollywood' to shine brightly - for a split second. My attention then returned to the angels in encased balls hovering by the funnel of yellow light at the other side of the room. The second angel began to move towards me. As it got closer, it too glowed brighter.

I'd been confused and puzzled by the first angel's message - auguries and pedagogues? What could this possibly have meant? It seemed the second angel had sensed my bewilderment.

"Our words seem confusing now, but we shall lock them away in your subliminal memory until the time comes for you to use them." The disappearing act was identical. The Hollywood sign flashed and a third angel began its journey from the funnel of light.

"We must appear now while you are innocent and un-prejudiced by your surroundings and other people's bigoted attitudes."

Another coruscating flash and a fourth pious being.

"You must rise above all. You are different. You will be learned, having a profound love of knowledge and a strong desire to fulfil your dreams. You must use this knowledge to work out the messages we will instil in your mind so you can discover your divine destiny."

A fifth.

"You must love, care, teach and be happy. Be strong, be spiritual and serve the Lord. You must appreciate the world you live in and the sights you see. You must fight to discover your destiny. You must also appreciate you are one of very few Chosen out of the billions of beings."

A sixth.

"You must not rise above your station. You must always respect your position, not taking advantage of your Chosen status. Eat from the tree of knowledge and digest it well. Do not banish yourself from the Eden God has created for you with greed."

A seventh angel appeared, glowing brightly in its transparent capsule.

"Now we come to your first message. It is also one of the most important messages. When you understand this message you are half-way to discovering your destiny. We enlightened Socrates, who was also a Chosen One, with the very same message. He used it wisely, and so must you."

With a blinding flash the six other angels reappeared in their opaque balls.

"Wisest is she who knows what she does not know," they chanted.

No eighth angel. No Mexican voices. Only confusion, astonishment and a distant Hollywood sign.

chapter thirteen

I woke to see the orange and brown psychedelic patterns on the curtains swirling around each other. I chased one swirl with my eyes to find the end. But there was no end. When I thought about it there was no beginning either, like tomorrow never comes and yesterday never dies, a ravelling mystery of never-ending patterns. As mysterious as angels from lights, Mexican accents, eating from the tree of knowledge, Socrates and pedagogues. The angels were certainly correct in stating I wouldn't comprehend. Locking it away in my mind was a wise decision. But when would the incomprehensible information resurface? Why was I chosen? What was my destiny? Those were the thoughts swirling around my mind, like the never-ending pattern on the ugly curtains, when Mammy entered the room.

"Come on now, Orlagh. *WAKEY, WAKEY!*" Loud! She was always so loud in the morning. I was so terribly tired too. I was on the verge of telling her I needed more sleep because I'd been conversing with angels all night when one of the messages suddenly surfaced out of nowhere, '*We are each other's secret.*' I found this quite difficult to understand. My parents knew the angels existed, they were present at my birth. So why not let them continue to know? I was obedient to their wishes though.

"Our last day, Orlagh. Come on now, we must make the most of it. We've so much to see in Los Angeles."

"City of de angels."

"Yes, that's right, sweetheart, city of the angels. You're such a clever wee thing. Who told you that?"

"Oh it's just something I heard somewhere." Mammy laughed as she departed the room.

The vacation of donuts, Disney and day-dreaming days away was over all too soon. We were to fly from the city of angels with our diseased suitcases and minds full of memories of building log cabins, eating cereal for supper, evading Sambo, meeting enchanting Disney characters and of course - the apparition of angels.

chapter fourteen

As we were about to enter the familiar yet strangely unfamiliar surroundings of our home after the continual humming of aeroplane engines, the harmonious sound of the telephone rang relentlessly. We stood outside awaiting the chief key-holder to let us in. You could sense an unheard chant from the telephone: 'I will be answered - I will be answered - I will be answered'. Dad fumbled, bags hung around his shoulders, diseased cases at his feet. The more the phone rang the more he rushed and the more he fumbled. The key wouldn't fit into the lock. It was the right key, but it just wouldn't turn.

"Agh for Christ sake, what's wrong with the bloody lock now?"

"There's probably nothing wrong at all, Rory. Just calm down, whoever's on the phone can call back. They've had to wait six weeks, they can wait six minutes longer."

As magic had it, the key went in, and the phone still rang, rang and rang. We were all certain it was a life-and-death situation. Dad had the same problem with the key in the front door as he'd experienced with the porch, although it didn't take as long. He ran into the hallway dropping the hand luggage along the way, put his hand on the receiver and, yes... it stopped.

"Agh ya bbaaa..." Whatever Dad was going to say he held it in along with his breath, pursed-lipped and furious.

We all stood in the hallway looking around as if a major re-decoration job had taken place while we had been away. But nothing had altered. It was all as it had been six weeks previous. Although it did seem bare and empty and lacked the usual fresh cooking and laundry smells. Only fusty, stale air lingered.

Dad unlocked the lounge and dining rooms, pausing momentarily to glance around each room to check all was in order. He then let us into the kitchen. I ran straight to the refrigerator, despite not being that hungry. I stared inside as if it were a television, only to discover a disappointing emptiness, which was an unusual sight in our huge American-style refrigerator. A lonesome jar of Branston Pickle and a solitary jar of Heinz Salad Cream peered forlornly back at me.

The vibrating bell of the telephone startled us all out of our melancholic return-home-reality feeling.

"I hope to God that this is important, whoever it is." Dad stormed to the bulbous green telephone in the hallway. Before he had time to put the receiver to his ear the echoing Dublin tones of Nanna Bridie's voice bellowed into the luggage-strewn hall.

"He's going to cut me throat. The Ayadollah's going to cut me feckin' throat."

"What... the Ayadollah is what? Agh, Jesus, Mammy, what have yer been doing?... Okay, okay, calm down would yer." We could hear no more. Dad had placed the receiver tight to his ear so no additional bad language bellowed forth. Mammy stood with her arms folded across her chest breathing in deeply, shaking her head, realising we were well and truly home. "Yes, yes, yes... Jesus, shut up will ye now. Me and the kids'll be up in a minute. Just keep out of his way for God's sake."

"What in God's name has that crazy old coot done now?" Mammy asked, with a hint of sarcasm.

"Are you not going to give her the benefit of the doubt, Grania? She may be in the right this time."

"In the right? *In the right?* Rory Emmet, I never thought you'd be a sucker... She's a trouble-maker, well and truly. The day that woman is in the right I'll go to the moon. Go now, go on would you, I can do the washing while you're all outa me hair." Mammy shooed us out of her way. We had only been in the door a couple of minutes and she was getting on with the washing. She emptied the cases over the linoleum-covered kitchen floor like a woman gone mad. "Colours, whites, colours. Agh, be off with ye you lot, the Ayadollah might cut your grandmother's throat... Chance'd be a fine thing." She laughed as she disseminated the fusty-smelling clothes across the floor.

The Ayadollah was actually the Iranian tenant who lived above Nanna Bridie. He was a well-educated and clean-living family man, lecturing in Electronics at Birmingham University. It was his misfortune that Birmingham City Council had allocated him a flat within a converted pre-war house. He and his family upstairs and Nanna Bridie downstairs. They shared front and rear gardens.

A couple of months before the Ayadollah's arrival the real Ayatollah Khomeini had overthrown the Shah of Iran and started an Islamic revolution to rid Iran of all Western culture. The story was covered on every national news broadcast. So, when an Iranian moved in, Nanna took on her creative side and nicknamed her neighbour. She thought this hilarious. Although, as usual, due to her lack of attention and her ignorance, Ayatollah had been distorted to - Ayadollah.

When he first arrived - as with most people she initially met - he was the best thing since the proverbial sliced bread. She just couldn't get enough of him and his family. But familiarity soon bred contempt. She became bored with their friendship and quickly changed into the enemy. She was certainly an adversary nobody would wish for.

On their first meeting she showed him around her flat, fed him sugared cups of tea by the brass knick-knack-filled

105

fireplace, told him all her business - and everybody else's too. She then offered him her side of the garden. The gardens were split down the centre; left for upstairs, right for down.

"You have my side me luv," she said. "I've no need for it. Only to hang me washin' out now and then, on a nice summer's day, ya know. You can have it for the kiddies to play in."

It was just previous to us leaving for America that the novelty of being nice had worn off. No more child-minding favours. No more friendship. The seed of Nanna's loathing had been well and truly planted. She couldn't be pleasant for too long, not even to her own children; she had got up and left them in the middle of the night. Not to mention leaving her husband lying in bed, with the beads of his rosary embedded into the translucent skin of his palms, as he coughed up phlegm the same colour as the light of the sacred heart which hung above his head. You could say she had a very short boredom threshold - crossed with a very evil streak.

So, as I mentioned, for no apparent reason the seed of Nanna's loathing had been planted previous to us leaving - but what was the reason for it sprouting so furiously into bloom? Was there a reason? We were about to find out!

We drove into Nanna's dirty litter-strewn inner-city cul-de-sac full of ethnic minorities and prostitutes. She adored it. The filth, the poverty and the piles of Asian spices and pulses laid out on mats in front of shops which sold fifty-pence useless bargains. Being seventy years old, she should have been living in a clean, secure, warden-controlled flat, going to bingo on an afternoon and getting a blue rinse. Instead, she was committing petty theft in local shops, evading potential muggings on an afternoon stroll and causing havoc with the neighbours.

She stood waiting at her gate like a naughty school-child awaiting a punishment. She was as tough as old boots, but weak at the same time. She wore her gravy-stained striped apron over five cardigans. Whether it was summer or winter, minus ten degrees or a hundred and ten, it didn't matter - she would invariably keep piling on the layers, making her already huge frame larger. She waved her idiosyncratic three-finger wave, well, two fingers and a thumb. Her little finger and adjacent digit were permanently bent down, the ligaments severed in a power-press accident. Her wrist also appeared to be deformed, due to a huge lump which protruded in different directions. But that lump hadn't been created from a power-press accident - it had evolved from numerous used tissues which she continually stuffed up her cardigan sleeve.

"Where ya bin, Rory? I've bin waitin' ages."

"We came as quick as we could, Ma. We've just walked in the door from America."

"Oh, never mind that. That Iranian bastard's going to kill me and now he's feckin' prayin' to Allah."

"What do you mean he's prayin' to Allah? Slow down and tell me the story."

We proceeded into her flat; as usual the door had been left ajar. Nanna had acquired a limp, which she hadn't even mentioned up to that point. If she had a snivel she'd say it was the flu and that she was most probably dying. So, the limp could either mean she was seriously worried about the Ayadollah cutting her throat and she had forgotten about her injury, or she had acquired it by doing something she shouldn't have been.

The usual smell of stale Irish stew lay dormant in the small hallway. I swirled myself as always in the plastic-beaded strips that hung in the doorway which divided the hall from the lounge. They were like those I'd seen in the movies which a fortune-teller always seemed to walk through before predicting someone's future. But there was no crystal ball behind Nanna's beaded strips, only her jumbled collection of ornaments, brass whatnots and general junk which was scattered everywhere. The television sat blaring in the corner. A gardening programme

107

flashed across the screen with the volume turned up to a deafening level. I almost tripped on one of the many mats which covered every visible piece of carpet. I always thought the immense number of mats defeated the object of a carpet. I could never understand it, but there again I could never understand Nanna Bridie either.

"Sit yerselves down, I'll make yer's a nice cuppa."

"Forget the tea for now, Ma, what's going on? And for Christ sake would ye turn that television down."

I sensed she was avoiding telling Dad the real story.

"To tell you the truth, I think that's what started this whole fiasco. The Telly, ye know." She proceeded to tell us the story, in her animated, entertaining way. "You know I'd been lookin' after that kid and everythin' for them ungrateful Iranies? Well, after I'd done all that he had the cheek to come down the other week. It was *only* midnight and didn't he tell me - feckin' tell me - not ask me, to turn the telly down." Speaking in monosyllables, she tried very poorly to impersonate his accent. "'Mrs. Bri-die. Ple-ase. You. Must. Turn. Tel-ly. Down. I. Need. Stu-dy. Ve-ry. Diff-i-cult. Stu-dy. With. Tel-ly.' On each syllable she nodded her head abruptly. "'Tel-ly. Ve-ry. Loud. Mrs. Bri-die. You. Must. Turn. Down.' Study? Feckin' study? He's only a poxy electrician. What do elec-feckin-trcians have to study?"

"He's an electronics lecturer at the university, Ma. And will ye watch yer language a little, hey now?"

"Yeah, and he tried to feckin' lecture me as well," she replied, not taking a bit of notice of what Dad had just asked her. "And I give it to him... erm, yer know I mean even after he'd told me off I did nothin' at all in retaliation - honest. Absolutely nothin' at all. And then he has the cheek to start all this trouble."

Dad rummaged through the rancid rubbish heap of her lies for scraps of truth. He recycled the salvaged truths and came up with the most probable interpretation for the start of this whole fiasco. "Yer didn't do anything at all? Now for doin' nothing at all, is that the reason why he wants to cut yer throat? Do yer really mean, Mammy, that as usual yer did the opposite of whatever anyone tells yer and yer tormented him terribly from that moment on with continual harassment? Did the telly happen to go even louder? Did yer taunt him and his poor wife? Did yer call him names?"

"I did no such thing, Rory. Why ever would yer think that of yer own mother? This is what happened. May God strike me dead if it's not the truth. I wakes up this mornin' and I heard all this racket in the back garden. Ey, yaaaa, eyyy, yaaa. It was all that Packie wailin' music. Ye canny be listenin' to that racket, especially at ten o'clock in the mornin' - I was tryin' to sleep, for God sake. Well, anyway, I peers out the winda and what do I see but the Ayadollah and a crowd more of them uns all crouched down like they're about to have a shite or somethin', all in their dresses. Grown men in dresses, I don't know what's come of this world, I really don't. And the cheek of 'em, they were sittin' in my garden around a feckin' barber... what'd ye call them cooker things outside?"

"A barbecue." Dad shook his head.

"Yeah, and it was built in my feckin' garden."

"But, ye told him he could use the garden, Ma."

"That's not the point. I told him I'd changed me mind. But the ignorant Iranian bastard took no notice, did he? I showed 'em, comin' to my country and takin' over."

"You're Irish, Ma. Just as much their country as it is yours."

"Yeah, but I'm feckin' white and they're not and anyway I've been here longer. Whose side're you on? So anyway, I went out there and showed 'em who's the boss around 'ere."

"Did ye get dressed first, Nanna?" Patrick's voice was full of mischief.

"No, no, there was no time for that - I had to get them while they were at it." A vision of Nanna in her nightdress and curlers was frightening.

"Get them at what, Ma? What the hell were they doin' wrong?"

"Smokin' them drugs they smoke. Marawanga they calls it. So I ran out, told 'em to piss off've me property and I gave the barber cookin' thing a nudge and it all fell down."

Dad was like a code breaker as he once again deciphered her story. It was amazing how he knew what had happened without actually being there - I hoped to do this one day. "Do yer mean, Mammy, that in one of yer violent rages you continually kicked the barbecue until it toppled over? Which would explain that limp yer've got. The barbecue which sat in the corner of the garden which yer've never set foot in. I bet ya embarrassed that poor Iranian to death."

"Embarrassed him to *my* death yer mean. That brings me on to the threat." She ignored Dad's accusations. "So there I am, innocently chattin' away at the gate this afternoon, ye know to that prostitute at number twenty-seven, the one with all them scruffy kids."

"Yes, yes, would ye carry on?"

"He was making his way through the gate past me and the old-bag when he grabbed me round the throat and whispered through his dirty yella clenched teeth; 'Mrs. Bri-die. I. Cut. Your. Fuck-ing. Throat.' And that's when I called you. Where the hell were ya? I could've been lyin' here dead." Dad didn't even bother to answer. "Now he's feckin' prayin' to Allah before he does me in."

We all proceeded into her back room. There were three wardrobes and piles of suitcases with clothes bulging out at every angle, seeming to try to escape their overcrowded, claustrophobic surroundings. On her bed four mattresses were piled one on top of the other. I thought of the princess and the pea, but stopped when I couldn't imagine Nanna Bridie being the princess. Her war-time impoverished childhood had given her an unrelenting addiction to hoard. 'You can't throw anything away, you never know when you may need it,' she would always say.

We followed Nanna to her viewing position. We all

110

knelt on the floor under her window which looked over the controversial back garden. The orange, fusty-smelling, satin curtains were drawn, but at the base there was a gap where they didn't quite reach the window-sill. From the gap we were going to view the ritual prayer to *Allah* which Nanna was so very convinced the Ayadollah was performing - 'on and off since the threat,' she'd said.

Sure enough, from our limited viewpoint we could see the Ayadollah's upper body. We couldn't see if he was standing, kneeling or crouching, we could only see his torso moving up and down every few seconds. We could only see part of his arms, from shoulders to elbows, which were moving along with his torso. Up and down, pause, up and down. His forearms and hands were out of sight, hidden behind Nanna's musty curtains.

"Woooo-weeeee, wooooo-weeeee," was the muffled noise we could hear coming from behind the window. I truly believed the Ayadollah was preparing to kill Nanna.

"See, I told yer's, he's gettin' ready, look. He's probably got the knife in his pocket. Go and sort him out, Rory, this is gettin' outa control."

"It's probably all innocent Ma, he may just be prayin'." I thought Dad was underestimating the seriousness of this situation. As crazy as Nanna was, I didn't want the Ayadollah to kill her.

"Innocent? Knackers is he innocent. You can see it with ye own eyes for God sakes... LOOK!" Her final word was accompanied with her index finger pointing at the window. But she had misjudged the distance between the end of her finger and the pane of glass - and hit the window, lifting the curtain to uncover our spying position to the Ayadollah himself. Our five sets of eyes hovered above the window-sill, caught in the act.

The Ayadollah was positively infuriated. He dropped the bright red ball he had been throwing to the toddler who had been out of our sight, which explained the intermittent up and down movement of his upper body.

111

He ran to the window. Dad's face was a picture; embarrassment and anger all mixed up into one confused expression, like a small boy being found out organising a school-yard prank.

"YOU DRIVE ME CRA-ZY MRS BRI-DIE. WHY YOU DRIVE ME CRA-ZY? NOW YOU BRING YOUR FAM-ILY TO SPY TOO. YOU ARE ALL CRA-ZY. CRA-ZY. CRA-ZY," he screamed at the top of his voice, expelling every bit of oxygen in his lungs. His beautiful brown skin formed a glow as red as the ball, which had been discarded in the drain, as he banged his palms on the glass in frustrated anger, causing it to violently vibrate. He stopped suddenly, placed his forehead on the glass and his arms above his head with his palms stuck to the window; as if a cowboy had told him to 'stick 'em up', and began to sob uncontrollably.

Nanna had taken it to the limit this time.

Nanna looked at us all, then looked out of the window at the distraught Iranian. Her false teeth bit her bottom lip. "Oh, bollockinhell - I've done it now."

Dad couldn't get out of there quick enough. She gave me a bear-hug that took my breath away, helped along with the stench of whiskey on her breath. She slapped the side of my face where my birthmark was situated and rubbed it so hard it hurt. "Never mind luv, it'll be gone soon, then you'll be normal," she said, as she usually did each time I saw her.

Nanna nonchalantly waved us goodbye at the gate with her three digits, as if nothing of any significance had transpired in the last hour. But that fiasco was just another in the long line of Nanna Bridie disasters, so I suppose it didn't really make any difference to Nanna's day - as long as her throat hadn't been cut.

Ayatollah Khomeini had overthrown the Shah Of Iran and Bridie Emmet had over thrown the Ayadollah. News came two weeks later that he was gone. "Lock, stock and barrel. The lot of 'em - gone. I don't know why." And she really meant that!

chapter fifteen

The fun and insanity continued endlessly in the Emmet household. Through the final weeks of summer and as the leaves turned orange on the horse-chestnut-tree-lined streets. The discoloration started on the outer tips of the branches, like a flame had been ignited, and then it spread, engulfing the whole tree in an extravaganza of autumnal fire. The conkers grew large in their bulbous, green, spiky, protective cases, which we split open to discover shiny, brown orbs. I was convinced they grew merely to fill our autumn days, as I ran and climbed trees with the boys to find the largest and the strongest of them all. We couldn't wait for nature to instruct the conkers to fall; there were too many children hunting for the biggest, the best and the strongest. *But*, if I couldn't find a strong one, Dad would fix that, like he fixed every other problem in our lives.

His eyes shone brighter when the idea first entered his mind, and when he put the inspiration into action the same eyes radiated a mischief which you would only associate with a child. He didn't have a master plan of vinegar-soaking or oven-baking; but car-body-filler-filled conkers. He sliced the conker at the rounded core with his Stanley blade and like a surgeon with a scalpel was cautious not to cut anything that he shouldn't. He kept the shiny brown skin intact while scrupulously hollowing out the white centre. On a string he threaded a nut (as in bolt).

"We'll need to put the string in now, 'cause once the fibreglass is set, there'll be no breaking through it!" Around the nut he filled the conker shell with his mixture, then threaded the string through the cut-out circular core and stuck it all back together. You would never know it had been tampered with. Forget conker seventy-eighter, I had a conker two-thousander.

Autumnal breezes encouraged those fire-coloured leaves to fall to the pavements and chase each other in circles, like a dog does its tail. Strong wintry winds blew those rusty-coloured leaves into drains and gutters, creating soggy mush as the rain waters flowed away. Jack Frost then made his enchanted crystal appearance, making everything fresh and crisp once more. He nipped at every inch of uncovered skin and turned the grass a sparkling crisp and clean winter white. The roses from the previous summer were adamant about not decaying into the cycle of life, but standing their ground. They resembled springtime dandelions; the frost appearing to be the white fluffy seeds of the dead weed, preparing to be blown far away into the fairy-tale landscape. People clad in gloves, scarves, hats and overcoats rapidly scraped at frosted windscreens so they could be seated in the warmth of the car interior, with the heater blowing out hot stuffy air. But it didn't matter, the bare trees, the frost and the cold, mornings of shivers and rubbed hands, because the wonderland window displays appeared. The musty-smelling Father Christmas suits were retrieved from dusty store-rooms and cloudless blue skies prepared for Santa and his sleigh to fly through and bring wonderment to all. It was Christmas.

I adored Christmas. It was a time to hang shiny decorations in symmetrical patterns on the ceiling, make a cake or a jelly or maybe a trifle sprinkled with hundreds and thousands for the school Christmas party. It was a time to open the advent calendar and write lists to Santa and, of course, time for the nativity play.

It meant so much to me, being chosen to be the

Archangel Gabriel, to wear a flowing white dress and imitate one of my pious beings. It was only fair I be an angel; after all, I was a Chosen One.

Rehearsal after rehearsal went on twice a week throughout December with Mrs O'Reilly, who was no longer my teacher but co-ordinator for the yearly play. She seemed as excited as we were.

Everyone considered 'Our Lady' to be the primary part in the play. I didn't care; I had to be an angel. Siobhan was cast for the leading-lady part; Mrs O'Reilly had said her olive-coloured skin was perfect.

Mammy had made my special dress from a set of Great-grandma Mary's net curtains. It flowed like a princess's and had the purity of an angel's. The arms hung wide and graceful, giving the impression of wings. It was strewn with glitter and pearls. Mammy knew how very special this was to me. Dad had devised a contraption from an old metal coat-hanger so I could have a halo of silver tinsel bobbing above my head. It was all going to be perfect. I would make the most exquisite Angel Gabriel, prompting the nativity organisers to call me back each year to fill the part.

Dress rehearsals took place the night before the big day. Mrs O'Reilly said everything was wonderful and she would see us the next day at the church hall where we were to perform. But disaster struck. Mrs O'Reilly had skidded on black ice in her Mini, but luckily had missed going under an articulated lorry and wrapped herself around a lamp post instead. They said in an emergency assembly on the morning of the nativity that she wasn't critical, but would be off school until after Christmas. 'Who was going to organise this morning's most important play?' was the selfish thought flying through my mind. Surely it wouldn't be cancelled, after all our hard work and exquisite costumes. Father Maguire soon clarified the situation.

"Well, *MY CHILDREN*." He stood on his tiptoes and

paused. His bald head glowed from the winter cold. "We *MUST* pray to *GOD* in His kingdom to aid Mrs O'Reilly to a fast and *HEALTHY* recovery." We all bowed our heads as Father Maguire took us through a prayer for our wounded teacher, after which he answered the question which must have been on everyone's mind. "There is an important event taking place this morning, *WHICH*, of course, you all know Mrs O'Reilly was supervising. *WELL*, my children, I'm glad to inform you *THAT* the kind head mistress from the prot.... err um, school down the road, has volunteered to send Miss Crookson to help and take Mrs O'Reilly's place in the nativity proceedings. She knows what she's doing as she did her nativity only *YESTERDAY*."

Well now, that made everything all right, even if she was from the Protestant school down the road, which is what Father Maguire really wanted to say. But everything was far from being all right. We arrived at our church hall to find our jolly, kind Mrs O'Reilly had been replaced with the wicked witch of the east. Miss Crookson would probably have stood about five foot two if she hadn't been hunched over, losing four inches or so off her height. She had a hump as large as Mrs O'Reilly's stomach on the top of her back – well, not quite that big, but it was huge. Her fingers were long and thin, the bones of her knuckles protruding through the white translucent skin. Her fingernails were almost as long as her fingers, ending in sharp points. Her hair was coarse and grey with a few black strands sticking out, being defiant to the end, standing up wanting to be noticed amidst the masses of over-taking grey, or maybe they were on guard against losing their long-standing colour. Crooked old Crookson was my first impression of this cantankerous old woman. Cantankerous, nasty, pernicious, evil, there is not one single word that could describe this witch.

Excitement was building and the stage was set. Crooked Crookson was shouting orders while we got ready. I had taken off my winter coat, which had my woollen mittens threaded through the sleeves by a long line of wool, so I wouldn't lose them when they were not placed on my hands. When I didn't have the mittens on they hung adjacent to my hands looking like a spare pair, at the ready to offer their help. Uniform removed, I was about to put on my beautiful gown when I heard the high-pitched squeal: "Gabriel? Who is Gabriel? Show yourself unto me." Miss Crookson spoke like she was performing a Shakespearean play (like Dad did when we visited Stratford-upon-Avon), not conversing with children. She also acted like she was organising a production of *Othello* at the Royal Shakespeare Theatre, not a nativity play at Saint Columb's RC.

When I heard her request, I was stuck with the angel's dress over my head. I had got the arm hole mixed up with the neck hole. The more I struggled the more tangled I became. I could have done with that spare pair of woollen-mitten-hands now. Instead Siobhan tried to help, but she only made things worse. I answered a muffled "I'm here, Miss Crookson."

"Where? Where art thou? Speak up, child."

"Over here, Miss. Tell her I'm here, Siobhan."

"Errr, ummm, Miss Crooked, she's here, err dressing."

"Crooked? Crooked? It's Crookson, you insolent child. Are you stupid, stupid, stupid?" Siobhan didn't answer. "Come now, what art thou doing in there. Is every child in this school impertinent?"

"I don't know, Miss," I answered, still tied up in my beautiful dress. "I don't know what impertinent means."

"Sshh, child, it was a rhetorical question, not one for you to answer. Now come, let's get you into this thing."

She pulled left and right, grabbing a clump of my hair here and there. I thought it best if I didn't complain as she seemed riled at the smallest of mistakes and asked questions we were not to answer. I untangled myself from the lining, poked my head through the neck hole and came face to face with the wicked witch.

117

"Oh my goodness, no! Surely this cannot be?" She held her claw-like hands over her mouth, extremely shocked at the sight she had just witnessed. I turned around to see what this frightening spectacle might be, only to see multi-coloured painted palms transferred to paper which hung on the changing-room wall.

"What cannot be, Miss Crookson? What's wrong?"

"You... You cannot be."

"Cannot be what? What've I done?"

"Gabriel. You cannot be... Gabriel. Angels do not have red faces. Angels are *perfect* and *pure*, not marked with the Devil. Who cast for this play? It must've been that O'Reilly woman. She must be as stupid as her pupils. It is a stroke of luck that God's hand struck her down, for me, myself, to sort out this unruly mess."

"But I must be Gabriel, I was chosen. I am a Chosen One and Mammy made this dress especially for me. Please Miss Crookson, what've I done?"

"You are marked. You are deformed. You cannot play someone as pure as Gabriel. You should have been chosen to play the ass so we could cover your face. As for your dress - worry not about thy dress for we shall find a stand-in. A stand-in which is not disfigured." She had finished what she had to say; there was no arguing, no pleading. The rest of the group looked in shock as she pulled the divine dress over my head, leaving a trail of sequins and pearls strewn across the scratched parquet floor.

Clad only in my white pants and vest, I fell back as if I'd been pushed by an unseen spirit passing by in the mist of my dejectedness. The hand-printed wall behind me caught my fall. I was broken-hearted.

I had faced name-calling and taunts from children. This I had learnt to handle. To handle with an iron fist... literally. But to have an adult insult me, one of those I was supposed to venerate, learn from, even respect, was positively disconcerting. I couldn't lash out at an adult; I had been taught that this wasn't right, but surely what she

118

had said to me was wrong. Images of me beating her like I had Rubbery Robert and many which had followed in his footsteps were flashing through my mind. I decided I could not go through this with-out a fight. She didn't understand it was my duty to be an angel.

I composed myself and concluded the best defence would be to hurt her with words, like she had done to me.

"No wonder you teach at that prostitute school, because there would never, not ever be a Catholic as nasty and as ugly as you," I stated, with all the anger and bravery I could muster, holding my head high and nodding the conclusion.

"Nasty? Evil? I shall show the evil. Come everyone, we have a play to do."

Rachael Rafferty walked out with her head bowed, sad and embarrassed to be wearing my virtuous dress which swamped her miniature body. Siobhan, with a blue shawl hung over her head, was last to leave, dragging her feet to the door; which she was helped through by a tug on her ear from Crooked Crookson who turned out the light. The switch was situated outside in the corridor. As the light was extinguished she spookily recited an excerpt from Macbeth, as if she herself was one of the three witches: *"Out, out brief candle, life's but a walking shadow, a poor player, that struts and frets his hour upon the stage and then is heard no more...* But you, young lady, will not be heard at all. You shall sit here and suffer the consequences of your evil tongue." As the door was closed, her muffled speech ended in a long, eerie laugh. *"It is a tale told by an idiot, full of sound and fury, signifying nothing... haaaa haaaa haaaa."*

My protective child-safe bubble was burst. I sat alone and momentarily scared. I felt like the conkers broken out of their spiky, green, hard shells, facing the harsh elements and realities of life. My shell was shed and I decided at that moment I was going to be a winning conker, one that survives through generations. One that you would think was filled with car-body-filler.

CHAPTER SIXTEEN

I shouted until my vocal cords no longer played their tune and all the energy in my body was drained out through my fists as I banged the door in rage, fear and sadness. With my back to the teak-veneered door, I slumped to the ground. My forehead rested on my goose-pimpled knees. Tears dripped from my face, flowed down my thighs and nestled in my groin. I was like the only child not going to the tea-party, only no one knew. Mammy was sitting proud in the audience, knowing my cue, waiting for my appearance, anticipating the lines I had recited over and over: 'Fear not: for, behold, I bring you good tidings of great joy, which shall be to all people. For unto you a child is born, which is Christ the Lord. And this shall be a sign unto you: ye shall find the babe wrapped in swaddling clothes, lying in a manger.'

Fear not, fear not, fear not, reverberated around my head like an echoing sound in a lonely valley. Where were my good tidings? Where was anyone? Where was Father Maguire? Why had no-one noticed my absence? I squeezed my sodden eyes closed, it being as dark as when they were open, praying, praying, praying for my angels to appear. If there had been any light, I'm sure my knuckles would have been white, as I clasped my hands together in prayer. Just one angel would do. I begged for the flawless image in the opaque ball to appear and tell me what to do - to help me escape.

I don't know how much later it was when a booming noise entered my head. All that I knew was I was cold, *so very cold*, lying on the parquet wooden floor of the church hall changing-rooms. All I could hear was a loud boom, boom, boom sound. My head was spinning. It was pitch-black dark except for a thin line of light at the base of the door - a ray of hope, the escape from my demise. Boom, boom, boom, like the drum at the head of the Disney procession. Boom, boom, boom. Did this herald the latest enraptured entrance of my angels for which I'd been praying?

"Orlagh, Orlagh, my sweet child. Orlagh, we're coming!" My saviours! They fumbled and rattled what sounded like a huge set of keys, like jailers releasing the inmates. I was the prisoner when I should have been an angel. But my angels were going to set me free. Did angels require keys? I thought they would have been able to fly through doors.

The door opened. I was too tired, too disheartened, to move a muscle. I had cried so much there were no more tears to cry. My energy had seeped out of me. My energy along with my happy heart. The joyful excited butterflies in my stomach had been savaged, wings broken, vanquished by the wild cats. I lay curled in the foetal position. My saviours pushed the door open wide enough for a little figure to squeeze through. The light was switched on and I was blinded, like the first ray of morning sun blinds you as you open the curtains. I shaded my eyes until I grew accustomed to the light. The discarded sequins of my beautiful dress crunched under the feet of my rescuers, like the sound of crisp snow. It was not my angels as I had expected, but Mammy, Father Maguire and Siobhan, who was still dressed like the Virgin Mary.

"I'm sorry we didn't come sooner, baby, so, so sorry." Mammy sounded incensed.

What had seemed like an eternity trapped in the dark, cold room was in fact an hour and a half.

Firstly there had been the carol service. Everyone sang Silent Night, including Crooked Crookson, who placed herself at the front of the stage with her head held high. The hymn book sat in her claw-like hands, giving her the appearance of a pious pedagogue. "Silent night, holy night, all is calm, all is bright." I lay with much silence except for my fatigued snivels; but there was no brightness for me. Although, like in 'O little town of Bethlehem', I went into a deep, dreamless sleep.

Following the carol service there had been a short homily from Father Maguire, about the importance of goodwill to all, year round and especially at Christmas. Crooked Crookson audaciously sat on the mini-plastic chair nodding in agreement.

Then the play began.

"Oh, my poor, sweet child, I thought you were there, through the carol service and Father's wee talk, amidst the lambs, shepherds and other angels. When the shepherds moved into place and you were supposed to appear, I thought you'd forgotten your cue. I thought you forgetting was strange because we'd practised so much. Then when I saw that wee girl, swamped in your dress, being pushed from the wings I knew for certain something was wrong."

Rachael Rafferty had been pushed on by Crooked Crookson and was silent - no lines, no sound of, 'Fear not'. I suppose because she was the one in fear. The one in fear of a repeat performance from the wicked witch of the east.

I was wrapped in Father Maguire's black blazer, the bitter-sweet aroma of old spice emerged, 'a real man's scent' Dad always said. I was like a small child banished from its home due to fire, wrapped in a fireman's coat, cold, overwhelmed and grateful for the rescuers' presence.

"I ran out of me seat, over to Father here, well he was there... you know what I mean. I asked him where you were, he said he didn't have a clue and would find out. Which is what he did. He went up to that woman who's taken Mrs O'Reilly's place."

"Crooked Crookson." Those were the first words I had uttered since my emancipation had taken place.

"I know you're sick, sweetheart, but don't be disrespectful now."

"Sick? I'm not sick. There's nothing wrong with me, only not being allowed to be Gabriel."

"Whoa, slow down, slow down. What do you mean you're not sick? That's what Miss Crookson told Father Maguire. 'She's sick, too weak to perform,' she said. You look ill, and look you're sweating buckets and it's freezing in here." She was referring to the vest wet with my tears of sorrow, my tears for the loss of my secure, protective bubble.

Siobhan and I immediately set the record straight and informed them of Crooked Crooksen's cruel words. Mammy and Father Maguire listened, astounded and infuriated. The pacific priest's usual resplendent green eyes, like emeralds amidst diamonds, were clouded over and downcast as he shook his head and tut-tut-tutted his way through the account. He placed a gentle, calming hand on Mammy's arm when she attempted to interrupt. As patient as though he were in the confessional box.

Mammy sat purse-lipped and restless. She took sharp intakes of breath and numerous glances at Father Maguire, as if reminding herself of his presence. She shook her head in pity as much as anger while stroking, clutching and pulling my curls.

I was dubious of relaying the part about the prostitute school, but thought I may as well come clean as I was sure Crooked Crookson would soon tell them that detail. After recounting that part of the tale, the part I expected them both to chastise me for, they both smiled and Mammy pulled me into her breast so tight I could hardly breathe. I wondered if I would ever be able to understand an adult's way of thinking.

When I concluded the story with the citation of Macbeth - which talks of the useless efforts of human life

- Mammy's fury rose to its pinnacle. She was like a pan of water that bubbles from within, then suddenly - *blast* - it reaches boiling point. She was like a wild animal about to attack its kill. Like a lion stalking an impala.

chapter seventeen

"Grania, please, Grania, come now, leave it be. We'll sort this out... properly, you know," Father Maguire gabbled as he ran the long, bare-bricked corridor from the changing room to the stage, after my usually calm, but now profoundly irate mother.

"No, Father, I'm sorry, this woman... no, she's no woman, that thing out there is beyond redemption, beyond your help, anyone's help. She likes name-calling and bullying, let's see her stand up to the Devil's mother shall we? I'll give her marked with the Devil, she'll be marked with Satan after I'm finished with her. Father, forgive me for what I'm about to do." Her anger was rising as fast as mercury in a thermometer taken from arctic to tropical temperatures.

"Well that'll be a first, forgiving before the occurrence. I can't let you do this, Grania. Listen to some reasoning, will you?" At that she stopped dead in her tracks. We were not ready for the abrupt halt. Father Maguire, Siobhan and myself walked into each other like a concertina closing.

"Reasoning? *Reasoning*? Like she'll listen to reasoning? Crooked old Crookson out there... I don't think so. Please, Father, think of what she's done to my precious child here." I stood looking innocent and hurt in my pants and vest and the priest's jacket trailing behind me like Batman's cape. "We can't let her get away with it." The speed of her footsteps continued.

The hunter was at chase.

The play had continued as best it could, with a mute Archangel Gabriel and an absent Mary. Crooked Crookson had replaced Siobhan - 'Our Lady' - with herself. She sat centre stage holding a plastic doll, while cueing the rest of the child actors. The audience sat in bewilderment at this bizarre scene, but the most bizarre of scenes was still to unfold.

Father Maguire tried in vain to stop Mammy, but to no avail. She was like a racing speed-walker as she reached the stage wings, arms swinging, elbows high.

"Uh, lookie here... what a hypocrite. How can you enact a being as pure and perfect as Our Lady?" Mammy shouted as she walked on stage, "with that ugly hump on your back and more wrinkles than a crocodile. Do you recognise any similarities in any of my hateful words? Similarities to words you spoke to a seven-year-old child before you locked her in a cold, dark room, scaring her half to death? Now bully me, *please*, I implore you." Father Maguire stood in the wings with his palms laid on his cheeks and mouth wide open, as shocked as myself at Mammy's calm character taking such an impulsive, unpredictable turn.

"Get out of my way, you insane woman. Is everyone in this establishment asinine and moronic? Move, let me out of this asylum. Do a good turn and this is what you get. No wonder Henry the Eighth tried to rid this country of your kind: you doltish, backward people," Crooked Crookson screeched. She raised her bony arms and with her claw-like hands tried to push my furious mother aside. As her arm made contact Mammy grabbed her scrawny wrist and swung her round so she was now face to face with her adversary. Mammy then took hold of her neck, thumbs nestling around her Adam's apple. On each word Mammy uttered she jolted her arms forward, causing Miss Crookson's head to move back and forth. It appeared her

126

grip was getting tighter and tighter. Mammy's long chestnut hair flowed, the curls bounced around her face.

"I'll give you moronic, you hunchbacked, obnoxious old cow ye. You cross my child - you cross me."

The malicious Miss Crookson had no courage, she would not or maybe could not fight back. Her boldness was diminished, her bullying terminated. Her wrinkled face grew redder as each word flowed from Mammy's mouth, which gave her the haunting appearance of Satan himself.

All Mammy's anger was almost discharged when realisation of where she was and what she was doing became apparent. She released Crooked Crookson's neck, looked at the back and front of her hands as if not believing what practice they had just performed. And performed it was, in front of an audience of Saint Columbs parents, all equally in shock as they witnessed these proceedings. Crooked Crookson stood as mute as Rachael Rafferty had. Father Maguire was still in the wings, continually making the sign of the Cross and saying a silent prayer unto himself.

"Go on go, get out of here, you evil old witch. You shouldn't be allowed around children." Mammy pushed the old hag in her bony flat chest, which caused Crooked Crookson to lose her footing and fall back on to her backside. She scurried off stage on her hands and knees, like a rat heading for the gutter.

The show was over. The hunt complete.

chapter eighteen

Dad was bobbing and weaving past Mammy, feigning being in a boxing ring as she hurried around cooking dinner. He had received a full account of what had transpired earlier that day and was continually cracking jokes about Mammy being a force to be reckoned with.

"I didn't realise what a feisty little madam I'd married. Yes, I'd better watch me mouth a bit more." Dad threw a one-two combination, just missing Mam's head as she drained the cabbage into the colander.

'That's right and you can start now. *Enough*, Rory."

"Boiled bacon and cabbage, boiled bbb-hu-hu-acon and cab-ha-ab-age, boiled bacon and cabbage, for my bbb- ha-aby d-oooll, for my baby doll." Dad had now transformed from Mohammed Ali to Fred Astaire as he captured me by my arms to dance around the kitchen, swinging me around the cabinets and appliances, singing the ridiculous song about our meal. He was trying as hard as possible to take my mind off the unfortunate incident which had occurred earlier that day.

The confrontation between Mammy and Crooked Crookson had momentarily taken my mind off my rejected predicament. The day had been filled with unexpected excitement. Not excitement I'd hoped for, but nevertheless it was excitement. At the party following the botched nativity Mammy was the hero. She had banished the wicked witch of the east, taken the ruby slippers and aided everyone into a happy ending.

But for me, there was really no happy ending.

'The way to a man's heart, Orlagh, and remember this, baby doll, is through his stomach. That's why I married yer mother. Ye canny beat home cookin', especially, Grania O'Toole's home cookin'. Although, kids." He winked at Dom, Pat and myself before he continued. "Although, I did teach her everything she knows. This gravy... that's my recipe, so it is." He was like a fisherman waiting for the catch to bite the bait. He felt a tug on the line, then he wound the reel, round and round, until - the catch was his, well and truly caught.

"Is that right, Rory Emmet?" Mammy had tried not to bite the bait, but couldn't resist a taste.

"And boiling an egg, she couldn't even do that when I married her." He nodded and raised his eyebrows in a confirmed conclusion.

"Ohhh, Mr-let's use every pot, pan and utensil in the house. Mr-let's leave traces of the dinner on everything that we touch along the way. You're worse than Orlagh when she makes a cake and leaves icing sugar on the door handles, the phone, the fridge. I'll give you 'taught you everything I know', you only know how to do a fry-up: bacon, eggs and black pudding." The catch was his, flopping its slimy body on the shore, gasping for breath. We all knew what was coming next. Dom had received the cue for his line.

"How long have you been married, Dad?"

"Too long, son, too long!"

They were so much fun, my parents, but all the amusement, jollity and a special Christmas episode of the Friendly Farting Giant couldn't take away my sorrow.

The Friendly Farting Giant was now recited in my room. Dominic was much too mature for things like that now; he was almost thirteen and according to him pretty much a man. He now bathed on his own and slept on his own.

There was no way of sneaking into his bed when the frightening night people arrived. Just like Carmel in Canada, Dom had acquired a little bit of an attitude problem, temperamental to say the least. But this was no fault of his own. The villains of the piece were his hormones. They had taken over my caring, loving brother's body. They told his muscles and bones to buck their ideas up, get a little strength, to stand up and be counted, causing his body to ache in the most uncontrollable way. They commanded hair to sprout in the most unusual places, causing much embarrassment and confusion. His mind was now consumed with thoughts of girls rather than Freddie, our wonderful giant - girls preferably to anything really - especially his little sister. I couldn't come to terms with these changes so I don't know how Dominic coped.

I laughed my way through the account of Rudolph and the rest of the reindeer coming down with a terrible illness, making them incapable of flying on Christmas Eve, causing much distress to Santa. Freddie, who happened to be in Lapland, successfully came up with an idea of using his flatulence as power. Thus, he farted Father Christmas, his sleigh and presents around the world. So now Freddie had farting power and not the usual farting destruction.

I couldn't concentrate on screaming, 'FARTING POWER' due to my preoccupied thoughts of my missed chance of impersonating one of my angels. My hallowed friends on whom I had not set eyes or even heard in such a long time. Dad sensed it as always. There was no chance of keeping anything from him.

"Go on with yer, Patrick Emmet, use some fartin' power and get yerself into that bed of yours." Patrick's hormones were still normal and so didn't find any embarrassment in giving me a huge goodnight kiss before sprinting his bony body and blond cherub-like curls back to his room while screaming; "FARTING POWER."

Dad snuggled up to me under my imitation patchwork

quilt. I could sense a serious discussion was looming. I knew one of his insightful chats was coming because he wasn't singing an Irish rebel song or dancing his way around the room. He calmly lay next to me with his arm looped around my neck; I found I fitted perfectly in his arm pit. The electric light formed a white square reflection on his smooth shiny forehead and in the centre of his blue eyes - like the sun glistening over a tropical ocean.

"You know, Orlagh, golden princess of princesses, me goin' out to work and buildin' walls with big grey concrete blocks, or regular red bricks, is just like you growin' up. Each brick is held together with cement, or what we call in the building game - *compo*. The cement, well that's like an everyday occurrence, the cement of life, ye know?" I didn't know. "Ye see, the way I see it, everyone has a wall and that wall signifies your character. A wall of qualities that make up the formation of a person. Now, the cement holds the bricks together and everyone has a couple of bricks, even, believe it or not, that Crooked ald Crookson women. But her wall would be small and weak with shallow footings and no foundations. So shallow and small you can break the wall in seconds, like yer mammy did today.

"Yer footings, now that's what we dug for yer, diggin' em deep into solid rock, so there's no chance of subsidence, and no chance of sinkin' to the level of the Devil, like ald Crookson did. We then laid yer foundations, the concrete pad that contains: God, Jesus, the angels, love and happiness... Strong foundations are set, so now *you* can begin to build yer wall so strong and tall you'd be able to touch the heavens.

"The cement is like goin' to school or learnin' somethin' new like how to ride a bike for the very first time - or fallin' off. These are your basic character buildin' compositions... See, *compo* - cement. Get it? Now the bricks. My, my, the bricks, this is where it gets tricky. The bricks are the major incidents, the very good and the very

131

bad, and when each event takes place a brick is placed on your character wall. Every time you go for some treatment, there's a brick - on yer wall.

"So, in the long run that evil old witch Crooked Crookson has done yer a favour. I know it may sound silly now, but believe me I'm right. All that she's done is add a few more bricks to yer wall of character, tough, rigid hard ones, like concrete blocks. She's helped to build it higher and stronger. Building you as a person into a courageous, confident individual. You see, the higher the wall, the stronger the character. The stronger the character the more determined, persistent and successful the person.

"By the time you go out into that big wide world on your own, filled with many Crooked Crooksons, no one person or an army of them for that matter will be able to climb your wall and break your character, therefore makin' you a better person. The building bricks of life, Orlagh, darlin'... the building bricks of life!"

An hour or so had passed since Dad had departed, leaving my mind filled with thoughts of brick walls higher than those we have seen in the castles of Ireland. Even higher than the castle wall which holds the blarney stone, which I'm sure had worked its magic on Dad, as he definitely had the gift of the gab! But thoughts of a high wall with its staggered red bricks caused me some distress. I figured I would have to have more distressing occurrences like today to build up a strong high wall, but there again Dad said good things can build it up too.

But thoughts of today swirled around my mind, like bath water encircling the plug hole. Whatever Dad had told me to ease my suffering couldn't make me easily forget Crooked Crookson's spiteful words and exclusion from my dream role. I lay in bed sobbing as quietly as possible, while watching the moving lines of light that appeared on the golden floral wallpaper. Moving lines of light which were created by car head-lamps as vehicles

132

drove down the street. Momentarily the light would break through the gap in the curtains, making thin strips of light glide across the wall, casting eerie shadows around the room. This frequently kept me occupied for hours when I couldn't sleep. The sound of the car engines broke the intimidating night-time silence.

Out of the same night-time silence came a voice, as clear and crisp as Dad's had been as he'd lain beside me. I wiped away the tears trickling down my cheeks and sat up in bed, pulling up the quilt to my shoulders. I checked the doorway to see if Patrick had sneaked back in, but only the silhouetted images of John Travolta and Olivia Newton-John on the *Grease* poster pasted to the back of the door stared back at me. It wasn't a reverberating angelic tone, nor the voice of a Mexican man, but the sound of a high-pitched Irish man.

"Hey, what do you think you're doing, most vehement and valiant one?" With the next strip of car head-lamp light that skimmed across my wall, a leprechaun figure emerged from it. Not dressed in the usual green jacket and trousers, but a white tuxedo, as crisp and as pure as the driven snow. He jumped from my wall to sit himself on the end of my bed. "Orlagh, the Chosen One... *crying*?... Surely this cannot be? Oh, but my... my, my, my, yes it is. Sobbing? Pitying yourself? Tears are nothing but the Devil's work, my child. He thrives on tears. Laughter is the work of God, the work of the angels. The only thing that the Devil cannot bear is laughter of any kind, whether it be in yer heart, in yer bones or emerging from yer mouth. So, laugh, laugh, laugh and laugh some more. Laugh so we can see yer sparkling teeth, till we can see yer tongue and yer tonsils flapping when the laughing breath from yer lungs passes 'em by, like they be washing on a line."

His laughter was infectious. My tears ceased and a smile began to emerge on my damp face as I sat in awe watching this magical character jump from place to place. He settled himself in front of the bookcase, placed his elbow on one of the shelves and balanced his head upon his closed fist. His intense laughter stopped abruptly and he began to speak once more. "Now your mind is on the job, we must get down to serious business."

"But who are you?" I asked, confused at this hilarious elf-like character.

"We taught you a little of what we once taught Socrates. That most important message. Do you remember those wise words?"

"Wisest is she who knows what she does not know." I didn't know where I had found these words. I hadn't thought of them since the last appearance, when the angels came in opaque balls in a dingy motel room in the city of the angels.

He hadn't directly answered my question, but it was obvious he knew about my previous teachings, so he must be one of my angels

"Yes, my clever pupil, well done! Now time for words we taught Plato: tempus omnia revelat - time brings everything. You must never forget these words. Use this to your advantage. Patience, my child - patience. Patience and laughter. Patience and laughter.

"The butterfly's cocoon is spun from silk, your cocoon from the innocence of childhood. Like the butterfly, you now have broken out of your cocoon. So, like the butterfly does, go and spread some beauty and joy in this world. Laughter and patience, these are the keys - laughter and patience."

"But, how... erm, what....?" Before I could finish one of the many questions I had for him a car passed and he jumped into the strip of head-lamp light gliding across the wall and was gone. Leaving me with more enigmatic wisdom and a smile on my face.

No more tears were coming from me - I was not going to fuel the Devil's fire!

CHAPTER NINETEEN

"Oh! Wonderful, Orlagh's a happy wee girl today. What did they put in your breakfast, sweetheart? Or has your mother not been able to conceal her excitement and told you my surprise?" Father Maguire enquired, hands clasped together while fidgeting immensely, as excited as a small child on hearing the jingle of an ice-cream van. He was jigging from left foot to right foot as if walking on hot coals.

I had been summoned to see Father Maguire on the morning of Christmas Eve, the day following my ostracism from the nativity proceedings. The priest had seen me depart the previous day in a melancholic mood, so upon the sight of me skipping my way to him with my lips up-turned and my teeth and gums jubilantly exposed, he was understandably shocked.

"No, Father, I've had Sugar Puffs and a glass of milk. And no, Mammy said nothing of a surprise."

"So why're you so happy, my child? Not, erm not, not that I'm complaining about your happiness. Not at all. But I was told you were still sad and upset from the actions of that, that, erm, err teacher from up the road." He made the sign of the Cross and mumbled something under his breath. I figured he'd had a bad thought of Crooked Crookson and was asking God for forgiveness.

"Well, Father, you must be happy. You must *always* be

happy. Sadness is the work of the Devil and happiness is the work of the angels. So, Father, I decided I was not going to help the Devil in any way at all. Anyway, it's just another brick in my wall." While I was repeating the teachings I had received off two of my mentors yesterday a bewildered look appeared on the kind priest's face.

Father Maguire shook his head in a leisurely way, removed his flat tweed cap from his bald head, gripped it tightly and placed his index finger over his top lip. "Surely to goodness you're right, it's the Devil's work, so it is. I couldn't have put it better myself. Accepting defeat, Orlagh, is an ingredient that makes success worth striving for and by golly I think you'll be striving for success more than anyone. Another brick in your wall - I know that one. You kiddies think us priests don't keep up with pop music, but we do, you know. I can't think of what you call them who sing it... but I will!"

Now it was my turn to look confused.

I proceeded to relay what Dad had told me about building character walls. Father Maguire stood smiling, nodding and repeatedly saying, "Grand, grand." He then began to tell me about my surprise: "As you know, Orlagh, only boys can serve Mass."

"Yes, Father, I know. Dominic and Patrick were once altar boys."

"Yes and didn't I know it!" He raised his eyebrows. "Well, tonight, Orlagh, we're going to bend the rules of the church a little. You, Orlagh Emmet, are going to be the first girl in Saint Columb's parish to serve Midnight Mass, or any Mass for that matter. Do you know what else?" Before I could say a word he answered for me. "You're going to wear your beautiful dress that you were supposed to wear yesterday. It'll be positively appropriate you serving Midnight Mass dressed as an angel, so it will. Oh, and Orlagh, it's Pink Floyd. I told you I'd get it!"

He was a strange, but extraordinary man.

Serving midnight Mass was better than I could ever have imagined. I might even go as far as to say better than the play itself would have been, if things had gone to plan. I had a much larger audience and got to wear my dress for an even longer period.

The leprechaun angel was right - time does bring everything.

Life out of my cocoon was proving to be wonderful thus far, but were there wild cats lingering in the shadows waiting to savage my delicate wings?

Chapter twenty

"Orlagh, I've got some fantastic news, so I have. There's going to be no more magic elephant's breath for you."

"Mammy, I'm nine now. I'm a little too old to believe in magic elephant's breath. What're you on about anyway?"

"You're never too old to believe in magic elephants," Dad commented.

"I've just got this letter. I think it may be the light at the end of the tunnel." Mammy waved the letter in front of my face. "It's from a doctor named John Callaghan who's accepted you on his waiting list, even though being nine is a bit young for the treatment."

"So who is he, Mammy? And what treatment?"

"He's actually an ear, nose and throat specialist whose own daughter has a port-wine stain birthmark. Well, Doctor Callaghan took it upon himself to go to America for one year and learn all about the treatment for removing birthmarks with lasers."

"It's terrible, isn't it, that he had to go all the way over there and fund himself to learn a treatment that's going to help thousands of British kiddies?" Dad interrupted. "What did you say it was, Grania, one child in a hundred is born with some kind of facial birthmark? Now you'd think the bloody government would've paid for him, wouldn't ye?"

"Let's not put the world to rights now, Rory, even though you're right."

"As always, Grania. As always."

"Anyway, Orlagh, when Doctor Callaghan came back from America he set up a clinic in Southampton where he treats birthmarks with this new procedure using an argon laser. But he still has to treat his ear, nose and throat patients and they take priority. Plus he's training other doctors to use lasers too, so he's really busy, which makes the waiting list a bit long. This letter says you've been added on to his waiting list and that an appointment for your first test patch will follow shortly. I think this is the appointment in this envelope, because it's got a Southampton postmark on it." Mammy opened the envelope.

"So when're we on our way to Southampton, Grania, me darlin'?"

"Not at the moment, I'm afraid. They said that there's an enormous demand for the treatment and Orlagh here is one-hundred and ninety-nine on the list." Mammy sounded really disappointed.

I felt sorry for Mammy; I didn't want the light in her tunnel to disappear. "It's okay, Mammy, I don't mind having a birthmark, honest."

"That's me girl." Dad attempted to smother me in kisses.

Mammy pushed Dad out of the way, kissed the crown of my head and whispered. "We'll sort something out, Orlagh."

She was always trying hard to sort something out. Her research letters had been randomly dispersed as rapidly as cross-pollination seeds in a gale. The fruits of her labour had grown into *genetically modified* proportions, when she'd stumbled upon laser treatment. The most consequential product in her harvest-of-research was, of course, Doctor John Callaghan. In fact he wasn't just the prize crop, but the harvest moon - the guiding light for the masses to follow. But the growth spurt of Mammy's prize crop had been stunted. It didn't cause Mammy to be despondent though. After the disappointing news she kept farming with exuberance. She examined every avenue, every crescent, every cul-de-sac. She was immersed in the A to Z road atlas of laser investigation when a couple of months after Doctor Callaghan's letter she stumbled upon an auspicious advertisement.

"Oh Orlagh, look at this. It sounds great." Mammy passed me a medical magazine, pointing at a large advertisement:

PORT-WINE STAIN BIRTHMARK REMOVAL
BY LASER
As used by stars and entertainers throughout the world.
contact: Aberdeen Clinic LTD. 42 Bronte Gardens,
Romford, Essex.
Contact - Mr.McLean - Tel - 01-784-4664.

"I'll call him straight away. I can't wait 'til your dad comes in from work, I'm too excited." Mammy dialled the number as she spoke. "Hello there. I'm calling from Birmingham in relation to your advertisement regarding port-wine stain removal for my nine-year-old daughter."

"Oh yes, only too happy to answer your enquiries. At your service, as they say!" the man at the other end of the phone replied.

"I've just a few questions."

"Fire away, I'm wearing a bullet-proof jacket, ha, ha, ha."

"Right... erm, who does the actual treatment?"

"Oh, I do."

"You do?!"

"Yep, I'm the butcher, baker, candle-stick maker, chief bottle-washer and cleaner." The expression on Mammy's face read as easily as a child's book; she was obviously not impressed.

"Have you treated facial port-wine stains before?"

"Have I treated them? *Have I treated them?*... The question should be, my dear - how many?... and the answer... hundreds, my dear, hundreds."

140

"Oh, right. So may I ask who you know in the medical profession relative to laser treatment?"

"Oh certainly, my dear... I'm not sure if you're familiar with Doctor Callaghan?" A fire of fascination had been ignited in Mammy's mind and, like the grey smoke roaring from the fire, Mr McLean had risen in Mammy's esteem.

"Of course, Orlagh's been on his waiting list for the past couple of months, so she has."

"In actual fact Doctor Callaghan is coming to see me again tomorrow. We have these little tête-à-têtes from time to time. Wonderful man, wonderful. I know it's short notice for you to come from Birmingham, but maybe I could fit you in for a consultation and you'd be able to say hello to the old fella."

"Right, we'll do that. Fit us in."

"Oh!" Stuttered coughing was heard. "Erm... okey-dokey... right. It's a long way, you know?"

"That's not a problem, Mr McLean. Seeing Doctor Callaghan would be wonderful."

"Righteho, ermm yes - tomorrow it is then... 12 noon."

"Will Doctor Callaghan be there at that time?"

"Ermmm, yes, yeah-se, of course. Erm, see you tomorrow."

I was fascinated by the aspect of being treated by a laser, for so many different reasons. For one, I would be associated with the light-sabres used by Luke Sky-Walker and Obi-Wan Kenobi. That would really make Dom and Pat jealous, I thought. I also wondered if I might beep when my birthmark was lasered, like a bar code being scanned over a supermarket check-out laser light. I was looking forward to the trip to London to find out.

The Aberdeen clinic was located in a suburban road next to Romford railway station, in a run-down semi-detached house. Torrential rain did not enhance its appearance. Heavy rain droplets cascaded headlong, ricocheting out of enormous puddles which covered the mud-filled garden. I silently hoped the surgery would be cleaner inside than it was out. Mammy viewed it with the same apprehension.

"It's shockin' lookin'. There must be something good about the place if Doctor Callaghan affiliates himself with it."

"Don't be worrying yerself, Grania, I'm sure it'll be fine. All will be revealed soon enough." Dad was being optimistic, as usual.

We were greeted at the door by Mr McLean, a small, stout-looking gentleman in an early Seventies brown-flared trouser suit. If there were no white stains on the lapel and he'd put on a ruffled white shirt and velvet bow-tie, he would have been a perfect presenter for *Come Dancing*. He directed us immediately into his file-strewn office for our consultation. He had grime under his fingernails and a moustache that made him look like a Mexican hombre in an episode of *Zorro*. I was expecting him to salute me with 'Hey gringo!', then produce a sombrero from behind the cheap veneered desk, place it on his bald head and smile a kitsch grin with a white star in the corner of his teeth. But that was not so. His head remained bare, except for the strands of hair which grew from beside his ears, greased and brushed over the bald spot, trying to give the appearance that hair loss really wasn't a problem. And his teeth didn't sparkle, only glowed the same nicotine-yellow as his fingers.

"Now he really doesn't put the *clean* into McLean, does he?" Dad whispered, while Mr McLean rummaged through files.

I scanned the room to find grime made appearances in places other than under his fingernails.

The consultation was as short and shabby as the man himself. He didn't seem to know much about birthmarks. When it was over, Mammy asked, "May we have a word with Doctor Callaghan now?"

"I'm sorry, Mr and Mrs Emmet, but Doctor Callaghan had to cancel his appointment, due to *unforeseen* circumstances. He said he may pop along tomorrow, or whenever... you never know with John. I'll just go and get my appointment book, I can't seem to find it in any of these boxes. With the clinic being overrun with patients, I don't have time for filing and that sort of thing. I'll be back in a tick"

"Ach, Jesus, I'd like to know where he keeps all these patients he's overrun with. I haven't seen a soul." Dad seemed riled. "He's a cowboy, this one."

"Yeah, of Wild Bill Hickok acclaim." The fire of Mammy's fascination had been extinguished and the smoke was on a mushroom-cloud descent, evaporating and polluting the atmosphere. "There's not a chance we'll be coming down here again. He's never removed a birthmark, only tattoos. You know that's a totally different procedure to removing port-wine stains, don't ye? I should know, I've done enough research... probably more than him. What a waste of time it's been. Let's just pretend we want the appointment so we can get away quickly, Rory. We don't want to catch all the traffic on that M25."

Mr McLean made exaggerated friendly parting gestures, clasping Mammy's tiny hand with both of his grime-filled palms, in the hallway filled with miraculous before-and-after photographs of tattoos, treated by the Aberdeen laser. There was no sign of port-wine stain removal. Suddenly Mr McLean had a strange change of demeanour, one filled with urgency and panic.

"Okey-dokey then, off you all go, have a lovely trip up to Birmingham. Hope to see you soon, so we can get some work started on Orlagh here. Okay then... yes, erm, bye." He released his double-handed grubby grip and tried to guide us expeditiously out of the door into the pouring rain.

Upon exiting the saloon of this deranged broncobuster, we passed an immaculately dressed, distinguished-looking man with hair as grey as the present sky, shaking his cane-handled, black umbrella. It reminded me that I'd left my

143

Marks and Spencer umbrella, which matched my green hat and gloves, in the Aberdeen Clinic. I proceeded to retrieve my lost property.

"Hurry, Orlagh," Mammy instructed, "meet us at the car. I want to be as far away from this place as soon as possible and on that motorway before all the office traffic."

I ran back through the paint-chipped doors, thinking they should definitely be replaced with louvered saloon doors. Upon entry I viewed the distinguished-looking gentleman holding out an impeccable, manicured hand to Mr McLean; "Doctor Callaghan," he stated. I considered this a strange greeting to a friend with whom you often share, as Mr McLean put it - *tête-à-têtes*. "Afternoon, so sorry I'm late. I had an emergency. I do apologise. You are Mr McLean, are you not?"

Now this was strange, although, I may be jumping to conclusions - he may not be *my* Doctor Callaghan after all, I thought. I had to confirm his identity, in view of the fact I may be meeting him in the not too distant future.

"Yes... yes I, erm am... I'll be with you shortly," Mr McLean replied nervously, and then directed his attention to me. I had been engrossed in their conversation, watching like a spectator at Wimbledon, back and forth, back and forth. "What do *you* want?" he asked rudely, trying to push me out of the paint-chipped door into the storm outside, like a bad dog being punished.

"I've forgotten my umbrella," I answered as rudely as he'd asked. I then directed my attention to the Cary Grant-looking gentleman; "Are you the Doctor Callaghan who treats birthmarks?" Before he could reply Mr McLean interrupted

"Doctor Callaghan is a very busy man, so go and get your umbrella and get on your way now."

"No, it's quite all right, Mr McLean," Doctor Callaghan replied, concern showing through his well-spoken tone. "Yes, my love, I'm that very man. I can't remember that pretty face. I don't treat you, do I?" His soft fingers brushed over my birthmark. I liked him immediately and would choose him any day over the hombre-looking Bill Hickok who was standing chewing his grime-filled fingernails like they were tobacco.

"No, I'm number one hundred and ninety-nine on your list, so hopefully you'll be treating me soon."

"Yes," he smiled, "very soon... What're you doing here?"

I explained the situation to him while Mr McLean neurotically dined on his dirt-filled digits. Doctor Callaghan notified me he would be around an hour in the clinic and to inform my parents to wait for him outside.

Upon telling Mammy the intriguing story she cupped my head into her hands, kissed me all over and stated: "You've the cheek of the Devil, so yer have... and it'll get you everywhere!"

It was less than half-an-hour until Doctor Callaghan emerged, shaking his head along with his umbrella and advanced to our car, where Dad was in the middle of one of his hilarious stories.

"Here's your umbrella, dear." I hadn't even realised I had forgotten it again; it must have been all the excitement clouding my brain. "I don't think you'll be going back in there again, not if I have anything to do with it." He rubbed his manicured hand through my curls. If only all the doctors could be like him.

We arranged to meet in a cafe in Romford town centre where we ascertained the obvious...

"I've never met the man before," Doctor Callaghan began. "Mr McLean contacted me to look around his clinic. Which is solely for the removal of tattoos, by the way."

"Yes, Rory and I gathered that, doctor."

"He thought I might pass on any patients not happy with the National Health waiting list and prepared to pay private. I had to investigate the avenue, of course. He knew all the spiel all right. He knew I was trained in California, so concocted a story of himself being trained in New York. He knew all the doctors' names, their credentials... *everything*. He just didn't know his stuff, unfortunately for him, but fortunately, I must say, for all those potential patients - like yourselves - who would be prepared to pay. Luckily you came to the conclusion yourself that he's a con man. But some people are so blinded by the concept of birthmark removal, they'll probe any possibilities and, with this man, who knows what disasters he could cause. With the rambling drivel he had the audacity to invade my mind with, I could guarantee it would be of an astronomical degree."

"I agree! As Orlagh told you, doctor, she's one hundred and ninety-nine on your waiting list, and you know better than anyone how fast it's decreasing - or more to the point... how slowly. Could you recommend a *reputable* doctor who would take Orlagh as a private patient? Get the wheels in motion, so to speak, and then continue on with yourself when her number comes up. To get it done quickly we'd love to take her private one hundred percent, but it boils down to money, unfortunately."

"Of course, of course. Unfortunately at the moment I'm the only trained doctor in this country, which was why I was so eager to meet Mr McLean. I'm usually too busy for such requests. I'd generally send someone else who could evaluate the situation, but his set-up sounded so wonderful I needed to see it with my own eyes. I was a little perturbed this morning when I couldn't make the 9am appointment, which is why I rushed over this afternoon. Anyway, doctors... The only ones I can recommend are in the States. Drop me a letter to my surgery - marked personal, and I'll see you get a list of them."

The doctor departed, leaving Mammy smiling broadly. "Now wasn't that a strange coincidence?"

As Mammy completed her sentence, a bumblebee flew in front of my eyes. I waved my arms around and jumped from the wooden chair, attempting to avoid being stung. "Get it, Dad, quick!"

"It won't hurt you, Orlagh. Bees are workers; they

only sting when they are in danger. Just ignore it and it'll go away."

Mam and Dad proceeded with their conversation as I tried my hardest to ignore the huge bumblebee which was so close to my eyes I could see every black and yellow stripe. I then just about interpreted another voice.

"Your father is right again - the bumblebee will not hurt you, especially not this one. Not when it has a messenger from God on its back it won't!"

I looked on the bumblebee's back and sure enough, the tiniest angel I'd ever seen sat straddled, sinking into the furry composition of the bumblebee's body. The wings of the angel moved as rapidly as the bumblebee's, as it hovered in front of my eyes.

"Do not speak, Orlagh, you know about being each other's secret. Do you, like your mother, think it was a coincidence? Was it a mere chain of coincidences, a line of dominoes falling with continuity, or was it God dispersing his Angels of Fate accordingly? Coincidence or God guiding the article on the clinic into your mother's path the day before the doctor you desired to meet was due to go there? Coincidence or God which caused the champagne of the sky to bubble over its immense glass and send its effervescence cascading down to earth; providing a purpose for a *Marks and Spencer* umbrella? Coincidence or the angels whispering silent instructions in your ears causing an umbrella to be forgotten? Coincidence or the Omnipotent Being urging the doctor to miss his scheduled 9am appointment? Coincidence or God making that same doctor appear as you were leaving?

"God certainly does work in mysterious ways and, as long as you believe it's God's work, the longer you will have reason to believe that there's always something better waiting to be encountered in God's paradise pantry filled with divine delights.

"To believe you humans are a mere brief being - a more

147

complex version of the dandelion, which is grown from a seed in the soil to become a bud; then a beautiful but brief flower which soon turns grey and fluffy and is dispersed in the wind, distributing the seed which will grow into the next generation of buds. To think your tears and laughter, your goodness or your mischief do not contribute to the transition of the soul to reach the paradise plains of heaven. To think the seeds you sow as your only way to extend the existence of your being - would be wrong. Very wrong and very sad. You must have trust in your faith. You must take comfort in your faith. You must feel safe in its secure, compassionate arms. You must always remember *everything* is God's work... there's no such thing as a coincidence!"

And the bumblebee buzzed away, taking the miniature angel with it. Why couldn't they speak to me in words I could understand? In sentences which made sense? Would I ever comprehend their teachings?

CHAPTER TWENTY-ONE

The doctor was as good as his word. Mammy's request for doctors' names was answered and an added bonus was that, with the imminent expansion of the laser programme, I had quickly been renumbered on Doctor Callaghan's waiting list. I became known as 'forty-nine'.

"How does this letter sound, Rory?

"Dear Doctor,

"You have been recommended to ourselves by Doctor J A D Callaghan of the Royal South Hants Hospital, Southampton, England, regarding treatment for my daughter's port-wine stain birthmark to her cheek, chin and neck, using the argon laser.

"You can imagine how traumatically a birthmark to the face affects a nine-and-a-half-year-old, so we are anxious to get it removed.

"I would appreciate it if you could send us some procedural details of the treatment and information regarding cost. Providing it is not beyond our reach, we shall make arrangements to bring our daughter to the U.S.A. at your earliest convenience.

"Thanking you in anticipation,

"Yours faithfully,

"Mrs and Mrs Rory Emmet.

"Now, I've sent that to the five doctors that John Callaghan recommended. What'd you think?"

"It's great, Grania. But I think you've forgotten one detail."

"What?"

"Well, I think you should sign it - yours faithfully, Mrs Emmet and her extremely handsome husband, Mr Rory Emmet."

"More like, Mrs Emmet and her eejit of a husband, Rory Emmet. Seriously, is it ok?"

"I think it's great, Mammy. When do you think we'll be going to America? Will we go to Disneyland again?" I couldn't wait to return to the City of the Angels and meet with *my angels* once again. But I couldn't tell them that, so I pretended to be enthusiastic about my treatment.

"I agree with Orlagh, it's wonderful. I always knew you were a genius. And, I'm sure it won't be long until we're on our way to the States, Orlagh, me darlin'."

From the day after Mammy posted the letter I ran to our porch every morning, searching for the reply which would instigate a trip across the Atlantic. But time regarding my laser treatment sauntered on slowly, like clasped-handed lovers in the indigo twilight. I knew a few letters which I'd given Mammy to open came from America. But she never told me what was in them. I considered they were about something else. But I knew the last letter I'd given her was definitely something to do with my treatment, because it had 'Harvard Medical School - Laser department' printed on the envelope.

"What's it say, Mam? Is it from one of them doctors? Are we going to America?"

She didn't look up from reading her letter; "Orlagh, don't be so nosy, I'll tell you what you need to know. Go'nd get ready, we'll be going out shortly."

I dragged my feet out of the kitchen. As the door closed behind me I heard Mammy whispering. Now, whispering

150

parents always caught my attention. It usually meant something exciting was going on. I crept to the door, avoiding any creaking floorboards and strained to hear.

"It's been four bloody months since I sent all those letters to the doctors in America. This is the final doctor to write back and guess what? He can't help us either. There was the one from Chicago who couldn't help because he said she was too young. The one from California who'd retired. The two from New York; one couldn't help us for at least four years and the other one wasn't doing laser treatment any more because of other commitments. Then this last one today from Boston who doesn't treat anyone under eighteen. Being prepared to pay doesn't make the slightest difference in the quest to find a suitable doctor."

Not being able to contain my disappointment about not seeing *my angels* in the City of the Angels, I broke my cover; "Does this mean we won't be going to America, Mammy?"

"For the moment, darlin', yes. But I don't think it will take too much longer for you to become number one on Doctor Callaghan's list. And anyway, you shouldn't be ear-holing on Daddy and me."

"Oh, but I really wanted to go to America."

"I know you did, baby. Maybe we'll do that anyway. But the most important thing for you to remember, Orlagh, princess, is that while you're waitin' to become number one on Doctor Callaghan's list, you'll always be number one on Mammy's and my list."

Dad always made things okay.

book two

chapter twenty-two

"If you'd have been a boy, Orlagh, you'd be British champ, I tell ya. You've got the best pound for pound right hook in this gym. Make that left hook and right cross too. Come on, show me some power, girl," Dad bellowed as he slapped the black punching pads together. I focused on the central white dots on the black-leather pads and tried to execute my punches flawlessly. I manoeuvred my body so each ounce of my weight was transported through to the end of my arms, through the cracked red fifteen-ounce gloves and on to the white dot. The louder the booming base tone of leather on leather, the more desirable the punch. With each punch thrown I would try to improve with the next, with a "uzzt, uzzt, uzzt" emanating from behind my clenched plastic-covered teeth. From deep within me, the power and the will escaped from behind my belly button, rose through my lungs to expel the "uzzt" which exiled all tension, like red hot lava from a volcano.

I had well and truly fallen in love - hook, line and sinker. You could say I was obsessed. Mammy was concerned with my obsession. She had protested somewhat. She said I shouldn't be spending so much time with my new-found

155

love. She said I should be concentrating on my school work or doing my Irish dancing and gymnastics. Dad on the other hand encouraged the romance. He tried convincing Mammy that it was a diverse learning curve, teaching me lessons which school didn't have in its curriculum.

My infatuation wasn't blond-haired and blue-eyed - it wasn't even male. God, no - chance of that would be a fine thing. As far as boys were concerned, I was 'one of the lads'. I suspected it would be a wondrous feeling to have admiration from a boy for *how* I looked, not because I knew the off-side rule or because I genuinely cared who won the FA cup, or who came top of the league, or because I got excited at who was on the transfer list. Not because I knew a perfectly executed left hook when I saw one, or because I knew who floated like a butterfly and stung like a bee. I would rather the boys admired me for my sparkling emerald eyes, not because I could climb a tree as fast or faster than them. For my golden curls, not because I could pop a wheelie on my BMX for longer or jump more steps on a skate board than they could. But as I watched all my friends fall in puerile pubescent love, I acted indifferent. I convinced myself that I would rather experience romantic rendezvous while encapsulated within the plot of a Catherine Cookson epic which I covertly borrowed from Mammy's paint-chipped bookshelf. My romantic encounters were illusory clandestine meetings with a character from one of these books, not in the mud and soggy fallen leaves amidst the trees in the woods behind our school, or in a squalid urine-smelling tower-block flat where other teenagers I knew congregated and drank cheap peach wine as one of the gang babysat a small child while the mother went to bingo, oblivious or apathetic of the virginities being lost in her fetid bed.

However much I attempted to convince myself that I was totally impassive about romance, gnawing away in the pit of my stomach was an incarcerated adolescent urge. It hauled its shackles through my loins, shrieking its innocence, proclaiming a romantic miscarriage of justice as it witnessed what appeared to be the whole world in an awesome relationship. I blocked the incarcerated adolescent urge's escape plans as hard as I possibly could.

I managed to avoid all that adolescent confusion by escaping to the arms of a replacement love. To the sanctuary where my frustrations were pounded away, where my dreams and desires were contrived and where that whining captive urge was silenced. My haven was the boxing gym.

The rancid but peculiarly ambrosial aroma of sweat trapped in battered leather gloves and on the worn canvas besmirched with spit and blood was to me - tantalising. Upon smelling the sweet fragrance of boxing a satisfied smile would sneak upon my face, my eyes would close, my mouth would lubricate, my shoulders would rise and a warm anticipatory shiver would run down my spine, like the sensation experienced when you see and smell a craved delicious delight. I was uncontrollably drawn to the arduous abode of pugilism - like metal to a magnet.

The omnipresent muscular defined physiques which frequented the gym were like sculpted pieces of modern art. As they pounded the boxing bags with all the strength, anger and skill they could muster, their muscles seemed to want to escape through their skin, like a drowning cat trying to escape from a tied hessian sack. The powerful magnificence, harmless aggression, mixed with boisterous excitement astounded me so much I would have spent every last minute of my spare time there, which to an extent, I did. I constantly yearned to be among the boys, among the sweat and punches, amidst the hanging black and red boxing bags and poster-covered walls plastered with champions of both present and past.

Dad was correct in assuming the boxing gym would teach me things school most certainly couldn't. I would quietly listen to the boys' teenage exploits as I stood with my orthodox stance - left foot forward, guard up, happily jabbing away at the flock-filled boxing bag as it swung back and forth causing me to bob, weave and dance with agility out of the way. I learnt the ins and outs, every detail of a man's mind in the hours I spent at the gym. They were the key to my imprisoned urges. I took mental notes as they spoke of what they preferred and abhorred in the opposite sex. I defined a slapper, a slag, a tart, what is acceptable on the first night, became confused at statements like: 'No really means I want to but I just can't', or even, 'No means yes'. I was baffled that if 'no' really did mean 'no' then the girl in question gained more respect. So, why did they ask in the first place if they really wanted her to say no? I pondered long and hard as I pounded the bag.

I soon learnt these rules (or thought I had) and dreamed of putting them to use, proclaiming myself to be the most eligible catch - everyone would want me! Then my dreaming would come to an abrupt end and I would remember a certain little burgundy patch of skin on my cheek, chin and neck, which most certainly put boys off romantic trysts. I was just a great mate. They all merely regarded me as one of the lads, a sister, a confidante. Romance... that was, well, that was a ridiculous assumption.

For the time being I was content with punching the bags or the hand-held pads at Dad's boxing gym. I didn't want to be one of those 'no means yes' girls the boys conversed about in the hours of the gym; I wanted to be the one they would want to marry. My ideals of a perfect woman were based on the opinions of a group of teenage pugilists. But my urges could not be imprisoned. They wouldn't stop protesting about unlawful incarceration. They wouldn't give-in - they were plotting escape!

I longed for Dad's prediction to be British boxing champion, but unfortunately - no girls allowed. The closest I came to competing apart from in the gym was visiting the eccentric, half-senile boxing doctor.

Maybe it was sheer fate, or maybe it was Dad's magical magnet to eccentric characters at work once again, that Doctor Awad Sudki was the appointed doctor to the West Midlands boxing board.

Each boxer had to go through what was supposed to be a rigorous medical to confirm physical and mental fitness before a competitive boxing match was permitted. But you could hardly call Doctor Awad Sudki's medicals rigorous.

Doctor Sudki, the oldest practising doctor in Europe, was four foot ten inches tall. His spine was permanently bent from hours of stooping over a desk with a candle as his only light. His olive skin surprisingly glowed in the depressingly dim room, certainly not looking ninety-six-years old. Large brown freckles were scattered over his lustrous bald head, due to excessive exposure to the severe Egyptian sun.

Doctor Sudki adored boxing. In his seasoned years he pulled his oversized trousers above his chest, clipped his braces to the waist, tucked in his soup-stained shirt, placed on his pork-pie hat and sheepskin coat and sat ringside. Equipped with an antediluvian brown-leather case, rusty stethoscope and ancient Egyptian remedies, he was prepared for any unfortunate incidents which might occur where a doctor would be required. For the love of boxing he'd do it seven nights a week, if need be.

Three of Dad's new boxers were ready for competition. They had been training three times a week for six months and were extremely dedicated. Dad decided they were ready for competition, for which a medical was essential. Upon passing, a medical card would be issued and the boys could commence competition. Expecting they would pass their medicals, Dad had set up matches on the next club show for the three new boys. They were to come training as usual on Sunday morning, after which we were all to proceed to the oddball household of Doctor Sudki.

"Okey-dokey, two down, two to go. I wish they'd all come on time," Dad stated.

Two boys had turned up to training but the third boy, Errol, a black twelve-year-old, was strangely absent. He was elated when Dad had told him he was going to be examined and in the ensuing period be able to compete. Dad was a little perturbed that Errol had not shown. He had high hopes for him. Had a big heart, Dad said, with a great left hook to back it up.

"Errol'd better show, I've got him matched with that golden boy from Kerl Hall. They won't know what's hit 'em when he takes that left hook out the bag."

"Who's the fourth, Dad?" I asked as I sat on the edge of the ring, with my chin leaning on my forearms which were balancing on the bottom blood-stained rope; the distinctive sweet aroma of hard-won stale sweat invaded my nostrils.

"Did I not tell ye? Paddy O'Riordan from the Ring Gym in Derry called me up last Tuesday and asked me if I'd take this young lad under me wing. He's supposed to be a great little fighter, with the heart of a lion. I arranged for him to be here half-hour ago, I canny be waitin' any longer."

"Well, why would you need to train him if he lives in Ireland?"

"Sorry, sorry, I didn't explain, did I? Him and his family are movin' back over here Apparently they're backwards and forwards from Birmingham to Derry. Talkin' of backwards, that's what they all are up the north anyway, if ye ask me." Dad chuckled at his own joke. At that the paint-chipped door closed and a small figure came jogging towards us.

"You can talk, yer culchie ya. You Free Staters, ya're all the same. Paddy said I'm to watch yer!" While Dad shook his hand and welcomed him to the Birmingham Irish Boxing Club, I was - for what seemed like an eternity - glued to the rope. I was like a child pretending to be a statue. My breathing slowed and muscles froze. I was in awe at the sight of Mother Nature's prime example of the perfect specimen of a male figure which was standing before me. Paddy from Derry omitted to inform Dad that this new lad wasn't just a great boxer, but that he also had the most exquisite smiling eyes; not the ocean blue of Dad's, but a cloudless summer-sky blue. The pupils were like blackbirds flying through paradise. A tiny reflection of yellow light near the circumference of his pupils was like the blackbird's beak. His protruding cheekbones gave the impression they had been carved from stone. Those cheekbones along with the strong defining lines of his jawbone accentuated his radiant white skin, slightly flushed from a short jog. A thin line of perspiration sat like a crystalline-jewelled moustache atop his full terracotta-coloured lips. But there again, I assumed Paddy's main priority wasn't the heartbreaking status of his boxers.

I was fixated on a drop of the perspiration moustache which had broken away from the thin layer of stubble and had begun a journey. It broke ground over the perfect heart-shaped top lip and was just about to enter his mouth when his tongue shot out like a lizard's and eradicated the salty droplet. His lips began to move consistently and his white tombstone teeth sporadically came into view. It was like a silent movie, with a mouth moving but no sound following - although there was noise emanating from his mouth, but I was in such an hypnotic state I couldn't hear anything. My mind had packed itself a wicker hamper, plastic cutlery, paper plates, a chequered blue and white cloth, mounds of delicious delights and headed off on a picnic. I tightly squeezed my eyes together and shook my head, attempting to shake myself from this ludicrous daze. I resembled a cartoon character after being hit on the head with an over-sized sledge-hammer. I'm sure like in the cartoons there were huge stars flying erratically from my head. Sound then began to form, but I still couldn't decipher the rounded vowels being made up into what I imagined to be wonderful nouns, verbs and adjectives. The sound then developed into the monotones you hear when immersed underwater.

"Mmmmmwaaawm, mmmmmwaawm."

Panic replaced the trance when realisation hit me like the cartoon character's over-sized sledge-hammer, that he was speaking directly to me.

"Mmmmmwaaawm, mmmmmwaawm, angel-face."

What? Angel-face? Oh, how could I be so stupid and miss the start? I straightened my arched back, lifted my chin from my arms, which were now tingling with numbness - much like my brain.

"What?" Aggg, how could I say *what*? Where was my courteous decorum? How embarrassing. I was, after all, trying to make a good impression. I quickly caught my bad manners in a net and replaced the indignant *what* with a stumbling fake cough and a stuttered; "Pppparrdon, em pardon?"

"Hows about 'cha, angel-face?"

Now I hung on his every word, like washing pegged to a line. *Angel-face!* Out of all the nouns he could have chosen, why angel? Did he detect my Chosen-One status? I was uncharacteristically stuck for words. My vocabulary was stranded on a mud-sodden deserted beach. Attempting to retrieve it, I sunk deeper and deeper into the thick, dirty brown puddles of discarded rock formations of ancient geological aeons.

"Now what's a pretty thing like you doin' in a boxin' gym? I must say things're definitely looking up. I was sad, so I was, leaving all those pretty Derry girls behind. But it looks like Paddy has landed me well and truly on me feet. Sure, I've the prettiest girl around, right here in the gym, so I have."

Time was moving like a runner trying to reach the finishing line in a slow-motion review. I needed my fast-forward button pressed and a quantum leap back into the real world.

"Hey there, Derry man, keep ye eyes off. That's me daughter, Orlagh, Orlagh Emmet. What's your name, son? Paddy did tell me, but I'm terrible with names."

"Oh my, you're a princess as well as an angel?" I

162

couldn't believe my ears, he knew the meaning of my name too. With each word he uttered he rose in my esteem, like the piece of steel on a fairground strength test; the hammer is slammed down - ten, twenty, fifty. "Emmet... Emmet O'Malley's the name." Ding! The steel could go no further - the bell had been struck. The ringing reverberated around my brain, bouncing from one side of my skull to the other. How could Dad forget that... Emmet, his own name? There again, how did Dad do any of the things he did?

Out of all the names in the universe why was his Christian name the same as my surname? Why? Why? Why? - Destiny? - Fate? I knew there was no such thing as a coincidence, the Bumblebee Angel had made sure of that. So what was the reason here?

I was hot, blushing and bashful. I was having an out-of-body-experience, or something of that description. I felt peculiar, weird... in love? Love at first sight was a romantic's delusion, not the harsh reality of a teenager with bee-sting boobs, puppy-fat and a facial deformity in a sweat-smelling boxing gym.

"Are ye shy, wee one?" he whispered, then puckered his lips and nestled his chin into his muscular defined chest. His paradise sky-blue eyes stared out from under elongated dark eyebrows as he traced a long finger-nailed digit from my forehead, over the bump of my cheekbone, around the contours of my face where it fell at my jawbone. I placed my palm over the side of my face which had just been stroked, mouth ajar, like he had just sliced me with a razor blade.

"Show him a left hook, doll. That'll show him how shy ye are. Come on, let's get this show on the road. We canny wait any longer for Errol. You'll just have to stand in for him, Orlagh."

"But he's a boy," I protested, snapping out of my bewilderment.

"And ye think that'll make any difference to ald Sudki?

163

He's as blind as a bat and senile to go with it. You've only bee-stings; he'll never know the difference, boy or girl."

I cringed from within, anger bubbling like a volcanic mud pool. Why did he have to embarrass me in front of my new-found love? The issue of my boobs was such a jovial subject in our household. I prayed to God and the angels that my boobs would not sprout like vegetables in an allotment, but stay right where they were, locked away, bra-less - bump-less. I prayed for a chest like Nadia Comaneci, not Dolly Parton.

"But Errol's black."

"Ach, Orlagh, that's a mere formality. Come, lets go."

We were greeted at the green door by Mrs Jones. On approaching the door a Shakin' Stevens song always shot to the forefront of my mind. Although, today I didn't do the usual recitation of *'Green door, oh, what's the secret you're keepin'?'* I couldn't reveal my juvenile musical knowledge to such a mature man.

Mrs Jones looked more than the seventy-two years she actually was. Doctor Sudki had delivered Mrs Jones when her mother had the job of Sudki's housekeeper. I wondered how good Mrs Jones's mother would have been at the job. I only hoped for Doctor Sudki's sake that she was at least better at the post than her daughter. I wondered how long the hallway, with its brown and orange psychedelic patterned wallpaper peeling haphazardly off the damp walls, had smelt musty. We knew how long the newspapers which had turned yellow and crisp with age had been lying on the dirt-filled parquet flooring because Dad picked up an ancient sheet, examined it closely and exclaimed facetiously - a little too loud; "Oh, and what's happened today? President Kennedy was shot? Jesus! that's terrible news."

Mrs Jones nodded in delirious, Alzheimer's agreement - nearly twenty years after Kennedy's assassination. "Terrible news, I thought that. What club are you from, love?" she asked Dad, not recognising him from his weekly visits to the nonsensical house.

"Aston Villa."

"Oh, I like them. They're my favourite." She nodded her hoary head in affirmation, with her wrinkled, almost translucent hands clasped under her chin.

"But we're the Birmingham Irish Club, Rory," Dermot whispered.

"I know, son, but this one's away to the woods, so she is. She has no clue who we are."

The eclectic group of people congregated in the newspaper-strewn house was at home with Doctor Sudki's eclectic mix of furniture. Confidential medical records of old were, like the newspapers, scattered around the room. Pictures of ancient mythological figures, surrounded by hieroglyphics woven with golden thread hung on the walls. Old black and white photographs, like the newspapers, faded to yellow behind the fingerprint-smudged glass, showed distinguished-looking men in tweed suits and open-necked shirts. They all sweated while standing in the desert trying to hold a shimmering, haunted-looking mask.

"I'll just call the doctor. What club are you from, love?" she asked yet again, oblivious of her recent enquiry.

"Birmingham City, Mrs Jones," Dad answered, confusing her all the more. That is, if the answer was absorbed in her absent-minded brain cells. Some days he went through the whole of the Birmingham district clubs. She never failed to ask again and again.

"Oh, Birmingham City, I like them. They're my favourite."

"Go you stu-pid woman. GO!" Doctor Sudki screeched, as he emerged from behind one of his doors which was speckled like an old cow. It was dirty beige with large brown blobs, where the old paint had fallen off to be walked into the cracks of the wooden floor. His bald head still managed to shimmer in the dingily lit abode. His ears, as globular as his lips, stuck out like handles on a mug. His stained trousers were invariably pulled up above his chest. "Com,

Emmet, com," he clamorously instructed while gesturing with a long, wrinkled finger. The spittle off his bulbous lips sprayed into the beautiful face of Emmet O'Malley. Emmet diligently followed the old man into the room.

"No, Emmet - com. Not you, you stu-pid boy. Emmet, com."

The divine Emmet was about to defend himself when Dad - the other Emmet - placed a hand on his strong shoulder and informed 'Emmet the divine' through a clenched-teeth smile; "He means me, the barmy ald bastard. Just smile at him. I'll cheer him up. I'll get him to tell us his favourite story. You'll love it, so yer will."

I'd heard the inevitable story one too many times. I didn't want to absorb it all over again because I didn't want to risk Doctor Sudki realising I wasn't black and I wasn't a boy. I tried my hardest to become invisible and look equally distinguished - for Emmet's sake, of course!

"Before we get down to business, doc, do me a favour would ye? Tell us that story about the tomb." Dad bellowed at such an intolerable level even Doctor Sudki cringed - and he was half-deaf.

Doctor Sudki, in his heavily accented English, excitably proceeded to tell us - yet again - his favourite tale. "The discovery of Tutankharmen's tomb was the greatest and strangest day of my life. It was the last tomb to be found, because all other excavations were taking place around it and they'd mistakenly hid the tomb by placing all the rubble from the tombs of Ramses one, two and three on top of Tutankharmen's. But it was mainly Ramses six rubble that stalled discovery of the boy-king's tomb.

"The Egyptian Minister of Health needed to be present upon entering any newly discovered tombs. This job belonged to my far-ter and I was a young handsome doctor a few years past my training who had the privilege of accompanying him.

"Death is everywhere in the Valley of the Kings and I thought I would be near it if How-ard Carter and Lord

Carnavon did not get a hurry in them. You see, Carnavon had tired of Carter's dig for the insignificant boy-king's tomb and had left in a - what do you call it? Strop? Yes, strop. He was like a spoilt child. But, upon discovery of Tutankhamen's tomb, we had to wait for Carnavon's arrival back at the excavation site before we could enter. The cliffs of sand surrounding us were scorching, like the hot Luxor sun. I'm from Alexandria, where the sea breeze makes everything good." His liver-spotted hands moved up and down as he advanced with the story, like a conductor instructing his orchestra. Spittle flew in each and every direction from his spherical lips. With the bottom lip protruding further than the top he looked like he himself had taken a few too many punches in the ring. "Carnavon eventually arrived and we got the all clear. We proceed down the dusty steps of the newly found tomb. The temperature soon changed from very hot... to cool.

"The seal of the first door was broken and we all enter: Carter, Carnavon, my far-ter and me. You could hear the pure three-thousand-year-old air being sucked out." He placed his wrinkled palm behind his mug-handled ear, as though he were again listening for the noise sixty years on. Sucking in his ancient cheeks he devoured the musty air around him, making a slurping noise as he did. "Ssslurrrrrr," - like when you take a petrol cap off a car desperate for gas, this was the noise. Then it was so quiet you could hear the silence. We all proceeded with much excitement and anticipation down a very long cool corridor. On the limestone walls either side there were beautiful paintings of Cleopatra-looking Egyptian ladies, with their hands above their heads as if they were dancing, or with them cooking on ancient stoves, or holding the head of a strong wild beast. We come to the end of corridor and there was yet another door with a seal unbroken for three-thousand-two-hund-red and forty-seven long years. The same ssslurr sucking noise and silence. Our torches fell upon a golden-jewelled vase full of the lotus flower, standing tall and strangely alive. The lotus flower was associated with the life-giving power of the Nile, so maybe the ancient people thought its presence would guarantee them powerful life in the next world. Then, slowly at first, the flowers began to wilt. The long green stems folded over and after all those years the pink flowers hung dead over the shimmering golden vase. We then turned right, heading towards the sarcophagus... Did you know that all sarcophagi are larger than the entrance doors of the tombs? A strange phenomenon."

"Never!" Dad commented, although he certainly did know; he had gone through the fine points of this story many times. He then winked at Emmet and out of a tiny gap in the corner of his mouth he whispered: "You have to humour the ald man, he has nothin' else!"

"Yes!" More spittle escaped captivity from the corner of Doctor Sudki's moist mouth. His bony index finger pointed to the ceiling, like a mad professor after making an amazing discovery. "The sarcophagus... the coffin, made of thick cold stone, housed the body of the boy king. Do you know the meaning of sarcophagus?" Before anyone could respond, he continued. "It is Grrr-eek!" Rolling his 'r' and spitting some more. "Grrr-eek for flesh-eating. But none of the boy-king's flesh looked as though it had been eaten. His mummied body lay still and haunted-looking, covered in gold and precious stones and wearing the mask we're holding there on the wall." He gestured at the old black and white, faded-to-yellow photograph of the sweating men; Doctor Sudki was recognisable in his youth, with his bulbous lips and mug-handled ears.

I was still dreading my medical, but I didn't mind hearing the conclusion of his story. It was more haunting than an episode of *Tales from the Crypt*.

"We gathered around the corpse and we all felt so much elation at the discovery of such a magnifi-cent tomb, for such an insignificant king. Then... one by one we passed out. It was not just a black-out. I felt like I was falling to sleep. I slowly began to spin. The gold in front of my eyes shimmered into a whole mass and began to look like golden waves of an ocean, and out of the golden ocean I swear I saw the wings of an angel; solid gold, but strangely buoyant. My feet tingled, then my shins, my knees and by the time the tingling in my thighs had begun I had fallen on to the jewels spread beneath our feet. Was it lack of oxygen? Or was it the curse of Tutankhamen?"

"Ach, doc, it gets better each time I hear it. Isn't it great, Emmet? What d'ye think, Orl... ermm, Errol?"

"Fantastic," I replied in a masculine tone. Because of course I was a boy and I was black.

"Emmet O'Malley up first, doc. Like me another Emmet, so he must be a good man. And he's Irish too. It's only a re-medical so don't go too mad." Dad slapped Emmet's muscle-defined back and pushed him in the direction of the hunched doctor. Like the camels of his native country, he had acquired a hump; I wondered if his carried an emergency water supply.

"Ah, Irish like you, Emmet. I like Irish. England stole your country like they did mine. They were only interested in Egypt for Suez Canal project, so they could make a shorter route to India. Ah, India, yet another country they decided to steal. They weren't interested in the Egyptian people who worked themselves to near death in Egyptian sun producing cotton to feed British textile mills. It took us until 1954 to get English out. You're still trying, eh? Com, I now do medical, Irish."

I didn't know whether to stay in the musty, mothball-smelling room or retreat to the grease-strewn kitchen, which was a putrefying museum of mould. Tea-stained china cups stood next to a battered old teapot which appeared to have emerged from Tutankhamen's tomb it looked so aged and dirty. The inside was the same chocolate-brown colour my skin was supposed to be. Milk bottles full to the brim looked like mini-mosques. The

UHT silver tops, which had been pushed to full capacity by the ancient milk which had coagulated to a solid mouldy mass while trying in vain to escape the glass bottle, represented the onion-shaped domes. Standing adjacent to the mini-milk-houses-of-worship were full urine-sample bottles which had been located there for months, years maybe - I dreaded the thought. Next to the urine samples were strips of *used* litmus paper, which had been used to test boxer's urine sugar level, dipped in and discarded on the kitchen worktops. The same worktops where Doctor Sudki insisted on making us tea in his filthy pot. Mouldy Turkish delight lay untouched, which Doctor Sudki's family sent him in ornate boxes from Egypt. I found it strange that they were not red and covered in chocolate, but a mouldy shade of yellow, doused in icing sugar. Oranges had acquired a green fungoid moss. Green apples had turned yellow and brown in the final stages of decomposition. Everything had been attacked by the germ of age. Time, as always, had won in the race of life.

Should I go to the kitchen and converse with a delusional Mrs Jones who sometimes mistakes me for the daughter she never actually had, or sit and watch a sculpted body take off its shirt and wince at the touch of the cold stethoscope? It was a difficult decision - Mrs Jones, who invariably smelt of boiled sweets and urine (or maybe that was just the urine samples)? Or Emmet, who smelt like a fresh sea breeze and replicated the illusionary figures of my dreams? I would never usually leave while a medical was taking place, but I cringed when I glanced at Emmet's body. I was convinced he knew I was glaring through him and daydreaming my way to his lips...

I decided to stay and endure the torture of Emmet O'Malley removing his crisp white T-shirt and revealing a perfectly defined torso. I watched as his deltoids, trapezius and rhomboids rippled at his every move, like water over a calm pond being disturbed by a small falling pebble. Attempting to distract myself, I picked up a decaying yellow newspaper and pretended to be engrossed in the 1971 introduction of British decimalization.

Emmet's perfect physique sailed through its medical and Dermot followed trouble-free. Jack caused the doctor distress. Adversity I could have done without. My anxiety was mounting and I didn't want a perturbed doctor examining my female contours for fear of discovery. Jack's bony teenage figure stood shaking before the hot-tempered spittle-spraying doctor. He had completed all stages of the medical except the eye examination. There wasn't a board pinned to the wall like in an optician's examination room; instead there were letters placed on a piece of cardboard, its edges curled with overuse and age. The doctor held the card ridiculously close to Jack's eyes. We could all sense Jack was struggling. You wouldn't have thought he had a sight problem.

"Hurry, boy, you can see, or not see - tell me?"

"Amoglmmmmtuuc," Jack replied.

"WHAT?!"

"Amogl…" He glanced at Dad, eyes damp from straining or frustration. "I can't read too well, Rory." His head hung low.

I thought I had problems… Jack thought he had to make a coherent word from the accumulation of haphazard letters. His eyes brightened upon Dad's explanation of only having to decipher each individual letter.

"A, M, O, G, L, M, T, U, C."

"Why did you not do this five minutes ago? Go. You're done. Quickly, who's next?"

"Errol is, doc. Great *LAD* he is, although he can be a bit of a *GIRL* at times." Dad, Emmet, Dermot and Jack folded over in convulsing laughter, alleviating Jack's humiliation and intensifying my consternation.

Through his enormous magnifying glass he read my - well, Errol's file. As I approached, the bold, defying words of **AFRO-CARIBBEAN** glared at me in spherical letters. My long hair was scooped up into a Toronto Blue Jay's

171

baseball cap, turned backwards so I could view the sight test unhindered. The cap was on so tight the plastic strip which was supposed to be at the back of my head cut into my forehead. A few unruly blonde curls were peeping through the semi-circle gap in the hat, also trying to witness the hilarious scene.

"Com... take off your shirt." I glared at Dad.

"Go 'nd make us a nice cuppa with Mrs Jones will ye, Jack? And give him a hand there, Dermot," Dad instructed the two younger boys. It wasn't them I was bothered about - it was Emmet. I didn't want him to view my boobs... or lack of them. Emmet must have sensed something because he turned to the wall and showed exaggerated interest in Doctor Sudki's pictures. The delay incensed Doctor Sudki somewhat.

"Hurry - I don't have all day for you people. I'm a busy man."

I quickly unbuttoned my shirt revealing my little bumps. My Nadia Comaneci prayers had been answered so far. I flinched as he placed the rusty stethoscope on my chest; it was as cold as an ice-cube that wouldn't melt. The only thing melting was my mind at the thought of Emmet behind me, and - of being a boy and trying to be black. With my mind on important issues I didn't hear if Doctor Sudki had instructed me to inhale or exhale. So, I took the fifty-fifty chance and bet on inhale.

"I said EXHALE, you stupid child. Emmet, why do you bring these black people to me? They're so half-witted. Their brains have not formed inside their skulls." He pounded my skull with bony knuckles. My cover was almost blown when the baseball cap tilted off my head. "These black people are just like Neolithic man. You only have to look at their faces and the colour of their skin to see they are backward."

Phew, I thought, at least I'd convinced Doctor Sudki of my blackness. He pointed at the skin on my arm, which was three shades fairer than his own - trying to prove his point on black people to Dad!

The sound of raspberries being blown on a child's stomach emerged from the mouths of Dad and Emmet, who was still busy viewing the ancient photographs. They couldn't suppress their laughter. I even saw the funny side of it.

Luckily for me, my black stupidity disgusted him to an extent that he rushed the rest of the examination. He pushed my female, *white* body in an arrogant fashion. Blood pressure, ears and eyes were done like a hundred-metre sprint. Dermot produced Errol's urine, which the doctor tested with his litmus paper in the kitchen - or maybe he was testing the coagulated milk. I'm sure he wouldn't have known the difference.

Doctor Sudki passed Errol, the twelve-year-old black boy with flying colours! I prayed none of the boxers would ever need his medical help in an emergency.

chapter twenty-three

I couldn't sleep. I was trying, but I merely tossed and turned and watched the red illuminated figures on my clock-radio increase. You see, I had to come up with a plan. A magnificent plan which would alleviate some of the torture I knew I was going to endure when my brothers and extended brotherhood at the boxing gym discovered I would soon be wearing a bra. Yes, my Nadia Comaneci flat-chested dream was all too soon banished. It had been struck down and murdered, like a rabbit's inevitable fate when it stands on its hind legs in the centre of a busy road transfixed by the car head-lamps... it was well and truly dead. My boobs sprouted like summer blooms and continued on their growth spurt, not stopping for air! I attempted denial, but they refused to resume their previous deflated position. My bee-stings now appeared to be bee-hives and it was emphatically embarrassing, especially in my brotherhood circles. They hampered my skipping, my running, my bag punching - most probably due to not wearing a bra... A bra? Ugh, I cringed at the mere thought as I traced my finger around the hexagonal shapes on my quilt cover. It wasn't the only dilemma I was facing either. Other than rapidly growing boobs, thoughts of periods loomed in the distance, which would soon, like a multicoloured kite trailing around in a deteriorating wind, come crashing down to earth and rock my already wobbling world.

I had recently watched so many of my classmates go ashen, looking like the proverbial death-warmed-up, asking to be excused from class because they had 'come on' - come on what, I always thought. To tell you the truth, I would rather not know its meaning because I was dreading my periods more than a bra! I had reason to be worried too. I had watched a documentary covering girls starting their, as the presenter so eloquently put it - menstrual cycle. It was set in a swimming baths where many girls had been interviewed in the stark changing cubicles. They all held their bare knees with their heads tilted sideways, as they sat in their swimsuits and verruca socks on the wet benches, explaining how they had all begun their - menstrual cycle. It perplexed me rather than informed me. I was then under the impression that I would start my periods in the swimming baths, with blood trailing behind me as I swam. I imagined the spectators and swimmers pointing and eeeee-rrrrr-ing at me as I innocently swam with my blood trail. The *Jaws* theme could certainly have been playing; this thought was just as frightening.

Mammy had endeavoured to inform me of the accurate explanation many times. Whenever her always happy face took a serious turn attempting the 'facts of life talk' I did an escape act Houdini would have been proud of, while cringing with embarrassment at the mere thought of *the* discussion.

I avoided swimming until receiving inside information from Siobhan as we walked across the large school field which always smelt of freshly cut grass and resembled a green glacier lake. She discovered the dreaded redness when she woke one morning - so swimming resumed. Although I was still somewhat dubious of the red flag rising - thus, being unable to enter the water.

Our walks to and from school produced numerous important conversations, other than the growth spurt of my boobs and her forthcoming blood loss. Each morning

I aimlessly strolled past the enormous horse-chestnut trees which looked like they had jumped out of an Enid Blyton enchanting adventure, past the cherry-blossoms which resembled over-sized fairground candy-floss in their spring-time efflorescence, down and around the block to rat-a-tat-tat on Siobhan's grandma's house. In fact, the house now belonged to Siobhan's Mam as Grandma Murphy had sadly died. Her death, although sad, did give Siobhan and myself added freedom. Mrs Connor left for work at 8.30am and didn't return until 6.30pm. Of course Siobhan couldn't be left alone. I had to keep her company - it was only sensible! We did miss the two Fox's Glacier mints Grandma Murphy presented each of us with on our departure to school. 'A boost of morning sugar,' she always said, as she tapped the crown of our heads. 'To get your brains in working order.' Our brains worked well enough to converse about our most favourite topic - boys. Emmet and Patrick specifically.

Now here was *yet another* dilemma staring me stubbornly in the face. Since the arrival of Emmet O'Malley I had been dumbfoundedly smitten. If he had been the Messiah himself, I don't think I would have been any more overwhelmed. He'd hit the number one spot in 'Orlagh's Top Ten'. Sales were high and it looked as though they were not going to fall. But Emmet just didn't notice.

It hadn't taken Emmet long to fit into life within the realms of the Birmingham Irish Boxing Club. He immediately became 'one of the lads', spending endless nights with my brothers. I always managed to find out when he was coming to pick them up or when he was to be dropped off. I'd be there, smiling sweetly. Through my clenched teeth I would silently beg God, beg my angels, beg anyone really, for him to just take notice of me in the way that I wished. Because he did take notice of me, but it was the usual scenario - I was just a great mate. One of the lads.

I sat in feigned awe when Patrick filled me in on Emmet's and the lads' misdeeds. When he told me about the girls they had picked up, I'm sure I turned one of the many shades of Ireland's green. There just seemed to be so many 'no-means-yes-girls' around. He didn't tell me these stories just for the sake of it either. He pretended he just wanted to let me know what they were up to, but I knew different - I had Patrick sussed. I knew he only told me certain aspects of each tale and made sure the stories were a lesson to myself. There were silent instructions woven through his accounts of how boys would use every trick in that proverbial unwritten book and more besides to get you to just say that one treasured word they longed to hear... yes.

"You know never to fall for any of those sweet-talkin' lines guys dream up, Orle? You have to wait. We all like the girls best who're waiting. They're the ones to get," Patrick often stated in his authoritarian brotherly manner. I only wished the 'sweet-talking lines' would be practised on me, so I could get the chance to say no.

I wondered whether Patrick sensed my secret desire for Emmet. Did he see the sad puppy-dog look in my eyes as he recited their tales? Did he add in the extra, 'Oh, she was an ugly pig who Emmet landed with,' for my sake?

But, as I lay in bed unable to sleep, tracing the same hexagonal shape for the millionth time, I decided I didn't have a chance with Emmet O'Malley. I was just a little girl to all Emmet's experienced women. A little girl with a red face. I had to come to terms with that particular dilemma - I didn't just not have a chance, I wasn't even in the running.

Suddenly all my pessimistic thoughts disappeared and the most shocking pain ripped through my head. Replacing every thought and mental picture was a spinning wheel which orbited through my mind. Engraved deeply into it were the enigmatic words of Plato. An image of the little leprechaun in his white satin tuxedo then appeared and his words echoed around my brain at an intolerable pitch: "Patience and laughter... patience and laughter. Tempus omnia revelat... tempus omnia revelat. Time brings everything... time brings everything."

I hadn't encountered an actual angel for a while, but I strangely sensed an angelic presence in whatever I was doing. I always had a weird feeling of never being alone, having to look behind me quickly to check if someone or something was there. It was always nothing, only the bare vacant space through which I had just walked. I ceaselessly felt their strength behind me. I felt I had something to wish to when in desperation I wanted my desires to be granted.

I placed my opened palms across my ears, attempting to block out the leprechaun angel's unbearable volume. But it didn't work. It seemed to be internal. "Patience and laughter... Time brings everything... Tempus omnia revelat!" Then as quickly as the noise began - it ceased.

It wasn't the first time something like this had happened. Not so long ago I had preposterously begun to doubt my angels' existence. I was like a Thomas - three times before the cock crows. When certain situations hadn't gone my way and I'd called upon my angels for their help - which didn't come forth - I considered that they were just a figment of Dad's divine imagination and the visions I believed I had witnessed were only my childhood imagination playing vivid illusory tricks with me. But strangely on the couple of occasions I had denied the angels' existence, a locked box full of the infinite teachings they had bestowed upon me had mysteriously made its presence known. The key to this box hovered in a faraway cosmos begging to be discovered. Then, like just now, my mind cleared of all other thoughts. The vision in my mind's eye was an abandoned ocean which was bluer than the purest sapphire. Out of that deserted sea an enigmatic teaser, a snippet of information appeared: an enlightening statement which had floated to the surface having been released from the sunken treasure-trove. The message bobbed along on the surface of the sea of my subconscious waiting to be discovered and understood. I longed for the key and wondered whether the treasured box would ever be fully opened, revealing its abounding contents, giving me the ability to rummage through them like an old lady does through clothes at a jumble sale. I wanted to examine its abundant riches - those invaluable treasures of knowledge, so I could ascertain why I had been chosen, which would then take me a step closer to discovering my divine destiny.

I didn't really care about angels tonight, though - I was over them. They only popped up when they felt like it - not when I asked. And they were certainly not helping me out of any of the dilemmas I was encountering at the present time. The leprechaun angel could shout his profound messages as loud as he liked because if he wasn't going to tell me where the key to my treasure-box of knowledge was, then I wasn't interested in what he had to say. He could stick his 'tempus omnia revelat' wherever leprechaun-like angels stick things, because time wasn't bringing me anything I wanted.

As I finished dismissing the leprechaun angel in my mind and I was just about to recommence contemplation of my bra-wearing plan the striking pain returned. Here we go again, I thought, more patience and laughter and promises of time bringing everything. But there was no shouting, only a feeling so agonising that I had to sit up and hold my head in my hands. I screwed my eyes shut, held my breath and apologised over and over in my mind for not respecting the angels. The pain ceased. I slowly removed my head from my hands and tentatively opened my eyes to be met by a scary, huge figure, which was shadow-like. It had no features but appeared to be male, with enormous arms and a head that had blackness deeper than the night-time obscurity it had appeared from. It stood in the corner of the room like a soldier on guard. Then, like the angels, it transported itself miraculously, ghost-like, around my room. This thing appeared above me, lying horizontal, hovering in the dim, eerie silence, although a strange force-field kept it at a safe distance. But this safe distance did not stop me from being petrified into a corpse-like stiffness. I didn't know if I could move, even if I'd wanted to. From nowhere he or it produced a golden key which caught the light of the moon as it was swung in front of my eyes, like a pendulum on a grandfather clock.

"Tick-tock, tick-tock, tick-tock... Let's discover together... Come with me... *Come with me...*"

"What are you? Who are you?" I squealed at the top of my voice, hoping Dad, Dom or Pat might hear.

"We can explore the treasures... Come with me... *Come with me...*" it implored, still swinging the golden lock-opener while laughing an echoing, contemptuous laugh which the greatest operatic bass could not have obtained, procuring a note which sounded three octaves lower than middle C. It sounded like a tune acquired on a termite-hollowed didgeridoo played by an ancient Australian aboriginal - but lower and more menacing. "You must come with meeeeeee." It held out its arm. "You *will* come with me."

"Where? Where do you want me to go? Where? I'm going nowhere. NOWHERE." I pulled my patchwork-covered quilt up to my neck for added protection and screamed for help. "Quick, there's someone in my room - come and get him. I'm not asleep. I beg you. He wants to take me. Please help, Dad, Dom, Patrick... *pleeeeaaaasssse.*"

Its laugh got louder and more intimidating. Why could no one hear this sinister sniggering which was at an unbearable volume, causing me to smother my ears with sweating palms as I screamed for help? "All that wander are not lost. But all that wander have something to discover. Let's discover together..."

Patrick, looking angelic with his blond, cherub-like curls falling around his face, appeared at the door. He sat next to me on the bed, held me in his arms and rocked me back and forth like a new-born baby. Kissing the crown of my head, he told me everything was going to be just fine now he was here.

The demon of the night silently watched my brother holding me. Why couldn't Patrick see it? It disappeared as quickly as it had emerged. Ebbing into the floral pattern of the wallpaper, it moved like the swaying reflections in a fairground house of mirrors.

When Patrick returned to his own bed, I lay apprehensive of sleep. If my angels were real (which, of course, I now truly believed they were), why did they allow this to happen? Where did it want to take me? There were so many unanswered questions. Would I ever obtain the key to this treasure-trove of knowledge? Was that the key which that thing had been swinging? I became extremely anxious. I had a peculiar feeling of vulnerability which I tried to annul by filling my head with thoughts of my prevailing daytime-nightmares. Of course, the most prominent was the thought of acquiring my first bra!

Why was I cursed with so many dilemmas?

chapter twenty-four

After hours of contemplation I eventually devised an ideal bra-wearing plan. The plan which I figured would alleviate some of the inevitable anguish and embarrassment the introduction of the supplementary garment would bring with it. A significant transition was about to occur and I didn't want it viewed in the public gallery filled with brothers and boxers where I would have to listen to their ridicule. Where I was sure they would teasingly holler gibes and jeers through mock loudhailers made from their cupped palms placed around their sarcastic moving lips. My mind wondered into a confused stupor at the thought of such taunts and I imagined being shackled in rusty chains and guided through a crowded courtroom, with squashed tomatoes and halved potatoes being tossed at me as I was charged with 'Wearing a bra before necessity'. If there was such a charge, I wished I could have been up on it - because the bra was *most certainly* necessary.

But, none of that teasing was going to occur because my shrewd plan was to purchase the bra prior to the school ski trip. There were two reasons for my ingenious plan. Firstly, I could get myself used to wearing the alien garment while away from the prying eyes of my tormentors. Upon my return I would be indifferent about the whole bra-wearing transition and the taunts would fly over my head in an unconcerning manner, heading to a faraway place where someone may care. Secondly, I would have been the only girl on the trip - bra-less. I couldn't be the odd one out. Being bra-less would just exhibit a shortcoming in my maturity.

The clandestine trip I was to take with Mammy to *British Home Stores*, for the sole purpose of starter-bra purchase, rapidly came around. She made the smallest of things exceedingly special and this important transitory occasion was no exception. We had a wonderful morning of shopping: *Dorothy Perkins, Miss Selfridges; Top Shop.* I knew Patrick would have told me they were full of rubbish for Shazzas and Traces but I didn't care for being cool - I was having too much of a good time.

The sole purpose of our trip soon approached. It was weird; even with Mammy I experienced a peculiar feeling of embarrassment at buying this garment. It was like the talk of periods - I wanted to avoid it. But there we were in the underwear department of *British Home Stores* examining: white, black, red, lace, cotton, and silk-cupped garments. Mammy ummed and arhhed, pulled at the seams, testing their strength as though they might be required in an emergency to tow the car. I didn't realise it was such a difficult decision. I just wanted a pretty-looking white broderie-anglaise one I'd seen pre-pubescent girls wearing in Siobhan's mammy's glossy catalogue - and get out of there. Too many people were paying attention to me- too many people could tell I was shopping for my first bra.

The distinctive aroma of Estee Lauder scent invaded my sinuses, which always reminded me of my Sicilian Great-grandma Mary. I then heard a high-pitched voice. "Do you know your size, darlin'? Can I help ya?"

I rotated to discover a graciously attractive lady, who I instantaneously decided was definitely working in the right department. She had the most enormous rounded breasts I'd ever seen on a slim lady. I figured with the size of them she was an expert on bras. She resembled Mammy's egg-timer. Even the cerise colour of her tight blouse was the same colour as the sand which trickled down through the egg-timer's glass neck into the empty identical space below. I imagined her cerise colour slowly draining from her huge breasts, through her microscopic waist and turning the divine curves of her hips - which were covered in a tight black skirt which hugged each and every contour - cerise, leaving her bright top colourless.

Mammy was lost amid the lace, so I decided to confide in this egg-timer-like, voluptuous lady.

"No, I'm sorry, I don't know my size. This'll actually be my first bra."

"Your first? My, my, you're a brave one. You look like you could've done with a bra a while ago. You've a nice little figure on you, haven't ya? How old're ya, sweetheart?"

"Fourteen."

"Oh my, you've left it late. We get 'em in here when they've only bee-stings on 'em. My figure was about the same as yours when I was your age, and now look at me! All boobs and bum. The boys'd better watch out, 'cause when you're in full bloom you're gonna be a stunner." She made me blush, but I liked her comments. I only usually heard these kind of remarks from people I knew, especially Dad. He told me every day how I was the most beautiful girl in the world. That didn't count, though, because he was too biased. But this lady didn't know me from the next stranger. I respected her opinion because she was so beautiful.

"Do you really think so? I haven't had a boyfriend yet. They all just want to be my friend."

"Oh, you mark my words, sweetheart, you'll be breaking all their hearts soon enough. There'll be an awakening in those young lads, I can assure you of that."

'If only,' I thought as I went into the musty-smelling changing room. The egg-timer lady shook her head in a slow, rhythmic way and continued talking, almost to herself.

"Men?... I don't know, confusing as kids and they don't change much when they grow up, luv... Come on, let's get ya measured up."

The name printed on her badge was Lola. She should have been a showgirl with a name like that, dancing at the Moulin Rouge in a sequinned bikini and a head-dress made of peacock feathers. I lifted up my T-shirt and she placed the cold tape-measure around my chest. I'm glad Mammy was lost somewhere outside amidst the lace; it would have been too humiliating, but Lola made me feel calm and, in her beguiling way, strangely beautiful.

"32B! See, what did I tell ya? You've left it quite late. No A, or double A's for you, sweetie. Have ya seen a bra ya like yet?"

"No, but I know what I want; white broderie-anglaise."

"Ummm, very classic. You wait here, we've got just the one."

She came running back a couple of minutes later, ecstatic with her find. Her hips wiggled sensually on each step she took in her six-inch stiletto heels and her breasts bobbed like luminous buoys in the ocean. She closed the ghastly patterned curtain and let me try on my very first bra. I placed my arms one by one through the arm holes, pulled the base of the bra under my bumps and like a professional fastened the hook and eye. I felt extraordinarily mature as I twisted left and right to view every angle of the new garment in the floor-to-ceiling mirror. It made my boobs look bizarrely bigger - but I didn't care because I felt wonderful - distinguished even. I straightened my spine and raised my chin... I was now a lady.

"Ready yet?" Not waiting for a reply, Lola pulled back the curtain. "Oh, look at you. Now isn't that pretty? I've got to go now, sweetie. Lunch-time calling. Got to feed this." She smacked her bum and laughed. "Janet'll look after you now." Lola pushed up the end of her nose with her long, red-nailed index finger, opened her blue eyeshadow-covered eyelids wide and with her full red lips exaggeratedly mimed, "snob." In a suspiciously loud, guilty voice, making sure everyone heard she was talking, she added;:"You mark my words, you'll be a heartbreaker."

She pinched my cheek, winked her blue-covered eye and wiggled her way out of the changing room.

As I emerged from the changing room with my freshly acquired mature feeling (and new bra), I spotted Mammy looking frantically around the rows of knickers and bras. Her brown curls fell around her face. Unlike Lola she wore no make-up, but I thought she was just as - if not more - beautiful.

A lady of uncanny resemblance to Mrs Slocomb from *Are You Being Served?* was wiggling her chubby body in our direction. Her hair, a bouffant blue-rinse of cotton wool, bounced itself in a controlled hair-spray-held kind of way. The ruffles of her blouse cascaded over the lapels of her dated Fifties suit. She was holding her plump arm in the air which revealed a large circle of sweat in her arm pit. I was expecting her to scream 'I'm free' in an *Are You Being Served?* camp manner. But to my surprise, in a ridiculously feigned posh accent which accentuated the Birmingham intonation she was trying so hard to conceal, she shouted; "Oh, Grania. It is you, isn't it? Grania, darl-ing?"

"Oh no," Mammy uttered in a ventriloquist fashion, through a clenched-toothed smile, "just my bloody luck."

It must be bad, Mammy had cursed. I awaited the justification. It wasn't too long before it was unveiled like a bride at the altar - in all its grandeur.

"Hello, Janet. Long time no see." Mammy now moved her lips.

"Yes, well of course it has been quite a while since we moved. We had to move out of the area quickly, you know. Going down it was. Had to get out before the rot set in. Too much riff-raff there now. Oh, no offence to you dear, we could afford to leave, you know ... to better ourselves ... Know what I mean? Although you were wonderful neighbours."

"Mmmm." Mammy nodded in an unbelievably controlled manner. Her eyes were wide as she took a deep breath and bit her bottom lip. She certainly sounded the snob Lola had accused her of being.

"So how are the kiddies? Boys must have left school now? Did they follow in their daddy's footsteps? You know, doing odd jobs."

"No, Janet, they didn't bother doing the five-year apprenticeship Rory did to be a registered tradesman... oh, I mean odd-job man. Dominic's at Birmingham University studying architecture. Patrick's a trainee Quantity Surveyor, weekly day release to Uni. and Orlagh here is still at school." I detected an uncharacteristic patronising tone in Mammy's voice.

"Goodness me! That's never Orlagh?" She rubbed her gold-strewn fingers through my hair like I were a five-year-old. I acquired a sweet wry grin. The horrible stench of body odour emanated from the wet, white-rimmed circle of her arm pit, which was then replaced by the sweet smell of Great-grandma Mary. Lola must have returned. Janet continued; "Oh, hasn't she come into herself?"

What was that nonsensical saying actually all about? Whose was I *in* before? It seemed this pompous lady was full of delightfully degrading sententious maxims.

"You've really blossomed, become quite the swan, you know taking everything into consideration... erm you erm know." Sensing Mammy's obvious consternation, her words began to stammer.

Mammy's face was the cerise of Lola's tight blouse. I noticed she had taken a long deep breath through her nose during most of Janet's sentence, her tiny diaphragm ready to burst. The last time I'd seen her anger rise to such levels was at the nativity debacle when I was a child. I imagined a similar astoundingly captivating finale with Janet being tossed into the stainless-steel racks of underwear, with her ankles skyward, doing a wonderful impression of a dying fly as lace panties fell about her candy-floss blue-rinsed head.

"No, Janet, I'm afraid I really don't know... Enlighten me. Taking *what* exactly into consideration?"

"Ermmm, you know, that horrid red mark. Well, you must admit, it's not at all pleasant to look at, is it?"

"You mean as pleasant as you, Janet? You wrinkled, blown-up old prune... well, rotting giant orange more like, with your ridiculous fake tan and your B O as revolting as ever. It's just a shame Orlagh's mark is prominent. Or no, it's actually not a shame, because she's a beautiful person with or *without* it."

"Hear, hear." I was right, Lola had returned, stumbling upon our tête-à-tête and defiantly joining in.

"*But you*, you're marked more than Orlagh could ever be. Marked with the shame of your hoity-toity, ex-school-teacher husband being fired after having an affair with one of his fifteen-year-old students. Marked with the shame of losing his job and spending your savings on a solicitor who could get you out of the mess when the parents tried to prosecute. I actually feel sorry for the excuse of a man he is - having to live with you. Are you still having an affair with his brother? The brother I saw a few too many times sneaking out of the bedroom window half-naked when your husband arrived home surprisingly early.

"Had to leave before the rot set in? Is that new terminology for banking foreclosure? Is that what they call *bettering yourself* these days - a clapped-out, rust bucket of a caravan that you had to move to, sinking and *stinking* in your mother's garden?"

Mammy was only interrupted by the squeals of laughter from Lola. "I don't believe it, the trumped up old bag. Caravan... I love it!" Lola slapped her leg in excitement. "Tell us more. Thank God I forgot me purse because I would've kicked meself if I'd missed this."

An audience of *British Home Stores* staff looked on with satisfied grins. Mammy had hurt Janet in the most wonderful of ways, reminding her of a few home truths. Janet, well, she was dumbfounded, mouth ajar and for the first time in our short re-acquaintance - lost for words.

It always seemed the egotistical, superficial people made

the most degrading, hateful comments about my birthmark: Rubbery Robert, Crooked Crookson and now Jaded Janet. The big-breasted Lola didn't give it a second glance. Emmet too had never made a comment.

Mammy as ever was my saviour. I didn't look at her as merely my deliverer into this world, but she too was one of my guardian angels, only of the visible, human species. She was always watching over and protecting me from those wild cats which were still prowling around corners, waiting unannounced to pounce.

chapter twenty-five

Mission accomplished! One 32B, white broiderie-anglaise bra was purchased for me, fourteen-year-old Orlagh Emmet - and didn't I feel a lady! Well, it wasn't exactly purchased, more like given as compensation so as not to take the Janet insults further - as the manager had subtly suggested to Mammy. Of course there was spare money which was supposed to be for the bra. It lay with the Queen's face gazing out of Mammy's purse, silently pleading to be spent. I found it surprisingly easy to respond to the silent Queen's supplicating gaze and purchased myself some finger-less lace gloves; because as well as thinking I was now a lady, after watching *Desperately Seeking Susan* I also thought I was Madonna.

I didn't really have time to be despondent about the Janet insults, I was too preoccupied with buying new Madonna attire. Apart from that, it was Nanna Bridie night, and the only thing you could focus on when Nanna Bridie was around, was... Nanna Bridie.

She still chose to live in the degradation of her inner-city, ground-floor flat. It was housed in an area which was a perfect example of a place politicians conveniently disregard after election day.

The Ayadollah long since gone, replaced with a senile old lady who still thought her husband was alive thirty years after his death, laying out his clothes daily and squealing, 'Not there! Can't you see Charlie?' if you attempted to sit on the wrong decaying seat. Dad aptly named her Psycho's Granny. For Nanna, Psycho's Granny was yet another easy target to torment. She had acquired quite a few more sitting ducks in her cul-de-sac of dysfunction. To reside there you would have to be either a psychopath, a prostitute, an illegal immigrant or... Nanna Bridie. And to live there and love it, to me, exhibited a fundamental flaw in their brain matter.

I walked up the litter-strewn cul-de-sac, past black bin-liners bulging open with a congregation of supplementary residents - of the maggot kind, toppling over each other for a taste of the discarded madras curry or late-night kebab. I proceeded through Nanna's wooden garden gate, which hung on to the status of being a gate by one bolt of one hinge, overcome by the struggle to survive as small scuffed feet swung their way to a dismal, uneducated life, while their mothers were paid for sex in their homes. Down the urine-smelling path and in through the invariably open door, twisting myself in her useless multi-coloured fortune-teller's beaded strips as I passed. Pigs' feet boiled rapidly on the grease-covered stove. In an adjacent pot an ancient stew had coagulated to a mass of white fat so dense you could do an Irish jig on it. Nanna Bridie patiently waited in her five cardigans, striped pinafore, with twenty tissues rolled up her sleeve, watching her unbearably loud television set, with a large stained bandage across her nose. It proved my point on basal brain blemishes - she was crazy.

Nanna Bridie honoured us with her remarkable presence each week, sucking the fat of her lamb chops, like a baby on a dummy, dripping gravy on to her brown-and-white-striped pinafore, looking as well as smelling (despite the gravy and grease) like a packet of humbugs. She would recount hilarious stories about the prostitutes, the Ayadollah and her new boyfriend Fred. Even my septuagenarian granny had a boyfriend, although she probably would have been better off without him. The most recent fiasco, which Fred had prompted, would explain the bandage over her nose.

On our return home, clutching the secret clothing, I proceeded to my bedroom and locked the door. I put on the new garment, cupped my breasts in my palms and repeated what I'd done in the *British Home Stores* fitting room; I twisted left and right to view every angle of my womanly contours. I was so excited at the thought of having the chance to wear it. It was still a secret from the men in my household - I was sticking to my plan. Mammy thought I was being a little absurd, but she just didn't understand the torment I would go through if they knew.

I went down to dinner that evening clad in my new lace garments, not of the bra variety, but of my finger-less, Madonna-like gloves.

"Are ya cold, lurve?" Nanna Bridie asked, as I joined them all at the table. Her chin was already covered in gravy. Dominic and Patrick could not contain their laughter.

"Like a virgin, ohhhh - touched for the very first time," Patrick started singing.

"Like a virrrrr-er-er-er-gin, when your heart beats, ah, ah - next to mine," Dominic continued. Nanna Bridie was oblivious of anything going on. Dad simply continued the conversation with her, also not knowing what had inspired the singing. I tried to ignore their mockery.

"Tell Grania and the kids about the disaster Fred caused then, Ma."

"Fred didn't cause it, Rory. It was just a freak accident."

"Jesus, you've experienced a few too many freak accidents, hey, Ma? Go on, Grania'd love to hear your side of the story."

A week previous we had received yet another of Nanna's SOS phone calls. This time it wasn't the Ayadollah who was going to cut her throat - the enemy wasn't even human. The adversaries were the electric volts which were chasing her naked, wrinkled body around the bathroom!

"There I was in the shower, havin' a great wash, mindin' me own business."

"Oh, so now I know, that's when you mind your own business, is it?" Dad retorted.

"Leave her be, Rory. Go on, Ma, ignore him." Mammy laughed as she rushed around preparing our dinner.

"*BOOM!*" Nanna dramatically continued, "the plastic cover off the shower hit me smack in me mush. Bits of plastic were flyin' everywhere. I couldn't believe me poxy eyes. Then it started, I thought I was in an episode of a space show. Blue flashes of light were flying from the shower box, which was now open with all the wires comin' out've it, through the water... to me and then back to the box agen. I was gettin' electro-feckin'-cuted. Everywhere I moved in the bathroom the blue flashes got me. When I ran into the livin' room all the pissin' lights were going *up* and down, *up* and down. The telly was going almost off and then back to normal. Off and back on." Tears of laughter trickled down from her bulbous blue eyes, over her corrugated face, past the bandage which covered her broken nose and off to be soaked up with the rest of the stains on her striped pinny.

As Nanna told her tale, I was aware that the boys hadn't recited any more songs for the benefit of my gloves. I thought my mature stance of ignoring their taunts had worked for once.

"When I arrived there," Dad began, "the silly mare was sittin' in the livin' room like a drowned rat, with a sheet wrapped around her, and blood trickling down her nose. The lights and the telly still going up and down and the shower still running full blast with sparks flying everywhere. I turned off the electricity and investigated the cause. She was lucky she hadn't been killed. All the fittings inside the shower were welded together. Fred the ald eejit had crossed the live wire over the earth, so everything was running live. I'd told her to wait for me to fit it... but noooo. 'Fred'll do it, Rory. He knows what he's doing,' she'd said. Didn't ya? Like hell he knew what he was doin'. He can hardly see to read the newspaper, let alone wire up an electric shower, which he's never seen the likes of before in his life!" Dad chuckled. It wasn't worth telling her off, she was too old and stubborn to change.

"Holiday!" Patrick started, behind a clenched-teeth smile. I had been a little hasty in my taunt-ignoring assumption.

"If we took a holiday," Dom continued, while chewing his food.

"It would beee-eeee - it would be so nice." Patrick danced to his song as he took his empty plate to Mammy at the sink. His head swayed from left to right on each syllable.

Due to my new lace gloves I was being persecuted by Madonna songs. And Mammy thought I wouldn't receive any taunts from wearing a bra.

"When is your holiday, doll?" Dad asked, thinking the whole performance was directed at my forthcoming ski trip. This comment encouraged Dominic and Patrick into a laughing convulsion.

"Ya'all pissin' barmy, you lot," was Nanna Bridie's contribution, as she picked up the rind of my lamb chop and began sucking on it.

"Next *Sunday*, Dad." With my chin held high I ignored my taunting brothers. Dad was oblivious as to why there was an air of pompousness about my demeanour.

"What's happenin' Sunday? Are ya going to get rid of that thing?" Nanna pointed to my birthmark with the chewed end of lamp-chop fat.

"No, Nanna, I'm going skiing. My treatment's on Friday. I'm having a test patch then."

"What-ing?" she asked while a droplet of gravy escaped from her greased lips. It slid down on a fast descent and clung to her bristled chin; like a rain droplet on a furred leaf.

Explaining the concept of pleasure skiing proved too difficult. "I'm going to Italy, Nanna."

"Ya'all spoilt rotten you lot... spoilt rotten. But it'll be good when ya get rid of that thing on yer face." And she continued on with her silent pledge of attaining a cholesterol level above and beyond anything that could ever be recorded.

I had quickly decided to discard the Madonna-like, finger-less gloves and allow them the honour of joining: the Aston Villa sweat bands, primary-school tie, a cheap seaside T-shirt with my front-toothless black and white image transferred on to it, along with the set of nylon nightdresses which stated in enchanting form my age. Angels, fairies and flowers entwined themselves around numerical figures which went from two to seven. All items were magnificent to observe at times. I loved removing them from their drawer and smelling their fabric-soft scent, nostalgically remembering the times I wore them. But it would have been unwise to wear anything which belonged in that drawer - especially if you had brothers like mine. I was hoping the bra wouldn't be joining them in the bottom drawer of rejection.

While I neatly folded the finger-less lace gloves in preparation to enter my drawer, I reflected on what had occurred earlier in *British Home Stores*. Although I marvelled at the destruction of Jaded Janet, I had a feeling which I figured my gloves must have been experiencing - one of rejection. My happy and mature, bra-owning feeling had been besmirched with melancholy. I understood that Janet was a shallow, hateful person, whose opinion I shouldn't take into consideration, but it was hard not to when there was a never-ending supply of such heartless people. People who had evaded being pulled off the continual conveyor belt of life by the hands of the creator and dumped into the rejected-goods pile.

I knew it didn't mean the whole of mankind had tendencies to be a Janet or a Crooked Crookson, but it made me wonder how most people saw me through their eyes. I had learnt to see myself through the eyes of my parents, with beauty, strength and dignity. But slowly their inherited vision was beginning to mist over as I heard too many of these comments. I was beginning to really dislike myself.

When I opened the drawer full of memories I realised that if the new addition was to have an unsquashed position it would require rearranging. I picked up the pile of neatly stacked nylon nightdresses. They hadn't been moved in quite a while and it looked as though they'd accumulated a layer of dust. I lifted the top nightdress and shook it out of its folded position. A thin blanket of dust departed the surface and ascended skyward; some made its way up my nose, making me sneeze.

I reopened my eyes after sneezing to discover the thin blanket of dust had formed into a replicated figure of the angel which was entwined around the number seven on my nightdress.

She floated around the room without appearing to move a part of whatever it was which formed her being. While she floated she spoke so softly I could hardly hear. "Self-love, Orlagh. Do you think it is a significant part of our spiritual make-up?"

I was too dumbfounded to reply. However many times angels appeared in my presence, they never ceased to shock me.

She was unfazed by my astonishment. "I'll answer for you. Yes! It's imperative to have self-love. To reach the highest level and live life to the full you have to know your own beauty. It's imperative you understand this rule, so you may lead a happy life and do the job we require you to do. Not being happy with yourself means not being happy with the world around you.

"It's a long, hard journey on the meandering road to self-love. But having self-love will make you admire your surroundings, thus giving you the divine gift of appreciating God's splendour. Learning to love yourself is most certainly the greatest love. It's not about being a narcissist, it's about seeing beauty, feeling beauty and being beautiful.

"But you're losing your way. Your sense of self-love is diminishing. You've wandered along the path of doom. You have to get back on the right road for the benefits are certainly worth reaping. The pot of gold is lying in paradise under the rainbow of happiness, yearning to be retrieved. You need to find the map along with the lost key and open your box of angel-bestowed knowledge. Stay on the right road and that pot will be yours."

"Yes, that's easy to say, but how do I do that?"

"You'll eventually learn. Just remember, time brings everything... Tempus omnia revelat. And most importantly... wisest is she who knows what she does not know."

"I don't understand. Please tell me what this means. And what's the job you have for me?"

There was no further conversation. Her composition fell like particles of dust illuminated in bright sunlight and dispersed over the clothes in my bottom drawer full of happy memories.

CHapteR twenty-six

Nanna wasn't the only member of the Emmet clan experiencing space-like laser flashes. I was finally going to have my argon laser treatment with Doctor John Callaghan. It had taken five whole years until I became known as number one on the South Hants Hospital waiting list.

The hospital differed only in location to all the others I had visited on my expedition of birthmark elimination. They all had the same disinfectant-smelling corridors with the intermittent fleeting aroma of over-cooked hospital food, the same scratched rubber doors and perpetual corridors. There were the kind, wry-smiling nurses present and nurses who looked at you like you were an inconvenience, a look which mirrored their dismissive thoughts of more needy, sick children requiring their expert care.

In the waiting room I saw for the first time a congregation of port-wine stain possessors. There were: small, large, raised, dark and light birthmarks. I saw a little girl cowering in a corner - her parents seemed to encourage her cringing camouflage. She was evidently embarrassed by her markings, and so were they. There were too many downcast eyes, not in a discreet waiting-room manner, but in a way where they all appeared to have an air of shame about themselves. It seemed it had been instilled into them that they were different, not different in a good way, but in a misfit-of-society-way. When I looked around and saw the only smiles present were those of my parents, I realised for the first time the silent job they had undertaken of making my birthmark a secondary concern in my life; how they had dug deep footings for the formation of my character wall. I was now more determined than ever to make them proud.

There was one pair of eyes not staring at the rubber flooring – and they belonged to an elderly lady. To me her eyes unveiled a powerful familiarity. They were like a scent which evokes nostalgic memories. I had never seen this lady before, but I'd seen those bulbous eyes. A square patch of red covered the left eye, like a pirate's patch. Their tropical-sea-blue colour glimmered through, similar to Dad's - but identical to Nanna Bridie's.

I felt myself staring, which in usual circumstances I would never do. I don't stare, because I dislike being stared at. But this lady protruded from the crowd, she stood out like a skyscraper amidst a row of terraced houses. I was mesmerised.

Her eyes caught my stare. I felt abashed.

"Orlagh Emmet, please." The nurse had saved me from my embarrassment. As I was about to look away, the old lady gave me a smile. A smile as familiar as her eyes. A smile which belonged to Dad's sister. It was definitely an Aunt Assumpta smile.

Doctor Callaghan had changed little in the years since the Aberdeen Clinic. His hair was a little greyer, well not so much grey, more like a shimmering silver. His eyes showed a hint of fatigue, but his stomach revealed contentment, and his warm welcoming smile indicated his boundless benevolence.

It was only the treatment which was changing; the situation was the same. Mammy's pain reactor had cranked itself into action once again; she had to remain in the waiting room.

"I can't bear it, Orlagh." Mammy glued her lips together, shook her head and squeezed her chestnut eyes shut at the mere thought. "It hurts me too much. I can't bear to see you in pain, baby. Your dad'll be with you."

I didn't really understand it; as it was me having the treatment, not her. I wasn't too bothered though because Dad made his presence known enough for me to forget about Mammy's absence - in actual fact, almost enough for me to forget the whole distressing process.

As Doctor Callaghan administered the anaesthetic, Dad acquired a Latino accent and honoured us with his rendition of Viva Espana. Dad was in the middle of sunny Spain as I was in the midst of an overcast gloom of embarrassment. I couldn't tell him to be quiet because I had a needle sticking out of my cheek. It just didn't seem the wise thing to do at a time like that.

"Here goes then, Orlagh; place on these goggles so we don't damage your eyes. Don't worry if you feel some pain, it's normal. We can't block out all of the pain with the anaesthetic."

Doctor Callaghan also placed on ridiculous-looking goggles; he only required a white scarf and leather helmet to completely resemble Biggles. I was actually surprised to discover the needle had been administered. I'd been too busy being humiliated by Dad's song to worry about pain, although the doctor's speech *had* temporarily silenced him.

The laser I expected to resemble a *Star Wars* light sabre was more akin to a Parker pen. I visualised the doctor signing his name across my face.

When Doctor Callaghan put the laser to work, he seemed to have also pressed Dad's *play* button. If Dad hadn't been standing at the bottom of the bed annoyingly tickling my toes, I would have been convinced he had a skipping rope doing fancy jumps and tricks. He sang an Irish skipping song so enthusiastically it was almost beyond belief that he was standing still: "She is handsome. She is pretty. Orlagh's the girl from Birmingham city. She's

200

a courtin' a one - two - three, please won't ye tell me who is she. I'll tell my ma when I get home, the boys won't leave the girls alone...."

He really was like the constant ringing of tinnitus in my inner ear; however hard I tried not to concentrate on it, it just wouldn't go away... or so I thought.

The invasion of burning hair into my sinuses struck the first chord in the melody of pain. The second, third and fourth chords soon followed. The pitch of agony falling and rising in perfect melodic contours, covering every note on the instrument of discomfort. It was like a sharp knife stabbing and a stainless-steel kettle full of boiling water hitting the area simultaneously. Dad's skipping song would now sound euphonious, if only I could hear him, but he was now merely a faraway echo in the valley of my mind.

I endured the pain which shot through my body like electricity through a circuit of multi-coloured wires. As the current-like pain reached the pinnacles of my limbs, it caused my hands to form a fist and my fingernails to dig deep into my palms, compelling my knuckles to turn the colour of a virgin bride's dress. My pelvis sporadically twitched as I clenched my buttocks together and pointed my toes as taut and straight as a prima ballerina preparing for a perfect pirouette. Then the current lit up my brain, revealing the reason behind my pain toleration, "If I endure this," I thought, as I gritted my teeth and held my breath. "If I go through this, maybe, just maybe Emmet O'Malley would consider looking at me." It was my mantra, which I repeated over and again, meditating through my pain.

The meditation worked, taking me to another world, where I could see the blackbird flying through Emmet's paradise sky-blue eyes, where I could see his bright smile filled with mischief and where I could faintly hear humorous words rolling off his tongue.

I was immersed in thoughts of Emmet when I sensed Doctor Callaghan had removed his Biggles goggles, placed down the Parker-pen laser and was affectionately rubbing my tummy, as though I were a new-born baby. Dad had finished telling his ma about the boys not leaving the girls alone and was saying; "Isn't she brave, doc? Not a complaint out've her. That's my girl."

"She most certainly is brave. It'd make my job a whole lot easier if all my patients were like her. That's the test patch completed, Orlagh. I'm afraid there's a little more waiting involved until we can assess if this intensity works on your mark. But it won't be too long - as soon as we can possibly fit you in."

I'd heard that before... '*as soon as possible*' . I had waited from February 1982 until February 1987 for Doctor Callaghan's '*as soon as possible*' appointment slot. I hoped it wouldn't be such a prolonged period until the next.

chapter twenty-seven

Mammy referred to Emmet as a lovable rogue. I referred to him as simply *lovable* (secretly, of course). Dad's most common name for him was eejit.

Emmet had become a common fixture at our dinner table. Spin the spoon had been replaced with - Who knows the most about current affairs, sport, politics and history? It was trivial pursuit without a game board, and Emmet was a major-league player, contradicting Dad's jovial eejit nickname! I was invariably the one without any slices in my pie, with no points - unless Dad slipped in an easy question, for me that is; which is what I thought he had done on this particular day. I had, after all, just had my test patch and needed an easy time.

Like the well in ancient villages, our house was the meeting place of the masses. It appeared to be the central location en route to just about *anywhere*. Although our well didn't produce mineral water which had lain buried in volcanic rock, untouched for thousands of years, it produced abounding hospitality from Mammy in the form of current-filled soda bread and chocolate biscuits, and ceaseless witticisms, enthralling stories and laughter from Dad. Mammy always said we had more comings and goings than Grand Central Station.

There always seemed to be something occurring in our

house, but this particular week was an exceptionally eventful one. There had been my test patch in Southampton for one. There was preparation for my ski trip going on and tonight was the semi-finals of the British Amateur Boxing Championships. But still, everything appeared so calm and normal, except for Mammy being a little more subdued than usual. The reason for that was that her intuitive pain reactor had been ticking over since my treatment and gone back into full action at the thought of the boys boxing. She could feel every jab, uppercut and left hook without even watching - before they were even thrown. She adored the sport, but couldn't bear to think about, let alone see Dom or Pat in the ring.

Emmet's arrival gave Dad the perfect opportunity to take the boys' minds off their forthcoming bouts, storing their nervous energy for the ring. He started a game of dinner-table pursuit.

I revelled in the thought of a boxing show, but was more excited at the thought of spending the whole night with Emmet. He stirred emotions in me which I was just experiencing for the very first time, affecting areas of my body I never even knew existed. Merely the thought of seeing him made me take slow, deep breaths and an invisible force slapped a smile upon my face. The only problem was, the allurement grew stronger every day.

Emmet came to our house directly from work. Covering his mahogany-coloured hair was a sheen of wood dust and wooden curls, and just like Dad after a day of manual labour, he had that bitter-sweet smell. He hadn't even bothered to have the afternoon off work to rest his body for the battle which was to take place in the ensuing period. He was about to do three rounds of three-minute duration and all day he had been using his arms for sawing, hammering and mitring. He was as bubbly as a shaken-up bottle of champagne on a formula one podium and seemed more concerned with Dad's trivia than boxing. Mammy, as usual, had squeezed him in a chair at the table in-between Patrick and myself. This meant he had to sit open legged, as the wooden leg of the table was in his way. There were no complaints from me at being so squashed, because his knee, or if I was really lucky, his thigh, touched mine. It was only a slight connection, but I was so conscious of it I sat like a statue so none of my movements would disturb his leg. I wanted it exactly where it was, resting (for him, unconsciously) on mine.

"Okay then..." Dad rubbed his hands together as if it were twenty degrees below freezing. "Let's see what this Derry man knows today. Is he worthy of a place at the quizmasters table? What'd reckon, Orle?"

Why did he have to ask me when it came to Emmet? I tried not to make my obsession with him noticeable. I tried to act as normal as possible, with limited movement so as not to disturb - the leg.

"Do Derry men know anything, Dad?"

As I concluded my audacious comment my heart skipped a beat, in fact it almost stopped; Emmet had nudged my knee with his (so maybe he wasn't as unconscious about the connection after all) and concluded by grabbing my thigh with his hand and squeezing until I screamed in pain. I wasn't sure whether my thigh was tingling with pain or from excitement at his touch.

"I'll show you what Derry men know, *Miss Emmet*. Me - the Derry man, against all yers bogtrottin' Emmets."

"You're on, O'Malley," Patrick confirmed, laughing in mock condescension.

"Right, where does the saying 'sent to Coventry' derive?" I considered Dad had chosen a difficult starter question. I was clueless, but Dominic and Emmet had both slammed down their forks - forks substituted buzzers. It was like a complete mad house, especially if everyone knew the answer; our dinner table then sounded more like a wild-horse stampede.

"To be fair, Dom, I think that O'Malley forked it first." All the boys cracked up laughing; I'd missed the innuendo.

"Hey calm down you lot, you're mammy's over there. Go on then Emm, throw it at me."

"Yer know, Rory, ye need some harder questions, so ye do, if ye think your lot'll beat me. It was from the Napoleonic wars, will that do ye?"

"No, we need details. There'll be no slackin' around here, boy." Dad laughed and winked at me.

"All right then... When the British forces captured Napoleonic forces they sent 'em mainly to the Midlands, Coventry in particular - so they'd be land-locked and would have less chance of escapin'. They chained all the prisoners of war together and locked 'em in the churches and instructed them they couldn't speak to one another, just in case they were plottin' an escape. Well, being as they were in churches, if they whispered it would be heard. Oh, but you may not comprehend that, Rory. When was the last time you were in a church, yer heathen Free Stater? Anyway, that's that. They weren't allowed to talk, so when you send someone to Coventry, no one's allowed to talk to 'em."

"Correct answer, but a point deducted for insultin' the quizmaster!"

"But just think," Emmet added.

"Don't do that, Emmet. Lord knows what'll happen if you do."

"What if Nelson hadn't won at the battle of Trafalgar?" Emmet dismissed Dad's sarcasm. "What if Napoleon had been successful and colonised England, makin' the English speak French and placin' their Gendarmes on English streets. Do you think the English would revolt? Fight against the invaders? Or would they sit and watch the crushin' of their culture and the annihilation of their identity?

"No, metaphorically speakin' like... the English decide - enough is enough and they fight for their beloved country. After quite a few tumultuous years the French decide that it's more trouble than it's worth, so they yield the *majority* of the country back to English rule. But sure, don't the French insist on keepin' ... lets say: Cornwall, Devon, Dorset and sure don't they want Hampshire as well - 'cause there's been a French majority in all those counties since they came and invaded and stole the land off the English, who'd been there an eternity. They want those counties 'cause it's where all the money is, and they hold all the jobs, although, they won't give any jobs to the English; they want frogs ribbertin' around in the tin mines and the dock yards - what they also stole from the English. Do you think the Brits would sit back and allow their beloved, beautiful country to be separated? Sit back and let decisions regardin' English soil be made by French politicians in a Parisian parliament? I don't think they would, do you lot?"

I didn't miss the innuendo in that little speech. Everyone agreed, even Mammy who was hovering over the stove. "You've hit the nail on the head there, Emmet, love."

"I've hit a few today, Grania. I even missed once and hit me finger." His dimples made an appearance as he winked at Mam.

"Jesus, Mary and Joseph, why did I mention Napoleon?" Dad asked laughing, while slapping his leg. But whether it was Napoleon, Wellington, Kennedy or Thatcher, it wouldn't have mattered - Emmet would have found an Irish connection.

The trivia continued through steak sandwiches, salad and baked potatoes. The boys only ate half and had the other half packed for after their boxing weigh-in. It continued without me having had the chance to answer one question; without me having had the chance to impress Emmet with my astounding intellect - if only. They'd travelled from Napoleon to Attila The Hun and on to Che Guevara.

"Did yer know, Rory, that Che Guevara's real name was Seamus O'Hara?"

"Ach, get away with yer now, Emmet."

"Sure it was, Rory. He was yet another great Irishman."

They travelled from Ireland to Indonesia, Kathmandu to Timbuktu. They had circumnavigated the globe within the hour. Forks were being slammed at astonishing speed. They were just too quick for me, and too knowledgeable. Then I saw my opening. I viewed my chance to go straight through the guard and knock them out with the speed and force of my wisdom.

"Who is to blame for the debacle known as Bloody Sunday?"

Finally I knew one. I regarded it easy in relation to the preceding questions. I also considered Dad had structured the question a little erroneously; because in the eyes of the youth it wasn't a disaster at all, but a popular art form. He was just being an old fuddy-duddy.

"I know. I know this one. Please let me answer, Dad."

"Slam yer fork, Orlagh, ye know the rules."

I shoved the fork in my mouth, clearing it of baked-potato traces, almost piercing my tonsils in the process, and slammed it on the table. The boys hadn't even attempted to intervene, they were giving me a chance.

"Bono!" I emphatically proclaimed and nodded in affirmed conclusion.

"What?" A second chin formed as Dad pushed his head back to view me with more clarity.

"Okay, if you're getting finicky, then - U2," I answered, giving a wry, derisive 'yeah-I-am-smart' smirk.

"Hold on a second, princess, you lost me with Boneo."

"Bono," I corrected.

The boys had all developed smiles as they obviously knew what I was talking about. I knew Dad didn't have a clue what he was on about when he had said *debacle*. How could anything U2 had done be considered a debacle? He was just trying to show off, pretending he was hip and up on all the popular music.

"All right, Bono, you lost me anyway. I think yer on a different wave length, baby doll."

"No Dad, I think you are. Tell him, Pat."

"I think he's on about the civil-rights march, Orlagh. Dad's clueless on U2!" Patrick answered, simultaneously bursting into fits of laughter with Dominic and Emmet.

"If U2 or Bono, or whatever, had something to do with Bloody Sunday, then you can have a point, princess."

"I don't want a point, Dad. Don't patronise me."

"Ohhhh, patro-n-iiiise," Dom and Pat sang together. Emmet just sat and smiled. If he wasn't there I could have got over it. It was no big deal to humiliate myself in front of my brothers. If I didn't ridicule myself, they would always find something to wind me up about, casting their lines and reeling, slowly at first and as soon as I bit their bait the reel turned as fast as the wheels on a speeding car. But at that point I was burning inside, my inner fire had been kindled and Dominic held the poker.

"So, Orle, tell me, was Bono in the Paras at the time? Or was it The Edge dressed as Father Daley, you know the old priest waving a white hankie?"

Dominic was driving the poker in hard and fast, flaring my anger until it became an inferno. My blood felt like it had boiled and had risen to my head. I could feel my face burning. I'm sure for a change I was one complete shade of red. Because of Emmet I couldn't have a tantrum, shout and complain and run out of the kitchen slamming the door on my departure.

"Will someone tell me what this Bono fella has to do with Bloody Sunday? I've read all there is to read on the subject, both sides of the story and Bono has never cropped up in any of the accounts." Dad appeared mystified.

"They sang about Bloody Sunday, Rory, that's all, so Orlagh was right in a sense - hey, babe?" Emmet nudged me with his elbow and winked. His dimples were deep and enduring. The ecstasy of his touch took away the imminent mortification. My fire just smouldered. I smiled and nodded. As the fire was being smothered in the rapture of his touch, someone just had to give it one last poke.

"We should have you here as a calming influence for

missy more often, Emmet. I've never seen her calm down so quickly." After poking my fire Mammy continued with her task of wrapping food in silver foil, chuckling to herself.

"So, come on, it's the last question before we head off. Tell Orlagh here the correct explanation I want - although, she should know, I've spoken about it enough."

My mind had gone totally blank; all I could think of was Bono in his beret ... 'Sunday Bloody Sunday'.

"As I was only a few hundreds yards away from the whole, as you so rightly called it, Rory - debacle, I think I should inform you of the correct account." Emmet tapped his fork in the centre of the table. "You see, Orlagh, it was all about internment, well in fact it all boils down to British rule full stop, but we won't go that deep."

"No, make it quick, O'Malley, we have a show to go to. I sure hope your hands work as quick tonight, as yer tongue has today." Dad grinned and nodded for him to continue.

"January thirtieth, 1972, it was, and the Civil Rights Association organised a peaceful - I must stress that - *peaceful* march, which was protestin' against internment. Internment can only be described as an unlawful law written in Britain's presumably fair judicial system, which was only viable in Northern Ireland. Where men, some innocent and - granted - some not, were taken from the streets on *suspicion* of being connected with the IRA. I say *IRA* specifically because not *one* unionist extremist was interned.

"The police can't hold a man suspected of murderin' his wife, children and throw the mother-in-law in as well, for more than forty-eight hours if they don't have sufficient evidence. But the interned men were locked away for months and can yer believe it, years at a time without charge - or trial, guilty only of the religion bestowed upon them at birth. It was tyranny of the crown in an unprecedented form.

"The British decided the only illegality was the civil-rights march against internment and they put a ban on it.

When a crowd of some three-hundred-thousand took to the streets of Derry, defiant at the breach of their simple civil rights, the authorities deployed the Paratroopers, who were reputed to be the toughest regiment in the army. Yeah, they were real tough against a group of unarmed protesters when they had their Self-Loading-Rifles in their hands - which, without warning or provocation they fired indiscriminately into the fleein' crowd, killin' fourteen and seriously injurin' loads more. The majority were shot in the back; one of which was me Uncle Malachie, but he lived to tell the atrocious tale. That's how tough the Paras are and that's what U2 sung about, Orlagh. So now yer know who it was behind the debacle of Bloody Sunday."

He relayed the account with so much emotion, you could see the sorrow shimmering in his eyes, and hear the passion echoing in his words. I wished he could love me as much as he adored Ireland.

chapter twenty-eight

I sat alone amidst the hustle-bustle of boxing officials, ring assemblers and half-naked boxers. No other spectators had yet arrived, but I loved being a part of it all.

I thought of Bono and cringed inside. I closed my eyes and shuddered at my imbecilic comment. How could I have been so stupid? I decided that I was going to put aside my love-story novels and immerse myself in the history of Ireland. I would learn the smallest details of the genocide engineered by the English, better known as the Great Famine, of Trevelyan's corn rations and the subsequent prison ships full of the starving, heading for the prison colonies of Van Diemen's Land and New South Wales. I would fill my head with Irish revolutionary sayings - I already knew Robert Emmet's, who my grandfather Dominic Emmet claimed to be a direct descendent of. Which is why he apparently chose to recite Robert Emmet's words each night: '*Let no man write my epitaph... When my country takes her place among the nations of the earth, then and only then shall my epitaph be written.*' But I wanted to know why he'd said that. I wanted to know why James Connolly was tied to his chair in 1916 and killed with no trial. I wanted to know how Arthur Griffith formed Sinn Fein. I wanted to know all about Michael Collins, along with how Eamon De Valera had stabbed him in the back and sold us down the river. In fact, I simply wanted to know everything and not just Irish history either, but world history and world revolutionaries. I wanted to know who Che Guevara was and if his name really was Seamus O'Hara, or whether that was another of Emmet's jokes. I needed to impress Emmet with my intellect and that was the route I was going to take to find the way to the heart of my infatuation.

Dad had a team of boxers known as The Birmingham Irish, who were envied within the amateur boxing circles. A team who were loyal, strong and skilful. They all had a hunger which sucked away at the marrow of their bones - an appetite they fed with victory. Virtually all of them were unbeaten. But Dad's boys had to dig deeper than those in most clubs, delve to the bottom of their boxing boots to produce a performance that would in no uncertain terms decide the winner; because there was a lot of jealousy which generated underhandedness. There were too many corrupt judges or biased referees in the Midland district, who were prepared to give the decision to the loser merely because Rory's lads had won too much, giving the other lads a chance. They didn't have the sense to realise the psychological damage it caused a boxer to be robbed of his victory. To have his win snatched away as he stood sweating and tired while the loser's arm was raised by a white-clad referee. They didn't realise that the opponent had his chance before entering the ring. They didn't realise Dad's lads never missed training. They skipped, sparred, shadow-boxed, did hours of roadwork and adhered to all the rules. They wanted to make Dad proud, make their own dads proud. The majority of Dad's boxers were from dysfunctional families and his boxing gym contained an adopted family. Dad was their mentor who instilled an unlimited amount of amusement, benevolence and fun into their lives; a kind which most had never experienced. They were a brotherhood of extortionately devoted proportions... A brotherhood with one sister.

The championships was a chance for them to shine, to not only box opponents within their district, but exhibit their skills countrywide - that was if they progressed past the preliminary rounds of the Midland district.

Most clubs entered two or three boys to represent them, selecting only their finest boxers. Some clubs encountered difficult decisions in deciding if their boxers would be good enough to last through even the first round. The Birmingham Irish possessed so many boxers of a high standard Dad's only difficult decision lay with selecting the most capable boys within the specific weight classes. He obviously didn't want friends and in some cases brothers boxing each other. Fifteen of Dad's lads had been entered at the beginning. Fifteen had reached the Midland Counties' Finals. Ten triumphed to box in the British semi-finals, which unfortunately were being held in the Midlands, where too many sneaky officials knew Dad's boxers' winning reputation.

All the boxers had made the weight and passed their medical check-up, which ascertained whether all the boys were physically fit. With Doctor Sudki being the resident doctor for the evening, the medical wasn't really an issue to cause fear.

It was Errol I spotted first holding his stomach and laughing, his white teeth dazzled against the contrast of his dark chocolate-coloured skin, chocolate which had been moistened with saliva so it emitted a gentle shine It was ludicrous to think Doctor Sudki had examined me believing that I was Errol, but he did, giving Errol a Medical Card which enabled him to box competitively. Errol went on to beat the golden boy of Kerl Hall who Dad had matched him with in anticipation of him passing the medical; in fact he defeated the golden boys of each club. Following Errol out of the changing-room area, Dad's lads appeared one by one, all laughing, some wiping tears from their eyes. The laughter and fun which Dad's boys displayed in huge amounts would spawn more

214

envy than a family of frogs does tadpoles. Dad always made sure they were relaxed, composed and under no pressure - but this bout of hysterics hadn't been induced by Dad.

"What's going on?" Patrick's honey-coloured curls bobbed like the spiralled cord of a telephone as he plonked himself on the seat next to me.

"Oh, Orlagh, you should have been there, it was hilarious. We were all lining up to see the doctor as you do, in our underwear. As you know, he checks your eyes, ears, inside your mouth and finally places his rusty old stethoscope on your stomach. It's supposed to be your heart he's checking, but his arms won't reach that far when he's sitting down, and he can't be bothered to move, so he just puts it on the first area that he can reach."

"Yeah, so what's so funny about that, Pat? It's nothing new."

"Wait a sec, Orle, you haven't heard the best yet." Patrick shook his head and laughed as he remembered the hilarious occurrence. "Old Sudki had gone through about twenty boys when he reaches us lot, so he's fed up and just wants it over with. Mickey Duffy decides he's going to have a laugh. We dared him. We said that he'd bottle it when it came down to it. But he didn't, he did it... the eejit."

"Did what?"

"When Mickey reached the doctor, Sudki looked in his eyes, ears and mouth. Sudki then turned his head away for a split second to place his magnifying contraption down and to pick up his ancient stethoscope. In that split second Mickey turned his back to the doc, dropped his underpants and bent over - his hairy bare arse was right in the doc's face."

"What did Doctor Sudki do? Didn't he go crazy?"

"You'll never believe it... Sudki placed his stethoscope right in the crack of his arse - and that's not all, Mickey pushed it that little bit further and started swaying his arse from side to side. Sudki shouted, 'Keep still boy, I need to do my job.' Then he shouted, 'Next!' He certified Mickey's arse fit to box!"

The jollity subsided and an air of seriousness ascended in a cloud of anxiety, like the cigarette smoke which hovered above the boxing ring in swirling ghost-like patterns, which were enhanced by the bright lights. Thumbs were twiddled, toes tapped and nails bitten as the boxing matches commenced.

chapter twenty-nine

The young boys boxed first and they always caused a stir, battling it out toe to toe. The junior division were aged between eleven and seventeen years old, boxing opponents up to a year older, with up to a seven-pound weight difference. Dad's junior boxers had been evenly matched and all our boys had won on points, except Errol. Errol's fight didn't have a chance of going to the score cards, not after the first opening punches were witnessed. His opponent was eleven months older, six pounds heavier and a foot taller, with two junior titles under his belt. None of the psychological or physical advantages discouraged Errol. The bell rang for the opening of round one and the referee shouted, 'BOX!'

Rather than deterring Errol, his opponent's advantages instigated a lightning charge of adrenaline which flowed through his veins and generated a flurry of perfectly executed punches. A single left jab to judge his distance, a double left jab followed, opening the champion opponent's guard to the straight right cross which flowed horizontally down the invisible pipe. The champion's head went back and his arms dropped; Errol stepped in to immediately administer a left hook, but as he threw it his opponent was already falling to the dirty canvas. It was the first real upset one of our boxers caused that evening - a novice knocking out a champion in the opening seconds.

Our five junior boys had won; of course we were all jubilant, but we were only halfway there and the hardest fights were yet to come. The tension mounted in the interval for the outcome of the senior boys' tournaments. There was Dominic, Patrick, Emmet, Sean McCabe and Mickey Duffy to box. I silently hoped Mickey's backside had no bearing in his bout, especially not landing on it.

The senior boxers were categorised in weight only. They could be from seventeen to thirty-one and box anyone of any age as long as they were in their weight group which, as in the junior division, stepped up every seven pounds.

Emmet emerged from the changing room area, from where earlier in the evening they had all emerged laughing. His exit was less jovial, but whether smiling or not he was still so beautiful. My nerves were racing around my body at the thought of Patrick boxing next, but I still felt that distinct tingle in my tummy as I always did when I sighted Emmet, especially the vision of him in his boxing attire. On his every move the emerald-satin shorts he wore shimmered, like a soft summer breeze brushing over a green-grass meadow. His white boots accentuated his tanned muscular legs. I couldn't see his defined torso unfortunately, as it was covered with a baggy sweatshirt. He was boxing directly after Patrick as they were in consecutive weight groups; Patrick was featherweight and Emmet lightweight.

Emmet moved Mickey Duffy's brother, who was seated next to me, and sat in his place. Dominic ran out of the same changing-room exit minutes later, dressed in the same attire and moved a McCabe brother out of the way. This now meant I was totally squashed in-between Dominic and Emmet ringside, awaiting the commencement of this crucial bout.

These were Patrick's first championships as a senior boxer. His first real encounters in the ring with men, and they unequivocally were men in comparison to Patrick's seventeen years. Tonight he was boxing an opponent who was twenty-five years old and had reached the final rounds of the championships the previous three years running. Matty Rollason was a notoriously formidable opponent who was a fighter, unlike Patrick who performed artistic pugilism. Patrick danced, entertained, caused laughter and tears, (depending which side you were on). He was like a Shakespearean actor, except his stage was the ring. Patrick was the showman of The Birmingham Irish.

If Matty Rollason had not been donning cracked red-leather boxing gloves and was not standing in the blue corner of a boxing ring, he could easily have been mistaken for a Russian Cossack dancer. Rollason was crouching as though he was hovering over an Asian toilet, while bouncing intermittently on his toes with tattooed robust arms stretched out at his side maintaining his balance. I was expecting music to start and for Matty Rollason to begin kicking his hairy mature legs out in front. But there was no dancing, merely limbering and the only noise was a repetitious hum, with no significant distinction of sound, coming from the anticipative spectators. Matty Rollason then stood, balanced on his heels and held the ropes with the bulbous gloves and began to stretch his arms. Then he commenced to spin his head clockwise, anti-clockwise and clockwise again - it looked as though his head was about to fall off.

Pat was a natural featherweight, weighing in at eight stone eight pounds, but it was hard to believe Rollason was anywhere near a featherweight. He had just made the weight class by tipping the scales at nine stone. He had used the old professional trick and had dropped a weight class or by the look of him, maybe two. Matty Rollason appeared as though he walked around the street at ten stone and the week or so running up to the championships he would have had to diet and train in black-plastic bin liners to reduce his body fluid, thus reducing his weight. Dad wouldn't allow his boxers to entertain this weight fluctuating stratagem; 'It's unhealthy and messes up the metabolism. They can fight at their natural weight,' Dad insisted.

Patrick entered the ring with an aura of calm and at the same time mischief about him, to a scream of support from the spectators. My high-pitched squeal was a distinct contrast to the shouting masculine tones. My brain had hit the gas pedal to the ground and the adrenaline accelerated around my body at speed comparable with a rocket ship.

Patrick's spiralled curls had been scraped back and tied into a ponytail; he was considered too pretty to box. The diversity in appearance was astounding. It was like Beauty and the Beast, with Patrick's boyish looks and bum fluff compared to Matty Rollason and his three-day growth. Patrick's tall and slender, perfectly postured body with each muscle defined in a flawless sculpted form, was in contrast to the short, stocky, rounded-shouldered, crude tattooed physique of Matty Rollason.

The greying MC dressed in his mothball-smelling tuxedo announced the boxers. Equal cheers greeted each of them. The referee called Patrick and Matty Rollason to the centre of the ring. Being too enthused about the pending performance of my brother, I had forgotten the close proximity of Emmet O'Malley - that is until he grabbed the flesh around my knee, which he squeezed unbearably hard, and stated, "He'll do good, Orle, don't worry."

I couldn't contradict him and tell him I wasn't worried, but totally ecstatic, so I silently nodded in agreement.

The ref stood with his arms stretched out separating the boxers. It was immediately obvious that Matty Rollason was a bully. He glared at Patrick, trying to weaken him with intimidation. It didn't work, Patrick smiled, winked at me and we all waited for Jack-the-fat-Dublin-timekeeper to ring his brass bell for round one.

"Ding, ding."

"BOX!" shouted the referee, clapping his hands together as he jumped back out of the boxers' way.

Patrick and Matty Rollason slapped their right gloves

together and immediately returned to their respective orthodox, left-foot-forward, guarded stances.

The fight began - Rollason immediately threw a four-punch combination, left, right, left, right. Patrick boxed off his back right leg, retreating gradually so the punches skimmed Patrick on his arms. Rollason followed through with another two-handed attack; this time the flurry of punches were directed at Patrick's head, but they fell short because Patrick glided on his feet retreating in the direction of the rope. As soon as Patrick felt the rope skim his back he knew the 'Rory Ruse' had to be put into action. The Rory Ruse was one of Dad's favourite counterattack manoeuvres, but you had to be fast to execute it.

As much as Matty Rollason resembled an angry pit bull terrier, stout and stocky and almost dribbling at the mouth, Patrick was a greyhound, lean, agile and swift.

Rollason was on the attack. He almost telegraphed Patrick, telling him that he was going to throw his best right cross. Patrick had to think quick. When the rope touched Patrick's back he stepped his back right leg to his right side, quickly moving his body and his head out of the way of Rollason's anticipated right hand. Patrick had been too quick for Rollason's brain to register the move, so Rollason still threw the punch with all the strength he could muster, expecting the force to connect into Patrick's head, but instead it was thrown into the smoky air; causing Rollason to lunge off balance and fall in-between the top and centre ropes - this was the Rory Ruse's intention!

Patrick was now in the centre of the ring basking in the glory of humiliating his tough opponent in the first fifteen seconds of round one - without even throwing a punch. With his left arm across his stomach and his right stretched skyward he bowed like he was the conductor of the London Philharmonic Orchestra. We all screamed and clapped our appreciation and instructions.

The referee attended to the disgraced Rollason, helped him up off the canvas, grabbed his wrists and wiped the punching area of the gloves over his white shirt, removing any grit that might be embedded from the fall. He brought Patrick from the neutral corner and instructed them to box on. Matty Rollason was humiliated and incensed and this was just what Patrick wanted - since anger that has risen to such levels causes mistakes, timing is lost and a fight plan is totally forgotten.

Rollason approached, attempting yet another two-fisted combination-four-attack, but his anger had blocked out his defensive skills and had left his arms wide apart, his face on show like an artefact in a museum. Patrick entered through the centre of his opened guard to throw a perfectly executed left jab, followed by a right cross. Rollason's head reclined like a flip top, his eyes were looking at the cloud of smoke hovering just below the nicotine-stained ceiling, but his feet were still on the floor. His nose had erupted, a stream of ruby blood flowed into his mouth, dying his gumshield red, making him look more of an animal than he already did.

For the second time in the first thirty seconds the referee, to Rollason's dismay, had to step in to clean up the remnants of Matty Rollason's mistakes.

We were all on our feet as Patrick was once again relishing his pugilistic glory in the neutral corner. Rollason's supporters were all in stunned silence at the disastrous degradation of their boxer.

Again the referee brought Patrick and Rollason to the centre of the ring. If the noise from the crowd hadn't been so thunderous I'm sure you could have heard Rollason growling like the pit bull he resembled. For the remainder of round one Patrick picked his punches like you would the finest juicy apples on a tree.

"Pat got that round, no problem, He's got to keep out of the way of that right though; it'd be dangerous if it connected." Dom's agitation was apparent.

We were close to the red corner where Dad was calmly feeding Pat water through a bottle which appeared to have

222

a bent straw protruding from the top. In his right hand he spun a towel at high speed generating a breeze to cool Patrick down. The excessive movement vibrated Dad's green and gold tracksuit bottoms, initiating a slow descent, revealing the beginning traces of a builder's bum. With his ambidextrous activities and his falling pants, he still managed to instruct Patrick on how to execute his punches in order to win the next round.

"Don't wait for him to *make* a mistake, Pat, yer've got to make him make them. Work him off that jab, pop it out so fast he won't know what's hittin' him. Fast hands! Bamboozle him with combinations, then move out of the way of those windmill punches he throws, let him chase you and start again. Fast hands, son."

And so Patrick did. Round two saw Patrick throwing his left jab so fast you couldn't see it, like the piston moving on an engine and the steam generated was that which was rising out of the top of Matty Rollason's head in anger and frustration. Pat's arm appeared twice as long as it actually was. With the speed of his punch the image of his arm was still visible connecting to the face of Rollason, although it had returned back to the guarded position and then thrown once more, twice more... consistently.

The crowd were on their feet. I was clapping my hands so much they were beginning to hurt. Patrick just continued producing the goods. He played with Matty Rollason like he was a puppet, pulling all the right strings; he could move him, left, right, back and forth with ease. Patrick danced the Viennese waltz; if Strauss's most famous waltz composition - *Rosen aus dem Suden* - had been bellowing out of the speakers, Pat would have been in perfect timing: one, two, three, one, two; one, two, three, one, two. He spun his partner into a disorientated daze, utilising every inch of the ring; one, two, three. As Rollason threw counter punches Pat's feet had glided back and to the side, making Rollason miss: one, two, three, one, two. Pat's feet had found a new comfortable position which allowed his arms to discharge another array of prodigious punches. He was like a gold medal Olympian archer; his punches like their arrows hit the bull's-eye each time.

In the third and final round the referee was a common sight pulling the frustrated Rollason off Patrick. Every punch Rollason threw, missed; Pat dodged each one, frustrating and tiring Rollason to an extent that he had to hold on to Patrick in order to survive, and to avoid the punishment of Pat's lightning shots. Rollason's fight plan had been mislaid in the first round and had not been recovered, however hard he tried looking in the maze of his mind.

"I'm headin' back there now," Emmet whispered, avoiding distracting Dom and myself from the match. "Pat's got this in the bag, no problem. I've to get ready meself."

"Good luck, bro," Dom said, as he and Emmet gave each other five. I stood, hugged him then kissed his stubbled cheek. I could smell the fading scent of his aftershave, mixed with the distinctive bitter-sweet smell of perspiration; it sent a shiver down my spine as though I'd just eaten a thousand fizzy sweets.

"Thanks, princess," he replied, pinching my cheek and walking away to prepare for battle.

"Ding, ding." I had missed the closing punches, but with the vision of Patrick's triumphant face and the sight of Matty Rollason punching the corner pads in anger, with blood dripping from his nose, it appeared they had imitated the preceding ones - they had all been executed by Pat. Matty Rollason's fist sunk into the blue-sponge corner pad. Why hadn't he tried to throw a few of those punches during the fight, I thought, or maybe he had, but unlike the corner pad Pat moved out of the danger zone.

The crucial couple of minutes waiting for the decision seemed to pass by slowly enough, but when there was an ancient MC having difficulty climbing into the ring - it seemed like a lifetime. Dad had removed Pat's gloves to reveal his protection bandages. His white vest was splattered with Rollason's blood. As the MC successfully made it through the ropes, the referee called Pat and Rollason to the centre of the ring and held each of their hands.

"And the winner of the featherweight division, who will continue to the finals of the Amateur Boxing Association championships is..."

I was holding my breath, so was Dom. It was obvious Pat had won, but you just couldn't trust some of these judges. Pat stood resembling a little boy as the referee held his hand. His head was held high and proud. His spiralled curls had fallen free from the ponytail. Rollason was observing the fresh blood which was splattered over the canvas.

"Oh... which was kindly sponsored by..." the MC continued.

"Get on with it," a spectator yelled.

"Kindly sponsored by Snap-On Car Repairs; by a unanimous decision... Patrick Emmet from the Birmingham Iri..." His commentary was engulfed by the roar of cheers. Patrick's hand was raised in the direction of the nicotine-stained ceiling. He shook hands with the loser and his trainers and made a jubilant exit from the ring. As he descended the wooden steps I greeted him with an array of kisses, the salt of his sweat covered my lips. I was so proud.

"I'll go 'nd get changed quick so I can see O'Malley," Patrick informed me as people were shaking his hand. My elation immediately turned to one of anxiousness when I remembered - Emmet was on next.

chapter thirty

Patrick emerged a few minutes later looking refreshed, as though he had just been on an energetic run, not having done three rounds with a pit bull. The roles were reversed; Pat took Emmet's seat as Emmet entered the ring.

When I looked at Emmet in the corner of the ring nodding in silent comprehension at Dad's quiet instructions, I had a feeling similar to hunger pains in my stomach, hunger pains mixed with dancing butterflies. For all Emmet's jollity out of the ring, he was the opposite within it. He was concentrating hard on how to execute his fight plan. His opponent was of equal weight at nine stone seven pounds and even height and was known to have a similar style to Emmet. He wasn't a dancing boxer, like Patrick, nor a fighter like Dominic; he was a hard punching-boxer. He was a boxer who shuffled his way around the ring, trying to dominate the centre of it. Emmet would get in close and release hard, artistic punches.

Emmet's cropped chestnut hair reflected the bright lights from above, as did the skin of his opponent, Derek Johnson. Johnson was a shade darker than Errol. His skin was a shining ebony which prominently depicted his muscular physique.

The judges were finally settled at ringside, the crowd were silenced and announcements made. The ref once again stood with his arms wide apart; now he separated Emmet and Johnson.

"BOX!" the ref shouted, clapping his hands and retreating quickly out of their way.

Johnson started the round with a single left jab which, as soon as it was returned to its guarding position, Emmet returned with the exact same punch. Neither punch connected - they were both measuring their distance. These single ejected punches continued throughout the first minute and a half of round one, some connecting, but not with the great power of victory behind them. They didn't generate much excitement at all.

"What's he doing? This isn't Emmet, he's being too cagey." Rage hugged Dominic's comment. "LET THAT RIGHT GO, EMM," he screeched, as he let his own right hand fly into the hot air. I was anxious; this really was unlike Emmet. He had usually judged his distance and had begun throwing some combinations at this point in a fight. They were obviously evenly matched; why was he holding back? It then got worse - disaster struck.

Emmet had all too obviously got settled into the slow pace of the bout and the nonchalance of it all closed off the usually skilled defensive part of his brain. Johnson threw yet another left jab and, as Emmet started the journey of his return jab, Johnson followed through with a straight right to hit Emmet directly on his unguarded chin. I felt the blow and my heart sank. I couldn't believe what I was witnessing. It took Emmet's head back for a split second. That was his wake-up call, his bedside alarm clock where the ringing reverberated around in his brain. He couldn't press the snooze button; he had to instantaneously wake-up and commence his own campaign if he wanted to stay in the fight.

Emmet thankfully wised up to the situation, lifting his right guard to cover his chin as he manoeuvred Johnson to win the centre of the ring. Johnson had accumulated some confidence and began throwing the same combination - left jab, straight right - consistently, but not connecting like before.

"After he throws that straight right it's dropping slightly and it's taking its time gettin' back to cover his chin," Pat excitedly informed Dom and myself. Just as we were about to shout instruction, Emmet had read this himself and capitalised on the fault.

Johnson threw his jab, followed by his straight right. Once again Johnson's right hand dropped a couple of inches on the return to its guarded position and it left his right side wide open. Emmet led with a straight right hand and caught Johnson on his chin. Johnson's left guard now dropped slightly too, in shock at the awakening of Emmet. Emmet followed through with a left hook, opening Johnson's eyes as wide as saucers. They looked like two full moons in a midnight sky. The first round was now even. Emmet had earned respect from Johnson.

Dad was as bewildered as we were at Emmet's uncharacteristic slow start, bewildered and frustrated. He pulled up his tracksuit bottoms as he stepped over the rope to enter the ring. As he started on his towel-spinning, water-spraying quest, the bottoms predictably dropped once again.

"O'Malley, ye've to buck yer ideas up, son - if yer want to win the fight yer do. Ye have to rise to the occasion, 'cause if ye don't, yer out. Think faster, ye know yer better than this. Throw some of your punishin' body shots. Go up and down - body to head. His right hand's droppin' all the time and ye only exploited it once. Step up a gear, Emmet, and dominate this fight."

It appeared that Johnson had been given the same pep talk, as he also came out with a vengeance. The punches being thrown were hard, vigorous punches. Their waists turned to incorporate the weight of their whole body into the blows. Their feet were planted like the roots of an ancient oak. They were toe to toe, both trying to dominate the centre of the ring. Emmet then turned the fight around yet again.

While they were toe to toe in the centre, Emmet took the chance to ride a punch. You have to judge this to perfection; it's imperative you have precise timing, because if you don't it could be fatal.

As they were exchanging their punches all Emmet's weight was leaning on his front left leg. Johnson threw a left jab which Emmet parried by pushing it with his right glove to his own left side. As Johnson threw a dangerous straight right, twisting his waist as much as possible to add that little more power, Emmet transferred all his weight from his front left leg to his back right leg, by bending his knees slightly and leaning his upper body back, so now his front left leg was almost straight and his back right leg was bent at the knee, supporting all his body weight. The dangerous punch fell just short of Emmet's face. The crowd gasped in amazement; some because they thought the punch had connected, as it was so close to Emmet's face, some because they couldn't believe the swiftness of the move. Johnson thought Emmet had actually stepped out of range, so stupidly he took a step closer to Emmet, not realising Emmet hadn't moved his feet a fraction, only transported his weight and reclined back. All Emmet's weight was now expelled as he released his right hand. The body weight transported itself from the back heel, which he lifted, to balance on the ball of his foot, up through his strong calves to straighten his back right knee, and carried on its accelerated journey to execute a straight right which on every millimetre of its rise absorbed every pound of his weight. It ascended into heaven and connected with Johnson's chin. The punch moved Johnson from the centre of the ring. He staggered back and was caught by the centre rope which he clung on to with his open arms. The referee jumped in before Emmet could execute any more punishment.

"One. Two. Three. Four. Five. Six. Seven. Eight." The referee extending a finger on each number, like a kindergarten teacher tutoring his pupils. "Are you okay to box on?" Johnson nodded a delirious reply. "What day is it?" the ref continued, checking if his brain was alert.

"Saturday."

Johnson was relishing the rest. The ref then extended three fingers. "How many fingers do you see?"

"Three."

"Okay - box on!" he instructed, bringing Emmet from the neutral corner. Unlike Pat, he didn't bask in his glory, but merely concentrated on the rest of the fight.

For the rest of the round Emmet dominated the centre of the ring, like a circus ring master - striking combination threes as fast as the ring master cracks his whip, making Johnson run on the retreat, which used up his energy supply. It seemed when Johnson did not command the centre of the ring, his confidence lessened, his heart was not in it.

The finale of round two saw Emmet exhibit more pugilistic skill. He released a left jab, followed by a straight right. He then dipped down over his left leg and threw a strong left to Johnson's body, which landed just below Johnson's rib cage, taking his breath and rocking his stance. Johnson was clearly hurt. He automatically tried to protect his body. He moved his elbows south, which left his chin as accessible as Nanna Bridie's flat; it was wide open for Emmet to rise from his left to the body. With his weight still on his left side he connected on the side of Johnson's jaw with a perfect left hook. Johnson once again sprawled on to the ropes and the full moons were again present. The ref intervened - but Johnson was saved by the bell.

In the third and final round Johnson came out fast and furious. He knew he needed a knockout to win the fight. Johnson administered a strong two-fisted attack. Emmet's chin was brushed with Johnson's left jab. Emmet had to once again think quickly to get out of trouble because a dangerous right from Johnson was on its way. Emmet, by bending at the knees dropped six inches. Johnson's right hand which was aimed for Emmet's chin skimmed the top of his chestnut hair, which was now drenched in perspiration. Emmet then released a single shocking upward right hand,

230

which like the punch of round two increased in speed and power as he straightened his bent knees. Subsequently, there was an action replay of round two; Johnson was against the ropes, again a standing eight count, more full moons and I'm sure an array of stars in front of his own eyes. But he survived, he didn't surrender easily, although the round progressed with Emmet totally dominating it. Johnson drew Emmet into clinches where he tied up Emmet's arms so he was no longer on the receiving end of Emmet's catastrophic blows, until the bell sounded for the end of the fight.

Emmet and Derek Johnson were brought to the centre of the ring. The MC had successfully made a swift-ish entry and the announcements began.

I was mesmerised by Emmet's tired, athletic physique and the hypnotic rhythm of his moving diaphragm, as he stood awaiting the judgement of his impressive performance. His blue eyes against his flushed complexion appeared brighter and more dazzling - more alluring, if that could be at all possible. The protruding bones of his eye sockets and high cheekbones were slightly grazed and swollen, from skimmed punches or clash of heads. It gave his refined boyish-looks a rugged but appealing edge. Through the ropes of the ring Emmet caught my eyes and winked - I shuddered with exhilaration; 'if only,' I thought, for approximately the millionth time that day.

"And the winner of the lightweight division, who will proceed to the finals of the championships, by a unanimous decision - in the blue corner..." Derek Johnson's head lifted in shock - he was the blue corner. My heart sank like the setting sun over the horizon. It was darkness in my mind. Patrick rose beside me to protest. Luckily Dominic had proceeded to the changing area; he had such a short temper, who knows what may have happened if he was present? Emmet looked as though he had taken Johnson's right on his chin - he appeared dazed. "Calm down everyone please, so I can proceed. In the blue corner - Emmet O'Malley of The Birmingham Irish."

The MC was almost as senile as Doctor Sudki.

"He's the red corner, you stupid old bastard," a spectator shouted. Relief swept over us all, and the delayed cheers and laughter drowned the forgotten sponsorship announcement. Johnson looked relieved at the legitimate judgement. The blackness lifted in my mind, the sun had set, but the moon shone as bright as Johnson's eyes had. Emmet's arm was raised and the sight of his masculine underarm hair made me quiver. I was going out of control!

chapter thirty-one

Every boxer in Dad's club was special to me and I supported them all, but Dominic, Patrick and Emmet were my absolute favourites. They were the ones I followed with adamant, unyielding interest. I sensed their anguish and their elation. Even after being on the receiving end of their torment the majority of the time, it was quickly forgotten when they stood in the ring. Being wrapped in my preoccupation, I had even forgotten the earlier embarrassment of the Bono saga.

Patrick and Emmet successfully triumphed that evening with both demonstrating that boxing isn't merely the art of executing punches; equally important it's the art of avoiding them. It left only Dominic to perform his artist interpretation of pugilism, which once again was as different from Patrick's dancing style as it was from Emmet's hard-punching controlled boxing style - Dominic was a fighter. Dominic wasn't interested in scoring points to impress judges. Left-handed measuring jabs only wasted his time and energy. Every punch he threw was intended to connect. Connect and hurt. Ceaselessly he searched for the knockout punch, just like he continually pursued an opportunity to tease me! It was a dangerous way to box, especially if like this evening the opponent has the same style, there being a greater risk of walking on to unexpected blows. You had to be fast and alert so as not to receive severe punishment.

Dominic had met his opponent twice before, each having won, so with this fight it wasn't only the Midlands counties title which was at stake, it was their own personal competition too.

It was predicted to be a full-on war.

Where Patrick was attractive in a pretty-masculine way, with his cherub curls, emerald eyes and sweet smile, Dominic was handsome. Neither Dominic, Pat or Emmet possessed any stereotypical boxing traits. Dom at times was mistaken for Emmet; he too had the chestnut hair, the sharp facial bone structure and had inherited the tropical ocean-blue eyes from Dad.

Dominic had to be quick to avoid receiving any of Markie Forester's ten stone seven pound punches, because it would be more than his admirable looks in jeopardy.

I felt more anxiousness for Dom's bout than I had for any of the others. Was it merely anticipatory nerves about my brother's fight that made every inch of me uncontrollably shiver from head to toe? Or, as I suspected, did Emmet sitting next to me, after I had given him an array of salt-tasting kisses in the excitement of his win, have some bearing on my trembling body? I decided on a bit of both while I endeavoured to roll Emmet's bandages, quite unsuccessfully, when the bell was rung for round one.

Dominic immediately attacked with a left jab, a right cross and left hook to Forester's head. As Dom connected with the left hook, Forester retaliated immediately with a straight right to Dom's chin. All the punches were absorbed with no apparent effect - like water in a sponge.

I hated this ridiculous consuming of punishment. Why wouldn't he dance out of the way like Patrick, or ride them like Emmet? It was a blatant show to prove that his opponent's best punches didn't hurt.

When they should have been feeling each other out and determining distances, they instead stepped the fight up into another accelerated gear. It appeared there were going to be no re-fuelling pit stops.

Dom threw a four-hook combination: left hook, right hook, left hook, right hook. Forester's head rebounded side to side like a double-hinged door, but unbelievably Forester did not retreat from this punishment; he executed a right over the top and followed it through with his own left hook. They exchanged these aggressively hostile, hard punches for the next half a minute. Surprisingly the referee didn't step in to break the catastrophic combat. I, along with the rest of the crowd, was on my feet, shrieking directional instructions. Emmet's sweat-soaked bandages had been discarded on the plastic chair behind me. The aggression of the match generated an instinctive barbaric excitement within the on-lookers. The thunderous noise was both chaotic and exhilarating.

Dominic gradually retreated to the ropes. Forester appeared to be administering a flurry of lethal punches. "What's he playing at?" I squealed to Patrick to make myself heard over the clamorous male vocal cords. "Why isn't he moving, Pat? What's going on? He's going to get hurt."

"Calm down, Orle, he *is* moving, look carefully. It's Dom's deceptive move. His arms are taking the punishment, not his head or his body - watch and shut up."

I looked carefully and sure enough Forester's punches were being absorbed by Dom's forearms, as he rolled his shoulders forward and held his gloves in front of his face with his arms protecting his body. Dominic wasn't moving his feet, nor was he riding them by transferring his weight from leg to leg; he was riding them by utilising the ropes.

When Forester threw punches Dom was rolling his body back into the ropes so the majority of the power was lost. He rolled from side to side as Forester threw lefts and rights.

"I see what he's doing, but what's the reason?" I screeched to Emmet this time, because Pat had told me to be quiet.

"You'll see, Orlagh. It's the Ali rope-a-dope trick, so it is," he replied with excitement, his eyes still riveted on the ring.

The reason for Dom taking so many of Forester's

punches on his arms soon became apparent. Forester had thrown some twenty punches while Dom rolled himself out of trouble and rested his body weight on the ropes. Forester was exhibiting fatigue, his punches didn't expel the same strength and he was getting careless because he thought Dom was hurt, cowering even. Forester's left guard completely dropped as he threw a right cross which almost connected with Dom's left elbow. Dominic had sunk as hard and as deep as he could into the ropes and then emerged in his full glory, propelling himself with the elasticity of the ropes behind him with a right upper-cut which connected directly under Forester's chin; it was like a stone from a catapult. The crowd were silent apart from the Birmingham Irish boys. Forester rose off his feet as though he had jumped in the air; he appeared to hover for a split second before crash-landing on his back. There he lay, his arms and legs wide apart, his gumshield discarded at the side of his open mouth; only the whites of his eyes were visible in his recumbent position.

Emmet and Patrick gave each other five in front of my face. I stood as silent as the rest of the spectators, who were all in complete confounding shock. Dominic walked around the horizontal Forester with his arms held high, as the referee counted him out. On the count of ten Forester still hadn't moved a muscle. He was unconscious. Commotion commenced as the doctor was summoned into the ring.

It transpired that while Dominic was knocking Markie Forester into kingdom come, Doctor Sudki was catching himself forty winks.

"Yes, *yes*. What do you want?" Sudki bellowed aggressively, as they shook to wake him. The spittle from his bulbous lips sprayed into Jack-the-fat-Dublin-timekeeper's face.

Forester was motionless. Realising the seriousness of the predicament, Dominic ceased to walk around with his arms held high and took rest on the tiny stool in the corner of the ring. Only the clanking of beer glasses as they were being returned to the veneered tables after giant gulps had been taken, and the exhalation of cigarette smoke could be heard above the monotonous sound of deafening silence.

The ancient doctor in his stained sheepskin coat with his trousers pulled up to his chest, holding his antiquated battered brown briefcase attempted ascent into the ring. He mounted the steps with apparent ease, but overcoming the ropes didn't demonstrate the equivalent simplicity. Grasping the centre rope with his bony liver-spotted hands, he pushed it down and stepped his right leg and body over; he was straddled - one leg in the ring - the other out. But as Dominic had exhibited, the ropes were exceptionally pliable.

"Jesus, that's going to hit him right in the goolies," Emmet proclaimed, getting up from his seat to proceed to help the old doctor.

But it was too late...

His elderly hands just didn't have the strength to keep the rope down, it bounced back into its normal position and verified Emmet's prediction - it hit him in the goolies. It lifted him off his feet as Forester had just been by Dominic's punch and catapulted the old doctor into the ring. The spectacle was as surreal as a Dali painting. The doctor lay adjacent to the unconscious boxer. Strewn across the ring were the contents of his case - which you could hardly describe as life-saving: a few Roses chocolates glistened in their brightly coloured cellophane and foil wrappers. I always thought it strange how anyone could resist the delights of hazelnuts in caramel or hazelnut whirls. I could only imagine how long Doctor Sudki had resisted these chocolates that lay on the canvas - going by the food items in his home, it could have been months, even years. Adjacent to the chocolate lay some unwrapped humbugs, their gooey stickiness attracting stray hairs and fluff. The rusty bowl-shaped receiving end of his stethoscope had disconnected from the Y-shaped rubber tubing and had rolled like a coin on its side to the red corner, rotating in one spot at Dom's feet, and then gave up; it lay as still as the boxer and the doctor. But the strangest items were two chicken-leg bones, one bare, and one with pinky-brown meat still attached, gnawed at the end as if a mouse had been feasting. Strange, that is, to the majority of the crowd. But the Birmingham Irish boys, Dad, Jack-the-fat-Dublin-timekeeper and myself knew why the remnants of two chicken drumsticks found themselves in Doctor Sudki's case. It was one of many of Dad's wind-ups, one of his many jokes, which we all found amusing - especially himself! It had started with Dad placing uneaten sandwiches, drumsticks or maybe pickled onions in Jack-the-fat-Dublin-timekeeper's pockets. It had then evolved to Jack retaliating by giving Dad some of his own treatment. We would often leave a boxing show to enter our car and discover sandwiches under the windscreen wipers or pork pies jammed under door handles. Other people were then the brunt of their juvenile joke and on this night obviously Doctor Sudki was the candidate.

Everything seemed to be occurring in slow motion; the only movement was that of the small brown bottle of smelling salts, rocking in a dip in the besmirched canvas, like an abandoned playground sea-saw. The quiet sound of the mobile liquid in the miniature bottle was almost audible in the flabbergasted silence.

Dad was the first aide at this outrageous scene. He picked up the rocking smelling salts and in a magical-like display swept them under the nose of Markie Forester, who reacted almost immediately. The potent liquid unsuspectingly hit his brain as fast as Dom had hit his chin. His eyes blinked - like Snow White waking after the kiss of the prince - but the scene couldn't have been more different from how I imagined that fairytale event; Forester's trainer descended to his knees and drenched him with a soaked orange sponge as he placed his head beneath the rolls of his protruding beer belly - certainly not a prince and Forester had no resemblance to Snow White. A sigh of relief emerged from my mouth. As much as I wanted Dom to win, I didn't want Forester to be seriously injured.

Dad then attended to the doctor. His emerald tracksuit bottoms shimmered and of course dropped as he bent over Doctor Sudki. He placed a hand behind the doctor's shining head and the mystical sweep was displayed once again, but there weren't the same eye-fluttering movements. Dad left it a few seconds before administering another sweep under the doctor's globe-ended nose.

"I'm not a grave robber. *I'm not*. Look at the flowers... the lotus flower, it's dying... The ocean of gold is beneath us. I don't want to drown in this greed... don't let me drown. I don't want to wilt like the flowers."

"You're okay, doc, no one's dying around here," Dad assured the delusional doctor.

"Carter? Carnavon?" he sprayed.

"No, doc, it's Emmet, Rory Emmet. Yer know, from the Birmingham Irish club."

"Ah, Irish, I like Irish. The English steal my country like they stole the Irish."

"I know, doc, I know. Come on let's get yer a doctor."

"I am a doctor."

The ambulance arrived expecting to transport an injured boxer, but instead took a concussed, confused, ninety-six-year-old doctor who believed himself to be in Tutankhamen's tomb.

CHAPTER THIRTY-TWO

I was successful in wrapping Emmet's bandages, pushing in the centre when it had veered out of the perfect spiral, the smell of him being transferred on to my fingertips in the process.

"You don't wrap my bandages," Bernie McCabe commented, as I was tying a neat bow around the complete coiled bandage.

"If you gave them to me I would!" My tone was a little too defensive.

"I didn't see O'Malley give you his. I saw you take them from him."

Emmet was standing next to me smiling - I was sure he could sense my discomfiture.

"It's because I'm her favourite, right, Orle? Yer need good Derry looks like mine to be Orlagh's favourite, not the look of an inbred bogtrottin' Free Stater."

"Ah, ya mom wears army boots," was Bernie's retort.

"Ach yeah, but at least like yer mammy, she doesney pop wheelies on a BMX." Emmet's impeccable white tombstones became visible as he laughed.

'Your mom' jokes were a strange phenomenon within the club. The boys metamorphosed into a group of giggling children on the commencement of these wisecracks. The most extreme mom accusation generated hysterical laughter.

"Well, did ye know your mom's a sniper?"

"A sniper, like in Cross-Ma-Glen?" Emmet bantered.

"Exactly, she lies down and opens up!"

The mom jokes continued and the show ceased with the Birmingham Irish boys causing a few more upsets. Champions were banished. Sean McCabe delivered another impressive win. Mickey Duffy's backside didn't make an appearance. The only rear end which had any bearing in Mickey's bout was his opponent landing on his. I wondered if Doctor Sudki would have the chance to examine Mickey's hairy posterior once again, or whether he would be swimming in the swirling golden ocean of his delusional mind for the rest of his days.

I always hated the end of a fantastic evening. I never wanted them to end. I wanted the good times to endure, the jokes, the banter. I wanted to be surrounded by the wonderful company - Emmet particularly. Even though I didn't know them, the sight of people trailing out of the exit doors made me sad. Sports bags were packed waiting for departure: Head, Diadora, Adidas.

"After dinner I did a shit," Errol proclaimed, he being my only companion at the end of the evening. All the other Birmingham Irish boys had mysteriously disappeared.

"Errol, that's disgusting. What brought that on?"

"Yeah, but, backwards it's... soon after dinner I did another!"

"You've taken a few too many punches tonight."

"It's a rhyme for Adidas, stupid... after dinner I..."

"Yes! okay. Got it, I don't need reminding."

The microphone lay on a judge's empty table. The tuxedo-clad MC had left. The bolts had been loosened on the corner posts of the boxing ring, causing the ropes to hang limp and tired. There were dribbles of lager left in pint glasses and the cold February midnight air blew in from the opened fire-escape door, producing a layer of goosebumps over the bare skin of my arms. Although the majority of the spectators had left, a few groups of people talked excitedly of uppercuts, knockouts and delusional doctors. Dad was immersed in one of these conversations when his team of warriors emerged as they had earlier in the evening from the changing-room area - appearing suspiciously jovial. Emmet was among them, wearing a ridiculous-looking black beret.

One by one they entered the ring: Dominic, Patrick, Emmet, the four McCabe brothers, the two Duffy brothers, the White twins - who were actually black (Dad said they took the black Irish to another level) and Errol, who left my side to join their little group. Conversations ceased and once again the room was almost silent, the only sound being the distant clattering of glasses from the kitchen as the bar staff rushed to go home.

What were they doing? Why was Emmet wearing a beret, appearing so ridiculous? A little tribute to Dad - that would be nice, but there were a few junior boxers missing and not enough people to appreciate it, I thought.

Emmet picked up the discarded microphone from the judge's table, flicked the black switch; "Testin', testin', one, two, three."

"I didn't know ye could count, O'Malley!" Dad joked. Emmet glanced in his direction and winked.

"We've just put a little something together for our greatest supporter," Emmet began. All the boys had their heads partly bowed; almost visible were mischievous smiles plastered across each of their faces. "This person never misses a show, gives us the best advice when we're in the ring." It sounded like he was talking about Dad - but Dad isn't merely a supporter, he's their trainer. "This supporter even rolls our bandages... well, mine anyway!" Was my comprehension of that final comment correct? I took a deep breath and awaited clarification.

Emmet drew the microphone up once again to his sensual, terracotta lips, squinted his paradise-sky-blue eyes and uttered in a game-show host way, "This, Orlagh, is for you, princess." My goosebumped arms were now not due to

242

the February cold entering, but of shock, bewilderment and thoughts of Emmet calling me princess in front of everyone.

Emmet began his rendition alone; the others swayed their torsos and heads from side to side in rhythm with his song;

> *"I can't believe the news today,*
> *I can't close my eyes and make it go away.*
> *How long, how long must we sing this song?*
> *How long? Tonight we can be seen as one.*
> *Broken bottles under children's feet,*
> *Bodies strewn across a dead end street,*
> *But I won't heed the battle call,*
> *It puts my back up, puts my back up against*
> *   the wall."*

I acquired a defeated sarcastic grin. I placed my elbows on my knees, I cupped my chin in my opened palms and nodded in agreement with their joke. The rest of the clan joined in the rendition, sounding wholly inharmonious.

> *Sunday, bloody Sunday.*
> *Sunday, bloody Sunday.*

And so it continued, the whole of U2's Bloody Sunday was performed by the Birmingham Irish boys and the presence of Emmet's beret became apparent - I thought I had escaped ridicule a little too freely at the dinner table.

> *Sunday, bloody Sunday.*
> *Sunday, bloody Sunday.*

Would the day arrive when my every action wasn't shared with a party of pugilists?

CHAPTER THIRTY-THREE

The air was crisp and chilly, but the soft light cast by the sun which was on the verge of peeping its head over the horizon to give vision for the adventures of a new day, gave the morning a hazy, warm feel. Dad hummed the tune to *Bloody Sunday* as he drove myself and my slightly diseased suitcase in the dawn twilight. I had requested the canary-yellow stickers which depicted our address on each and every angle to be removed from the brown leather case, but gave in to Dad's persuasion and consented to one address sticker. I figured I could remove it amid the Italian Alps.

"Don't you think it's a little too early for sarcasm, Dad?"

"I haven't uttered a word, baby doll," he replied with virtuous sincerity, his tired eyes as wide as an innocent child in earshot of profanities.

"You don't need to, Dad, you're humming it instead!"

"I'm sorry, princess. I was doin' it subconsciously ye know... It's a dangerous thing that subconscious, dangerous!"

My exasperation at the continuing taunts about the U2 incident quickly vanished. My hostility had been conquered by the thought of Emmet's wet lips. On the conclusion of the Bono impersonation he had descended from the ring, approached me, cupped my head in his palms and placed a lingering moist kiss upon my forehead. A tingle travelled down my spine, stimulating each nerve,

244

rambling over all my vertebrae. It ended its exhilarating expedition like a river reaching its estuary and flowed into the ocean of my loins. "You took it well, Orle, you took it well!" he had said, pinching my cheek before the rest of the choral ensemble descended from the boxing ring and gave me their array of back slaps and hugs.

Supplementary to Emmet's kiss, my calm reaction to Dad's torments towards the Bloody Sunday performance - (whether intentional or not), was somewhat due to it taking the onus off my newly-donned mature garment.

Today was D-day or B for bra day - in my case it was 32B-day. I had placed my rapidly growing bumps into the broderie-anglaise cups, clasped the single hook and eye and performed my usual twirl in the mirror to view all angles of my now mature body. I felt the same distinguished feeling I had when I had first tried it on under the attentive eyes of Lola: the kind of feeling you acquire when you progress to the next school year; the notch up of the chin feeling; the I am an adult feeling; the too big for your boots feeling. The feeling that I found lands you in too much trouble...

Dad transported my diseased case to the awaiting orange and white coach. Grey smoke whirled from its exhaust, giving the fresh dawn air a tainted diesel malodour. The frozen grass of the school field crunched under our feet as he held my hand as we walked in silence to the school foyer - I was still his little girl, with or without a bra! I tried to determine if his silence was due to tiredness from the previous late night or whether he worried about me leaving the nest. I could never ascertain such things with Dad, for the only feeling he externally showed was that of happiness.

"Hey there, Rory." The greeting broke the morning silence. "I'm sorry I couldn't make it last night, but Bumble couldn't get it together. How did the boys do?" Mr Kennedy held out a huge hand to Dad.

"Ach, don't worry, Sean, all the boys in the club won.

Patrick unanimous and Dominic in a first round knockout." Dad shook Mr Kennedy's hand with the two of his as he spoke.

"Fantastic. Oh, Jese, I'm sorry I missed it. Are *you* ready for a knockout time, Orlagh?... On the slopes, of course." Mr Kennedy excitedly rubbed his hands together. "Oh, we're gonna have some fun, that's for sure!"

"Orlagh, keep him outa trouble, hey?" Dad facetiously declared. A strange request for a pupil to a teacher - but Mr Kennedy was no ordinary teacher. Apart from being too good-looking to be one, he was too much fun. His nonchalant, humorous demeanour with the pupils obtained him the kind of respect all teachers aspired to. Although, paradoxically, Mr Kennedy could have been the least proficient teacher in the school, the strictest and most arrogant and the female students would still have radiated pubescent desire when he was in close proximity: from their eyes and their fidgeting adolescent bodies. He was the teacher whom everyone fancied, whom everyone's Mammy made that extra effort at parents' evening for - a little more lipstick, a touch more rouge. His dark brown - almost black, unruly curls fell about his tanned face. His lengthy, muscular legs were permanently on show as he paraded the school gymnasium or sports field. Extraordinarily, I didn't have the same infatuation. Maybe that had something to do with me already having one unobtainable crush. Also, there was the issue of me being personally affiliated through my parents and brothers - although that didn't prevent me lying awake at nights dreaming of Emmet O'Malley!

Mr Kennedy and I didn't have a teacher-student relationship. I saw him on a personal basis too often to regard him merely as a teacher. He was an avid boxing fan and fervently followed Dom and Pat around the country, provided Bumble, as she was tenderly referred to, could make it.

Bumble was his sweetheart. She had stood by him

through university, waited patiently through the year sabbatical he took in America, where he had a brief but meaningful love affair with the country; instilling in him the longing to return on a permanent basis. He said that was when all the trouble had started; he'd left her alone and untouched for too long and joked that she may have sensed that her joining him in the land of milk and honey was a long shot.

I had first heard this distressing news after he had annihilated me in a table-tennis game. I had been protesting, saying it wasn't fair and that he should go easy on me. But he wouldn't give any concessions, regardless of age or ability. "It'll teach you to develop. If I let you win points, you'll never improve your game. Life just isn't fair, Orle. You have to practise to be the number one at anything. You'll be the best little table-tennis player around by the time I leave for America," he stated, smiling flippantly. To control my anger rising, I squashed the hollow white table-tennis ball tightly, causing permanent indentations and replied in a barely audible voice;

"You're leaving?"

"Pretty soon, Orlagh. Pretty soon."

Dominic was the first person I had encountered after I'd received the devastating news. "Did Mr Kennedy tell you he was leaving for America?"

"Orlagh, Sean Kennedy's a dreamer. He started at the school doing his teacher trainin' in my final year there. He confided in us he wasn't really interested in teachin' there, but needed to be a registered teacher, so he could teach soccer school in the States. That's two years ago now and he's still there. He's goin' nowhere."

Dom's prediction had proved true thus far. I was now in my third year of senior school and Bumble was consistently, without fail, the last vehicle on the staff car park each day. Her canary-yellow Volkswagen Beetle body with black bonnet chugged through the blue steel gates, came to an abrupt halt, emitted a bang from the exhaust, followed by a gush of greyness which Mr Kennedy invariably emerged from tired, rushed and quite often hung-over.

This morning Bumble was absent, but the tiredness was apparent. The dancing extravaganza his changing eye colour performed was in intermission - presently they were sleepy and brown. As the day progressed, a hint of green would creep upon them, like moss on a tree trunk and they would commence their mischievous dance once again.

Dad left after hugging and kissing me excessively. Mr Kennedy and myself proceeded to the assembly hall. Along the way I gave him a detailed rundown on the events of the previous boxing evening, omitting to inform him of the comical rendition of *Bloody Sunday*. He would have capitalised on my mistake, just as the boys had. I was sure Mr Kennedy would discover a suitable taunt without any assistance.

"Orlagh, you explain those moves as good as any fighter I know. You're the ultimate girl!"

Tell the boys that, I thought.

The school seemed strangely unfamiliar. The combination of smells were present - the concoction which produced the fragrance that is unequivocally *school:* the disinfectant smell, the floor polish smell, the odour from the canteen, the cookery-class disasters smell, the art-room paint smell, the changing-room staleness, they were all lingering; but a vacant, quiet eeriness loitered along the dark corridors and in the student-less classrooms.

Siobhan sat adjacent to her new boyfriend waving frantically as I entered the assembly hall. I wondered how much of her company I would be honoured with on the trip; with Steven being present, I figured it wouldn't be in abundance. They had recently celebrated their anniversary. *Two whole months.* "I'm in love... for real this time, Orlagh, *for real,*" she had informed me - again. I don't know how many times I'd heard that over the previous year. It didn't take much for Siobhan to fall head over heels.

Our friendship became secondary when things were going well, but soon got back on track for me to pick up the pieces when discovery exposed what I had initially detected - that they were complete losers. Albeit Steven was an improvement on her past consorts; although that wouldn't be a hard task to accomplish, considering her most recent ex-Simon was having a passionate love affair, not with another female - but with lighter-fuel gas canisters.

I had given up on showing interest in any of the boys at school, losers or not, good or moderate looking; it was as futile as a camera with no film. I remained a virgin to the kiss. With my body as well as my mind maturing, (along with my incarcerated, adolescent, sensual urge - which still hauled its shackles through my loins and gnawed away at my stomach and now considered itself to be serving a life sentence) I was beginning to get frustrated with the boys' apathetic reaction towards me romantically. I always tried so hard with myself too. The clothes I wore had to pass the Dominic and Patrick censorious test. I showered constantly, cleansed, toned, styled my hair and, to Mammy's shock and consternation, shaped my eyebrows. But, however hard I tried, the boys still couldn't get over the fact I had a birthmark on my face.

"Hey Orlagh, come and meet Steve's friend, he's new and he's a boxer too!" Siobhan's neck was in a stiffened position, with her eyelids wide apart. Her eyes then darted in the direction of the stranger. She was silently imploring me to look. It was an action which I detected was supposed to inform me that he was good-looking.

As soon as my eyes set upon his pale, slightly freckled face, which was framed with long strands of strawberry-blond hair, the memories of the previous evening vanished. Emmet's soft, moist kiss had been a picture on a child's etch-a-sketch, which'd had the swiping mechanism pulled across to reveal a blank grey plastic surface, ready for more wonderful pictures to be created. It wasn't that I considered this stranger to be any better than Emmet; it's just that I had packed my wicker basket one too many times. My mind had picnicked on fantasies of Emmet for far too long. That's all I considered my fantasies were ever going to be - a faraway dream picnic for my mind to feast on.

Week after week Emmet, Patrick and Dominic had different beautiful, voluptuous girls linked to their arms. I would smile sweetly and when Emmet left the room to hurry my brothers up I would secretly, with unblushing boldness, answer the girls' 'let's try to get information out of the sister' questions. Behind my smile there was jealous loathing. Although I was content in the fact I never saw the same girl twice. But I came to the conclusion I would never have the chance even to be one of those transitory girls.

It must have been the bra which had given me the added confidence, the reassurance which ignited my brain into thinking that this boy was different from the rest. The romantic interest in boys I had tried so hard to overcome - to obliterate, was back with an avenging force behind it - the pressure of temptation. I was in the garden of Eden, staring at the forbidden apple - shall or shall I not? Would this boy, Steven's friend, be the artist on my etch-a-sketch of dreams?

"Hey, Steve, so what's you're friend's name?"

"James," Steve replied, pointing at his friend with his thumb.

"Hi. Who do you box for then, James?" I tried to break the ice.

"Erm, Jaguar Boys Club," he answered, without making eye contact. An inconvenient tone was resonant in his voice. I needed a sharper pick - the ice was tough.

"Oh, right, so Ronnie Carpenter has you under his wing?" Agh, *under his wing*. That was a lame statement. But, if I had uttered the most articulate sentence, I doubt he would have shown enhanced interest.

"Who?"

"Ronnie, your trainer?"

"Oh, right, yeah."

"How many fights've you had?"

"Hundreds." Answered with the same apathetic feeling for the conversation.

"*Hundreds*? WOW, that's funny, I've never seen you around." I was also going to add that having a hundred fights for a seasoned boxer is a remarkable accomplishment; for a fourteen or fifteen-year-old schoolboy, it's simply phenomenal. With an obligatory three-day break in-between boxing matches and a three to four month season break, he must have boxed consistently twice a week for years - which could not and would not happen. I didn't say it though. I bit my tongue and let him bask in the notion of his invented, glorious record. Instead, I watched him remove his jawbone off his clenched fist, frown and glance at Steve with his Richard Gere eyes as if to say, 'What the hell is she on about? What would she know about boxing?'

That look told me all I needed to know - or should have done. The look that showed disinterest and disgust. He wasn't even (as most of the boys were) interested in merely talking to me. So why did an allurement still rumble inside me? Why did the force of temptation guide me towards the forbidden apple?

"Let's get this show on the road then, everyone. Make sure you have *all* your belongings. Hand me your passports on the way out of the door and head for the coach," Mr Kennedy bellowed above the sound of fifty ecstatic juvenile voices, saving me from the embarrassment of any more apathetic or simply pathetic conversation.

"So, what do you think? Is he gorge or what?" Siobhan excitedly enquired.

"Who?"

"What do ya mean... *who*? James of course."

"Yeah, he's nice, but he's not interested, Shiv."

"Of course he is, he's just shy. He's new, you know."

"I gathered. Where's he from?" I dropped my guard and showed some interest.

"He's originally from Birmingham, but he's been living

on some army base down south. Believe me, Orle, he likes you. Anyway, you've got a whole week to get to know him!"

I really don't know how Siobhan had come to that conclusion, but I truly hoped she was right. We made our way across the school field heading for the coach. The sun had risen over the horizon and attempted to eradicate Jack Frost who clung to blades of grass, bare branches and windscreens of sleeping cars. The sun reflected off the bedroom windows which housed their owners, imploring them to rise and enjoy the day which lay ahead - enjoy it just as Siobhan and I intended to.

We ceased the conversation on the newcomer and I informed her of last night's results. I briefly explained the *Bloody Sunday* incident, but she didn't get it, or just wasn't interested. All she was curious about was Emmet's kiss. When I relayed the details the memory prompted my pelvis to tingle and my stomach to ache - so maybe Emmet hadn't been completely wiped off the etch-a-sketch dream board.

The coach was already half-full, and the invisible magnet which entices teenagers to the back was active. Siobhan and I didn't have a chance of finding a free seat, so we settled for halfway, which surprisingly Siobhan wasn't concerned with. Clarification was swift when I discovered that Steve and his new acquaintance were in the row behind. We compromised on the window seat. I would have it going - Siobhan coming back.

chapter thirty-four

Siobhan and I had engaged in numerous conversations on the journey to the airport, regarding important issues such as my new bra. Watching the passing scenery fly by, I was silently contemplating such important issues when Siobhan broke the silence and dealt me the most shocking revelation.

"I think I'm going to lose my virginity this week."

"What! You're what?!"

"You heard, Orlagh. I've decided Steve's the one, and what better time than when we're away?"

It has to be said, in every aspect of life I was more mature and more knowledgeable than Siobhan - that is every aspect except sex. When it came to boys (on a sexual basis) she was the expert. Mammy said her want for a boy all the time stemmed from her not having a father figure. Little did Mammy know how I pined for one of Siobhan's many boyfriends. I'd had the details of Siobhan's first kiss, even of her boobs being felt. I'd listened in complete and utter shock as she described the male body. But what she was telling me now was way beyond my comprehension.

"Siobhan, don't rush into anything."

"I won't, I love him."

"How can you love him? You're too young."

"You love Emmet!"

"That's different."

"How so?"

"It just is. I've known Emmet forever and anyway, even if by any chance Emmet was interested in me, I wouldn't have sex with him after two months. Once it's gone, it's gone forever and boys look upon girls differently who've lost their virginity; Pat said so, they all say."

"Yeah, yeah, whatever... I don't care, I love him."

"Don't say I didn't warn you, Shiv. Just don't do anything foolish."

I hated arguing with her, but I felt I was right. My head was spinning, so I wiped an area of the coach window clean of condensation, rolled up my jumper, placed it and my head against the damp window and submerged into a deep sleep. The accumulation of excitement generated from the previous day's events and anticipation of what this day might bring, along with the late night and early morning, made my body feel like it desperately required a recharge.

I suddenly found myself in the boxing ring, in the exact same spread-eagled position which Markie Forester had been in after Dominic's rope-a-dope ploy. But there was no crowd noise; in fact there were no people. The beer glasses still had their slops in and the microphone still rocked back and forth on the judge's empty table. The mingled smell of sweat and nicotine lingered in the air. I heard something drop. I couldn't move my arms or legs; they were paralysed in a starfish-type position. I could only turn my head, which I did, in the direction of the noise. That was when I first noticed the chicken-leg bones. Haphazardly scattered around my recumbent body was an abundance of them, some stripped bare and some with uneaten bits of browny, pink meat still attached. Another identical sound, but this time I observed its source - a fallen chicken-leg bone.

Still motionless, except for my head, I tried to determine the origin of these bones which had fallen from above. Illuminated by the fluorescent ceiling lights, the cigarette-smoke cloud still endured above the ring. I watched the swirling motion of the smoke and to my surprise another chicken bone fell to the canvas, having emerged from the swirling-smoke cloud.

"Who's there?"

One by one, four chubby little cherubs fell from the smoke, all of whom took a seat on the top rope of the ring - one on each side. They chewed on chicken drumsticks.

"I never knew angels ate chicken."

"You don't know a lot of things, my child," one replied, tossing another bone into the ring as she spoke.

"Well done," shouted another, picking her mother-of-pearl teeth, "you have complied with an important rule - you've admitted ignorance of something."

"Wisest is she who knows what she does not know," they chanted in unison.

"Don't rush into anything," another proclaimed.

"I told Siobhan that."

The one who appeared to be the principal angel sat on the rope in front of me. She nodded and smiled, discarded another bone and continued, "Forget Siobhan, she's not Chosen, *you are*. Don't do anything foolish." I took a deep breath and opened my mouth ready to speak, about to tell them I'd also informed her of this too, when the angel placed a finger against her lips. Her finger was short and plump, and her nails, like her teeth and the whites of her eyes, were mother-of-pearl. They resembled the inside of an oyster shell, enchantingly shimmering the colours of the rainbow, while still appearing white.

"*Patience*, all will arrive in due time," the angel behind me assured.

"Patience and laughter... Tempus omnia revelat... Time brings everything... " they all chanted once again, as one by one they threw their bones around me, smiling broadly so the rainbow shimmered and their cheeks bulged into balls of chubby flesh. All except the principal angel ascended and disappeared into the cigarette-smoke cloud.

"The seraphim have endlessly endeavoured, but you forever decline their divine invitation. You must accept to determine the direction of your destiny." And she too ascended into the swirling cigarette-smoke cloud.

"Don't go," I pleaded, tears trickling down my face, "don't go."

"I'm not going anywhere," was the reply. But there were no angels and it was a masculine tone. I then realised I wasn't in a chicken-leg-bone-filled boxing ring, but on a coach - an orange, white and grey coach with a strawberry-blond-haired, Richard-Gere-eyed boy sitting next to me. He tenderly wiped the moistness from my cheek and said, "I'm not going anywhere for a while."

I quickly resumed an upright position and the jumper fell from the window on to my lap. Was I awake or asleep? Siobhan had disappeared and been replaced by James. I had been struck by a cartoon character's over-sized hammer once again. Stars flew from my head as realisation hit me that I was no longer asleep and James was actually sitting next to me. I wiped my moist cheek and discovered my chin was also wet. I must have been dribbling - how embarrassing. I wiped it as secretly as I could so James wouldn't notice the saliva dribble, when a moist droplet fell to wet the area once again. It became evident it wasn't saliva at all, but condensation dripping from the window.

"You were dreaming," James continued. It was a different person sitting next to me. He smiled - he touched me! With the new bra I considered my maturity to have increased, and with the enhanced maturity I figured my luck had changed too.

"Yeah, I must've been... sorry." But was I dreaming? It had all seemed so real. Still in a sleepy stupor, I glanced down at my lap, and my eyes fixed on the three pale-blue stripes on my navy-blue tracksuit bottoms, 'After dinner I did a shit', I thought.

"What're ya smiling at?" James snapped me out of the daze.

"Was I smiling? Oh, I was just thinking about this Adidas rhyme one of my dad's boys told me last night."

"So he's your brother if he's one of your dad's boys?"

"No, no, one of his boxers. Errol, Errol Johnson. You must know him, he's your age actually. Well, like you he's a year above me at school anyway. Hey, he's about your weight too. You may've boxed him at a show I missed, which doesn't happen very often - I'm always there. Anyway, he's got an amazing right cross and a shocking left hook." I became quite excited upon remembering Errol's surprising win of the previous evening.

"Boxer?!... Erm, your dad's a... boxer?"

"Yeah, of course, didn't Steve tell you?"

"No, no he *never*." His freshly acquired smile disappeared and was replaced with a vacant look, as he turned his head and stared out of the opposite window. I could now view the fine blond hairs on the back of his head, which disappeared into the nape of his neck.

"Dad run's the Birmingham Irish Club," I continued. "Ten of the boys are going through to the finals of the ABAs next Saturday. I'm so gutted I'm going to miss it. I don't miss any of their bouts and if they all win it'll be a first for one club to have so many champions. Were you not in them?"

"In what?"

"The championships?"

"No... No I wasn't..." James seemed preoccupied and distant. Absently he continued, "Anyway, have you been skiing before?"

With every other boxer I knew you had to force them *not* to talk about their sport, to *not* recite their favourite boxers in each division or the ultimate knockout of all time. *You had to* listen about the Rumble In The Jungle and the Thriller In Manila, of Sugar Ray Robinson and Sugar Ray Leonard, or of Mike Tyson, who the previous year had become the youngest ever Heavyweight World Champion.

257

Instead of his aloofness to the conversation on boxing causing me a strange feeling of rejection, it actually gave me some hope. I figured he was like Siobhan had said - just shy, that his demeanour in the assembly hall had been influenced by bashfulness not dislike for me. If he wasn't interested in talking about his own sport, he must be reserved, mustn't he?

"I haven't skied on real snow, no, on dry slopes yeah, but I'm told it's totally different." I then attempted one last shot at a conversation he would respond to. "Siobhan tells me you lived on an army base, how come?" I'd hit the spot, the ice was broken. His eyes lit up and the ice-cold water flowed. It bubbled to the surface, breathing the air.

"My dad's a soldier. He's the *ultimate* soldier - he's SAS. But that's between me and you, it's supposed to be a secret." Siobhan must be right, he must like me because he was sharing family secrets with me now.

"Why aren't you living on the base any more then? Has he left the army now?"

"No, of course not, Dad'll never leave the army. It's just he's gone to Ireland for a while, and Mom didn't want to be on her own any longer. So, we moved here to be by Mom's family." A self-satisfied smile came across my face. My fateful angels were at work once again. James wasn't *just* a boxer, but he was a boxer who also like me was affiliated with Ireland. We had more in common than I had first anticipated.

The conversation continued. He talked - I listened. I listened to descriptions of his favourite guns, of the best armies, even of the best army uniforms, the best wars, of his army-cadet training and of how when he left school he too was going to be a soldier. I soon concluded that I had Action Man sitting next to me.

"Where's your dad in Ireland then?" I interrupted, when he had stopped to regain enough breath to continue on with his combat tales. I was trying to get off the subject of army and sway it towards Ireland. To the land where I spent endless summers, amid the undulating fields of Mayo, surrounded by thatched-roof cottages and fairy-tale castles. Where salmon and trout-filled waters were scattered around which I was convinced were there merely to reflect the beauty of the surroundings. Where smiling locals inhaled the freshest of all air which blew in from over the Atlantic and turned their faces a healthy flushed red. Where men tipped their caps and bid, 'Good mornin' to ye, wee one.'

"He's all over."

"What's he actually do there?"

"Kills Catholics."

"What?"

"Shoots Catholics. That's the job of the army in Ireland, to stop Catholics tryin' to steal our country." I was dumbfounded. I was being immersed in the freezing water which had risen through the ice I'd broken, and it cut through my skin, its icy hands had taken a grip of my throat and ribs and was crushing my lungs. He had completely taken my breath away. I couldn't determine whether he was trying to wind me up or whether it was a joke to see if I had a sense of humour.

I didn't know much about the north of Ireland, but I'd decided last night to find out *everything*. Although I did know for certain that the British army were not there to kill Catholics.

"Do you know why the British army were sent there in the first place?"

"Yeah, to kill Catholics."

"No, to protect Catholics. They were and are *supposed* to be a peace-keeping force."

"I doubt that very much. They're there to kill Catholics for tryin' to steal our country. They could never protect them; every Catholic deserves to die."

"Every Catholic? Really? Well, I'm Catholic, Siobhan's Catholic, so's Mr Kennedy. Do we deserve to die?"

"But you're not Irish Catholics, so that's different."

"Of course we're Irish Catholics."

"But you gave Mr Kennedy a British passport in the school hall; I was right behind ya and saw it. So how can ya be Irish if you was born in England?"

"Jesus was born in a stable; that didn't make him a donkey. A German Shepherd dog can be born in Poland, but it's not going to be a Polish Shepherd dog, is it? My parents are Irish, my grandparents are Irish, my great-grandparents are Irish, all the blood which runs through my veins is Irish. It doesn't matter where I was born." I omitted to inform him about my Great-grandma Mary who was Sicilian but thought she was Irish - that would just have confused things.

"Hi guys," Siobhan interrupted, popping her head through the gap in the seats. "Gettin' on?"

"Yeah, like a house on fire." I was seething. I shook my head and glared out of the window at the passing landscape of wheat fields and mustard grass. I looked at the farmhouses and quaint cottages fly by, which once would have been immersed in the hustle-bustle of an ancient village, which had since been torn down and replaced by the haste, noise and pollution of the motorway.

I should have forgotten about him when I heard the bigotry and hatred. I wasn't that desperate for a kiss - was I? But despite his prejudiced opinions, the enticing apple still hung on the tree of temptation, swaying in the wind of emotional instability, or more accurately - immaturity.

The passing landscape rapidly changed from fields and flowers to the winding serpent-like concrete flyovers of Heathrow Airport, through the anonymous crowd of waiting-to-board air passengers, then to a cotton-wool floor and a blue sky only we who were above the clouds were privileged to see. Those same clouds hovered over the towering snow-covered mountains, like smoke coming out of a volcano, as we drove the climbing, winding roads to our alpine resort of Pinzolo.

The sleepy wooden-cabin-filled resort rested in a valley

amid the crystal whiteness of the mountains. The landscape was magical and almost undisturbed by human inhabitation. My excitement was roused when I imagined myself being transported on the chair-lifts I viewed which climbed the slopes, disappearing into the cotton-wool clouds. Siobhan's excitement was roused on a different ascent. When we climbed the terrazzo stairs of our hotel she soon discovered our room was next-door-but-one to Steven's room. I could only imagine why this thought encouraged her excitement.

"I can't believe it, Orlagh."

"Believe what, Siobhan?" I asked, sarcastically.

"They're there." She pointed at Steven and James' door. "How easy is this going to be?"

"What's going to be easy, Siobhan?" Mr Kennedy asked as he turned the corner and produced a key which fitted perfectly into the lock of the door which separated the boys' room from ours.

"Erm, er, tobogganin'... sir." Her face was an embarrassed shade of red as she stood like a statue, frozen in her pointing position.

"Oh, you think so do ya, Siobhan Connor? So, what's that room got to do with tobogganin'?" He bit his bottom lip, concealing a smile.

"I was, erm, just sayin' erm to, Orlagh, errr." She umed and ahhed until she invented a suitable excuse. Mr Kennedy waited patiently for her answer. "I was just sayin', wasn't I, Orle?" I nodded, although I didn't have a clue what I was in agreement with. "I was just sayin'."

"You were just sayin'," Mr Kennedy encouraged her. He was enjoying it, you could tell. And then, as I was about to save her from any further discomfiture, she quickly explained what she 'was just sayin''.

"Yes, I was just sayin' how easy it'll be to beat Steven and James at tobogganin'."

"Oh, right." He nodded in agreement. "I should hope so! Don't forget, dress like you're gonna ski, wrap up warm, 'cause it's gonna be cold now it's gettin' dark."

Our room was cosy, with a sloping roof, wooden walls and bunk beds. I chose bottom bunk, I couldn't really be trusted on top, as my nightmares (or what appeared to be nightmares) were getting worse. The night people – well, person, was a regular visitor, opening the door of my mind, wiping his feet and making himself quite at home. Always swinging his key and begging me to discover with him. I didn't wish to discover anything with a huge talking shadow.

"Orle, can you believe how close that was? Do you think Mr Kennedy knew what I was on about?"

"Probably!" As I wound her up, I opened my diseased suitcase and proceeded to unpack.

"What?! Are you serious? Oh mmmyyy God!"

"Oh no, Siobhan!"

"What? What's wrong?"

"I've forgotten my gloves. Oh no, what'm I going to do? I can't ski without gloves."

"Is that all, Orle? Ha, all - Orle... Anyway forget your gloves, if Mr Kennedy knows what I was on about, then there's no way I'll lose my virginity."

"Well, isn't that a good thing? You shouldn't be giving it up anyway. To tell you the truth, Shiv, I'm not really interested in your pillow talk. I've more important things to worry about right now." I was a little perturbed with her stupidity as well as the absence of my gloves.

I searched and searched through my case for the gloves, throwing its contents over the bed. By the time I emerged from being buried in my case Siobhan had disappeared.

"Siobhan, where are you? Don't get mad with me. I just think you're rushin' things, you know?" As I said it, chicken-leg bones and chubby cherubs fleetingly floated through my mind. Siobhan suddenly burst into muffled song and the chicken-leg image disappeared.

"Never 'onna 'ive you up, never 'onna let you down, never 'onna 'un around and 'urt yooooou." She skipped out of the bathroom singing what I suspected to be a

Rick Astley song, with a pillow placed over her head and my ski goggles wrapped around where her eyes should have been.

"What're you doin', you nutter?"

"'Illow 'alk!"

"What? I can't understand you with that thing on your head," I shouted, in hysterics.

"Pillow 'alk," she bellowed back.

We just couldn't argue, it was impossible. Either way one of us would make the other laugh. We had a pact, whoever is in the wrong must give in - we mustn't be stubborn. We dismissed the talk of irreversible virginity and I placed the pillow on my head to show her what she looked like - she wet herself. How someone could possibly consider losing their virginity when they still wet themselves at the sight of their best friend with a pillow and ski goggles over her head was way beyond me.

Still laughing, we descended the terrazzo stairs meeting Mr Kennedy, Steve and James on the way. James smiled as we met. My Irish Catholicism obviously hadn't disturbed him too much.

"I've forgotten my gloves, sir."

"What're you like, Orlagh Emmet? Don't worry, we'll sort you out, won't we, boys?" He reassuringly wrapped his huge arm around my shoulders.

Steve and James thought Mr Kennedy's comment was humorous, laughing as they told him they would be back in ten minutes.

"Well, don't be too long, boys, we're headin' off to the slopes in ten minutes, and hey... what's so funny?" He didn't receive an answer.

"Can we come?" Siobhan asked Steve.

"I'm okay," I said, not wanting to appear interested in their company. My right hand covered my chin as I tapped my teeth with faked apathy. Due to James being present I was conscious of the birthmark on my chin. But, why should I care what he thought?

With a dismissive tone echoing in his voice, Steve retorted, "No, Shiv, you can't come... we won't be long."

She pouted, but his absence promptly lapsed from her consciousness as Mr Kennedy introduced us to our bronzed Italian ski instructor.

"Lew-chi-arrr-no." he said, as he simultaneously grabbed one of each of our hands. I raised my eyebrows - Siobhan raised hers back. My mind had already begun to pack the plastic cutlery for the picnic to the land of unobtainable crushes. Siobhan and I were in silent agreement that Luciano alone was worth the trip.

"I've got my eye on you two." Mr Kennedy laughed, clicked his fingers, pointed at us, winked and walked to the bar. "I'm just havin' a quick bottle of Bud."

"Do they sell slow ones then, sir?" Siobhan and I said in unison. Our laughter was interrupted.

"Orrrr-lahh, I like sis name. Orrrr-lahh." When Luciano ended my name it sounded as though he had taken a huge sigh and was out of breath. He closed his eyelids languidly and kept them closed as he said my name slowly, over and again. His continual rolling r's made me bend my own tongue and try to imitate him, but it just wasn't as he had done it; the tip kept slipping through my teeth and breaking through my lips. I must have looked like a lizard on Valium. I wished I had the other characteristics of the lizard other than my escaping tongue. I wished I was a chameleon, so I could change the colour of my skin to suit the environment around me, so someone like Luchiano wouldn't merely be attracted to my name - but to me. My chameleon thoughts were interrupted by a tap on my shoulder.

"Orlagh, could I have a word?"

It was James, smiling and handsome; no, not handsome, Emmet was handsome, with his chiselled cheekbones and paradise sky-blue eyes. James was pretty in a boyish fashion.

He walked me to the base of the stairs where it was private and quiet. He had his opened palm on the base of my back, causing my spine to tingle. I liked his gentle touch, yet didn't want to. What was the point? More craving and more wasted time.

"These are for you." I could smell nicotine on the breath of his words. "To say sorry and everything, for what I said on the bus, ya know. You can't go tobogganin' without gloves."

A peace offering in the shape of green gloves to match my hat and salopettes... All was forgiven.

A bucket of sherbet had been absorbed by my taste buds, the effervescence bubbled down my spine, hit my tail bone and ricocheted off on an upward ascent, spreading at my shoulder blades and travelling down my arms, arriving in my ten digits simultaneously, causing me to stretch my fingers so the excitement could escape. He had taken the pen and had begun the new picture on my etch-a-sketch dream board. I yearned for a masterpiece.

James departed as Siobhan skipped and jumped in excitement, showing me her gift from Steve, a mother of pearl heart with an 'S' inscribed on the front.

"An angel's tooth," I said quietly to myself as I examined the heart.

"What?"

"Oh, nothing, it's nice, right? Look at this, James got me gloves. Can you believe it?"

"Aghhh, I told you. I knew it. I told you. Oh, Orlagh, I knew it." She was leaping up and down, hugging me - leaping. She looked at my gloves for clarification and leapt some more.

"Now what's she so excited about?" Mr Kennedy asked. "Don't tell me... tobogganin'?"

"I'm sorted, Mr Kennedy." I held my gloves in his direction, diverting his attention from Siobhan's excitement. I couldn't let him know about James, not only because he was my teacher, but he was too close to my family. It would generate endless taunting if any of them knew I had a possible admirer. I would even go as far as to say it would be more embarrassing than the males in my household knowing I had a bra.

"Grand, that's just grand. Now you'll look like a complete leprechaun," he concluded, and began to organise his pupils.

"This heart just proves he loves me. Now I'm certain," Siobhan whispered. She could have been the subject in a mist-covered photograph, with that vacant, romantic, distant look.

We came back from tobogganing wet, exhausted and hungry, but jubilant with our win. I was jubilant anyway; I suppose because I had done most of the work. Siobhan had complained while I pushed. We beat our boys, the other schools' boys, even Mr Kennedy, but I suspected he let us win. We sped down the slopes and ran the toboggan back up again. It surprised me how unfit James was, considering he was a boxer and Action Man. Perhaps he needed camouflaged combat attire, woodland and an obstacle course to exert his full physical potential, I thought.

We left Mr Kennedy with his wet, unruly curls falling into his chocolate eyes, which were as wide as saucers as he held another quick bottle of Bud while he conversed with a blonde-haired bimbo.

"We've got our eyes on you, sir!" Siobhan and I satirically stated, as we proceeded to bed.

Beds, darkness, clocks ticking past the midnight hour and two best friends generated conversations. Continual conversations. Conversations which we'd had on previous occasions. Conversation subjects which are dismissed in daytime, ones that are meant for midnight: weddings, babies, never splitting up, buying houses next door to each other. Details of Emmet's kiss on my forehead. Of James's Richard Gere eyes when he gave me my gloves... Were there any innuendoes? No! Siobhan assumed there must have been.

"Of course there was. He must fancy you, Orlagh, or he wouldn't be..."

266

"Wouldn't be what?"

"Nothing... wouldn't be nothing..."

Conversations of school, Mr Kennedy - his new girlfriend. Was she pretty? No, of course she wasn't. More of Emmet. Forget Emmet, she said. I supposed I should. A little of Patrick, but back to Steven.

"I can't believe they'd leave it so late, Orle. Ermm, errrr."

"What so late? Who? What're you on about?"

"Oh, nothing."

"It can't be nothing again. What're you talking about, Shiv?"

"A surprise. A little surprise. I thought it may be now, but maybe not."

"Tell me."

"No, I'm going to sleep."

I rolled on to my stomach, untangling myself from my twisted pyjamas which had wanted to stay in their previous position. I placed my arms above my head and slid my hands under the pillow.

"Agh, errrr, oh my God!" I banged my head on the underneath of the bunk bed as I jumped to my knees.

"What? What?... A spider! Is it a spider, Orle? Oh no."

"I don't know what the hell it is, but it's slimy and under my pillow." I flipped my pillow on to the floor. There were only shadows in the room: the outline of the bed posts, a hidden light behind the curtains, Siobhan's head hanging over the bunk bed, and a shadow of something long and thin where my pillow had just been.

"A snake, a fat worm, a centipede, urgh, errrr." I shivered, cringed, scratched and ran to the light switch to determine exactly what was under my pillow, which felt greasy, slimy and hard, yet soft in places.

We both squinted as I switched on the light, peeping our eyes - left eye, right eye - getting them accustomed to the brightness. Not wanting to be bitten by a greasy creature, I kept my distance in case the light caused this thing to jump.

267

It was still there, lying dormant. My eyes could now clearly make out the mysterious object.

"Oh, you're soooo funny, Shiv. So funny, ha ha ha. You're a comedienne, no - an actress with that performance of shock."

"What're you on about? What've I said? What is it anyway?"

"You know full well what it is, you put it there!"

"Put what there? What is it?"

"A chicken-leg bone, Shiv, with little bits of meat still on it, little brown and pink pieces of meat and even some black threads still on it! Just because I told you it was funny when my dad did it to Doctor Sudki."

"I never. I swear I never... honest, Orlagh. Where would I get a chicken-leg bone from? We had spaghetti for dinner, not drumsticks." Her plea of innocence appeared genuinely authentic, but she couldn't be trusted.

"Yeah, really."

"No, Orlagh, I promise. Who the hell got into our room to put it there? Unless..."

"Unless what?"

"No it couldn't have been. I can't ruin your surprise, but no it definitely wasn't me and it couldn't have been who I thought it was, 'cause who I thought it was wouldn't have done it."

"Okay, okay, I believe you, enough of he, who, what and surprises. At least it wasn't a centipede or a snake, urg." More scratching and shoulder shrugging. "I'll just make sure this door's locked. I don't want anyone droppin' any more legs into my bed, whoever it was."

"No, no!" She jumped up and banged her head on the sloping wooden ceiling. "I already checked that... it's locked." I gave her a strange, 'what are you up to?' look, wrapped the chicken-leg bone in toilet paper, switched off the light and took up the same position in my bone-free bed.

Siobhan's bed creaked as she tossed and turned above me, while muttering something to herself. With my eyes wide open I lay thinking. I could barely make anything out as my eyes hadn't habituated themselves to the darkness which now prevailed in the room.

I lay in the night-time silence wondering who had put the chicken-leg bone under the pillow if Siobhan hadn't, when a powerful unspoken force strangely invaded my mind, making me ask myself certain questions... Had I dreamt about chubby cherubs with chicken legs or had they really been present? Had those cherubs left the bone as some kind of sign? Was it a key to the box which held consequential angelic messages?

I was spinning in a whirlwind of angelic quotations: *"Wisest is she who knows what she does not know..."* It didn't make sense. If you knew what you don't know, then you knew it! Why was this such an important message? Why did the angels keep reminding me of it? Didn't they have something new to say? Something I understood? They only gave me riddles, riddles, bewilderment, more puzzles, more riddles which only led me into a labyrinth of grey, winding tunnels, with no light shimmering in the distance. *"Tempus omnia revelat. Time brings everything."* - not so far... My eyes were heavy, I was getting sleepy. *"The seraphim have endlessly endeavoured, but you forever decline their divine invitation. You must accept to determine the direction of your destiny."* Who were the seraphim? Nobody had invited me anywhere. *"Don't do anything foolish. Don't rush into anything."* I was rushing into nothing - except sleep.

chapter thirty-five

Just as the chubby cherubs had invaded my mind, someone was now invading my bed. Was *this* a dream, or was it real? I felt a warm palm slip across the base of my back. I knew this palm, it had been there before. But what was it doing there, under my pyjamas, in my bed? I thought I must be dreaming. I rolled on to my side to come face to face with the trespasser. I couldn't determine features, it was still too dark. Although, I did recognise the shadow. But what was it doing in my bed, with its warm, clammy palm on my back? It must be a dream... I closed my eyes once again and tried to ignore the hand. It wasn't really there.

"Do ya want me to go?"

I recognised that breath.

"Oh!" I sat up, leaning on my elbow. "Oh my God, I'm not dreaming. What're you doing here, James?"

"What'd think I'm doing here?"

"Did you put a chicken-leg bone under my pillow?"

"What? Chicken bone? No... hush, lie down."

I lay down on my right side. I lay rigid. 'This is it...' I thought. 'This must be it... I think it's it anyway.' His hand rested on the dip that had recently formed into a waist. My palm lay under my cheek, my left arm guarded my boobs - the barrier between his body and mine. I could feel his breath on my lips - it tickled. I had to lick my lips to stop the tickling sensation; the wetness my tongue left made his breath feel cold on my lips. There was then creaking and whispering. "What's that?" I asked.

"It's just Steve and Siobhan."

"Oh, right..." This was obviously my surprise. She could have told me, I could have been prepared - how, I didn't know, I just could have been. I was about to speak but James placed a finger on my lips.

"Sssshhh..." His lips were now in that puckered position, he brought them closer to my mouth...

Oh no, he'll know I've never done this before, I thought. I had watched it on television. I had received detailed descriptions from Siobhan. I'd practised on pillows. But I'd never actually done it. His lips touched mine, they were warm and moist, a little cracked, but they felt nice. I had finally bitten the apple and it tasted divine. Kissing was easy enough, until he changed his strategy. There were new rules - he had opened his mouth. Should I open mine? I didn't. I let him continue. He closed his mouth over my lips. The dryness of my lips pushed his top lip up and the bottom one down, exposing the soft, wet, fleshy inside. His wetness transported itself on to my chin, on to my upper lip. I wanted to rub it dry... obviously I couldn't. His hand rubbed up and down the side of my body. Goosebumps appeared. There was way too much to concentrate on at one time. He opened his mouth again, this time I opened mine with him. I could taste his breath - stale nicotine, but I didn't care, I liked it. I liked his moving hand. I liked his moving lower body which riddled slowly, sensually closer to mine. He nudged my protecting left arm out of his way and placed it slowly on the side of his own body. I could no longer hear the creaking of Siobhan's bed, only the noise of his breathing as he kissed across my cheek. His tongue cupped my ear lobe and his hand cupped my breast. Initially I wanted to resist, but I couldn't, it felt good - too good. A hardness penetrated into my pelvic bone, slowly; back and forth, back and forth. His tongue left a trail of wetness in the shape of a meandering snake that journeyed down my neck. His hand kneaded my breast like a baker manipulates his dough. My nipples were full of yeast and rose to the rhythm of his touch. My body was encountering sensual feelings it hadn't known existed. His lips met mine once again. I had almost perfected my technique. I was like a fish - open, close, open, close when the rhythm was interrupted by the tip of his tongue, it passed the perimeter of my lips and glided across my teeth, as though he was cleaning them of food traces. His hand slipped from my breast and his fingertips made the same meandering-snake shape over my lower ribs, on to my stomach, where he caressed my navel with his finger. The snake slithered south, pausing at a barrier - the drawstring of my pyjamas.

I should have been lost in the land of lustfulness, preoccupied on the plains of passionate pubescent desire, enticed in ecstasy, with images of his face floating through my mind as we frolicked in a field of multi-coloured, sweet-smelling flowers - but no. As his hand reached my drawstring the only image was - a chicken-leg orbiting through the blackness of my mind; spinning, rotating, dilating, like a spaceship in infinity. A greasy, half-eaten, chicken-leg.

"What're you doing, James?" I hastily removed my hand from his rough, spot-covered back and placed it on his south-bound hand.

"What do you think I'm doing?"

"I don't know, that's why I asked."

"Just wait and see."

"If it has anything to do with going beyond my pyjamas, I'm not interested."

"You will be, just let me show you."

I sat up and moved his hand from my stomach. "No, James, I won't be. I don't know what gave you the impression I would be, 'cause I won't."

"All right, don't worry, lie down, we've got lots of time."

And he kissed me again. We kissed each other. We

kissed to the sound of Siobhan's creaking bed and to the sound of nocturnal life. To the sound of a key in the door... *a key in the door?* Muttering, mumbling. A key in the door - *our door?*

Hurdling James's body, I landed with precision on my feet, tiptoed to the door and placed my ear against it.

"What're ya doin', Orle, you spaz?" Siobhan asked, at a hazardous volume. "Get back into bed."

I tiptoed back to the bunk bed. An aroma of perspiration assaulted my nostrils as I hoisted myself up to her bunk. My head was now level with hers.

"Someone's tryin' to get into our room. It must be the chicken-bone person," I whispered.

"Is she always so crazy?" Steve asked Siobhan. "Can't you see we're busy?"

When the rattling of the key commenced once again, they all heard it. The volume of the mumbling increased. I tiptoed back to the door.

"Concentrate," the would-be intruder said. "Focus. You can do it, son. You can do it."

I knew that voice a little too well, but like the hand I had discovered in my bed, I didn't know what it was doing there. "Ahg, for feck sake." It was the prowler getting frustrated. There was then a bang at the door, as though the intruder was trying to shoulder-barge it open - a bang that made the door vibrate. Then there was scratching or rubbing, one long sliding sound.

"Get the boys into the bathroom, Siobhan, 'cause we're in trouble," I instructed in an authoritarian whisper, well, as authoritarian as a whisper can be. "He must know. He's found out. I'm in trouble, *big trouble*. Oh my God, he'll tell my dad. Quick, quick... hide, put towels over you or something, anything."

"Who's there, Orle?" Siobhan was panicking.

"Mr Kennedy!"

"Oh fuck, well why didn't you say so in the first place?" James voiced, too loud. Much too loud. The boys ran into the bathroom while I tried to execute a plan in my chicken-leg-bone brain. Siobhan paced - naked.

"Will you put some clothes on, Siobhan."

"I didn't realise."

"No, you wouldn't. Listen, Shiv, this is the plan. I'm going to open the door and ask him what he wants." Siobhan hastily put on her nightdress.

"No, you can't do that, he'll see them."

"He's not going to come in and say, 'I want to look in your bathroom,' is he?"

The key rattling had ceased, only Mr Kennedy's quiet mumbles persisted outside the door. I imagined him calling me all the names I deserved to be called. How had he found out? Maybe he'd seen the boys coming in? I cringed at the thought.

I decided to go ahead with my plan, the plan which would invent itself along the way. Siobhan's grey silhouette covered its eyes as I unlocked the door and slowly pulled the handle down. I closed my own eyes tight; red dots and a fading chicken-leg bone appeared. The door creaked as it opened. It seemed heavier than usual. It was now open six inches. I peeped into the dimly-lit corridor - no Mr Kennedy. I opened the door wide, so I could step out and observe the origin of the mumbles. The door flung open and Mr Kennedy's slumped torso hit my goose-pimpled legs (not the same goose pimples from my arousal, they had departed long ago and had been replaced by their siblings, originated by fear).

"Mr Kennedy, are you all right?"

"Orrr-lagh, my sweet, what're *you doing* in my room?" he slurred, his unruly curls balanced on my feet.

"This is my room, Mr Kennedy. You're next door."

"I am?"

"You are!"

"I am, so I am."

"Too many quick Buds, too quick?" There was no answer because he was snoozing, right there on my feet.

"Shiv, I'm just helping Mr Kennedy to his room. Clean the bathroom while I'm gone."

"It's too late for that carr-carr-rry oooo-n. Much too late to clean. You're a gooood, good girl."

Not as good as you think, I thought, as I assisted him in standing. He couldn't do it, so he crawled, like a puppy dog on all fours; I had the leash which led him to *his* door. The key fitted perfectly, he crawled in.

"I love you, Orrrr-lagh, and I love your dad, he's a good man, good man."

"I know. I know, sir," I agreed, smiling. Smiling because he was drunk and smiling because I saw the profile of two figures run past his door.

There wasn't a chance of getting him into bed, so I put a pillow under his head and a blanket over his body. He curled up like a baby.

"You're a good girl, Orrr-lagh. A prin, a princ..." and he was asleep.

chapter thirty-six

The rusty shackles had been removed and cast aside. My intrinsic incarcerated, adolescent, sensual urge had been paroled, set free into the wide-open environment of experience.

I had a boyfriend. I, Orlagh Emmet had a boyfriend. The sky appeared bluer and smiles seemed a whole lot brighter, except Mr Kennedy's. He was tired, hung-over and hungry - as was I, except hung-over. Even my freshly acquired status as a girlfriend couldn't stop my stomach begging for food. Mr Kennedy, Siobhan and myself had over-slept, missed breakfast - missed James, missed his freckles, missed his Richard Gere eyes - they were on the slopes while we were in our beds.

Siobhan and I had sprinted down the stairs into the dining room to discover chairs upside-down on table-tops and cleaners sweeping the mess dropped by the diners.

"What're we gonna to do, Orle?"

"I can't understand why Mr Kennedy didn't wake us."

"He didn't wake you because he hasn't woken himself *yet*. Fine example he is. Fine example. Thirty children under his supervision, left up to me, and he's in bed."

Left up to the small, evidently incensed, bespectacled teacher from the grammar school who had accompanied us on the trip. He looked down on us. We were comprehensive scum, working-class riffraff - you could see it in his magnified eyes. The two-inch-thick lenses in their massive

276

black frames enlarged his eyes so much they appeared as large as the lenses themselves.

"He's sick, isn't he, Shiv?"

"Drunk more like," he mumbled.

"We'll fetch him. Come on, Siobhan."

We banged on his door. "Mr Kennedy! Sir! *Sean!*" No reply. More shouting and more banging - until Buckwheat answered the door. His unruly curls took the statement beyond its meaning - out-of-control, rebelling, insubordinate curls. His chocolate saucers had melted and smudged the sockets of his now sunken eyes. As Dad would say, 'like piss-holes in the snow.' An appropriate analogy in our present surroundings.

"Too many quick Buds too quick?"

"Tell me about it, Miss Emmet. Have I you to thank?"

"You do."

"You're a good girl."

"I know, you told me already, but it was slurred before!"

We eventually got to Luchiano and his bronze complexion, but I couldn't concentrate on his 'Bendze knees' instructions. My imagination was too busy rolling out its rainbow. James had been in my mind all day, but absent in substance; then I spotted him in his group.

"James!" I shouted, waving my ski pole above my head, "James, it's Orlagh." He glanced over without acknowledgement and skied away. I decided he hadn't heard me, or maybe I was mistaken; everyone looks so similar in goggles and hats. I continued painting his picture in my mind, but it was rapidly fading - it needed refreshing - required a touch-up.

It was just before dinner when the picture in my mind was finally restored. Siobhan had continued without me because I was taking too long. I was making the extra effort for James.

"You've got to look your best for your man, Shiv. That's what I say."

She looked at me in mock disbelief. "All right, Miss World, I'll see you down there."

With adornment complete, I left the room and closed the door. Simultaneously James closed his door. Mr Kennedy's door was the only thing separating us.

"Hey." I smiled. He ignored me and walked towards the stairs. "James," I called, fooling myself he hadn't heard me, "James, it's Orlagh."

He stopped abruptly. I knew he wouldn't ignore me, not after last night. "I know full well who it is. Leave me alone."

"What? You're joking, right?"

"I must've been jokin' when I agreed with Steve to go ahead with this."

"With what? I'm still your girlfriend, aren't I?"

He laughed and laughed and the rusty shackles which had imprisoned my now-freed adolescent, sensual urge shook.

"Girlfriend? Ya can't be serious? The only thing you mean to me is debt, and a big one."

Parole was being violated, apprehension of the urge was taking place.

"I don't understand."

"Well, I'll explain," he growled like an enraged mutt, when the night before he'd been a loving puppy. "I bet Steve that I'd be able to shag ya on the first night. You lost me ten quid, you scar-faced frigid Irish bitch. You need your head looking at in more ways than one, especially if you thought I'd be interested in you. When I look at you all I see is red. Oh, and there's a little bit of green too, you Irish-Catholic bitch."

An orange was in my throat and it grew rapidly; it trapped my vocal cords, blocked my windpipe. I too was seeing red, dazzling, blazing crimson - not in my birthmark, but in wrath. I slowly and calmly walked to where he stood on the landing. Chicken-leg bones, meandering snakes, dribbling mongrels and boxing rings crashed in my brain; they were bumper cars in a fairground colliding into each other. But out of the confusion came a clear message.

I gently placed my hands on his shoulders and he smirked, a contemptuous nicotine-stained smirk; the yellow of his teeth glimmered through the saliva. I hadn't noticed the stains previously. I smiled too, slowly, no teeth showing, just stretched lips - and his smile faded - maybe he too saw the message through my eyes. The message which had broken through all the commotion and had shone its precise instructions.

The gentle hands placed on his shoulders glided down to the tops of his arms, where gentle became fierce. My grip tightened causing my knuckles to turn white with the strain. I stepped forward with my left leg, bringing my body close to his. I thought I had detected a hint of fear in his eyes. Fear of the incarcerated sensual urge which had been told that parole was violated and had been placed back in its rusty shackles and thrown into the dampness of the cell situated in the pit of my stomach. My stomach which ached from the fighting and screaming of innocence. The urge was imploring me to fight back, which is exactly what I was going to do.

I could hear Dad's voice precisely in my head, giving me fight instructions; 'If yer don't think yer gonna knock 'em out with one punch then you must do this. You've got to be fast, Orle, but it'll knock 'em off their stride. Knee 'em in the goolies, then when they hunch over to protect 'emselves you've got to go up them stairs and throw yer punches up to the head hard and fast - uppercuts, hooks, the lot. Give it all yer've got, princess.'

My right leg followed through after the left which had stepped forward. But the right leg didn't merely take a step, it did as Dad had instructed in such situations. In circumstances where I thought the opponent needed to be weakened; which is what I anticipated with James. I thought, well he's a boxer, he'll bob and weave past my punches and follow through with his own and I wasn't going to give him any more satisfaction than he had already acquired at my expense.

With my hands on his arms I pulled his body closer to mine. My right knee rose and sank into the flesh between his legs. Into the flesh which hadn't been so fleshy the night before. Into the flesh which had wanted to take advantage of my innocence. He took a deep breath and his Richard Gere eyes opened as wide as they possibly could, followed by a high-pitched squeal, which was music sounding in my ears. The smile had now completely faded as he cried in pain. As Dad predicted, he hunched over and both his hands cupped that same flesh. But I was to give no further abuse to the damaged flesh in-between his legs; I began climbing those stairs.

In a hunched position with his chin on his chest, his head was now level with my shoulders, a perfect position for an uppercut. I stepped my right leg back, which left me with the perfect boxing stance. I transferred all my weight to that right side. I too hunched myself over and dipped down over my right side an inch or two and just as Dominic had done to Markie Forrester - I emerged like a stone from a catapult, like a compressed spring leaping with all the pliability it possesses and executed a perfect right uppercut, which connected in the centre of his face. I felt his nose crushing under my clenched fist and I was oblivious to his pain. There was moisture on my skin. Everything seemed to happen in slow motion. His hands now deserted their protecting position and I thought, here we go, prepare yourself for punches - hard, strong punches. His left hand raised itself, but instead of clenching into a fist, it bent into a claw and attempted to scratch my face - scratch? But he was a boxer. Boxers don't scratch - they punch - or they should anyway.

I leaned slightly to my left to avoid any feminine scratches, placing me in the position to render an exquisite left hook. A left hook Dad would have been proud of, one which Dominic, Patrick and Emmet would have been honoured with calling their own. A left hook which had metamorphosed from my anger and humiliation, and from the incarcerated sensual urge in the pit of my stomach. A left hook which sent James and his now wide Richard Gere eyes crashing into the wall, causing a cheap alpine-scene painting to rock on its nail, like a pendulum on a grandfather clock.

"I'm sorry... Please don't, I'm bleeding."

"Yeah, so now you're seeing red in a whole different way."

But I couldn't stop. My punches were flying fast and extremely furious. My anger wouldn't restrain itself. His blood was on my fists and I just kept punching. He fell to the floor where he tried to roll up into a ball, but before he could I straddled his body, making a nice comfortable seat on his lower stomach. His forearms protected his blood-covered face. My left hand grasped his neck, while my right pounded punches through his protecting guard into his face; his blood speckled my face on each blow. He wouldn't or couldn't fight back. He screeched his apologies, squealed for help, he cried in pain - but I couldn't stop. Every punch was releasing enslaved anger and frustration. Each punch was flying on the forceful wings of killing-Catholic comments, scar-face comments; they glided with the intensity of continual romantic rejection behind them.

Other than the squealing James I could just about hear another voice, but comprehension of actual phrases evaded me. The voice then became physical. It grabbed my hair from behind, pulling me from the straddled position.

"You animal, look at you. What're you doing? I despair of your kind. *Despair.*" Two gigantic magnified eyes glared at me. "I'll take this poor boy to the nurse. Do not move from this spot, I'll be back to deal with you." The bespectacled grammar-school master supported James who hobbled and limped, undecided whether to hold his head, his bleeding nose or mouth or the damaged flesh in-between his legs.

It wasn't the picture I had earlier hoped to paint.

I slumped against the wall and slid to the cold floor. The wall vibrated causing the swinging painting to drop into my lap; it was dislodged from the frame, as broken as I was. I hugged my knees and placed my head on them, sad and hurt. But why should I be sad? Once again I had won, beaten the villain. But had I really won? The physical - yes. The psychological - no. Every part of my mind was screaming for answers, begging for clarification. Would life get easier? Would romantic rendezvous ever ring with the sound of success? Why did the wild cats still prowl in dark corners of my mind, pouncing and savaging my immature wings?

Urgent footsteps climbing the stairs interrupted my line of thought. I was expecting the grammar school Gestapo, with their blue blazers and striped school ties to cart my common comprehensive posterior to the confines of a dark room where they would leave me to wallow in my own self-pity. But from the stairs a friendly smiling face emerged.

"So what did he do, Orlagh?" Mr Kennedy's piss-holes in the snow had been replaced by sympathetic chocolate eyes, with a touch of creeping moss.

"The usual."

"The usual? Is that all, Miss Emmet?" He slid down the wall as he had done down my door the previous evening. He hugged his knees as I was doing and shuffled his body close to mine. "'Cause I just saw the state of him and he's past the usual state you leave them in."

"Scar-face, red-face, what else can I say?"

"Come on, Orlagh, this is me you're talkin' to, Sean Kennedy, the drunken teacher you put to bed. This isn't just a fight for your hurt pride, a fight caused by name-calling idiots. What's it about, O?"

"How is it you teachers know everything?"

"I don't know everything, I just know you, and this girl sitting next to me here isn't the Orlagh Emmet I know. The Orlagh Emmet that radiates confidence and happiness like the ReadyBrek boy with his orange glow."

He wet the sleeve of his jumper with saliva and wiped away the blood speckles on my face.

I smiled for the first time and proceeded to tell him everything, (well almost). I told him the story, from beginning to end. From the assembly room to the coach and killing Catholics, to the gloves and even the visit to my room and finally to the bet.

"Do you know what, Orlagh Emmet? You're the most beautiful girl I've ever had the good fortune to set my eyes upon."

I sniggered sarcastically.

"I'm serious, Orlagh. Most beautiful, most talented - athletically and academically. And as for confidence, no one comes close, boy or girl. Don't you dare lose that confidence and don't be losing any sleep over that one either, Orle; he's trouble - with a capital T. Do you know what all these boys are going to do when they grow up?" Before I could answer, he continued, "They're going to get their legs, wrap 'em around their backs and kick 'em selves up the bum. They are gonna think, *'What was I thinkin'?* What was I thinkin'? *She's so beautiful,* so successful.' It'll mean nothin' now, Orlagh, but he who laughs last, laughs loudest! Your fists break noses and your eyes'll break a few hearts. Look at them eyes, they're like two emeralds shimmering on a bed of mother-of-pearl."

"Like the angels," I said to myself.

"You are an angel, and all this, Orlagh, happened for a reason."

"I know, another brick in my wall, a big huge concrete block."

"What?"

"Oh, nothing, something my dad once told me."

"As I was sayin', everything happens for a reason. God sends out his little angels to make things happen, to keep the world revolving."

"You believe in angels?"

"Of course I do. Anyway, it *was* just a kiss then?"

283

"It was, *thank God*."

"And what if the angels hadn't got me drunk and I hadn't arrived at your door, what would it have been then?"

"So the angels got you drunk?"

"They did. Don't avoid the question."

"Just a kiss."

"Good. You're a good girl."

"So you keep tellin' me! You won't tell my dad will you, Mr Kennedy?"

"Tell your dad? *Tell your dad?* Are you serious? Tell him I was drunk... angels' fault or not, outside your door while you had a boy in the room? He'd have me guts for garters. He likes garters your dad and he's not gettin' my guts to fulfil his fantasy!"

The James scenario had been concluded with my talk to Mr Kennedy. The bespectacled, magnified-eyed teacher couldn't believe I was not being disciplined. He informed Mr Kennedy he was an excuse for a teacher. Mr Kennedy told him he didn't have a clue. He said he wouldn't know the feelings of real children. Children who daydreamed their days to the sports field, not the exam rooms.

James and Steven made themselves extremely scarce for the rest of the trip. I suspected James did so because of the embarrassment of a broken nose, swollen lips and two black eyes - Steven with the fear of ending up looking like his friend. Why? What had he done? Surely he couldn't be guilty by association. No, Steven, like myself, had broken a few things, in a metaphorical sense as well as the literal.

Siobhan's heart had been broken along with her hymen. When Steven stole her virginity I suppose he had won the bet. But I didn't rub salt into her deep open wounds. I didn't say I told you so, you should have waited; we just talked and laughed, placed more pillows on our heads, pulled ridiculous faces, invented hilarious caricatures and she wet herself a few more times. I was the cement that fused the delicate pieces of her heart back together. I was strong for her, like I endeavoured to be strong for everyone.

As the week progressed I became anxious; all my thoughts were in England, at the finals of the boxing championships. I was enjoying my trip, but I was so annoyed that I was going to miss the finals. Annoyed that I was going to miss my brothers and my extended brothers box in the ultimate contest in the country. My anxiety was apparent, but only Mr Kennedy and Siobhan could understand the significance.

"Don't worry about the boys, any of them, they'll all do good. Enjoy your last night. It's the medal ceremony this evening and there may be a couple in store for you. I'll see you over there. Mr, erm, what's his name?... pompous grammar school guy?... You never heard me say that, Orlagh; anyway, he's organising you guys while I help Luchiano organise the ceremony."

My visions of victorious boxing matches were most certainly removed, though not by thoughts of a bronze, silver or gold for most improved skier, or fastest slalom, or superlative skier of the week, but by sinister accusations.

All the students from our school and those from the grammar school sat within a waiting area on the second floor of the hotel - all, that is, except James and Steven. They had conveniently arrived late or not at all for most events throughout the week, including, breakfast, lunch on the mountain and supper. Everyone knew what had happened. James was utterly humiliated. In the ensuing period I had been told by people I hadn't spoken to previously that he was a bully. Since he had arrived at the school six months earlier he had intimidated, threatened, demanded lunch money and generally made life miserable for numerous pupils in the school. They praised me, back-slapped me and I basked in the heroic adulation. There was another bonus resulting from the confrontation: thankfully there had been no further name-calling taunts. It was in such situations when I was surrounded by strangers that such taunts would usually arise: sports events, school trips, Saturday shopping excursions. School itself had quietened down as far as name-calling went. After a few people had received the treatment James had, no one bothered, or maybe I had become as ordinary as everyone else and had simply blended in.

But this medal ceremony was imperative, obligatory, so their absence from this gathering, along with the absence of the bespectacled grammar-school teacher, who was a stickler for accurate timekeeping, confirmed speculation of the earlier rumours which had stated they had been caught shoplifting.

"Steve told me he wasn't shoplifting any more."

"So he's done it in the past? And you knew, Siobhan?"

"Oh course he has, Orlagh," stated Michael, a friend of ours from school. "You're so street-wise in most ways, but so naive at the same time. I bought some ski goggles off them at the beginning of the week. Mine broke on the first day and Steve offered me a pair."

At that the magnified eyes appeared at the top of the stairs, on the landing where I had conquered James.

"It appears that we have a group of pupils who are inclined to purloin." The words came from his eyes, not his mouth.

"What's purloin?" Siobhan asked.

Before I could answer the magnified eyes continued.

"And here," he pointed to a black, leather-bound diary, "I've a list of the guilty, the culpable, the thieves, the pilferers and the fences - all you scum."

"What's fencing got to do with this? They probably do that in their posh school." Siobhan looked confused. I tried to clarify.

"Not fencers as in the sport, fences as in Fagan."

"I still don't understand."

"Receivers of stolen goods."

"Really?" Michael was horrified. "Then I'm done."

"When I complete this list of riffraff, the rest of you must

286

continue to your ceremony. Enjoy yourselves while the incriminated are under interrogation. First to be called... Adrian Webb." He spoke like a barrister in a court of law.

Adrian stood slowly, his head hung low as he mounted the terrazzo stairs. The group were silent. We watched his every move as he ascended into the unknown. As soon as his back disappeared, conversations struck like the spark of an ignited match.

Siobhan and I tried in vain to distract Michael from the fate he thought he was about to endure. Names were called one by one: Liam, John, David, Mark, Jason, Justin. All attenders of our school. Andrew, Paul, Danny.

"And finally."

"Oh no, this must be me," Michael trembled. "My dad'll kill me."

"The last name on our inventory of scum, which I must add is no surprise to myself... Orlagh Emmet."

It may have been no surprise to him, but I was astounded, along with Siobhan and Michael. Although Michael's astonishment was probably due to his name not being called.

"I haven't stolen anything, I'm going nowhere."

The silence was deafening. The idle chatter had ceased and every pair of eyes gawked at me: blue ones, green ones, brown ones and huge bulbous magnified ones which bellowed instructions from the top of the stairs. The light which radiated from the third-floor landing glowed behind him, giving him the eerie appearance of an omnipotent being.

"Are you defying my orders? Get up these stairs immediately, if not sooner, young lady." He was incensed. "Although, *lady* is hardly the title which can be used for your kind."

"Just go, Orle. Tell him the truth and it'll be all right." Siobhan was clearly nervous - I was angry.

I ascended the stairs and upon reaching the top I was amazed at the sight in front of me. Suitcases lay opened on

287

the landing floor, overflowing with multiple items of the same kind. The first open suitcase was Adrian's, teeming with ski goggles and sunglasses: mirrored, slightly tinted, dark black. There must have been forty pairs, all with labels still attached. Adrian was on his knees behind his case, his head hung to the floor. Steven was next in line, also kneeling behind his case which was overflowing with labelled items: Fila sweaters, Lacoste shirts, ski gloves, sunglasses. I could only see the top of his head; his chin was burrowed into his chest. His shoulders vibrated as he sobbed. Next to Steven was his partner in crime - James. His case was a treasure-trove and there must have been no evidence of ownership of its contents, not James's ownership anyway. Where the bruising was fading on the skin around his eyes, it appeared the same nicotine yellow as his teeth. The bandage across his nose was grubby and his lips resembled Mick Jagger's.

My mind was full of justifying explanations as to how my name would appear in the black diary. I could never steal anything; the genealogical line containing the thieving trait had discontinued itself when it reached Nanna Bridie. Those theft-ties had definitely all been severed. I just couldn't work out why I was there. I was back in my grey, winding labyrinth of avenues, running into continual dead ends. Elucidation lay in someone else's mind. In their maze there was a busy thoroughfare with the vehicle of clarification speeding by at a hundred miles an hour.

"I'm not one of these." I pointed at the three sorry cases kneeling behind their abounding cases. "I'm not a thief."

"One didn't accuse one of being a thief," the eyes stated.

"Well, what is *one* being accused of then?" My brazen comments would not stand me in good stead, but I didn't care.

"At least these boys admitted their wrong doings, but you, you don't contain one ounce of decency. You bought stolen items. *No,* I correct myself, you didn't just *buy* them - you placed an *order* for them." Spittle was attempting to escape from his bad-breath-smelling mouth, frothing in tiny white bubbles in the corners of his lips, as he stood inches from my face in-between James's case and myself. "You ordered gloves to be stolen, because you were stupid enough to forget yours."

At the mention of gloves, I glanced past the mad-dog froth, over his dandruff-covered shoulder to James, who was grinning through his Mick Jagger lips. In my labyrinth of winding grey avenues I crashed through a road block and had a head-on collision with clarification. As the magnified eyes finished their speech I ran around the bespectacled teacher and took a flying kick at James's head. I was going to wipe the contempt off his face. James ducked my kick and as I replanted my feet, for the second time in a week, the bespectacled teacher grabbed my hair and pulled me away from the reason I was obviously there. The karate kick along with my audacious comments didn't pave the way to an expeditious escape; instead, I was led to the corridor where my room was situated. Along the corridor standing against the wall, in-between each room's door, were what I suspected to be the fences. All were silent with bowed heads.

I attempted to prove my innocence, telling them the real story. I needed my witnesses - Siobhan and Mr Kennedy.

"Your teacher can't get you out of this one, like he gets you out of everything else. You're scum. The *scum* of the earth." His spittle sprayed in my face, as he waved my green gloves around in the tense air.

"How did you get those? They were in my room."

My question was promptly answered without the magnified-eyed teacher uttering a word. A tall, skinny man with a dark suntan and black slip-on loafers rattled a bunch of keys, like a jailer, as he emerged from another room occupied by a pupil from my school.

"You've got no rights to go into my room."

I was pushing my luck to the limits.

"Rights?" the loafer man said, with a heavy accent

hugging his words, "Rights? What about the rights of the people in my village who have been robbed by you English scum? Never in the thirty years I've owned this 'otel have I had English scum like you before." His eyes turned glossy as he squealed his abuse at me. I felt sorry for him. I wanted to tell him that I was Irish, not English, and that I have a little Italian in me too. I wanted to tell him about Great-grandma Mary and her Palermo roots. I wanted to tell him all the stories she had told me about Mount Etna's eruptions and of playing in the olive and orange groves. Maybe then he would understand I couldn't steal from them - I was almost one of them. But it didn't seem an appropriate time to inform him of my ancestry. He despondently shuffled his slip-on loafers along the floor and disappeared around the corner.

It seemed like I was going to be there for the night, in the cold banal corridor, missing the medal ceremony and the disco. Missing presenting Luchiano with a gift Siobhan and I had bought him. Missing saying goodbye to him and all the new friends I had made - missing the fun, all because I had defended myself against malicious actions and cruel taunts. I was incensed when I thought I was also missing the boys box in the finals of the British championships - not missing them to have a good time, but to sit alone and falsely accused of a crime. My incarcerated, adolescent, sensual urge and myself were both experiencing the same miscarriage of justice.

I prayed for my angels to come and help me get out of this predicament. I closed my eyes and begged - and still nothing. I prayed for a sign, a symbol like the chicken-leg bone which had given me pre-warning not to do anything foolish and to rush into nothing. The sign which I hadn't interpreted fast enough. I thought there might be a sign in the hotel corridor which I hadn't discovered. I sat on the cold floor and scanned every nook and cranny. I looked deeply into the cheap alpine-scene paintings which hung on the walls - there was nothing. My eyes searched in the intricate spiders' webs which filled each corner. I watched a fly fighting to escape, without any luck. I felt I had reached the same fate as the fly.

But then my prayers were suddenly answered. My angel had arrived - the key to my escape...

I heard my innocence being shouted. The story of my blamelessness being bellowed. I smiled because I knew my angel couldn't be beaten. He would fight until freedom was attained. And fight it almost was.

The magnified-eyed teacher placed his body in front of me, with his arms stretched out horizontally, like Jesus on the crucifix, preventing my rescuer from access. But his tiny body in his oversized dandruff-covered suit didn't have a chance against the muscular physique of Mr Kennedy. Sean Kennedy's strong arm pushed the magnified eyes to the side. He lifted me on to his shoulder in a fireman's lift and we skated over the ice-covered streets to the medal ceremony; where I was just in time to receive a gold medal for best beginner. A gold for fastest slalom time and, as I basked in my glorious win, I was called up once again to receive gold for overall best technical skier of the week.

As I received my final award, from the crowd Mr Kennedy became clearly visible, as though a spotlight had been shone upon him. I caught his stare and he winked one of his beautiful eyes, which no longer looked like pissholes in the snow, nor did they cry sympathy - they screeched pride, and I thanked God for once again sending his angelic agents to my aid.

CHAPTER THIRTY-SEVEN

"Who won then, Mammy?" I was so excited to know about the boxing-championship results that I was asking her before I'd completely departed the coach.

Awaiting an answer, I descended the steps of the coach, leaving behind me the sadness of the kissing experience, the new friendships and further mystifying angelic apparitions. Siobhan had been bewildered by the planting of the chicken-leg bone. I'm sure she had asked everyone in the entire hotel if they had placed it there under my pillow. The majority didn't even deny it; they merely wrinkled their brows, squinted their eyes and looked at her through puzzled, commiserating eyes. Eyes which reflected their thoughts of her being mildly insane. The same eyes she would have seen me through if I had informed her who had really placed the chicken-leg bone under my pillow, and more astoundingly - why!

"Well, it's grand to see you too, Orlagh."

"Oh, you know all that, Mammy, of course I'm glad to see you, but how did the boys do?"

"And how's the bra?"

"*Mammy*, stop winding me up."

"I'm not, I just wanted to know how the bra was."

"I don't mean about that. You're avoiding the question."

"Well, Orlagh, sweetheart, I've been sworn to secrecy. My lips are sealed, zipped, buttoned, locked and I've gone and thrown away the key."

"What're you talking about, *Mammy*? Just tell me. T*his isn't funny.*"

"Look, Orlagh, the boys want to tell you themselves... all of them. I'm not even allowed to tell you how Dom and Pat did. They've a little surprise for you tomorrow night at the gym."

"I'm sick of their surprises. It's only another way of them tormenting me and I'm *really* sick of it."

"Hey, are you sad and angry 'cause you're missing me already, Miss Emmet? And how did the lads do, Mrs Emmet?"

"Oh, aren't we the gentleman tonight, *Mr Kennedy*? Sean, you're never that polite. What're you after?"

"Okay, whatever suits you, *Grania*. How did the lads do?"

"It wouldn't matter if you called her Your Royal Highness, she still won't tell you."

"I said I was sworn to secrecy not to tell you, Orlagh. I can tell Sean what I like."

I shook my head, annoyed by the teasing, and stormed off to the car dragging my diseased suitcase on its broken wheel behind me. I slumped into the passenger seat watching Mammy inform Mr Kennedy of the previous evening's boxing event. It wasn't a simple case of wanting to know the win or lose outcome - I wanted to know the intricate details of how they had won or lost. Was it by knockout, majority decision or unanimous decision? Maybe it was ref stop contest or even the second had thrown in the towel? I had missed a momentous occasion and I needed to know the details.

I had been home for a whole night and day and the secretiveness had continued. Nobody would tell me the results of the championships, however much I begged. We were allowed to miss school the day after we'd returned home, so I had hours to ponder. Dominic and Patrick appeared too jolly to have lost in the final of the British Boxing Championships, although I saw no evidence of any new trophies having been added to the array of shimmering gold boxing statues which stood in the corner of the lounge. After hearing Doctor Sudki's tomb-opening story so many times, I had re-named it the Tutankhamen corner. I imagined the boy-king's tomb would have glistened as majestically as all the trophies. There were so many of them bunched together that when you stood near them the gold would transfer itself on to your skin, giving the impression of a golden tan, or more convincingly - jaundice. I stood near them so regularly - reading, touching, dreaming - that I often appeared to have such conditions. I knew the engraved writings on the small gold tags off by heart. I would sit and remember the contest, the punches, the flash moves, as though it had been me in the ring. I would treat them as though they were mine. There were large ones, small ones, ones with marble columns. There were wooden shields, medals, crystal bowls, glass tankards and I knew each of their stories. I wished they could have belonged to me. I wanted so much to compete in the ring. I trained just as hard as all the boys, in some cases harder. I knew I was as good, or in the majority of cases I surpassed their skill and ability. I was faster, stronger and frustrated that I couldn't exhibit my dextrous expertise in public. In the gym I really was one of the lads and they didn't take it easy with me while sparring. If I didn't want to be hit, then I should learn how to move, or not be there in the first place.

"Are yer ready, baby doll?" Dad rattled his keys, like the Italian hotel manager had, but under much different circumstances.

"Yeah, of course, I've been waiting all day, let's go."

"And are yer sure yer all dressed and ready, Orlagh?"

"You can see I am, Dad. What're you on about? Everyone's talking in riddles."

"All necessary garments fastened, buttoned and hooked?"

"Yes, *Dad*. Will you tell me what you're gettin' at."

"Nothing, doll, just makin' sure yer all done up."

I definitely couldn't detect anything from Dad's demeanour, because he was always the same: laughing, joking, singing. If they had all lost he would have acted the same as if they'd all won. That's why the boys all loved him - he never put any pressure upon them. But there was an added mystery to these events. There was too much secrecy involved in the withholding of championship results. Dominic and Patrick had sneaked off quietly after dinner and had proceeded in Dom's van to the gym.

As Dad and I pulled into the huge car park which was shared with the adjoining pub I spotted Luke McCabe running in through the gym door. The poster-covered door was quickly slammed behind him before I could get a glimpse inside. Dad took his time parking the car, pulling his huge, home-made, anti-theft device around the wheel. It was a ridiculously large chain which he had bolted to the floor of the car. He wrapped it around the steering wheel and put on a padlock almost as large as the chain. He swore by it, making sure Dominic had one on his van and I was certain when Patrick passed his driving test the next month, he too would have Dad's home-made device attached immediately to his vehicle.

Dad trailed behind me as I rushed to the gym door. The stale brewery smell lingered outside the gym, which always sparked off my nostalgic sensory perception. I knew which smell would follow - that rancid, but strangely ambrosial, aroma of trapped sweat in leather gloves. Of perspiration mixed with deodorant. Strong, male smells.

"You go on in, Orle, I've forgotten something in the car."

I opened the gym door apprehensively, because I knew they were up to something. As I walked into the small porch area, hanging next to all Dad's home-made 'Boxing Gym In Here' posters was a banner which stated 'Welcome Home Orlagh'. I smiled to myself and thought that wasn't so bad, quite nice really, especially considering I had only been away for a week. But all the secrecy for that?

I continued through the next door as I heard Dad's footsteps approaching outside. Along with the footsteps I heard a wolf-whistle and I just about recognised the pub-landlord's voice as he shouted in a feigned camp tone; "Errrmmmm, don't you look sexy, Rory?"

Pushing open the gym doors I tried to recollect what Dad was wearing - nothing out of the ordinary, I thought; or maybe in all my excitement I hadn't noticed. All was quickly revealed. My initial suspicion of tormenting-in-progress proved correct, as I stood in shock at the door. Initially, I didn't know whether to laugh, shout or even cry. When Dad pushed past me and he too came into view, I had to smile. I closed my eyes, deeply inhaled, shook my head and leaned up against the door. My lips stretched into an uncontrollable smile and I once again thought about a time when my every move wouldn't be shared with a group of pugilists.

Each and every one of those boxers: Dom, Pat, Emmet, Mickey Duffy, all the McCabe brothers, Errol, the rest of the gang, and even Dad (which explained his visit back to the car) all wore a supplementary garment, clothing which certainly wasn't associated with boxing, or even men. This time they didn't don a beret and imitate Bono... They all wore a bra.

All were still dressed in their regular clothes, but with a bra wrapped around their chests. Most of their bras were stuffed with their protection bandages or boxing vests, except Errol's bra, which was stuffed with fifteen ounce gloves, because the cups were that huge. Even with the gloves stuffed inside, there would have been room for some bag mitts!

I didn't comment; I just looked around at each of them as they awaited my response. I felt myself blush when I realised my eyes had fixed on Emmet. When my eyes absorbed his chiselled face, with those paradise sky-blue eyes, where the blackbird still fluttered through, I knew he would never, not ever be erased from my etch-a-sketch of

296

dreams. In the previous week I had tried to draw a fresh picture on the etch-a-sketch dream board but underneath, deeply embedded on the cellophane surface forever, was Emmet's face, his muscles, and with them the images of my desires. However many times I would try to draw over it, it could never be removed. I quickly recovered my composure, which was escaping into the Emmet dream-world, and made my first comment.

"I don't think my boobs'll ever grow as big as your mammy's, Errol."

"Well, her botty's as big as her boobs." Errol's white shining teeth appeared from behind his chocolate skin as he laughed along with everyone else.

It was an opportunity for Mickey Duffy to off-load one of his many mom jokes: "Yeah, 'cos the last time your mom saw *90210* was on the scales."

"Well, we Jam-ai-cans." Errol had acquired a distinctive Caribbean accent. "We like our women big and round, with big ass and big tittie." He sounded like a sexually-mature man instead of a teenager.

"Plenty of rice and pea," Mickey retorted, attempting a Jamaican accent, but sounding more like an Irish-Indian.

"Well, at least she doesn't eat grass from the park, like your mamma."

They were off and I felt well and truly at home. How had they found out about the bra? Had Mam told Dad? I doubted it as I'd asked her not to. Had Dad noticed it while we ate breakfast on the morning of my departure to Italy; *my* D-day - well, B-day? I didn't know and I didn't care now, the ice was broken and hopefully after this little performance I would hear nothing more.

"I suppose you'll be wantin' the results, hey, princess?" I smiled inwardly, I loved it when Emmet called me princess.

"I do, please."

"Well, ye canny have them. Right, boys?"

The row of boxers nodded in silent agreement.

"But why? I'm here now. What's the big deal?"

"Well, yer went off gallivantin' around Italy instead of watchin' us, so we thought yer don't deserve 'em, so ye don't."

"Well said, Emmet. She really doesn't deserve to know how we did." Mickey Duffy had discarded the Irish-Indian-sounding accent and was back to his normal Birmingham-Irish twang. But whichever accent he used, his statement would still have wound me up.

Before I could defend myself the row of bra-wearing pugilists separated in the centre, making two walls of underwear-clad males, creating a clear walkway and a vision of an amazing sight. It was like Moses stretching out his arms and separating the Red Sea, creating a pathway for the Hebrews so they could flee from hostile Egyptians. But unlike the ancient Hebrews there wasn't a view of a great mountain in the distance which would bestow ten commandments, only a television and a VCR, which would exhibit ten fights.

"We won't tell ye the results, baby doll, sure, ye can watch the whole thing for yerself." Dad pointed to the television. "Emmet's uncle was over from America with one of them new-fangled camcorders and recorded the whole lot. So take yer seats, it's Show Time."

I was in heaven, not merely because I was re-living the whole of the missed evening, but also because I was sitting next to Emmet, where the smell of his aftershave was sweet and alluring, and where I could clearly see how his fitted white T-shirt hugged his muscles.

I was sure the noise in the gym was as loud as the actual evening. If I'd closed my eyes, I could have pretended I had heaved the huge hands of time back two days and was actually sitting ringside. All the boxers screamed their instructions at a glass screen. They cursed the ref and applauded their wins. Mickey relished his pugilistic glory and bowed in front of the screen.

"Feck-off outa the road, Mickey, ya big eejit. We can see enough of ya on the telly." Mickey ignored their taunts and pulled his trousers down to once again reveal his backside. This time Doctor Sudki wasn't present to examine it.

The excited noise echoed around the gym. It bounced off the scuffed wooden floors and hit the high ceiling, which was covered with Georgian plaster-cornices. Bunches of grapes and majestic bowls of fruit were decoratively depicted on the ceiling's banquet table. The grand plaster moulds appeared so out of place next to the huge bolts which held the boxing bags in position. Before Dad had rescued the hall from drowning in the ocean of dilapidation, it had once been a place where couples waltzed and tangoed, quick-stepped and jived, but as a sign of the times it had died and been replaced by dancing of a different kind. Patrick's one two three, slip the punch, one two; one, two three, one two, was the closest the old dancehall came to a Viennese waltz. And waltz Patrick did in the finals, out of trouble as he had done in the semis, evading his opponent, causing him to trip, lose his fight plan, get frustrated and get hit. Patrick's punches were like machine-gun fire. He had fired a belt of ammunition in a few seconds, hitting the same spot and causing continual destruction, which attained him, by a unanimous decision, the title of Featherweight British Amateur Boxing Association Champion, 1987.

As the bell was rung for round one, I watched Emmet immediately come to life, unlike in the semi-finals where he had taken a straight right from Derek Johnson to act as jump leads to jump-start his aggression-engine. All his punches transported themselves on the wings of victory. They transported so much artistic punishment that his opponent's corner-man subtly skimmed a sweat-and-blood-stained white towel under the bottom rope. The towel came to an abrupt halt as it wrapped around the ref's shining black shoes, stopping the fight at the end of round two and earning Emmet the distinguished title of lightweight champion.

Dominic came out like the proverbial bull in a china

shop, ploughing down any obstacles in his way. The obstacle in question was a valuable piece of southern porcelain - the golden boy from Repton Boys' Club. The referee separated Dom and the ten stone seven pound china doll at every opportunity he could, protecting the Repton Boy from Dominic's brutally antagonistic punches. The referee bestowed upon Dominic, in the space of thirty seconds of round one - to the joy of the Repton Boy's supporters - not one, but two public warnings for unlawful use of his head. They were totally unjustified. In the London Stadium as well as the gym the ref was bombarded with appropriate denunciations.

A public warning meant each judge was to deduct one point from their score cards. Two public warnings meant yet another subtracted point, but a third public warning would result in disqualification.

Dominic looked bewildered by the warnings as he sat on the corner stool. As Dad performed his ambidextrous activities of towel swinging and *Gunga Din* impersonation, it soon became obvious that the public warnings had planted a seed of fury not astonishment in his brain. Dad's seed of fury had developed into a towel-spinning frenzy. Dad's gyrating body caused the inevitable, although somewhat accelerated, fall of the tracksuit bottoms, and the crack of Dad's backside put in its glorious appearance.

"What's it like having a famous arse, Rory?" one of the White brothers asked.

"Ask Mickey, he'll tell yers. His has seen more daylight than most!"

Dad's seed of fury must have cross-pollinated in the wind of the spinning towel and gestated itself in the womb of Dom's brain, because he came out for round two with an anger I had never before witnessed on his face. The seed grew fast and strong and out of it was born a babe-of-destruction in the form of a straight right cross which greedily fed on the annihilation of his opponent. The babe sat fat-bellied and full, as the Repton china doll lay on the

300

canvas, cracked from head to toe. We watched his punch, which had flowed down the invisible pipe, over and again. Stop. Rewind. Play. Stop. Rewind. Play. Dom had evaded another public warning and won the Welterweight A.B.A title, 1987.

Dad made almost as many appearances in the ring as the referee, accompanying, as well as my three favourites, his other boxers: Errol Williams, Luke McCabe, Frankie Duffy, Darren White, Gerard Nolan, Sean McCabe and Mickey Duffy. They all entered the ring and contributed their wins to make the Birmingham Irish Boxing Club the first single establishment ever to have won more than five British titles in one year. To add to that record, there were the largest amount of sibling winners too and once again they were all from our club: the Emmets, the McCabes, the Duffys.

Each and every boxer representing Dad's club had looked both stylish and formidable in the ring. But looking at that same group of boys in the gym, cackling like a group of broody mother hens, donning their mothers' underwear which was stuffed with protection bandages and boxing gloves - they looked ridiculous, and hardly what you could call indestructible. But looks, as I knew well, could be devilishly deceiving!

"That was yer first surprise." I could feel the slight stubble on Emmet's chin as he whispered in my ear. It made all the fine hairs on my body stand to attention, as though they were saluting his attractiveness, like soldiers on parade. When I overcame the initial thrill of his touch and comprehended his comment, my brain screeched *'at ease'* and the hairs resumed their slouching, idle post.

"No more surprises, Emmet, please. Don't you think I've had enough torture?"

"Yes, and yer took it well, so yer did. But this is an even better surprise. A little reward, yer could say. Come on, we'd better get off, or we'll be late."

"Be late for what?"

"Arrah, come on, Orlagh, where's your sense of adventure?"

"I think I have enough adventure with you lot around me. I don't need any more winding up, I'm going nowhere." I was an over-wound watch and my coiled spring was just about to break. But what was I doing refusing to go somewhere with Emmet? I'd go anywhere with Emmet, even at the cost of further humiliation. I quickly changed my mind. "Oh, all right then, let's go."

"That was a sudden change of heart."

"Well, I'm just warning you, Emmet, you're to blame if I don't like this surprise."

"Oh, there's not a doubt in my mind that yer not gonna love it," he said, while having trouble unclipping his bra.

"Shows how often you get to do that, O'Malley," Dominic bantered.

"Arrah, but, Dom, it's not very often I'm in this position doin' the unfastenin'. If you're an expert at takin' a bra off while yer wearin' it, we've got some worryin' to do." He glanced over to Dad. "We're off then, Rory."

"All right, watch yer driving."

We both walked out of the gym together, which wasn't an unusual occurrence; it had happened many times before, but what was unusual about it was that no one followed. As the poster-covered doors closed and we proceeded to walk across the car park, I glanced over my shoulder.

"What're yer looking for?"

"Where's everyone else?"

"Oh, there's no one else, Orle. There's just me and you and a dog named Boo." Grabbing my hand, he led me towards his car. I was mortified. Emmet and myself alone? I couldn't stand it. It was pure torture in itself, never mind the surprise he had in store. I adored every chestnut hair, every bone, every inch of skin (not that I'd been introduced to all of it) and every word which emanated from his mouth in his soft Derry accent.

"See that there, Orlagh." He pointed up into the cloudless

night-time sky, where it appeared a cyclone of darkness had swept through and left a debris of speckled stars. "Do yer know what that is?"

"Which? The Starry Plough?"

"My, yer a clever wee one. But who does the Starry Plough represent?"

"James Connolly... My Grandpa Dominic, that's Dad's dad, was supposed to have seen the Starry Plough as a sign to fall in love with my Nanna Bridie. He came out of the pub, saw it shimmering in the Dublin sky and decided it was a sign from Connolly himself to pursue her love. To fight for her, to work for her."

"I think a few people've fallen in love under it, Orlagh, and I suspect a few more will in the future." I silently wished it would be us, as I bet my grandpa had silently cursed the night he first set eyes on Nanna Bridie.

"Do you know what James Connolly stood for, Orlagh?"

"Yeah, for the freedom of Ireland. He was a leader in the 1916 Easter rebellion. Grandpa Dominic was actually under James Connolly's command in the G.P.O." Happy with my knowledge, I delivered a self-satisfied smile.

"But that's not all." Emmet ignored my jovial smugness. "He's not just about Irish freedom under war. He was for the people. He wanted to cease the exploitation of the Irish workin'-classes. He was fightin' for the workin'-class struggle against capitalism. The capitalists who were invadin' our beautiful Ireland from England, exploitin' the poor to near slavery. The same capitalists who weren't interested in givin' jobs to the Irish people, but interested in the control of the Irish economy to boost the British economy. Connolly fought for *their* rights - the ordinary *Irishman's* rights."

It sounded like Irish freedom to me, whichever way he put it. But I wasn't about to argue because he'd lost me at capitalism. But, even if I had wanted to, I wouldn't have been able to have my say, he was off - and there was no stopping him.

"You know what, Orle?"

"What?"

He pulled me by the hand to face him and with his free arm he gestured to the star-spangled sky and broke into song, "Oh, it's a marvellous night for a..." I was silent. Surely he didn't want me to sing with him? I didn't want to make a fool of myself. When the rest of the gang were there, I wouldn't have cared, I would have sung and danced the loudest and most outrageous. Us alone - I was strangely bashful. He spun me in circles, then under his arms and continued; "Come on, Orlagh, I know yer love Van The Man. What is it? Oh, it's a marvellous night for a..."

Sighing, I quietly uttered, "Moon dance."

"With the stars up above in the sky. A fantaboulous night to make..."

"Romance?" I cringed as I filled in his gap, because little did he know how much I desired it.

"Neath the cover of an October sky... Well it's March, but we can still make romance under it, Orlagh."

I was embarrassed, blushing and wishing he'd sing some more so he wouldn't notice. He may have been joking but I wasn't. Every second I spent with him I longed for more. He had injected his presence in my body like an addict injects their heroin. He pumped adrenaline around my body, which was transported in each and every capillary. It rushed through my veins, oxygenated in my lungs, run through my arteries and sprinted to my heart, making it pump faster and what I imagined to be *louder*.

"Oi, Emmet." I had been saved by Dave, the pub landlord. He didn't speak in a feigned camp tone as he had when he'd spotted Dad in a bra, but in his masculine Birmingham accent: "Well dun for winnin' Sat-dey, mate. I'd put all me money on ya and I won a few bob. I'll buy ya a drink, an orange juice or sum-ut."

I didn't want Dave to ask me why Dad had been wearing a bra; I'd sustained enough embarrassment regarding that issue. So, as their conversation continued,

I made a swift escape and entered Emmet's car. I slammed the door and the car rocked, causing the rosary beads which hung from the rear-view mirror to swing from side to side. Jesus was like a child on a playground swing; he gracefully glided to-and-fro. The silver crucifix caught the light from the street lamp, making it glisten like one of the many stars Emmet had just serenaded - back and forth, side to side. It placed me in an hypnotic state. Jesus was my hypnotist who was instructing me to show Emmet just how much I adored him. The driver's door was slammed and Emmet bounded in. Jesus swung out of control and I terminated my astral travelling and steered myself back down to earth. Emmet's fingers steadied the rocking Jesus and my attention diverted to his extremely long, clean fingernails. They were the pink of a baby's bum with perfect half-moons, the white part elongated above the tips of his fingers. A smile crept across my face when I viewed his nails, it always did. It's just that I could see Siobhan's face the first time she had noticed them. She had screwed up her facial features and bit her bottom lip as though she was in pain. She hunched over and grabbed her pelvic bone with her two hands. 'The thought of it, Orlagh. Awh, owe. It's gotta hurt.'

"What're ye smirkin' at, cheeky?" He pinched my cheek which inhabited the four-by-two-inch red mark. I wondered if he noticed it? Did it bother him? I could never work it out because he never mentioned it; he didn't even try to steal a secret look when he thought I was unaware.

"I wasn't smirking."

"You were, come on, throw it at me. What smart comment've yer got rolled up yer sleeve? There's usually one ready to pounce. Come on, I'm ready, give it yer best shot - on the chin." He pointed at his stubbled chin.

"I haven't, there's no comment this time... really." And there wasn't. Usually I could banter with the best - even Emmet. I would throw taunts at him as good as one of the lads. I *was* one of the lads - but that was when I was

305

encapsulated in the safety bubble of the gym, with the rest of the gang close by. Here it was just the two of us and for no particular reason he managed to turn me to jelly. I was in an almost permanent dumbfounded daze - like the first time I had set eyes on him. I had once again been hit with that cartoon character's sledge-hammer and the stars erratically flying from my head were on a journey to join James Connolly's Starry Plough, carrying in their trail my brain cells. But Emmet was at ease - as always. He sang some more, talked continuously and still wouldn't tell me my surprise.

We drove through the city centre, which was almost desolate in the midst of a lonely Monday night. Shoppers and workers were in the warmth of their homes, while the homeless snuggled up to their black and white dogs as they lay in urine-smelling doorways. A bottle of scrumpy in a creased, brown paper bag was their only company.

The advertising clock which flashed at the top of the Rotunda building was missing something. It flashed, 'oca-ola', and only the minutes of the time flashed on and off. What was the point in minutes without hours? Or Coca-Cola with no c?

We parked the car, slammed the doors and Jesus rocked.

"Where're we going, Emmet? Nothin' is open now."

"You'll soon see, so yer will."

We entered the popcorn-smelling Odeon Cinema and Emmet bought tickets for two to see, 'Dirty Dancing'. There was no entourage of bra-wearing boxers ready to pounce from behind the candy stand. There was no underlying witticism in the title, so why? Like the flashing sign on the Rotunda building - I was missing the point. Why was Emmet bringing me here? Alone? The bulbs of my own flashing sign required replacement. I needed clarification. I just couldn't work it out. I shouldn't really care, I thought - not everything can be explained. All that mattered was that I was with Emmet (with my knee touching his) watching Baby Houseman and the ruggedly

306

handsome Johnny Castle fall in love while doing some dirty dancing. I decided to light up my own bulbs, fill in my own gaps and make it whatever time I wanted it to be!

On the way home I'd found my tongue again and talked ceaselessly; my shyness had been strangely lifted. I informed him of *my* love for America and the fun I'd had there. About evading Sambo and of Teddy Bailey's 'Biga Rosa in Chattanooga, with the bigga da like a watermelons.' I thought that story appropriate, considering the earlier underwear performance. I even filled in his gaps without the slightest hesitation.

"The night we met I knew Iiiiiii... needed you..." Emmet pointed to me and Jesus bopped as we bounced along the road.

"So-oooo..."

"And if I had the chance, Orlagh... Iiiiiii'd never let you..."

"Go-oooo..."

"So won't you say you love..."

"Me!" I was wishing I could.

"I'll make you so proud of..."

"Me!"

"We'll make 'em turn their heads, Orlagh... every place we..."

"Go-o-o-o-o."

His volume raised and his left palm slapped my knee vigorously to the beat of the chorus. "So won't you ple-eaa-ease be my, be my, be my, come on, Orlagh, be my little baby."

We both sang in unison, "My one and only baby." We arrived at my house, my knee was slapped harder and Emmet serenaded me, face to face. His eyes danced to his song, his thick brown eyebrows were jumping, endeavouring to reach his hair-line. His voice deepened and he attempted a serious look. "Say you'll be my darlin'." He did his own echo. "My darlin'." While a voice in my own head shouted and reverberated, 'I will, I swear I will... Forever.'

"Orlagh, be my, be my, be my baby noooo-ow, oh, oh, oh, oh, oh..."

On his 'oh's' his chin had lowered a notch along with his

voice, and his hand clutched my knee tighter. He concluded with his chin on his chest while looking at me from under his huge brows. I laughed so hard because if I didn't I would have looked at him in a way where he could have looked through my eyes as though they were clear glass and viewed my every thought.

"Go on now, I'll be seeing yer at the gym on Wednesday." He placed his sumptuous moist lips on my forehead for what seemed like an eternity. I fumbled to open the door.

"Thanks, Emmet, that was great."

"Well, we're mates and that's what mates do. Goodnight and God bless, angel-face."

Every pessimistic thought in my head had been eradicated, wiped out - exterminated. The insecticide was a noxious dosage of Emmet O'Malley. It attacked the nervous system of every memory of the derogatory rejection I had experienced in Italy. Those memories wriggled and fought for existence, but melancholy was no match for the euphoria that Emmet instilled.

"So he didn't kiss you?" Siobhan interrogated the following morning, as the frosted grass crunched under our shoes as we made our way to school.

"No, not properly anyway." I grinned as I remembered each moment.

"But he must've. Why're you so happy, so, ha de har har har? You spend so much time with him anyway, what was so special about last night?"

"It just was, there was like this bond between us. We're in this like magnetic field and we're being pulled together by this magnetic force. But at the moment there's something blockin' the force. I think it's the age thing. I'm only almost fifteen remember and he's nineteen. It matters now, but when I get older the gap gets smaller and it's not as significant. Look at me mammy and daddy, there's ten years between them and you wouldn't think it. You'll see we'll be

308

like a magnet and a paper-clip. There's a force there, Shiv, I'm tellin' you."

"Oh, God, no. Get the violins out. You and your magnets, you've been spending too much time in your physics book if you ask me. I sure hope this paper-clip thing happens soon, Orlagh, 'cause I can't stand looking into those glossy eyes for much longer."

"It will... I hope."

BOOK THREE

CHAPTER THIRTY-EIGHT

'End of an era,' was Dad's most famous saying. It was uttered whenever something - *anything* - changed. When he recited the tales of when he permanently departed, first from America, then Canada, 'End of an era.' When each of us left primary school, 'End of an era.' When Dom, then Pat, left senior school, 'End of an era.' When Dom finished university, 'End of an era.' When Father Martin Maguire left our parish on his redemptorist mission to Africa, 'End of an era.' When Dom, Pat and myself had had enough of playing and hearing *Für Elise*. Our grades were passed and we no longer had any need for the piano and it departed along with Beethoven, Bach and Brahms. 'End of an era,' Dad said once again, shaking his head in his usual sad, nostalgic kind of way, as we transferred the ownership of the ancient Steinway over to our one-toothed, blind piano-tuner.

There were so many eras which I wished would come to an end but stubbornly they refused. The era I longed - more than any - to come to a close was the one which would witness the end of me saying '*No,* he didn't' in answer to Siobhan's 'Did Emmet kiss you?' question.

Almost two years had passed since *Dirty Dancing*. Each and every Sunday evening Emmet and I visited the cinema.

My diary was crammed with Odeon tickets taped to their pages, and next to them a detailed explanation of the journey, the hand touches, the leg touches, the song gaps I filled in, the pecks on my forehead or the end of my nose. At times Dominic, Patrick, Mickey Duffy, and a couple of McCabe brothers joined us, but generally it was only Emmet and myself. Two years had passed of me wishing my weeks away for Sunday to arrive. Two years of sitting through Mass and daydreaming through the Gospel: daydreams in which I visualised myself slowly walking down the red-carpeted aisle, to stand at the altar where I would vow to love, honour and obey Emmet. Two years of constant dreaming. Two years of frustration.

My sixteenth birthday - which I considered to be my arrival into adulthood - had arrived and departed without any acknowledgement from Emmet. So my theory of the age issue blocking the romantic magnetic force was destroyed. I cursed myself for selecting the most unobtainable infatuation. For picking the one who owned looks which surpassed those of the movie stars we would watch each Sunday. For choosing the one who had the blackbird gliding through paradise sky-blue eyes, which themselves selected the most sought-after girls: blondes, brunettes, red-heads - it didn't matter. All had perfect little figures and fluttering eyelashes. Emmet O'Malley was most definitely the Everest of obsessions to conquer. I hadn't even reached base camp of my Everest obsession and my breathing was laborious. Maybe I was rushing the acclimatisation period, because the altitude sickness prevailed: the headaches, the shortness of breath, the endless sleepless nights and the nauseating gnawing in my stomach. Perhaps I should be patient and evoke the words of Plato, which were first taught by the leprechaun angel. *Tempus omnia revelat. Time brings everything.* If I waited long enough, maybe my red blood cells which are stuffed with oxygen-carrying haemoglobin would multiply, aiding me to make it to the summit of my Everest obsession, where I could bask in the beauty of God's extraordinary creation... It was all relative to time. I had to wait for the seconds to turn into minutes, minutes into hours, hours into days - but the waiting game was getting frustrating. I merely wanted to squeal 'yeeeeessss' in reply to Siobhan's weekly question, until the muscles in my neck ached and my throat became hoarse. I desperately wanted to say, 'end of one era - beginning of another.'

Another era which wasn't ending was that of my birthmark removal, red blood cells which I most certainly wanted to eradicate - not multiply. But an era which did end was one I didn't wish to - one which saw me being treated by Doctor Callaghan.

"Orlagh, I've got some great news."

"What's that then, Mammy?"

"You're going to be changing doctor. You're leaving Doctor Callaghan and moving to Doctor Delaney."

"And can you tell me what's so good about that?"

"Well, for the first time in sixteen years we won't have to drive all over the country. The laser clinic is right here in Birmingham, at the Selly Oak Hospital."

"But Doctor Callaghan's great and he knows me really well. Why do I have to start all over again with some new doctor who doesn't have a clue about my birthmark? Doctor Callaghan knows everything about my treatment, he knows where my birthmark has been treated and how many times."

"That'll all be passed on to the new doctor, Orlagh, you know that."

"But Doctor Callaghan is the one that started this whole laser procedure over here, so he's the expert. This new doctor will be second best. Why do I have to change again?"

"I'm sorry you feel that way, Orlagh, but I think you're just being silly. We'll see how it goes next week on your first appointment. If you really don't like him we'll see what we can do, but I'm sure you will."

* * *

It had taken us a mere thirty minutes to drive from the north side of Birmingham, under the intertwining concrete serpents of Spaghetti Junction, through the incomprehensible underpasses, flyovers and one-way systems in the city centre and over to the south side of the city. We drove through the tree-lined streets of Bournville where the Quaker Cadbury family had built quaint cottages in a village-like area to house the staff which created their delectable chocolate - and on to the hospital I didn't want to attend, which housed a doctor I didn't want to be treated by. I was being a brat, but my unusual silence in the car didn't faze Dad. He dismissed my sulk and sang all the way, prompting Mammy to fill in his gaps. Mammy was also quiet and entirely apathetic in the filling of Dad's gaps, but unlike me she wasn't sulking. The key had been inserted and slowly turned, implementing the engine of her intuitive pain reactor to purr like the engine of a Rolls Royce. It never faltered, just methodically ticked over. Whether it was rain, snow or sunshine, the pistons were being pushed up and down by a never-ending supply of fuel. Her fuel hadn't originated from sediments of eras which had ended thousands of millennia ago, but by the mere thought of my pain.

On entering the new laser clinic we were taken by a receptionist nurse to an unused hospital room. Dad softly bounced on a single bed covered with white starched sheets that had 'Birmingham Health Auth' sewn through the centre, as though he was in a furniture shop testing the bed's capabilities with all intentions of buying it. The nurse was not amused.

That same nurse began to ask lots of questions: medical history, address, GP's name. Ridiculous questions which incensed me because she should have known them. But the most ridiculous question which ignited the furious fire which had been smouldering within me since I had discovered I had to change doctors, was:

"So, Orlagh, have you started your periods?"

"What!" It was a shocked, *what!* Not a pardon, *what?* Why did she have to ask me that? In front of Mammy would have been embarrassing enough, but in front of Dad it was unambiguously humiliating. I felt the flames of my furious fire rising and cooking my face into a red ball. My eyes fixed on the pale blue 'Birmingham Health Auth' being distorted by Dad's bouncing. I couldn't comprehend what this had to do with my being there; it was the blood vessels in my face which were causing the problems, not ones coming from my nether regions. Dad continued to bounce and stared out of the window into the full car park, trying hard not to reveal his own embarrassment.

"Have you started your periods?" More fuel on my fire.

"*No*. No I haven't."

As she ticked or crossed her box and continued the onslaught of questions in a nonchalant, conceited manner, my anxiety, anger and embarrassment metamorphosed into an internal inferno that I was convinced couldn't be extinguished. I had suspected moving doctors was going to be disastrous, but not that cataclysmic.

When she had finished, I departed the room with added animosity embedded into each step I took; my heels dug into the shining rubbery vinyl. I was almost pushing Mam and Dad past the point of their forbearance. I was embarrassing them with my infantile tantrum. I knew it was time to calm down, but I couldn't nudge the senseless anger from my mind. It was like an annoying ulcer in my mouth. If I had left it alone it would have healed and gone away, but I kept biting, chewing and gnawing. That was until another patient arrived in the waiting area. Not just any patient, but the patient who I had first observed two years prior in Southampton General Hospital - the elderly lady who had a red pirate's patch port-wine stain over one of her bulbous tropical sea-blue eyes.

After that first encounter two years previous, when her face had seemed to have a mysterious familiarity, I had

317

continued to see her. On each of my three-monthly laser treatments she would either be leaving as I entered or vice-versa. She always smiled and nodded.

When the pirate-patch lady entered the waiting room at the Selly Oak Hospital, my attitude immediately changed. She was the soothing, healing Bongela on my mouth ulcer of anger. She was the fire blanket suffocating my internal inferno. I felt she would be judging me and I wanted her respect, even though she didn't know me. So I smiled and pretended I didn't have a care in the world. Dad squeezed my hand which sat palm down on my thigh, in a 'that's a good girl' gesture.

I was quite surprised she was actually here as Southampton was over two hundred miles away. I thought what a strange coincidence it was that she too had changed doctors to Selly Oak Hospital. A striking pain suddenly cut through my head, causing me to screw my eyes shut and hold my head in my hands. The pain subsided as the tiny cherub straddled on the bumblebee's back took flight through my mind; "Remember, Orlagh, there's no such thing as a coincidence..." It departed my mind as quickly as it had appeared, leaving only the distant buzz of the bumblebee.

I was determined to speak to the mysterious pirate-patch lady. Mam and Dad obviously hadn't recognised her, as they most definitely would have struck up a conversation. I was about to interrupt her reading when the interrogating nurse summoned me: "Orlagh Emmet, Doctor Delaney's ready to see you."

As we walked past the mysterious pirate-patch lady, she glanced up from her magazine and smiled. Crow's feet landed in the corner of her eyes, but then took flight as she raised her eyebrows in mischievous recognition, creating a washboard on her forehead. I was definitely going to speak to her after my *undesired* consultation.

* * *

318

Doctor Delaney contradicted every offensive thought I'd had about him and his treatment. He was conscientious, extremely friendly, *and famous*.

"Are you that doctor off the TV who treats tribes people in the Amazon Rainforest?"

"Yes, Orlagh, I'm that very man."

"But on TV you treat rare skin disorders, severe burns and deformities, not birthmarks."

"Goodness, you sound like my number one fan. You must've enjoyed the series we did then, Orlagh? You're right, I do a lot of plastic surgery in the Amazon, but don't you worry, I know what I'm doing here. Doctor Callaghan's taught me all there is to know about removing port-wine stains with the Argon Laser. And together we've also been learning a whole new procedure done with a new laser called the Pulse Dye. It promises a ninety-five percent success rate in removing marks. It's much finer-tuned than this Argon Laser and doesn't cause any scarring at all."

"I think my mammy read something to me about that, but she's always finding out about new things, so I didn't take much notice. When can I start having that treatment then, Doctor?"

"The National Heath are trying to acquire a Pulse-dye Laser, Orlagh. Hopefully it won't be too long, though." I'd heard 'not too long' before - I wasn't about to hold my breath.

Doctor Delaney was still tanned from his latest expedition to Brazil - and handsome, in a mature middle-aged manner. But his admirable appearance didn't distract my mind from my usual agony-alleviating mantra which I recited over and over. 'If I go through this pain, maybe, just maybe Emmet O'Malley would consider me romantically.'

The Argon Laser was a despicable procedure, regardless of which doctor performed it. I could smell my hair and then my skin burn as the laser was guided across my face in small lines. The concept was that the following time I went for treatment the doctor would go in-between the lines he had previously treated. But it never worked like that, as there was barely a significant result. The procedure produced scar tissue rather than eliminating over-active blood vessels, so detection of the previous treatment was difficult and the same areas were being done over and over with no consequential effect. It was all getting very disconcerting, but I continued to go, resilient and optimistic.

My upset on that particular day was more due to the disappearance of the enigmatic, pirate-patched lady. Dad and I departed the operating theatre to retrieve Mammy, who sat nervously twiddling her thumbs and masticating her bottom lip.

"Where's the old lady, Mammy?"

"Which old lady?"

"Well, she's not really old, older than Dad anyway."

"There's no old lady here, Orlagh. Come on, let's get you home and wrapped up warm on the settee. Isn't it great that you're going to be home in no time at all?"

"Don't worry about the settee, Mammy. I know there's no old lady now; that's why I asked where she was. Did you see where she went?"

"Orlagh, I didn't see an old lady, or any lady for that matter. Why do you care anyway? Who is she?"

"I don't know; that's what I want to find out." I sensed I was confusing Mam and Dad as much as I was bewildered.

How could Mammy not have noticed her? She had been the only other person in the waiting area. Mam was usually so observant too. It made me wonder if I had really seen her. Or was it that I just wished to see her? Although I wasn't usually in the habit of seeing people no one else could see, except a strange shadow-like person in my sleep, and angels of course. Was *she* an angel? Was she there to watch over me through my treatment? Was she the one who removed my pain, who aided in silencing my psychological anger and gave me the strength to continue almost carefree through life, being different? I wanted to interrogate the *interrogating* nurse, but not surprisingly she wasn't around to answer *my* questions. So I left speculating about the pirate-patched lady's miraculous status.

Unperturbed, I continued Argon Laser treatment with my replacement famous doctor at the Selly Oak Hospital. Much to my disappointment, I didn't see the pirate-patched lady there again. To my further disappointment, I didn't see any results from the painful treatment either. I incessantly scanned my face in the mirror, hunting for white among the red. I pressed my fingers hard on the birthmark to watch it momentarily go white and then reappear in all its crimson glory. I pulled and stretched, prodded and poked, but the birthmark had hardly altered. Maybe the new treatment Doctor Delaney talked about would make a difference. Maybe it would mark the end of that particular birthmark-owning era.

chapter thirty-nine

The era which I was adamant was most certainly going to end did not make Mammy at all happy.

"Orlagh, I can't believe you don't you want to go to college. You're such a high achiever. It'll be such a waste for you to finish your education now."

"I see no point in wasting my time studying for something I'll never use, Mammy. But, if I get a job I can get an education and money all in one go. Out of everyone I know going to college, not one of them knows what they want to do. They're just wasting time. It's not that I don't enjoy learning, because I do, you know that. I'm always reading a million and one books a week." I didn't add this was because I was searching for fascinating ammunition which I could place in my cannon so I could blow Emmet away with my astounding intellect. "No one I know reads as much as me. But what's the point in going to college when there's no specific profession I want to study for? I can't comprehend wasting years studying for something I won't ever use." I also failed to add that there was an unexplainable force, with an obscure message, steering me in the opposite direction to institutionalised education. The force obliterated each thought I had about going to college. Its voice told me I needed to work, earn money and patiently await my orders. I hoped the opening of my box full of angelic-bestowed knowledge would make things clearer. I hoped clues would trickle out of the box, like the drip, drip, drip on a faulty tap, aiding me to deduce the angelic riddles which had been relayed to me over the years, so I could successfully discover my true, divine destiny.

"Yes, Orlagh, I could appreciate what you're saying if you knew what you wanted to do. But you haven't a clue what you want to do either."

"I know I want to earn money. I know I want to be my own boss. I don't know exactly how yet, but I will. I know there's something big in store for me. Anyway you or Dad didn't go to college or university and look how well you've done."

"Yes, but it was different in our day, Orlagh."

"That's always the excuse, Mammy."

"I did go to university anyway, baby doll."

"That's the first I've heard. Don't lie to me, Dad."

"I did, I swear. I went to the university of the *world*." He waved his huge, opened palm in a swirl above his head. "I travelled and followed my own curriculum. But that's the point - yer've to have some sort of curriculum. Yer can't just bum around. Wherever yer find yerself, you need to listen to the local people and learn from them. Read their politics and history and appreciate their cultures. I experienced it all first-hand, not out of some book. And there's still so much information out there which has never been documented. Information too *dangerous* to be documented! It's the easiest university to get into, but with the hardest work and the lowest success rate."

"Don't encourage her, Rory. You make it all sound so romantic."

"But I have to be honest, Grania. If yer do it properly, no education comes close to travellin'. That is, as I said, if yer do it right. Experiencing different cultures, tastin' diverse foods and visitin' the world's museums, where yer can see and smell the artefacts and masterpieces in real life is an amazin' way to learn. And there're all those geological sights waitin' to be explored, too. You know, the natural wonders of the world."

"I know, Rory... So what're you sayin'? That she should go off and travel the world, instead of being responsible and obtaining a career?"

"I'm not sayin' that at all. *At all*. Although, it wouldn't be such a bad thing if she did go travellin', as long as she was with someone responsible, like Dominic or Patrick. Neither am I suggestin' she should go'nd work in a cake shop or somethin'. But I can see her point. What's the use of her wastin' her time studyin' things she's no interest in?"

"Come on then, missy, what's your big money-making plan?" Mammy's pursed lips and wide eyes gave her that '*I know it all*' look.

"Well, I'm going to apply to the banks. I've no intention of staying there forever, but it's not a bad salary while I decide what I really want to do."

"It's not as easy as that; the banks are pretty selective you know, and you're even leaving before you've got in."

"I know, Mammy, but I was talking to the career adviser and she said that I shouldn't have a problem getting in. I would need to obtain five GCSEs with at least C grades. I'm taking ten and they estimate that I should pass all of them with C grades, or above."

"That's just my point, ten O levels and you don't want to go on to college and then university."

"I thought she said she was taking GC whatever they are, not O levels." Dad looked confused.

"GCSEs are the same, Dad, and if you obtain C or above it's the equivalent of the old O-level system. GCSEs were brought in last year. Anyway, if I want to get into the bank as soon as I leave school, I'll have to start applying now. Is that okay, Mammy?"

"Why bother asking me? It looks as though you've already made up your mind."

"Apply now, baby doll? But when do yer leave school?"

"Well, I'm doing my mock exams right now and I should

be taking the real McCoy from June onwards. So, probably July. Eight months then, give or take a few weeks."

"Jesus, the end..." Dad's head was already shaking as he began his saying, but Mammy and I interrupted him and said in unison;

"We know, we know... the end of an era."

chapter forty

Maybe my pain-alleviating mantra I repeated over and again while having treatment on my birthmark had had some effect, along with my own novenas to the Miraculous Martha, and my continual praying (well, begging) to the Lord. My suspicions that my prayers regarding Emmet and myself in a romantic situation were finally being answered had been excitedly roused upon returning to the gym after a short, unavoidable respite. I had been conscientiously studying for my mock examinations and had not been training for a couple of weeks.

"Orlagh, why don't yer leave that revising malarkey for tonight? If yer don't know it now, sweetheart, yer never will. Yer'll only be gettin' wound up. Why don't ye give it a rest and let off some steam at the gym?" Dad enthusiastically proclaimed, as he tucked into his mustard-pasted and Worcestershire sauce-drenched steak, bare-chested with his after-shower teddy-boy hair-do. He was right, I had been getting wound up, staring at what appeared to be identical mathematical equations and reading over the same English texts.

"What's the enthusiasm for, Rory? What're you up to?"

"Nothin', nothin' at all. I just don't want her brain overloading... that's all."

"That's not all, there's always something else. Come on, what is it?" On each syllable Mammy pointed the wooden spoon in Dad's direction, with her only rubber glove-covered hand on her hip.

"All right, all right. I'll *never* get one past yer mother, kids... never. How long've we been married, Grania?"

"Too long," Mammy stated, with her back to us as she stirred our custard in the pan.

"Oh, she's on form tonight, so she is."

"What is it then, Dad? Why do you really want me at the gym? Are there some new troublemakers or something?"

"You've got it in one, doll, and my God we'll teach 'em a lesson. They're worse than the usual ones that we get. They've been runnin' wild. They've been there two days and it feels like two months - whipping each other with the skippin' ropes, kickin' the bags, and they were tryin' to bully the little ones as well."

"Well, why didn't you just throw 'em out, Rory?"

"Because we have to teach 'em a lesson, Grania. A good beatin' with the added humiliation of it being delivered by a girl, is the best education these little toe-rags will learn. I'll be doin' 'em a favour in the long run. They reckon they've boxed at another club. I didn't question 'em though, 'cause a blind man could tell they'd never been in a ring before. Sure, they wouldn't know a left hook from a coat hook."

"But why does Orlagh have to be the one to teach 'em a lesson? She's busy revising."

"Grania, she's one of the best boxers - boy or girl - I've ever seen and I'm not just sayin' that 'cause she's me baby doll. I know she can handle herself in that ring, I wouldn't put her in jeopardy now, would I? Anyway, it separates the men from the boys. If they get through Orlagh givin' 'em a beatin' they won't forget in a hurry and they want to stay on in the gym then they're definitely worth teachin'. This time I think it's going to surpass all the other lessons we've taught bullies before because these boys are a nightmare, I tell yer."

"Oh, whatever, I've no say at all when it comes to you lot and that boxing gym. Just be careful."

* * *

327

"Hey, who's this stranger invading our territory, boys?" Emmet shouted from the porch area, as Dad, Dominic, Patrick and myself walked towards him. His white teeth shone in the evening sky.

"Listen, lads, before them new eejits arrive," Dad began to the crowd of his boxers huddled in the porch as he fiddled around trying to find the correct key on his bunch of many. "Don't pay any attention to Orlagh. Make sure everyone who arrives gets to know, 'cause we're gonna have a little light entertainment tonight, and we wouldn't want to spoil the surprise now would we?"

The air in the gym was colder than the December air outside. It was air which penetrated every area of uncovered skin, sneaking in through every open pore or orifice, to strangle your lungs and fight with your nerves. Air which turned your escaping breath into a visible, fleeing spirit. I must have unconsciously shivered because Mickey Duffy, who was walking in behind me, rubbed the tops of my arms.

"We'll soon get ya warmed up, Orlagh, me girl." Mickey ceased the arm rubbing and started massaging my shoulders as though I was a championship boxer about to enter the ring.

"Hey, hands off there, Duffy. She's mine, so she is," Emmet declared, elbowing Mickey in his kidneys as he passed.

"You wish, O'Malley." I was the only one wishing as I walked away laughing to hide my embarrassment.

The cold air soon warmed up as the gym filled with all my beloved boys. A Chinese whisper circulated and I was ignored as I silently shadow-boxed in the U-shaped alcove of mirrors. It had once been the cloakroom when the gym had been a dance hall, so it was private and secluded. I stood in my orthodox stance with my left foot forward and threw punches at my own image. I annihilated my muscular reflection, imagining it was the bully Dad would soon be placing me in the ring with. I picked my punches: body to head, jabs, straight rights, hooks and uppercuts. I watched my birthmark disappear as it gradually blended in with the mass of heated blood vessels which invaded my face. I admired my face when it was flushed.

"Hey, boys, calm down there, would yers? Yer've only been in five minutes and yers are causing trouble," I heard Dad shout, at what I suspected were the new boys, (the regulars knew better) as I continued with the abolition of my reflection.

"The bags are meant to be hit, ent they?" one of the bullies cheekily replied. I was sure I recognised his voice. I tried to catch a glimpse of him in the mirror, but there were too many swinging bags and bobbing and weaving bodies in the way.

"With yer fists yeah, not yer feet. This is boxin', not kick boxin' you fuckin' little prick," Mickey Duffy shouted, quickly losing his temper.

"Why don't I teach you a bit of both in the ring. I'll kick your arse," the bully fatuously threatened Mickey.

"Listen army-boy, I'll..." Mickey began.

"It's all right, Mick, we'll calm him down a bit now. Do yer fancy a little sparrin' then, son?" My heart began to beat faster; I knew this was my cue.

"Yeah, of course I do. I've bin 'ere all week and I ent got in the ring once."

I stopped my shadow-boxing and rested my arms by my side. I now had a good view of my imminent opponent. Dad had chosen the largest out of the three disrupters for me to spar. That would prove his point that little bit more. He must have stood four inches taller than me, and at least a couple of stone heavier. He was dressed in cut-off army-camouflage trousers with a 'do not ban the bomb' T-shirt. Flabby love handles protruded from his waist. His face along with his voice sounded familiar, but I couldn't quite place where I knew him from.

"So, yer've definitely boxed before then, son?"

"Yeah, I told ya that already."

"Where was that at now? Me memory's terrible, so it is."

He mumbled something under his breath and said, "Jaguar Boys." I'd heard that before. It couldn't be who I thought it was. But as each new sentence emanated from the nicotine-stained-toothed mouth, I suspected it was. "Yeah, and Glen Parva." he added, with pride.

"Is that supposed to impress me, son, that you've been in reform school? 'Cause it doesn't. All I need to know is your fight record, not your criminal one. I wouldn't want yer getting hurt in that ring."

"I've had loads of fights. Too many to remember."

"Okay then, as long as yer know what you're doing. Come and get gloved up. What's yer name again, son? I told yer, me memory is not what it used to be."

"Cause you're punchy, that's why!" Luke McCabe contributed.

Dad winked at Luke as my suspicions on the identity of the bully were quickly established. He had gained a few pounds since our last encounter, grown quite a few inches and the strawberry-blond hair now appeared the same browny-yellow as his teeth.

"Jimmy's the name. But everyone calls me Jimmy The Nut."

"Okey-dokey then, Jimbob, up yer get. Come on, princess, are yer ready?"

"What's going on?" He was evidently shocked as Patrick removed my baseball cap and my long spiralled curls bobbed up and down in my ponytail. "You're not putting me in with the girl?"

"Is that a problem? Yer said yer've boxed before, *right?*" Dad tried to conceal his smile.

"Yeah, I have and I'll tear her to pieces. Do ya know what ya doing? I'm ten stone ya know. She must be two stone lighter, and they don't call me Jimmy The Nut for nufink, ya know."

I nodded while jogging on the spot to make sure my face still kept its flushed appearance. It was obvious *Jimmy* didn't recognise me after the two-year gap. He had been expelled from the school along with Steven after the ski-

330

trip thieving episode, so I never did get my added revenge for the glove-theft accusation. Now was the time for nemesis to enter the ring! "Mmm, I'm eight stone, give or take a few pounds," I confirmed.

"Take it easy with him, doll," Dad instructed.

"Take it easy? Are ya serious? You're a crazy paddy man. It must be true what they say about the Irish!"

All the other boys stopped their bag punching, skipping and shadow boxing and congregated around the ring. I basked in the attention and lapped it up like a thirsty dog. James, or Jimmy, or even Jimmy The Nut, took his stance in the centre of the ring. A crafty smile crept on to my face because it was obvious he was clueless. His right foot was forward as if he was a southpaw, but his arms were set in the orthodox position, with his right hand guarding his face and his left ready to jab. The confounding conversation about boxing from our first encounter floated back into my mind; it all made sense now – he had never boxed.

Dad rang the tarnished brass bell.

Ding Ding.

Jimmy The Nut might as well have had a pitchfork wedged in his right red glove as he immediately threw a hay-maker. With my chin well tucked into my chest and my upper body leaning slightly back - no hay was collected. The excuse for a punch continued its descending motion, which left the right side of his face as wide open as his mouth was, exposing those nicotine-stained teeth. I then executed my first shocking punch - a straight left jab which connected with his nose. He frantically blinked, trying to regain his lost vision as water streamed from his tear ducts. With the demise of the excuse of a punch he had thrown, the excuse of a stance also diminished. He now stood square on.

I immediately worked off my back foot to get out of his technically preposterous, although presumably hazardous assault. He was incensed as he attempted a two-fisted attack, proceeding forward as he did, with his elbows at his shoulder level. He advanced to impersonate the oblique blades of a windmill. Still retreating, I shuffled on my back right leg and went straight though the middle of his windmill blades with a double left jab and connected once again in the centre of his face. My chin nestled into my chest evading his windmill punches, which were swinging as though they were producing a life-saving energy force; which of course they were not, the only production being his own frustration.

I had run out of ring. The thick centre rope dug deep into my back and the bottom one skimmed my calf as a heavy-breathing Jimmy The Nut collapsed his ten stone body on top of me. His windmill arms were now either side of my head, resting on my shoulders. His gloves gripped the top rope causing it to delve into my bare neck. It would have been a perfect position for him to smother me with an array of romantic kisses.

"No wrestling - box!" Dad shouted from ringside. "Back to the centre."

"You've fuckin' had it, ya bitch," he mumbled in my ear through his heavy breathing, as he removed his grip of the top rope.

"Don't hold back, O, throw some of your big shots. Teach him a lesson," Patrick whispered, as I walked back to the centre of the ring.

On my arrival in the centre, the scene was as hilarious as his botched stance had been. He must have convinced himself he could actually box. Once again standing square on, he was jumping up and down, with both feet coming slightly off the canvas, appearing like an over-weight kangaroo, his arms as stiff as the stainless-steel levers on an old fashioned one-armed-bandit. Although the black plastic ball was a red leather boxing glove.

"Box on!" Dad instructed, with excited vigour.

I immediately executed a combination four: straight left, straight right, straight left, straight right. My fast, adamantine punches connected with his own hands which were placed too close to his face. He metamorphosed into a self-mutilator, appearing to provide his own punishment. I instantaneously administered a duplicate combination four; the result was identical. I knew I would not be able to throw them again so I took a step back to view his reaction. His elbows were now back up to shoulder level, his forearms jutted out at a ninety-degree angle, one either side of his head - his head which was now face down to the canvas as he began his surge forward. The Paso Doble struck up inside my mind. I was the matador to the angry bull charging towards me. My aficionados screamed instructions from ringside. I teasingly swung my cape in front of the infuriated animal and sidestepped with precision to witness Jimmy The Nut live up to his name, as he charged head first through the ropes and into the poster-covered wall.

"Let him get his composure back, princess," Dad instructed.

His anxiety contributed to his laborious breathing as he retook his ridiculous stance, now placing his gloves six inches apart, one adjacent to each temple.

"Lead with the right, Orle," Emmet shouted.

I desperately wanted to impress Emmet as much as annihilate James. So, I threw a straight right which began in my back right toes and transferred itself through my leg into my waist where I pivoted, instilling all my body weight into the punch, which glided past his useless guard and collided with his mouth. I quickly retrieved my right hand which left me in the perfect position to execute a left hook which connected on the point equidistant between his ear and his chin. I followed with another devastating straight right hand which crushed into the tip of his nose and mouth. The explosion of blood was like a bursting pipe in a gory episode of *Hammer House Of Horror*.

He fell to his haunches, put the huge red gloves in front of his bleeding face and uncontrollably sobbed.

"Okay, let's call it a day now, Orlagh. I think he's learnt his lesson," Dad shouted.

"Orlagh?" he barely whispered, slowly removing his head from his gloves and reclining it to look into my face, astounded.

"Yeah, so that's the second time I've kicked your ass... *Jimmy The Nut!*"

He placed his right hand under his left armpit and struggled, pulling and yanking to quickly remove the glove.

"Come here, son, I'll untie the laces for you." The gym was silent, all eyes were on James. Blood was smudged across his entire face as he raced out of the ring, ignoring Dad's offer and joining his followers who removed a glove each.

"Make sure you don't steal those gloves." I was still in the roped enclosure as I shouted behind a self-satisfied smile.

The well-worn gloves were politely placed on the canvas of the ring and the disgraced James and his entourage proceeded to the exit.

"Hey, son, one last thing before yer go. What is that *they say* about the Irish?" Dad asked, mock-intrigued.

He scurried out like a cockroach when a light comes on.

"Da - da - da - another one bites the dust. Da - da - da - another bites the dust," all the boys chanted.

I was lying on a beach basking in the zealous, comforting rays of glory.

"May I have the honour of rolling thy bandages, miss?" Emmet asked, in the most ridiculous English accent. He bowed down, swooped his right hand in front of himself while his left arm was placed behind his back, as though he was a regal butler.

Laughing, I ducked under the centre rope and began my descent of the three wooden steps. On reaching the second step Emmet held out his arms as though he was going to whisk me away, like a handsome prince to a destitute princess. I fell into his arms, with my boxing gloves hooked around the back of his neck as he swung me from the steps and placed me on the scratched parquet wooden flooring. I could smell the distinct sweet odour of aftershave-enhanced sweat. My nerve endings reacted to the aromatic amphetamine and they tingled from the nape of my neck to my tail bone. This, added to the boxing adrenaline, produced an absolute ecstasy in my body.

"Are yer cold, princess?"

"No, I'm fine."

"Well, you're soakin', so yer are, and yer just shivered. You'll have to get out of those clothes before yer get a cold. Anyway, that was the best one and half minutes of punching I've seen in a while. You're unreal, Orlagh. That pretty wee face hasney a mark on it. I'd say yer better than ninety percent of the lads in here," Emmet proclaimed, as he proceeded to untie the fraying laces of my gloves, plucking an obstinate knot with his clean, long fingernails.

"Don't fool yourself, Emmet," I cheekily replied, attempting to distract myself from the shimmering sweat-coated, chiselled cheekbones.

"No, really, I'm not joking, yer are."

"No, really, don't fool yourself. I'm not better than ninety percent... I'm better than all of 'em!"

"With that much talent and all that confidence, you'd be dangerous. It's criminal that yer can't box competitively."

"Tell me about it."

"So what was all that about after the fight? Did yer know that kid?"

"Sort of."

"Don't leave me hangin' in the balance, Orle, I thought we were mates. Mates tell each other things. Was he yer boyfriend or what? I thought yer had better taste than that one. Like me, for instance."

My inherent infatuation was protesting impatiently to be freed, but it was as imprisoned as my hands in the damp leather gloves. Although my hands were, unlike my feelings for Emmet, due for imminent release.

I wanted to be able to skip along a dirt embankment

holding the reins of a horse singing about the release of my secret love. I wanted to shout from the highest hills, and just like *Calamity Jane* even tell the golden daffodils that my secret love was no secret any more. But I couldn't even whisper it in a crowded gymnasium. "Oh, don't flatter yourself, O'Malley." Was the best my brain could conjure. I then proceeded to tell him about my past association with James. I omitted to inform him of the kissing incident. Even if I wasn't totally beguiled by Emmet, I wouldn't have told him. Boyfriends, brothers and boxing-gym boys just didn't go together. They were over-protective of me, to say the least.

"Ach, the lad was an eejit then and an eejit now. He doesn't know a beautiful woman can be dangerous - in more ways than one in your case."

"Emmet, you're being awfully complimentary tonight. What're you after?"

"See beauty and brains all in one. Yer can read me like a book, so yer can."

"So, come on then, what is it?"

"Well, I could do with that beautiful face on another mission. It's me works Christmas do next Saturday night. It's a big posh affair over at Abbey Hall."

"Yeah, you said something about that the other day. What's my mission?"

"Well, I was wonderin' if ye wanted to come with me?"

"Me?" I searched around for the person he was really asking.

"Well, I'm definitely not thinkin' of takin' him. I know he looks like yer but they'd think I was the other way, so they would," he said, pointing at Patrick.

"But, why me?" It was out before I thought about it.

"Well, yer me best mate, are yer not? So, come on, I won't be askin' again."

"Yes, yeah, of course." Did I sound too enthusiastic?

Was my birthmark removal pain-alleviating mantra actually working? Were all my wildest dreams being granted?

* * *

"You look mighty pleased with yourself, missy."

"Oh, I am, Mammy. I certainly am."

"I take it your father's master plan worked. You got the result you were after then?"

"Most definitely! I've got to go'nd tell Siobhan."

"She doesn't usually care about the boxing."

"Oh, she will with this result!"

"Listen, before you go I forgot to tell you that an appointment came through for you to have your first treatment with that new Pulse-dye Laser that Doctor Delaney told you about. It's for next Monday, isn't that great?"

"Brilliant. I've gotta go, tell me the details later."

As I suspected, Siobhan certainly was pleased with my result. Emmet's Christmas party was almost as exciting for her as it was for me. Would her Monday morning 'Did he kiss you' question finally be answered with a long awaited - 'Yes'? Would the illustrious colours of the utopian rainbow of Emmet-induced euphoria soon appear before me? Was my birthmark-removal, pain-eluding mantra finally being acknowledged?

I lay in bed that night unable to sleep. Unusually my insomnia wasn't caused by the shadow-like appearance which most nights swung the golden key in front of my face, imploring me to discover with it, reducing me to banshee wails. No, I was wide awake because my mind was creating romantic scenarios with Emmet at his Christmas party. I constructed conversations we would have. I imagined the slow song he would ask me to dance to. How he would brush my hair from my face with his forefinger and kiss me gently. But then reverberating there, amidst the romantic images, somewhere in the morass of my mind was an exasperating whispering voice reminding me of the harsh reality of it all. The voice which reminded me that Mammy had said I had a hospital appointment five days before the Christmas party. I hadn't given it a thought since she'd told me; I'd been too consumed with telling

Siobhan about Emmet's invitation at the time. I hadn't ever dreaded a hospital appointment, especially when there was optimism looming in the form of a new treatment. But after my long-desired date with Emmet I yearned to evade my upcoming hospital visit because it was going to leave my face scabby and even more undesirable. I had been experimenting with make-up for a while. I hated it, though it covered my birthmark to a certain extent; but the unsightly scabs caused by the laser treatment would look like poorly concealed acne under make-up. I was sure Mammy would understand if I wanted to cancel the appointment, so I quickly got back on track to fantasising about Emmet.

"Can we change my appointment, Mammy? Until after Christmas maybe?"

"Oh, come on, Orlagh, you know we can't. It might be months before another appointment becomes available."

"But, you know I'm going to Abbey Hall with Emmet and I'll look a mess with scabs all over my face and I can hardly cover them with plasters at a place like that."

"No, this treatment doesn't scab, Orlagh, and sure it's only a test patch anyway. Get Doctor Delaney to do it by your ear, that's covered by your hair anyway."

"Really, it doesn't scab?"

"No, it goes into a black bruise apparently." She winced at the mere thought of it.

"Oh, okay then. That doesn't sound too bad."

"You're such a brave wee girl, Orlagh."

"Yeah, yeah, Mammy."

"Don't forget to give Sean Kennedy that note I wrote explaining about the day off you're having for your treatment. When's that one leaving to America anyway? We'll have to have him over for dinner before he goes."

"Not until the end of January. He's staying until the end of the Christmas term." I was devastated when Mr Kennedy had first informed me that his green-card had been sanctioned. Dominic had assured me years ago that he would merely talk about it for ever, so I conveniently indoctrinated myself with the same conclusion. But his dream departure was looming ever nearer. He was going to teach soccer in a school in New York. Not football - soccer.

"Sean's definitely off to the States then? Jesus, the end of an era..." Dad shook his head and the newspaper at the same time. "End of an era."

chapter forty-one

The days were seeming to drag with a monotonous momentum. My mock examinations thankfully finished and the hospital appointment arrived.

Although there was a change of treatment, there was no further change of hospital or doctor.

"Isn't it great that we only have to go to a hospital up the road? You'll be wrapped up on that settee in no time at all, baby doll." Dad never ceased to comment on how wonderful it was to have a laser clinic in Birmingham. I suppose I had taken the previous inconvenience of hospital visits countrywide for granted. But they hadn't once complained. I longed for their sake, as much as mine, for this new treatment to work.

Even on the cold December morning Mammy's internal pain reactor had purred effortlessly into action, and steadily ticked over.

I scanned the waiting area as usual, searching for the pirate-patched old lady, but she was absent once again.

"Do yer need the toilet or anything before yer go in, Orlagh?" It was one of Dad's predictable questions. I was usually fine. I avoided public toilets as much as possible; they repulsed me. But desperation overtook my aversion today.

I followed the simple signs to the toilets, but simplicity evaded me and I seemed to be walking around identical corners of identical hospital wards. The liquid in my bladder was pushing on the walls of my stomach and the absence of the toilet intensified the need. A nurse who I had presumed was excessively busy running from ward to ward, but had actually not moved, gave me directions to the toilet as though I were a moron. What seemed like an eternity later I arrived at the huge door with a silhouette of an A-lined skirted figure glued to it. Its stainless steel handle cried out germs, so I kicked the bottom of the door to see it career into the face of a woman who was about to depart. Her hands immediately covered the hit area of her forehead. I was mortified. My apologies flowed as fast and as furious as the door had.

"Shall I get a nurse?" I offered the injured lady, who was still covering her face.

"No, I'll be fine, sweetheart. Don't you worry. A little bump never hurt anyone. It may knock a little sense into me." She chuckled while taking a couple of steps in reverse and balancing her backside on one of the sinks, then removed her hands. I couldn't believe my eyes when I sighted her full face.

"Oh, hello. Orlagh, isn't it?"

"It is. But how could you possibly know that? I've never spoken to you," I answered the pirate-patched lady, who now had an added red line above her other eye.

"I never forget a pretty face, especially with such an apt name. You know, with it meaning golden princess?"

"Orlagh!" Mammy shouted from the bottom of the corridor, "come on, Doctor Delaney's waiting."

"Have you already been treated?" I anticipated I might see her after I'd had my treatment.

"I have, but I'm sure I'll be seeing you soon. I'm Angelica, by the way."

I daydreamed while Doctor Delaney explained how the Pulse-dye Laser worked. While he explained how the medium from which the energy source came in the Pulse Dye was a liquid as opposed to a gas in the Argon laser.

How the Pulse Dye was much finer-tuned and directed only at the damaged blood cells, unlike the Argon, which attacked everything in its sight. My preoccupation wasn't, for a change, about Emmet. It was about the strange meeting I had experienced in the toilet with *Angelica*. Angel – Angelica? Was my mind making a spectacular connection?

My preoccupying thoughts abruptly discontinued when the laser was cranked into action. It created an altogether different sensation to what I had previously experienced. The singeing of hair could scarcely be heard above Dad's invariable singing distractions, and the ensuing stench of burning skin was thankfully absent. The sensation the Pulse-dye laser caused was all so sudden and electrifying-like that it was difficult to concentrate on anything. The pulse of the laser which produced the blue/green ray moved my head back to sink into the pillow abruptly, as though I had been hit with a straight right cross with the sting of an enormous elastic band. Bang, bang, bang. On each pulse my hand squeezed Dad's.

"It's all right, baby doll." I almost detected suffering in his comforting words.

Bang, bang, bang, bang, bang. Eight pulses which left eight mini-circular bruises in a cubed shape by my ear. No blood. No imminent scabs. Just a throbbing in my head and thoughts drenched in optimism.

CHAPTER forty-two

Mammy slammed her finger underneath an article in the local evening paper. "Oh my God, Rory, you'll never believe this." She sounded shocked and excited.

"What's that then, doll?" She had caught everyone's attention with her fascinating statement.

"Come on, Mam, what's so exciting?" I asked.

"It's in the classified section. I really don't know what possessed me to read this, I never usually do; I always stop after the obituaries."

"And what possesses you to want to know who's dead amazes me," Pat stated.

"Forget all that rubbish. What won't we believe?" As ever Dominic was to the point.

"It's your grandmother. It appears she's wanted!"

"Oh Jesus, what's that one done now, Grania?"

"Which grandmother? Bridie or Maggie, or even Mary?" I don't know why I asked really because I had a pretty good idea which one it might be.

"Now, who would you put your money on, Orlagh? Who holds more secrets than a priest after years of sitting in the confessional? Which one's caused more trouble and upset more people in her eighty years?"

"Well, then I suppose it has to be Bridie."

"That's me mother yer talkin' about, watch what yers are sayin'. She's a respectable woman, so she is!" We all laughed along with Dad at the thought of Nanna ever having an iota of respectability.

"Well, Rory, that Aldi fiasco last week only backs up my point for the millionth time that your mother doesn't have a respectable bone in her body."

"What's the Aldi fiasco?"

"Oh God, Orlagh, did yer father not tell you? You've only been revising for those exams and it seems like you've been away. Well in one week she disproved her point on not having any respectability twice! Tell her, Rory, go on."

"Well, we get an early mornin' phone call from Nanna tellin' me I have to get round there right away. I thought, Jesus what's happened now? Is someone going to cut her throat? Has she been electrocuted? No, there she was waitin' for me like an excited little kid with a set of triple-extension ladders leaning up the side of her flat. 'Look what I got yer, Rory,' she said."

"Triple-extension ladders? Where did she get them from."

"Oh, listen, Orlagh, you won't believe it!" Pat shook his head in feigned disbelief. "There again, can you believe anything Nanna does?"

"That's a grand set of ladders, Mammy,' I said, 'but where've they come from?' Do you know what she'd done, Orlagh? You know that Aldi supermarket that they're building down the road from her?"

"Yeah, the one where she thinks just because Aldi's a German company that everyone who's workin' there's German?"

"Exactly! What about when she told us the workmen were wearing lederhosen? What a craic. Anyway, that's another story. Well the openin' of the supermarket was set for the end of the week and the workmen were finishin' off. As yer know she'd been down buggin' 'em everyday they were workin' on the place. So while inspectin' their work for the day she'd noticed this set of triple-extension ladders and thought they'd be grand for me. In some unfathomable way she returned that evenin', broke into the buildin' site, stole the ludicrously heavy ladders and walked

344

the eight-hundred yards back to her flat. When she told me what she'd done I went ballistic. I took them straight back to the site and do yer know, Orlagh, I was strugglin' with 'em on me shoulder, so God knows how she'd managed 'em. While Nanna stood next to me, all innocent-lookin', I explained to the site manager that she'd found 'em in her cul-de-sac and noticed the name of the company painted on the side was the very same as the one which was buildin' the new Aldi and figured they must've been stolen by some kids. He couldn't thank me enough and he could never have suspected Nanna. 'Why'd ya give 'em back to them German bastards?' she asked me. 'Jesus, Mammy, they're not German. How many more times?' But she didn't listen. 'I wouldn't have given 'em back, the trouble that them Nazi bastards've caused,' she said."

"But I thought Mammy said that she'd proved her point on having no repectability twice."

"She did and it was with Aldi again, on the day it opened. She'd gone in, stole a bottle of Irish whiskey, got caught and *conveniently* acquired a bout of senile dementia. The naive manager calls us up sayin', 'all she could remember is her son's phone number. She's very confused, she thinks I'm German.' That was the only truth she'd told him that day."

"So he let her off?"

"Yep, but she'll get her comeuppance one of these days, I'm sure. Anyway let me tell you all about this announcement in the paper."

"Yes, finally. Come on then, Mam, spill the beans." Dom was getting frustrated.

"It's in the lost friends and relatives section. O'Connell, Bridget, formerly of Dublin, Ireland, aged approximately eighty. Sister to Kathleen and Patsy. It says to contact the Evening Mail lost relatives to organise a meeting with the person in pursuit."

"Who do you think it is?" Dominic's attention had been captured.

Dad shook his head and raised his eyebrows, "With her history, Dom, me boy, God only knows. Remember when I was fourteen she left yer Grandda' the notorious note tellin' him to stick Robert Emmet, the Proclamation and the Starry Plough up his arse and left us all, disappearin' for twenty-odd years and reappearin' when Orlagh was a wee baby. The finer details of her years on the run have never really been ascertained."

"Maybe the mystery person is a secret bone beginning to rattle in the closet of her past."

"That was very poetic, Patrick," Mammy said. "And probably true."

We all mused over the identity of the mysterious person while we ate dinner, suggesting numerous candidates.

"Bridie, someone has placed an advertisement in the Mail looking for you. Do you want me to answer it?" Mammy asked Nanna over the telephone, after dinner.

"Lookin' for me love, 're yer sure?" echoed back. The older she became her tumultuous volume seemed to increase a few deafening decibels.

"It's in black and white right here in front of me." Mammy proceeded to read it out to her.

"I wonder who that could be. Maybe someone wants to leave me a bit o' money or somethin'?"

"Maybe, Bridie. Maybe."

The call to the newspaper was made the following day. Mammy's details were taken so that the unknown person could then make contact.

"Does this person, whoever it is, really know what they're letting themselves in for?" Dom remarked, chuckling.

"I don't think anyone could anticipate your Nanna Bridie, that's for sure."

The guessing game endured throughout the day, although I had no particular interest in it. My thoughts were not focused on the disclosure of this mystery person, as they had all been infected with remnants of Emmet. Each thought

346

passing through my mind would divert itself in some way and end up being relative to Emmet and our arranged date.

The telephone rang continuously. Mammy had taken the job of switchboard operator. In most cases she cut all callers short as she waited with expectant hope that it might be the mysterious seeker. While waiting for the phone to ring, she annoyingly tapped her fingertips on the table top. When the miniature bells did chime she appeared like a hundred metre sprinter, leaping into full stride from the starting block of her chair. Her rapid return indicated numerous false starts.

The starter's pistol was fired once again and off she went. But this time she didn't re-emerge moments later; it appeared the finishing line had been reached.

"You'd better sit down, Rory." Mammy looked ashen when she eventually arrived back in the kitchen.

"I am sittin', Grania. What's the matter, doll? Yer look like death warmed up."

"That was the person looking for that mother of yours. She sounds lovely and definitely wants to meet. This Saturday if possible."

My mind momentarily swayed once again to thoughts of my imminent Saturday evening date.

"Who's this mystery person then, Grania?"

"Your sister!"

"What? Why would any of them put an advertisement in the paper? We're in touch with 'em all, for God's sake."

"Not this sister you're not; your mother had her adopted when she was a wee child."

"What?!" all four of us screeched in bewildered unison.

"That was my initial reaction too. It sounds as though she gave her up around the time she went back to Dublin from Birmingham when she was twenty. I'd always wondered why she'd gone back to Ireland when most of her family had moved over to Birmingham."

"Are yer sure it's the same Bridget O'Connell?" Dad was absolutely astonished.

"It appears so. I'll have to confirm it with Bridie. Eighty and she's still shocking us. When will it end?"

Mam and Dad didn't bother confirming with Nanna; they went ahead and arranged the meeting for Saturday afternoon.

Were the tears of regret, which would magnify the elation of reunion, going to flow from Nanna's octogenarian eyes? Or was the pugnacious personality burrowed deep within her bones going to present itself in all its antagonistic glory?

With the meeting of my new aunt and my date with Emmet, it was going to be an exciting day for me in its entirety.

chapter forty-three

It was a fortunate omen in disguise that the secret relative chose that particular Saturday to tackle the controversial rendezvous with Nanna, as it had taken the focus off my date with Emmet. I couldn't have coped with Dad's boyfriend taunts; or maybe, since it was a date with Emmet, he didn't think of it as a boyfriend-girlfriend scenario. Unlike me, maybe romantic images didn't spring to Dad's mind.

After dinner and previous to the impending encounter Dad decided he had better inform Nanna of the identity of the mystery person. She was so unpredictable there was no trusting her. She wouldn't dream of holding her tongue for fear of offending someone. Could she have abandoned all her children (and one we hadn't known about) if she possessed an iota of a conscience?

When Dad delivered the shocking news to Nanna, we had all expected denial, hostility, maybe even a whiff of embarrassment as her decomposing skeleton rattled its forsaken bones inside the clandestine closet of her promiscuous past. But that lack of conscience proved itself once again. The only scent was a fetidness of apathy. A stench composed of unconcern, which made you hold your breath and wrinkle your brow and wonder how Dad had turned out such a phenomenally devoted father, born of a woman whose initial reaction to the news of an abandoned, secret daughter surfacing was: "Oh bollockinhell, I've bin rumbled." She shook her head, raised her eyebrows, shrugged her shoulders and smirked like a crafty child. "Don't worry about that, have yers heard about this AIDS thing that's spreadin' like wild fire?"

Don't worry about that.... She never ceased to amaze me.

"Which AIDS, Nanna? Lemon-ade or cherry-ade?" Patrick asked, laughing, as he was about to depart the room.

"You'll laugh now, but you might be next. It's all in them genes, so it is."

"Yeah, but you have to be infected by contaminated genes first, Nanna. There's no way I'll be anywhere near contaminated genes," Pat replied.

"But how do yer know? They say yer can't tell at first whose genes're infected. Yers could be on the bus sittin' next to someone with them infected genes. I saw it on the telly meself, if clean genes get near them dirty genes, yer a gonna, dead in no time."

"That's partly right, but I think there's a bit more to it than that, Nanna." Dominic attempted the diplomatic approach behind a hidden smile.

She was oblivious of Dom's comment and continued on with her very own scientific interpretation. "Them Homo Sapiens are the worst."

"Homo Sapiens?" Pat enquired.

"Yer know, them dirty bastards - men who have boyfriends. They don't *wash*, and after they've done whatever is it they do with each other and get dressed agen, *that's* when they infect *the genes*. You'll see, the lot of ya are at risk, and yer mother there."

Through laughing and swallowing tea at the same time Dad almost choked. Maybe Nanna knew something we didn't. Was Mammy having unprotected sex with strange men or was she an habitual heroin addict sharing dirty needles? I glanced at the innocent face of my teetotal mother, who was in flabbergasted shock at Nanna's statement, and dismissed the ridiculous declaration immediately.

"Bridie, how could I contract AIDS for God's sake?"

Mammy had momentarily been distracted from her continual dusting and pottering, intent on making a good impression on the new family member.

"Well, look how tight yer wear them things. If yer got near dirty ones the germs'd soon multiply under there. I'm tellin' ya it's a breedin' ground."

"Wear what so tight?"

"Them jeans. I blame it on them Yanks for bringin' 'em over here. We never had these AIDS problems in our day, 'cause we never had them jeans. Why do yers still wear 'em if there's the risk? For the love of God, I don't know anymore with you young uns?" Nanna slammed her deformed hand on the arm of the chair.

I foolishly endeavoured an accurate explanation, while suppressing my laughter. "No, Nanna, it's in the genes, not the *jeans*."

"Yeah, that's what Nanna's sayin', Orlagh. It's all in the denim." Dad winked at me.

"That's right, Rory, it's all in the denim. Yer never see yer father wearin' those jean things."

"I keep tellin' 'em, Mammy, but they won't listen. Washin' lines, washin' machines, ironing boards... they're all dangerous places. Them AIDS germs are in all them things somewhere, lurkin' around!"

The doorbell interrupted our biology discussion. It was like the music being switched off at a child's birthday party as a game of musical statues was being played - none of us blinked or breathed, all, that is, except Nanna Bridie. "What's wrong with yers? Why's no one answering that pissin' door? That bell'd drive anyone mad."

"Why don't you get it, Ma?"

"Why should I get it? It won't be for me, will it?"

"Ach but it is. It's yer secret daughter."

"Ohh..." The whites of her eyes grew as she seemed to shrink into the gold, velvet-covered armchair; her feet dangled almost a foot from the carpeted floor.

I left the armchair I had been sitting in to make room for

351

our guest who Dad was about to enter the room with, and sat on the warm hearth of the fireplace. The blunt coarseness of the red brickettes penetrated into my back as disbelief at the identity of my new aunt saturated my brain - like rain water being absorbed by the soil. Only in this instance the rain of disbelief was torrential and the soil of my brain had taken all it could for the time being. A waterfall cascaded from a flood of clarifying ideas. Was I hallucinating? Was she an angel? Or was she a fake - a weirdo?

"What's going on? What're you doing here?" I asked in total and utter shock.

"I'm sorry, she's not usually rude," Mammy explained, behind an embarrassed smile, glaring at me through piercing angry eyes.

"It's all right, I think Orlagh's just a little shocked," my apparent new aunt stated.

"How do you know Orlagh?" Mammy sounded almost as flabbergasted as I had been.

"Hello, lurve," Nanna Bridie piped up, attempting a preposterously posh accent. "Which one are you then?"

"What do you mean, *which one?*" Dad added to the all-round astonishment.

"Yer mean there's more than one adopted child?" Nanna Bridie seemed to sink further in the chair.

"I'm Emily, the younger one."

"Jesus!" Dad shook his head to the rhythm of bewilderment. "So *there is* more than one?"

"I thought you were Angelica," I proclaimed.

"Well remembered, Orlagh. I am now; my name was changed when I was adopted."

"Hold on, let's slow down a bit here and start from the beginning," Mammy suggested. "I'm totally lost."

"Well, it was in the Great War, see," Nanna started.

"Not you, Ma, we'll hear from Orlagh first. You've a lot more explaining to do, madam," Dad insisted.

"Angelica is the pirate-patched lady..." I regretted that immediately. "Oh, sorry, I didn't mean to be rude."

"I've been called worse than that, sweetheart," Angelica replied.

"What's happened to your birthmark anyway?" I noticed the red pirate patch wasn't over her Nanna Bridie-like eye.

"Oh, that's covered with make-up, Orlagh. We'll speak about that later." She then directed the conversation to my confounded parents. "I've been seeing you since Orlagh started having Argon laser treatment in Southampton. Of course I didn't realise who you were at first, but straightaway there was this familiarity about you, Rory, and Orlagh here." Angelica's huge turquoise-ocean eyes trickled languidly into their shore. "But being adopted, I was always searching. Every stranger could be a potential relative. Then it was a little while until I saw you again in the Selly Oak Hospital here in Birmingham. When Orlagh walked in, she had matured, become a little lady, become an image of what I remembered of myself at age. It was like looking into a mirror of my past. I was tempted so many times to put the advertisement in the Evening Mail, but something was stopping me. Then when Orlagh hit me with the toilet door the other day I saw it as an omen, a wake-up call. It certainly knocked something in my brain into place!"

"The toilet door?" Mammy asked, confused.

We explained.

"So you've a port-wine stain as well? Jesus, yer wouldn't know it," Dad remarked.

"I have make-up on, but I'm also having pulse-dye treatment, like Orlagh."

"But, still an' all, you wouldn't even know yer had make-up on. It's amazin'."

"That's what I thought, Dad. You can see when I put make-up on."

"What're yers on about?" Nanna Bridie was bemused.

"Angelica here has a birthmark, like Orlagh," Mammy informed her.

"What, one of them horrid red things?"

"Yes, a port-wine stain, *Ma*." 'Use a little tact' reverberated in Dad's tone.

"Don't you remember? It was over my eye," Angelica reminded Nanna.

"That was a long time ago, lurve. I'd forgotten you, let alone yer eye."

A foggy dawn dew of embarrassment and pity hung over us all, but Dad brought out the sun from behind the cold greyness of Nanna's rudeness.

"Well, that's two beautiful people in the Emmet clan with little red marks. 'Cause that's what yer are now, Angelica - an Emmet. You're the only person to be adopted twice!"

"Who's Angelica? I thought yer said yer name was Emily." We ignored Nanna.

"It's strange, Angelica, that there are two people in the same family with port-wine stains. I was told it wasn't an hereditary condition."

"No, I don't think it is hereditary, Grania. Maybe it's just Orlagh and I have both been kissed by angels!" Angelica replied, glancing at me and winking one of her Nanna Bride-like eyes.

"She's pissin' barmy, this one," Nanna whispered to Dad at a level we could all hear with exceptional ease.

My opinions generally differed from my grandmother's, but in this instance they didn't just differ, they were beyond the realms of human infinity apart; fluttering on the virtuous wings of my angels.

CHAPTER forty-four

"It's like pissin' New Street Station in here, who's that at the door now?" Nanna enquired at the bell being rung with the tune of a familiar guest.

"You never know, it might be more of your abandoned kids," Dad jocosely remarked, behind a sarcastic smile which didn't quite hide the underlying tone of resentful earnestness.

"No, I think it'll be Emmet," Mammy corrected. "You'd better get yourself ready, Orlagh."

"Oh no, no, it can't be." I panicked. Disorientated, I jumped up, undecided which way to turn. "He must be early. He's never early."

I glanced at my watch and realised he wasn't early at all. Since he had asked me to the Christmas party I had been wishing my days away. But ironically, as the final hours ticked by, he had escaped my mind. I had been engrossed in engaging conversation. Firstly I listened to the hilarious botched account of Nanna's past, where she expertly skated, like Katarina Witt, over the finer details - as in Aldi she feigned memory loss, although we were not as gullible as the naive supermarket manager. Then I listened to some of Angelica's accomplishments. She was a remarkable raconteur. Her stories were almost as engrossing as Dad's.

When Emmet walked through the living-room door, to say my heart fluttered would be an understatement; it was in a full flight of ecstasy, gliding through the open skies of wishful thinking. It was the first time I had ever seen him in a suit, a black one with four buttons and a high lapel, with a two-tone tie which shimmered as he walked. He looked as though he had transported himself from the glossy pages of a fashion magazine. Dad wolf-whistled him, Dom and Pat slapped his hand, Mammy kissed him and Nanna called him a Derry bastard - he was part of our family. I thought Angelica must have sensed that feeling and she too greeted him.

"Hello there, Emmet."

I considered her attentive too, taking note of his name.

"Hey there, Angelica. What're you doin' here with these nutters?"

"A long story, Emmet," she replied.

We all looked at each other with the same shock which had circulated the room hours previously. Nanna remained oblivious and concentrated on the television.

"You know each other?" Mammy finally broke the stunned silence.

"Sure, she's my neighbour."

"Now isn't that a nice coincidence?" Mammy concluded.

A striking pain invaded my head; I knew what was coming next. The bumblebee buzzed through my mind with the tiny cherub on its back. "Remember, Orlagh, there's no such thing as a coincidence..." It departed my mind as quickly as it had appeared, leaving only the distant buzz of the bumblebee.

I remembered all right - with so many appearances the Bumblebee Angel was making sure of that. I knew it was God's Angels of Fate at work once again. I knew God has organised everything to happen for a particular reason. He leaves it to us to find the fundamental connection. We're all pieces in a huge jigsaw; some pieces fit, but just don't create the correct picture. Then there are the pieces which are so far away from each other there is no association. There are then pieces which are intimate, fitting snugly together. These seemed to be the pieces of Emmet and my

356

families. With us, one piece fitted perfectly into another, which would then accommodate another and another and more were being discovered each day in the jumbled-jigsaw-box of life, creating a picture which was still unclear, but one which I painted in my mind everyday.

Paddy, Emmet's boxing trainer in Derry, who was a good friend of Dad's, had initially sent Emmet to our gym. Then we discovered Dad's best friend, Tommy Two Saints, had been neighbours with Emmet's mammy in Belfast. Emmet's Uncle Finnian had been Two Saints' childhood best friend. When Finnian had first moved from Belfast to Birmingham he had taken over my dad's bed (when he went off to Canada) at Two Saints' parents' place. Subsequently Finnian married Two Saints' sister, Bernie, who was also my godmother. Now we discover Nanna's abandoned child is Emmet's neighbour. One way or another we were bound to have crossed paths. Why did God's Angels of Fate organise all of these connections? What did they have in store for Emmet and me? What was our fundamental connection?

I charged up the stairs to get myself ready. I had pampered myself earlier in the day, doing my hair, painting my fingernails, as well as my toenails, since they were to be exhibited in my exquisite open-toed sandals. I had to reapply the make-up which covered my birthmark and put on my divine black dress. Mam had been the one to insist I wear something extra special. I suspected she had used her motherly intuition and had detected that I was totally infatuated with Emmet. It had been an unconfirmed suspicion until one night recently while returning home after attending a cousin's wedding. Siobhan and I were enthusing over the bride's dress, the cake, and the wedding in general. We then progressed to discuss my own wedding. I had it all planned out: the venue, the dress, the bridesmaids, the flowers - everything. Mammy looked over her shoulder from the passenger seat and commented, 'You'll have to find yourself a husband first.'

'Oh, I've already done that!' I replied with a wry smile. Siobhan nodded in agreement beside me.

'He wouldn't happen to be an Irish boy and have the same trade as Joseph, as in Jesus, Mary and Joseph, would he?'

'No!' Siobhan and I, a little too adamantly screeched in unison, ending our talk of weddings.

Mammy had suggested renting a dress after I had experienced a major clothes crisis, emptying my entire wardrobe to find nothing suitable. She had ideas of a ball gown. I didn't want to look like an inflated crepe-paper Christmas decoration, so I opted for an elegant, ethereal, black satin shoe-string strapped ankle length dress, which was accompanied with a long-sleeved flowing over dress made of black chiffon.

"Wow!" Emmet, with wide eyes and raised eyebrows commented, as I entered the room.

"You look great, Orlagh," Dominic said. That made me smile as he didn't usually comment. Patrick was customarily the openly complimentary brother.

Dad shook his head with pride. "Arahh, you'll be the belle of the ball, baby doll. It's a shame you're with that eejit though." I was beginning to get embarrassed. "Let's get some photos."

My embarrassment escalated as Dad resurrected the camera, which was invariably loaded with film, and proceeded with his David Bailey impersonation. He didn't have a clue how to use the majority of the camera's functions, although he pretended he did. But he looked the part, altering his lenses and taking his time - too much time. My smile began to ache as he moved himself up, down, left and right. There were photos taken of Emmet and myself in front of the fireplace where he secretly, behind our backs, hooked his middle finger around mine, squeezing it and winking. I took a deep breath and attempted to keep my composure. There were photos of Emmet, Angelica and myself in front of the fireplace, then us next to Nanna Bridie squashed on the settee. Dom, Pat

358

and Emmet in front of the boxing trophies. All of us together - then apart. After continuous coaxing Mammy joined the pictorial commotion.

We eventually escaped the family portrait session and began my dream date. Emmet even linked my arm as we walked to the car. I felt like an American teenager being taken to the prom; all I needed was the corsage wrapped around my wrist.

Jesus greeted me as I entered Emmet's car, swaying from side to side.

"She's great, Angelica. What's the story there then, Orlagh? I didn't like to ask again."

I told Emmet the unbelievable tale of my wayward grandmother.

"I should have guessed, Angelica has those huge Bette Davis eyes that you've got, so she does. What's your granny like, hey? My grandparents were almost as bad. They had their kids in Ireland and left them there with me great-grandmother to raise while they lived it up in England. They reckoned they were workin' over here in Birmingham 'cause there was no work in Belfast. They said they were makin' money to buy a house for their kids... thirteen in all, me mammy is the youngest. It seemed all they were bothered about was makin' kids, not money. Thirteen kids and me great-granny in a one-up, one-down. Yer wondered how they ever coped. But the difference with my granny and yours is, yours doesn't give a shite and doesn't deny what she's done; mine thinks she's owed the world, the feckin' old witch. But there again, I suppose me mammy's lot all knew who their brothers and sisters were and even though they didn't see much of them, the mammy and daddy too. She's full of surprises old Bridie, hey? What happened to the other child she had adopted?"

"Angelica said she'd tried to track her down, but lost the trail quite early on as it seemed her adoptive parents had moved overseas, America they thought. It must have been terrible though, Emmet. It wasn't as if they were new-born babies being given up; Angelica was three and the other child was four. But I don't suppose we can be any more shocked with this, not after she left my dad, Assumpta and Una. Una was five when she left and has never seen Nanna from that day to this."

"What made your da' make contact with her after she'd done a runner?"

"Oh God, it wasn't Dad, he wasn't interested. Nanna had arrived back in Birmingham after being God knows where. We still don't know the finer details of that story, or maybe Mam and Dad do and just haven't told me! I think she would have been too old to have any more kids, though, thank God. Anyway, she arrived on her sister's doorstep, my Great-aunt Patsy's, as if she'd never been away. Mam and Dad obviously heard on the family grapevine she was around. Dad was adamant about not seeing her again. Mammy was curious to meet her, but Dad would have none of it."

"So, what changed the eejit's mind?"

"Uncle Seamus. He was visiting here at the time she'd arrived back on the scene. I suppose because he wasn't around when Nanna had done a runner it didn't really affect him. He hadn't seen what she'd done to Grandpa, well to all of 'em, I suppose. With him living overseas Mammy reckons he wanted even more to hold on to that family bond that didn't exist any more. To cut a long story short, Uncle Seamus talked Dad into seeing Nanna.

"She walked into our kitchen twenty years after she'd left the family in Dublin. Dad had last seen her leaving the house to go shopping when he was fourteen. He said, 'You went out for bread twenty years ago; it must be stale by now.' And that was that, she was back on the scene."

"Do yer think that's why yer da' is so great with his family and all those dysfunctional kids at the gym? Yer know, 'cause of the shite he had to go through. Hey, and don't be tellin' him I was praisin' him. Jesus, I'd never hear the last of it."

360

I smiled. "I suppose it is, I've never really thought about it. But what I was thinking about was how messed up it would've been if say my dad had dated Angelica, without knowing they were brother and sister. I know she's a lot older than Dad but they could've got married and had children and I would've ended up looking like one of those sunken-eyed, inbred hillbillies."

"Yeah," he said with thought, placing his left hand on my knee, "but you're not, you're just beautiful, look at yer." His long fingers wrapped around my knee and squeezed it, then left them there limp for a few lingering and what I categorised as amatory seconds. My brain along with my body went numb. The frost of silence wrapped around my body and I shivered. It felt like I had been silent forever; I was desperate for something to say.

"You didn't tell me you knew anyone else with a port-wine stain birthmark." Was the best I could do.

"I didn't know I did. Who do I know?"

"Angelica."

"Really? I didn't know that. Where?"

"All around her eye."

"Really? That's amazing. She must wear make-up, but yer wouldn't even know that, would yer?"

"I know, isn't it fantastic? She's going to sort me out with the exact same make-up. It's supposed to be for horrific burns and scars, that's why it covers the mark so well. It's not on the market, though; you have to go to a special consultant and then get it on a doctor's prescription. It's waterproof and doesn't sweat like this rubbish that I have on now and it'll only come off with a special cleanser." I hadn't stopped once for air. My mind had been so abducted by the ecstatic thought of acquiring the new make-up that I became unaware that I was engrossed with informing Emmet about a subject I wouldn't usually broach with him. Make-up wasn't really his thing. But he listened patiently, and I could just about detect a smile as the car sporadically flashed with white light as we passed under the street-lights.

361

"Well, you don't need that make-up shite at all if ye ask me."

"That's nice to say, Emmet, thank you." He had been so sincere it warranted an expression of gratitude.

"Well, I'm only telling you the truth. You look great. You always do." And I felt great; he made me feel comfortable, beautiful... real.

We drove off the main road, on to the unlit private driveway which led to Abbey Hall. The moon was hidden by the tall trees which lined the driveway either side. The tree-tops met in the centre of the driveway, forming an enclosed canopy. The car headlights gave vision to the fallen, decaying brown leaves which swirled and cavorted in the winter wind. I had driven down the winding approach many times, but never feeling the way I did. I was still basking in the effervescent delectation of Emmet's compliments, which caused ecstatic adrenaline to pump around my body as though I were wired to an electric circuit of excitement.

My preceding visits to Abbey Hall had been as a spectator at the boxing shows. Twice a year each men's club like the Rotary or the Masons held a boxing-evening dinner: men's clubs for men who were not so manly - old-school-tie righto-boyos, with their finger-twiddling handshakes and their 'We're not a secret society, just a society with secrets' silly slogan. Every boxer I knew hated these atmosphere-lacking dinner shows, with tables full of middle-class penguins who thought the boxers were beneath them, mere entertainment fodder to have a little bet on. They were not at all appreciative of the boxers' artistic dexterity. It was something to talk about at the office or on their round of golf, other than their herbaceous boarders. The tuxedo toffs had more interest in the tacky pre-show comedian, who told clichéd 'keep the wife in the kitchen' jokes.

"You've gone quiet, princess. I think yer need a little wakin' up!"

362

A few seconds after that comment he switched off the headlights, creating an isolated darkness and pulled his handbrake until the click, click, clicking stopped and we spun around for what seemed like an eternity. I squealed, "Emmet!" at the top of my voice and he laughed, flicked the headlights back on and sped off with a wheelspin down to the open gravel-surfaced car park; where he once again utilised the handbrake, spinning and reversing to end up parked perfectly, like in a stunt scene from a Bond movie, between a Ferrari and a TVR.

"I bet the tossers who drive these cars canny drive like that!" His face, now perfectly visible from the light being emitted from the cast-iron Victorian lamp-post outside, reflected mischievous rhapsody.

"Do you think they'd really want to? I thought I was dead back there. Won't you wreck your car doing stuff like that?" I was still shaking, uncertain as to whether it was from my previous ecstasy or mere fright!

"The car's not mine from tomorrow. I sold it, so I don't give a shite. And as for dying... in my presence, Orlagh, that could never happen. God and me have a deal. I do good by him; he does good by me. You could say I'm one of his angels," he stated, as he kissed Jesus on the Cross, who had gone totally erratic in the three-sixty, handbraker-incident; He had swung out of control on His rosary beads which hung from the rear-view mirror. Emmet then tapped his left trouser pocket which contained his holy medals wrapped in a tattered handkerchief given to him by his granny, which The Pope had palpated. Wrapped inside were: Saint Martin, Saint Columba, Saint Anthony, Saint Patrick, Saint Bridget, Our Lady's miraculous medal, a rosary ring and many more. There were prayers to Padrae Pio, Saint Joseph and Saint Jude. He never ventured anywhere without them. "You stick with me, Orlagh Emmet, and you'll be all right."

I had every intention of doing so.

Abbey Hall was architecturally aesthetic. Each time we

came my dad enthused over the renaissance stone masonry. I had been shown every brick and informed of the era of each extension. I had no choice but to love it. It was built like a miniature castle out of local quarried clay bricks, with circular princesses' turrets at either end. A moat surrounded the entire building, adding to its idyllic fairytale mystique.

We entered the ballroom to an ensemble of air-kissing, 'oh luvvie', 'dear poppet', 'oh dharrr-ling' women. They were dressed in their gold and bronze shoes, leopard-skin shoulder pad-filled outfits, bygone bouffant-ed peroxide hair-do's with sagging jaws and excess wrinkles sewn behind their ears, giving them that wide-eyed, permanently alert look. This was the Birmingham bourgeois-bullshit bunch that had escaped their tedious life as lunching-ladies, for their husbands' Christmas party, their annual excuse to be excessively extravagant. I scanned the room while Emmet was at the bar and promised myself I would never turn into one of them.

Emmet worked for a relatively small family construction company, constituted mostly of real men, with real wives. Maybe the bourgeois-babes, as Emmet referred to them, were all real in their own way; it's just I couldn't relate to the pretentiousness they possessed.

Each company present was specifically grouped on tables which were set in a medieval banquet style, with ostentatious fruit-bowls teeming with winter fruits. Evergreen foliage decorated the centre of the tables from top to bottom, with sporadic acorns sprayed gold, sprigs of holly and bunches of red berries placed within. There were goblet-style wine glasses and impeccable polished cutlery. I picked up my dessert spoon and checked my lipstick in the reflection. I wondered if supermodels had the same shocking convexity when they looked into spoons. I dismissed my spoon distortion thoughts when I heard the owner of Emmet's firm direct his attention towards us.

"Is this your wife then, Emmet?"

"Future one, yeah." My heart leapt like a cavorting moth captivated by the firelight. I did an imaginary punch in the air and through my toothy smile I whispered a triumphant *'yes'* to myself.

"Well, introduce me to the beautiful lady, Emmet. Where're your manners?" the owner said, as his wife looked uncomfortable at the attention I was acquiring. She was one of the leopard and lamé air-kissing, 'oh luvvie', 'dear poppet' ladies I had witnessed on my entrance.

"This is, Orlagh. Orlagh Emmet."

"That's a beautiful name for a beautiful girl." His wife looked away in disgust.

"And she's exactly what it means... a golden princess." And underneath the red-baize tablecloth he did what he had done in the car and squeezed my knee. It had the same exciting effect, but this time I had people to divert the attention from myself. Why I wanted his attention distracted from me I couldn't quite understand, because I had prayed for moments like this from the first time I had set eyes on him.

"So where do you know young Emmet from, Orlagh?"

"My dad's his boxing trainer," I replied, grateful for the touch-averting question.

"I didn't know you boxed, Emmet. You couldn't have done much, not with that pretty face," the owner patronisingly proclaimed, laughing heartily at his own joke.

"I can't believe he didn't tell you he boxed. He's an amazing boxer, and he's so pretty because he doesn't get hit. That's the art, you see."

"Oh, do you know a bit about the old fisty cuffs then, Orlagh?" the owner interrogated, continuing his condescension through clouds of his cigar smoke, implying I should be ignorant of the sport.

"Well, she knows a wee bit more than any man I know and can throw a left hook better than most of 'em too," Emmet interjected, as I was about to answer.

"I knew a bricky called Emmet who was a boxer," a flushed-faced, pot-bellied man further along the table commented. "An Irish fella he was. Haven't seen him for years. God we had some craic me and Rory." He shook his head and smiled as he silently reminisced.

"Rory Emmet?" Emmet and I asked in unison.

"Yes. Is he some relation?"

"That's my dad."

There was another piece slotted into Emmet's and my jigsaw.

Barry the Bricky commenced to tell us hilarious stories of past experiences with Dad. The owner's wife's boredom with the builders-bum-banter was obvious. She huffed, puffed and clicked her scarlet-painted fingernails in the air to summon the waiter. The excess skin flapped from her triceps like wrinkled sheets on a washing-line as she ordered a bottle of wine. I felt embarrassed; I didn't want the waiter to think I was associated with her. I didn't want him to think that my manners were just as bad. The waiter promptly brought her a bottle of Cabernet Sauvignon and asked if she would like to taste.

"Oh course I would," she indignantly replied. He poured, she swirled, then sniffed. "Oh, it's very... tart. Bring me another."

"She's gettin' mixed up; she's the tart," Emmet whispered to me. I struggled to suppress my giggles.

Another bottle was brought and then another. She moved from tart, to woody and on to insipid.

"She wouldn't know the difference if the waiter'd pissed in it... which he probably has. I would if I was him! The pretentious bitch won't have so much pretence when she gets a bit more of that *woody* wine down her gob," Emmet predicted.

He was right; as the night progressed we witnessed a scandalous transfiguration in the owner's wife and the rest of the bourgeois-babes. The 'dharrr-ling, luvvie' finishing-school girls' perfect posture plunged into the pool of inebriated hunched shoulders, with limp wrists clutching their goblets, while their closing eyes peered into the disappearing alcohol, believing all the answers to their problems were lying in the bottom of their glasses. Their talk of holiday homes in the South of France, credit card limits and nannies metamorphosed into husband profanities and their own detailed vulgar sexual fantasies. Their cigarettes were no longer held extended at arm's length like a Twenties film star, but stuck to their bottom lips, now like a gangster's-moll, as they ran to the dance floor in pure drunken excitement to boogie to YMCA and the birdie song. All their supercilious dignity swirled around, drowning in the slops of their Cabernet Sauvignons and Chardonnays.

"Shouldn't your girlfriend be at home doing her homework? I could teach you a thing or two that she couldn't," the owner's wife propositioned Emmet, drawing patterns on his cheek with her scarlet fingernail. "You know what they say about older women."

"Yeah, that they sag and gape in all the wrong places." My response was lost in her enthusiasm at the introduction of Aga-Doo, and she ran arms held high to join the mass of plastered plebeians decked in their fake feline fur. Leopards that were most certainly not going to change their spots.

"Let's get out of here, Orle. I can't take much more of this disco-down-with-Dave shite."

The tacky tunes were annoying me too, but as long as I was with Emmet I didn't care. My heart sank when I thought the night was over. My last-dance dreams were denied. We made a covert escape through the ballroom of intoxicated work-mates, who would probably all regret their overly affectionate actions at the office on Monday morning.

The cold air hit us outside. The mist from the moat and adjoining lake hung over everything like silent, swirling ghosts. Emmet wrapped his muscular arms around me, like all the cars which had been cloaked in the white phantasmal mist, and rubbed both his hands up and down the chiffon sleeve of my dress.

"Quick, princess, let's get you into that car and get yer warmed up."

I would have been quite happy with a continuation of the present friction heating method. My nervous system had danced back into action, prompting my blood to circulate quickly through my rapidly beating heart, causing me to glow internally. I was sure if he did persist, our bodies would soon fuse together.

The light being emitted from the Victorian lamp-post was also shrouded in the fog, giving Emmet's car which sat underneath a halo-ed aura. I didn't want to complain about anything, even the cold leather seat of his MG, so I silently winced, jigged about and placed my hands under my thighs.

"We'll soon have yer warmed up, Orlagh, don't you worry." Emmet started the engine, giving me one of his beautiful white-tooth smiles accompanied by a slight wink, and once again left the car to scrape the thin layer of ice from the windows.

"Still cold, babe?" he asked, jumping back into the driver's seat as I sat shivering from the cold air which was blowing in from the heater vents. Before I could answer he began to unbutton his suit jacket. "This should keep yer warm until the engine gets warm." He wrapped it around my shoulders. The pleasantly redolent scent of his aftershave aromatically warmed my cold nose as I rushed to inhale as much of his smell as possible. His hands rested on the steering-wheel but strangely he didn't attempt to move the car. He appeared deep in thought. I wanted to speak so badly, but I couldn't think of anything suitably impressive to say.

"Are you all right, Emm?"

"Oh, I'm just fine, but, do you know what? We're not going anywhere, Orlagh."

"Why? Do you think you should go back in there until

the end?" Visions of a slow smoochy dance flashed through my mind.

"No, not at all, we're not going anywhere, not until you lean over here and give me a kiss," he instructed, with tenacious mischief.

It was astounding how the coldness immediately departed my body and the passionate warmth of apprehension entered.

"Come on, I'm serious."

How was I to know how he defined a kiss? I didn't want to lean over there and begin a kiss of unyielding passion, humiliating myself to an extent I could never look at him again because all he had meant was a peck. So I played safe. I placed my right hand on the edge of his cold seat, my fingertips slightly touching the fabric of his trousers. I leaned and quickly executed a peck on his soft lips.

"Sorry, we're still not movin', wee girl. I said a *kiss*."

How long had I awaited this moment? How many times had I enacted it in my head? But, like water down a plug-hole, all my plotting visions had swirled down a dark drain in my mind, combining in an open sewer of befuddled anticipative desires.

I replaced my right hand on his chair, slipping my fingertips that little bit further so I could feel the warmth of his leg. As my face slowly met his all my saliva had mysteriously evaporated. I was convinced my lips had suddenly become dry and chapped, but I continued. My heart raced as once again our lips met, this time lingering on closed contact. Then the slow, passionate, repetitious movement of our lips began. His right hand slipped under my hair and gripped my neck. His fingertips nestled into my nape. His thumb sensually stroked my ear-lobe. My pelvic bone throbbed and my stomach performed somersaults as though I was standing on a cliff edge and my lungs felt as though they were emptied of air. The moisture from his mouth transferred to mine as his tongue caressed the perimeter of my lips and then ventured past my teeth and explored my mouth. The tips of our tongues met and ecstatically frolicked. I had just cupped his slightly stubbled jaw into my hand when he startled me, abruptly ending our kiss. He then captured my nose in-between his teeth and slowly tossed his head from side to side growling like a playful puppy with a cuddly toy. The blackbirds flying through his paradise sky-blue eyes cavorted.

What could I say to follow what had just occurred? I was cringing inside and my brain was screaming 'You've just kissed Emmet O'Malley... EMMET O'MALLEY!'.

"Yer don't know how long I've wanted yer to do that, Orlagh Emmet."

"Not as long as I've wanted to, Emmet O'Malley, that's for sure."

CHAPTER forty-five

Angelica obviously wasn't the immortal winged angel I had initially thought and hoped she was when I had repeatedly witnessed her, what was to me at the time, mysterious presence at the hospital. *Although* she was assuredly an angel, but of the human kind, I believed her intrinsic influential angelic mission was that of introducing me, as she had promised on our first proper meeting as my estranged aunt, to the German fräulein-looking cosmetics consultant, who dealt in the miraculous camouflage make-up.

I had been expecting a bimbo-looking dizzy blonde, with blue-eyeshadow-decorated eyes and cherry-red lipstick. I thought she'd be dressed in a tight white nurse-type uniform, which would reveal the outline of skimpy underwear, with white stilettos that would parade a solarium suntan and a high-pitched voice which matched her fragile figure. Alternatively, a surviving member of the Gestapo would enter our house, with a huge, black ominous-looking briefcase, clad in an A-line battleship-grey skirt and double-breasted jacket to match. There were no white stilettos on dainty feet - only durable, flat, black-leather lace-ups. The only tan she possessed was the 'American Tan' nylon tights which slightly wrinkled at her ankles.

"Would you like a cup of tea or coffee, Miss Rutlage?" Mammy asked, as she guided her into the dining-room.

"Tea. Black. None of that watery stuff. Strong. Very

strong. Two sugars. Thank you," she requested, in an extremely deep, to-the-point, brusque tone. "Let's get down to business then; I haven't got all day. Where's the young lady in question?"

Patrick raised his eyebrows and pulled one of his, 'Oh no, what're you letting yourself in for?' faces, as I departed the hallway and went into the interrogation pit.

She had seated herself at the dining-room table and was rummaging around inside her portentous black case which was placed in front of her, its lid open but the contents concealed from myself. I envisaged that implements of torture were going to be removed forthwith. She did not appear to notice my entrance.

"Right, I have some questions to ask you," she declared, acknowledging my presence for the first time. She looked lingeringly at my birthmark, then in a brisk action closed her eyes tightly, pursed her lips, shook her head and as she completed her look of disgust she sighed, then redirected her attention to the clipboard she had placed on her knee. I was expecting her to grill me about having anti-Nazi opinions, arrest me and place me in a concentration camp. Instead, she questioned me about my skin. In each enquiry her continuing abruptness was resonant. 'I haven't got time for this,' reverberated in every word (although, Mammy was paying handsomely for her presence).

From her case she unveiled her transforming make-up. It didn't look so impressive to me: a tray of dull circles ranging from light tan to chocolate brown. I was certainly dubious as to whether Miss Rutlage could transform anything artistically; her face looked as though it had never been in contact with moisturiser, let alone foundation. It had the appearance of old tan leather that was as well weathered as a matured saddle.

"You don't know how lucky you are," she said, breaking the overpowering silence, as she oppressively applied the solid foundation on to my face. I couldn't feel any creme substance being applied, only a hard dabbing with her middle finger.

"Excuse me?" I was bewildered as to what my good fortune might be.

"This." She pressed that little bit harder on my mark. "It's like a pimple in comparison to what I've seen."

Her earlier look of contempt was clarified. I didn't know whether it was her way of being nice.

After the brutal dabbing, she removed yet another box from her briefcase, this time containing numerous shades of powder, each only a slightly different shade to the next. As she had done with the foundation colours, she eliminated the majority of shades instantaneously and dabbed a smidgen of the remaining ones on my skin. Expeditiously choosing the match she presumed suitable, she proceeded to cover the area of my birthmark with powder. I sneezed and upon opening my eyes I was met with a look of disgust; I felt like a chastised child. Mammy entered to witness my responding incensed gaze (which, incidentally, was covered with white powder). Mam silently instructed me to be patient.

This powdery procedure only further clarified the sceptical thoughts I was having about this make-up. I thought I was going to look like one of those women Dad says look as though they have applied their make-up with a trowel. Perplexity persisted as she reversed what she had previously performed, by taking a huge brush and dusting off the powder she had just applied. Then, wetting a clump of cotton-wool, she dabbed the whole area. A couple of water droplets clung to my chin; I was hesitant about wiping them off, worried I would upset her temperamental disposition, but then I decided I didn't care how she judged me as she wasn't helping me any. I considered the whole procedure was turning out to be a complete waste of time. As I was about to wipe the droplets away, she dabbed them dry. It was all dabbing, no wiping. She then produced yet another brush from her bag of tricks, dipped it into what appeared to be blusher and dusted all over my face as though she was clearing cobwebs from an insect-inhabited corner with a feather duster.

"There you go," she said. "All done."

"Really?" I dubiously questioned, doubtful of anything being *done* other than my parents. At that she produced an oval mirror which was to reflect a sight I had wishfully envisioned for years.

"Wow! This is amazing. How did you manage that?" I was in a state of shock. My port-wine stain birthmark had gone. Disappeared. Not even a shadow was present. No outline - nothing.

"Well, I've practised on *serious* cases up till now. I treat burns victims, bomb victims. I was in the army for thirty years, you know."

You'd never have guessed it, I sardonically thought, but I didn't allow the sarcastic thought to turn into words and pass the threshold of my lips; I was too grateful. She had every ounce of my respect. For she had achieved in two hours what numerous doctors had attempted for almost seventeen years. I was indebted to her. I touched my face in astonishment and was wonderfully surprised to find there was no creamy, sticky feel to it, just all-over smooth skin.

"Mammy, come here - quick!" By the look on Mammy's face as she rapidly entered the room I think she had taken my euphoric scream to be one inflated with wrath, since my last facial expression she had observed was one of anger.

"What? Whatever's the matter?" she asked, distressed that Miss Rutlage had pushed me that little bit too far.

"Look!" I pointed to my concealed birthmark. "Look!"

"Oh!" Mammy continuously shook her head. "Oh, oh." Articulation eluded her. "Oh, Miss... Oh, Miss Rutlage, thank you."

Mammy hugged me, then hugged Miss Rutlage, who was unmistakably embarrassed. It was apparent she had never received an Irish embrace quite like it.

"You're welcome," she meekly whispered, "very welcome." And a hesitant smile slowly sneaked on her hardened face to make her look not so austere.

How could I ever have doubted her? I more than anyone should know looks can be deceiving.

Two months elapsed until my life was completely transformed. I had to wait for the miraculous make-up to be ordered through the National Heath and then to be obtained from the German manufacturers. I hadn't told Emmet about my make-up as I wanted to surprise him. So, on the day the cosmetics arrived I had conveniently arranged to visit Angelica. With Angelica living next door to Emmet it was another perfect excuse for Emmet and myself to spend time together. But he didn't notice my perfectly concealed birthmark when I jumped into the passenger seat of his new car. I had been so excited about hearing his reaction; consequently, I was extremely disgruntled when it went unobserved. When we arrived at Angelica's she didn't notice either. I desperately wanted to hint. After lots of small talk I said; "Notice anything different, Angelica?"

She looked me up and down, searching for the difference she couldn't detect. I then noticed a flicker in her eye, a realisation of a simple observation which had gone unnoticed through looking too hard.

"Oh, Orlagh, I'm sorry I didn't notice. The make-up's wonderful."

"What? What's the difference? What am I missing here?" Emmet stared at me.

"Orlagh has new make-up on," Angelica informed him.

"What's the difference?" My disappointment intensified. Angelica explained.

"Ach, Jesus, I never noticed. What am I like?"

I desperately tried to hide my disappointment and attempted conversation, but Angelica detected the despondency reflecting in my eyes and said to my embarrassment: "I think you should maybe take Emmet not noticing as a wee compliment, Orlagh."

"Sure you should, princess, you always look beautiful to me, make-up or no make-up. Right, Ange?"

"I don't think I've heard you say a truer word, Mr O'Malley!"

Our clandestine kisses had continued throughout the months following the Christmas party. Emmet and I were having a secret love affair. The exploration of our mouths escalated to that of our bodies. I was emotionally embraced in a perpetual state of rapture, and *every* occurrence would associate my mind with Emmet. I would stand in the shower rubbing soap into my body and think, 'Emmet has touched these same curves.' A shiver would run up and down my spine and I would excitedly cringe at my once inconceivable dreams coming true. As I placed on my bra, I would think of the bra-taunting episode and smile an accomplished smile when I thought Emmet had now slipped his hand inside the garment I had once most dreaded placing on my body. His name would be mentioned by at least one person in my family each day, and I would have to stop myself from acquiring a self-satisfied smile when it was. Patrick didn't know. Nobody knew... except Siobhan - of course!

I had woken up on the Sunday morning after the first kiss with Emmet at Abbey Hall, trying to decipher if it hadn't all been a divine dream. When I soon realised it wasn't, Siobhan consumed my thoughts. She was the only one I could share my excitement with.

Siobhan's Mam was one of those get up and go out early on a Sunday morning type people, and on that particular Sunday she had dragged Siobhan out with her. So, it wasn't until the Monday that I got to see her. I had been overwrought with excitement at telling her the unbelievable news, but I contained myself and acted as normal as possible when I knocked on her door.

"Quick, quick, come in." I had anticipated that she would be excited to hear all the details of the evening; she usually was on a Monday morning after a Sunday night with Emmet at the movies. With the Christmas Party I suspected she was almost exploding with questions.

"How was your weekend?" I asked, prolonging her impatience.

"Great, great, I'll tell you about that in a minute, I need you to tell me something first." She dragged me into the living room and I laughed at her exaggerated elation. "What's so funny?"

"You, you're so excited."

"Tell me about it." She threw an Argos catalogue into my lap. "Danny said he was going to buy me a *ring* for Christmas. A *ring!* Can you believe it? I've only been seeing him, what? six weeks? Oh, I think he's the one, Orle, I really do." I'd lost count how many times I had heard that now. "Anyway, I want you to help me choose which ring I should have. Look on page two-hundred and tell me which one you like best."

My Saturday evening obviously wasn't the most important incident on Siobhan's mind. After we decided on a ring, I had the entire details of *her* weekend. It was unusual for us not to see each other at all over the weekend, but with Angelica and the party there was a lot going on. She was such an airhead, she had forgotten about everything.

We walked our regular route to school, which would, in the subsequent months, come to an end. We passed through the navy-blue school gates, past the graffiti-covered louvered doors of the mini-electricity substation, where as a child I had viewed the older kids bunking each other up to sit on its pebble-dashed flat roof and thought they were so cool; realising now that they were boring time-wasters. Siobhan proudly pointed out the fresh tag on the louvered doors which Danny had sprayed, clearly proclaiming his undying love in graffiti art.

"I could just see Emmet doing you a tag like that. What'd you think he'd use as his tag? Boxerboy or something?"

"I doubt he'd tag, Shiv. It's just not him, is it?"

"True. He'd probably cut something out of wood. Oh

377

my God, I forgot to ask. Sorry, Orlagh. What am I like? How was his Christmas party?"

"It was good, very good," I nonchalantly replied, with a shrug.

"Did he kiss you then?" she asked as she always had each and every Monday morning since he had first taken me to the cinema.

I uttered the response I had been bursting to for years: "Yes."

"So what did you have to eat? Turkey, I suppose. Did you have loads of different courses that you had to eat with all different knives and forks?" We continued to walk across the field and I smiled inwardly; my information hadn't sunk in. "Was it dead posh, or what? WHAT!? Did you say, YES?"

I slowly nodded my head as a smile spread across my face and I screamed, "YEEEEESSSSS!" stretching my vocal cords to their limit and causing every other person on the school field to stop and stare. We both dropped our school bags on the dew-damp grass, grabbed each other's hands and danced around squealing like excited little girls.

The era end I had prayed endlessly to my angels for had finally been granted.

chapter forty-six

Orlagh Emmet. Orlagh Emmet. Orlagh Emmet. It was the wallpaper of my school books, written on every hair's breadth of paper in: blue ink, black ink and red ink, in script, in bubble letters, in tag. 'Orlagh, I'm thankful your books are not covered in Orlagh for Johnny - or whoever, but you do have a wild obsession with your name. There're people who can decipher what it means writing your name over and over,' a teacher commented about the decoration of my books. She along with everyone else had omitted to notice a tiny line which crossed the h in Orlagh to form a plus sign which linked Orlagh and Emmet together.

Our relationship (if you could call it that, at this point) was as covertly concealed as the little cross which linked our names. It was an unspoken decision we adhered to. In the boxing gym, in my house, in his house, we acted as though nothing had changed, as though our lips had never met and our hands had never ecstatically explored or impulsively investigated. As though he had never delectably delved over my contours to prompt my back to rise in absolute ecstasy to appear like an expertly engineered arch bridge.

In a way I was quite happy with it being our secret; I don't think I could have endured the torment and teasing I would have experienced at home and at the boxing gym. I assumed it would have been difficult for Emmet also to admit to my brothers that he was having a relationship with their little sister, and to Dad that he was dating his little girl - his baby doll. But there was also the flip side to the coin of concealment. Emmet had kept his usual social calendar with my brothers and the lads. He still had to be one of *the boys,* which of course included their persistent philandering antics. However, I had been used to that when I hadn't had the privilege of being one of *Emmet's girls*, so it was a case of tolerating it. I had one iron in the fanciful fire and I didn't want to complain and have my iron removed to go cold. I had listened for years to what the boys liked and loathed in women and I was putting all I had ascertained into action. Although my toleration didn't annul the gut-wrenching feeling or that blistering iron burning within my heart when I heard their womanising tales.

At least I knew I had his company more than any of the other girls. If I wasn't actually with him, in some way or another I could find out exactly what Emmet had been up to, without him even knowing I had been investigating. If he wasn't in my presence, he would usually be with Dominic or Patrick, or other lads from the gym like Mickey Duffy or one of the McCabe brothers. With none of them knowing about us, I could easily slip an obscure Emmet enquiry into a conversation to collect the information I required.

I did have comfort in the knowledge that each and every Sunday I would be with him almost all day. I had him all to myself on Sundays - no exception. For this reason I dreamed my weeks away for Sunday to arrive.

I awoke to attend Mass with Mammy. Patrick or Dominic, or both sometimes made an appearance at church; but they had drastically lapsed, and unlike myself - were permitted to do so. Dad, 'the ultimate pious being', didn't ever attend. He maintained that if he were never to go to Mass ever again, I could never in my lifetime, going every week, catch up with the amount of times he had been.

How he arrived at this conclusion I didn't know. Mammy had given up arguing the case and would merely shake her head at that particular feeble Mass-avoiding justification.

I didn't really mind going. I habitually daydreamed the hour away. Staring at the red-carpeted aisle, I transported myself to a day I had organised in my mind a thousand times. My head was an easel to a moving masterpiece being created. I always had to begin with the same scene - waking on the morning of my wedding day. I couldn't start half-way through my dream wedding day and I couldn't skip a detail; if I did, I would start all over again - to the flutter of my eyes opening to the vision of my fairytale wedding dress. I began my scenario in the first reading of Mass and had it to such perfection that the climax of myself reaching the altar to come face to face with my fiancé would occur as I was to stand to recite the Creed -

> *We believe in one God,*
> *the Father, the Almighty,*
> *maker of Heaven and Earth,*
> *of all that is, seen and unseen.*

After vacating the grandeur of the gothic Saint Columb's, with its white-washed stone statues and stained-glass windows which depicted worshipped Christian icons, leaving behind me the fervent scent of burning incense - I actually came face to face with the protagonist of my wedding daydream. I entered a building not so grand, which displayed icons not of a bygone millennium, but of twentieth century idols relevant to the surroundings: Ali, Sugar Ray, Iron Mike, Marvellous Marvin, Macho Camacho, The Clones Cyclone. The odour of burning incense was absent, but there was a burning odour which was just as delectable to myself - that of encased sweat in battered leather gloves. Sweat which had been shed with the *burning* desire to win.

It wasn't merely Emmet's company I adored at the

boxing gym on a Sunday morning. I still revelled in the entire atmosphere: the stories of the boys' Saturday nights, the team spirit, the brotherhood, the friendships, the nonchalant expression of heartfelt laughter when they threw their never-ending 'mom jokes' around, hurled as fast and as furious as their punches. 'Your mom eats grass out of the park.'

'Well, your mom is a skateboarder.'

'Arh, but at least she doesn't wear a donkey jacket like yours.'

'No, yours is more interested in wearing tattoos. Sure, she has more tattoos than teeth.'

None of the lads ever seemed lost for words.

And in recent months there was an added objective to my assiduous attendance at the boxing gym. With someone caressing my curves and testing the tautness of all my extremities, the importance of keeping in shape was paramount.

After Angelica had come into our lives I decided I would like to get to know her better. I came up with a great plan which incorporated seeing more of Angelica - and Emmet.

Because Angelica was Emmet's neighbour I decided that Emmet could take me directly from the boxing gym to Angelica's house. There was also a supplementary bonus resulting from the visits to Angelica's in that when Emmet's mammy, Niamh, found out I was going next door, she insisted I have Sunday lunch at their house before I went to see Angelica. This plan suited me fine and I almost became as much a part of his family as he had of mine

So the diversity of my Sunday progressed from boxing battles in my beloved retreat to braving another kind of battle: one which I had diligently devised in my mind. A battle which I hoped would witness the conquering of Emmet's family. Conquering them in a way in which I would gain all their respect and affection, and thus, inspire them to inform Emmet that he would be a fool to miss the chance of capturing me... If only!

Over dinner Niamh told me endless childhood tales of

her carefree life growing up in Belfast. With twelve siblings there were a lot of stories. My favourites were those which included her neighbour as a child, and later in life Dad's best friend, Tommy Two Saints.

While Emmet showered I went next door to Angelica's. Visits regularly transformed from an intentional half an hour, into endless hours of inspirational conversation about her years spent travelling around the world. She was certainly an equal match for Dad in the storytelling department as they were both enthralling raconteurs. Along with those eyes, they obviously shared additional genes.

I listened to how she had worked on missionary sites in Africa. She relayed her memories with such enthusiasm she made you feel the intense African sun burning on white alabaster skin and with the whiff of her words she could transfer the smells that famine or civil war bring along with them. I marvelled at how she had helped Mother Teresa through the humid days in 'Nirmal Hriday Home For Dying Destitutes' in Calcutta. "What's Nirmal Hriday?" I asked, intrigued by her moving stories of lepers, and chronically crippled children who were purposely mangled at birth, so their parents could make a living by begging. "It means pure heart, Orlagh, and that's what Mother is, pure heart." I smiled when she uttered those words - at least she eventually found a mother that *was* 'pure heart', because her own birth mother, I'm convinced, didn't even possess one.

I especially loved her tales of Australia, of its golden beaches and indigenous people. A favourite anecdote was when she attended the opening of the Sydney Opera House. She had been a care assistant of an Opera House trustee who needed her permanent aid, giving her the privilege of attending the 1973 opening concert. "As I approached the magnificent building," she recalled, "the spring October wind was strong and I was convinced its white sails were going to flap and vacate their position at Bennelong Point and sail away, out of the harbour into the

Tasman Sea, transforming the Harbour Bridge to a distant view. But it didn't, and I heard the angelic voice of Lauris Elms, mixed with the baritone of Raymond Myers as they sang Beethoven's Symphony number nine, instilling in me an undying love of classical music."

"Why did you go travelling in the first place, Angelica?"

"It was my destiny, Orlagh. It was what I was meant to do. The angels pushed me on my way. They gave me that nudge to *realise* my destiny. To chase it. I was lost in Birmingham, so I thought I might as well try to find myself on an interesting journey."

"And, did you find what you were looking for?"

"I think I just recently did that. But I had to come home to do so."

As Angelica answered the question, the comment which had been relayed to me so many times, by the shadow-like appearance which emerged in the night, came to the forefront of my mind. *'All that wander are not lost. But all that wander have something to discover.'* Did I have something to discover? But I wasn't wandering - although I did long to visit all these locations and all the places Dad told me about. I yearned to smell the spices piled along the dusty Indian roadsides. To smell the fresh breeze blowing off the Tasman sea into Sydney harbour. There was so much to do and see; I didn't even want to begin getting lost, and then trapped, in a bank in Birmingham.

Maybe I was beginning to realise my own destiny. Maybe unbeknown to me the locked box full of angelic-bestowed knowledge was leaking, and bobbing along on the surface of my subconscious were clues to the realisation of that very destiny, which blatantly begged recognition. I desperately wished to understand the clues.

I could have stayed with Angelica all night. There was so much to tell and so much to hear. But I didn't mind leaving, considering I was departing to spend my evening at the cinema with Emmet.

Sundays for me were truly *divine*, but they flew by too

fast: as fast as time seems to pass when you have a project dead-line, a lunch hour, a holiday, or ten minutes on the alarm-clock snooze button.

chapter forty-seven

Belfast tales which Niamh relayed over succulent Sunday roasts had been exceptionally interesting to me of late, in view of the fact that I had talked Mammy into allowing me to attend the semi-finals of the Amateur Boxing Association championships in Belfast. My mock examinations were long since over and I had attended numerous interviews for all the High Street banks, all of which had auspicious results. I could have my choice of which I wished to join, as long as I passed five GCSE examinations, with C grades or above, with a stipulation of two being mathematics and English. Those exams were not for another three months, leaving plenty of time for revision - that was my argument anyway.

When I arrived in Belfast, the tales Niamh had recited could have been of another distant place. The skipping-song-sentimentality and blissful Belfast existence of carefree children stuffing their faces with the city's baked delicacies, which boasted comical names Niamh would enthuse over, such as Paris buns and bannocks, coconut-covered snowballs, sore heads, diamonds and flies' graveyards - were non-existent. These scenes had been replaced, or wiped out, by the presence of armoured vehicles; by Saracen tanks which roamed the tarmacked streets like prehistoric monsters. Their green, patchy camouflage told me they shouldn't be roaming city streets, but long, wild grass tackling warfare in faraway jungles. Belfast wasn't a jungle, not even a concrete one; rows of sturdy red-brick terraced houses lined the roads which housed an art gallery of repression. On each gable wall on every street, whether in Catholic or Protestant neighbourhoods, there were murals painted in green, white and gold or red, white and blue, of: IRA, UVF, INLA, LVF or UDA - abbreviations of a denied war. There were enormous effigies painted of Bobby Sands, Joe McDonnell and Robert Emmet; or King Billy and his horse, the red hand, or the Derry apprentice boys slamming the city gates shut. There were doves of freedom and slogans of hatred.

There *were* snotty-nosed kids present - but not of the innocent kind, as *I* had first witnessed when Emmet had taken Dominic, Patrick, Mickey Duffy and myself on a guided tour of the city on the morning of the boxing championships. As we approached Niamh's sister's house by the Queen Victoria Hospital, we stopped at a zebra crossing. I smiled and waved at the cutest, curly-blonde-haired child who was swinging on a rope attached to a lamp-post. She couldn't have been older than six.

"Who'd ya think yer lookin' at, ye English fucker you?" she screeched, and instead of sticking out her tongue or wiggling opened palms at the side of her head, she raised her middle and index fingers to form a resolute V.

"How could she possibly determine I'm English from a smile and a wave?" I asked, intrigued at her assumption.

"It's all about symbols here, Orlagh. Symbols mean everything in a war zone and she has been taught to recognise them," Emmet replied, unfazed by the occurrence.

"But what kind of symbol does a smile and a wave give? Do I smile in an English way or something?"

"No, babe. You're sitting in an English plated vehicle and you're a stranger surrounded by more strangers. That shouts out enemy to her," Emmet clarified. "But she's not to blame, and neither are any of the other children - Catholic or Protestant. They've been hardened by the conflict which permanently surrounds them in every aspect of their lives: in the colours they use, the songs they sing, the roads they live in, the schools they attend, or the names they bear. They are divided by a history which precedes them. They are divided by endless segregating symbols, like the corrugated iron fence which is named 'the peace line'. I see no peace in that Belfast-Berlin-wall, do you lot? I only see a representation of suppression - repression. By being born within the six counties these children have been denied the rights of a normal childhood." As Emmet concluded, an air of contemplative silence fell upon us all.

"But the man from Delmonté, he say YES!" As we entered the city centre and continued our tour of Belfast, Emmet's remark ended the elongated silence and caused us all to jump out of our skins.

"Ya, eejit ya, you scared the life of me!" Mickey said, holding his heart. "What're ye on about now, Emm?"

"And yer call yourself an Irish man, Mickey Duffy? You southerners're all the same." Emmet winked at me in the rear-view mirror of the minibus we were touring in. "It's the City Hall, look." He pointed at the white, limestone building. It was almost a replica of the White House, only it had a copper dome in the centre and a copper turret at each end.

"And? What's that got to do with Delmonté tinned fruit?" Mickey asked, bewildered.

"The banner hanging above the door which states 'Ulster says no' has been hangin' there since the Anglo - Irish agreement was signed at the end of '85. The unionists put it there to show their objections of the agreement; another blatant sign of their continuing unwillingness in peace negotiations. So, Ulster says no, but, the man from Delmonté?"

"He say - YES!" we all shouted and laughed in unison.

Maybe, away from the many fortified army bases and barbed-wired, corrugated-iron-fence peace lines, under the hum of helicopter blades, hidden in their own backyards or in the folds of the Divis or Black mountains which surround the city like a large protection barricade, there were children innocuously playing, experiencing the blissful Belfast life which Niamh and Tommy Two Saints had experienced; it's just I hadn't witnessed it yet.

The jollity subsided on our return to The Europa Hotel, the venue of the most important championships. The championships were particularly significant this year; not merely because the winner of the championships would be regarded as the best boxer in Great Britain at their respective weights, but they would be eligible to enter the British team, which would work towards representing the country at the 1992 Los Angeles Olympic Games.

The evening started out on a note played by an instrument which was in desperate need of tuning. A note so bad it required you to cover your ears with the palms of your hands and screw up your eyes with the pain of the catastrophic cacophony. And as the evening progressed the notes continued to play - deafening, sinister and desperately inharmonious.

Errol and I were both sixteen, but there wasn't a chance I could impersonate him now. There again, it was quite unbelievable how Doctor Sudki had mistaken me for a black, twelve-year-old boy back then. Although, except for our colour and gender, of course, we were pretty comparable in size and weight, and I did only have bee-sting boobs. Now, along with my boobs sprouting, so too had Errol, to a staggering six feet tall, while weighing in at twelve stone. But tonight, at the official weigh-in, the officials claimed he had grown even more rapidly - seven pounds more, to be exact, tipping *their* scales at twelve and a half stone. Turning Errol from a middleweight boxer to a light-heavyweight, thus, ineligible to box; resulting in instant disqualification. Dad protested profusely, knowing all too well that Errol had most probably dropped a pound or two - not gained seven. Dad was merely met with dismissive, 'it's the rules' looks.

Due to Errol's unfair disqualification, Patrick was the first of the Birmingham Irish boys to box. Also due to Errol's unjust decision, it meant that an air of anger and demoralisation was hovering over us all. An air which was to grow thicker and heavier as the evening progressed, clogging our lungs and crushing our hearts.

While anticipating Patrick's long-awaited entrance into the ring Dominic, Emmet, Errol, Sean McCabe, Mickey Duffy and myself sat in the abnormal conversation-free atmosphere which surrounded us. Maybe a win would cheer us all up, I thought. Pat had been due to box at eight o'clock but it was now nine o'clock and still no sign. Each of the boys had investigated the late commencement of the bout, all returning from the changing rooms with the same account: Patrick was warmed-up and raring to go, but there was no sign of his opponent.

"There's something dodgy going on, I know it," Emmet proclaimed.

"Yeah, it's strange how all the other bouts have all been on time," said Dominic.

"I know what they're trying to do, they want Pat to get psyched up and warmed up, and then drag it on and on, so he loses his focus," Emmet surmised.

A commotion began ringside. None of us could comprehend what was transpiring. *Dominic's* opponent was making his way over the centre rope and into the ring; gloves on, gumshield in, ready to box. He had obviously received pre-notification of the altered program.

"What the fuck is going on?" Dominic, Emmet and Mickey shouted in unison.

Dad appeared next from the changing room vicinity, with a pair of red boxing gloves hung around his neck, which bounced with ferocity at his incensed pace. Encapsulated within his eyes that hot midday sun glistening over the turquoise tropical sea, which extends its aquatic fingers to caress the shore with hypnotic, insouciant rhythm had disappeared behind a set of tempestuous grey clouds; and the calm tropical sea was, slowly but surely, changing into a tidal wave.

"Come on, Dom, me boy, these fuckers are trying to pull a fast one. You'll have to warm up in the ring, son, 'cause *you're* on now."

Dominic, silent and bewildered, proceeded to the ring. He removed his tracksuit in the corner, to reveal his shimmering emerald satin shorts and vest.

The MC, wearing a tuxedo and a self-satisfied smirk, climbed into the ring. "Due to unforeseen circumstances, the featherweight bout has been rescheduled and will proceed after the next bout, which shall be the welterweight division. Between, Dominic Emmet in the blue corner, representing The Birmingham Irish Club of Birmingham and William Wright in the red corner, representing The Shankill Boys' Club of Belfast."

"You mean lightweight bout," someone in the crowd shouted.

"Yeah, what about the lightweights? They're supposed to be after the featherweights," another spectator stated.

"Not tonight they're not, the welterweights are, " the MC responded, and climbed out of the ring, with no explanation as to why Patrick's featherweight bout had been rescheduled, or why Emmet's lightweight match had been skipped in favour of Dominic's division.

"Fuck," Emmet began, "I knew it, they're tryin' to catch us unawares."

While Dad hastily wrapped Dom's protection bandages around his hands and placed on his gloves, he gave him rushed instructions. Dom lightly jogged on the spot and silently nodded. Dominic too had that anger in his eyes. The instructions were worthless, as the decision had been made before Dominic had entered the ring. In the space of the first and only thirty seconds of round one Dominic had received three bogus public warnings: one for attacking

391

too soon after the bell had been rung, a second for misuse of his head, and a third for a low blow. Dom had done none of these things, the warnings were all uncalled for. They were all predetermined by the referee. Patrick had arrived at our table in time to hear the announcement that on account of three public warnings, Dominic Emmet of the Birmingham Irish Club had been disqualified. I don't suppose if Dominic had boxed within the correct time slot the decision would have differed any.

While Dad once again protested about the mistreatment of his boxers, Patrick returned to the changing area to warm up for his delayed bout. But the proceedings merely matured in absurdity.

The MC once again made a confounding announcement, with no justifying reason; although to us it was clear what they were attempting to achieve. "I apologise for the disruption, but we're still unable to proceed with the featherweight bout. So, can the lightweight boxers please proceed to ringside."

Emmet's opponent instantly appeared ringside, gloved up, and by the looks of things, warmed up. As with Dom's opponent, he had obviously received pre-notification of the altered programme. Emmet had boxed this particular opponent on three different occasions when he had been living in Derry, all in the schoolboy division. Emmet had won each bout.

"Yer can refuse to box if yer like, Emmet, 'cause it's all a fix, so it is. It's up to you, Emm. God knows what else these bastards've got up their sleeves." Dad was more enraged than I had witnessed him in a long time.

"No, Rory, I'll box. I've worked too hard to get to this stage to let them get away with it that easily. I'll beat this orange bastard, no problem."

Emmet and Dad entered the ring and I observed for the second time in succession an occurrence which in all the boxing shows I had ever attended had never before been seen - a boxer removing his tracksuit, placing on

392

protection bandages and gloves while warming up - all in the corner of the boxing ring.

I hadn't even had time to give him the usual good luck kiss.

As the bell was rung for round one both Patrick and Dominic took their seats beside me. Patrick was still in his boxing attire, prepared to box, while Dominic was showered and changed after his unfair disqualification. Both were visibly and uncharacteristically demoralised.

"BOX!" the referee shouted, in his strong Belfast accent.

Emmet came to the centre of the ring and met his opponent, Craig Wilson. Emmet appeared strong and somewhat incensed, and rather than measuring his distance with his left jab he immediately led with his right hand which connected with Wilson's chin, causing him to take a couple of retreating steps. Emmet also took those steps, but on the attack, and followed the straight right cross with a perfectly executed left hook, which met Wilson's right cheek and sent him sprawling off balance to his left side and subsequently to the canvas. We cheered and clapped as Craig Wilson was given a count of eight. As soon as the referee had authorised Wilson fit to box on Emmet delivered two shocking left hooks which landed underneath Wilson's ribcage sending Craig Wilson's guard down to protect his body, and so Emmet emerged with a right over the top which met the left side of Wilson's face, which he followed with a lethal left hook which landed on the right side of Wilson's face. With his head moving from one side to the other it appeared Craig Wilson was giving the signal for 'no', but before Emmet could land another punch on the left side to continue Wilson's 'no' signal, the referee jumped in to bestow another standing eight count. It appeared the rush to get ready and box had caused a sudden anger within Emmet, which usually takes time to surface. The official's underhandedness had backfired on them, because if Wilson received one more standing eight count in this round the referee would have to stop the fight. Making Emmet the winner.

Thirty seconds hadn't passed and the referee was once

again wiping the punching area of Wilson's gloves on his own white shirt after Emmet had knocked him down yet again. Emmet was in the neutral corner, looking as frightening as one who is so beautiful can possibly appear. The film of perspiration on his face enhanced his defined cheekbones, and his flushed red colour made his eyes appear bluer, with the blackbird focused on its prey. Emmet came out to stun Wilson with yet another array of prodigious punches. It was obvious that the third and final standing eight count was looming ever closer. The referee could not allow Wilson to receive such punishment, so we had the security of at least one of our boys proceeding to the finals of these championships, I thought, when another underhanded manoeuvre was performed - not by the referee - but by someone in the wings, someone close to the power box which runs the lights. It was suddenly darkness. Only the orange tips of cigarettes could be viewed, like dancing fire-flies in the night-time darkness.

"Bear with us, ladies and gentleman," the MC's voice sounded in the darkness. "It appears that the lights' fuse has failed. It's presently being changed."

"Yeah, likely feckin' story, more like purposely switched off, you cheatin' shower of bastards," Mickey Duffy screeched.

It took a couple of minutes for the so-called fuse to be changed, or rather, for the culprit to switch the lights back on after Craig Wilson had received a good two minutes' rest, and the need for a third standing eight count had been forgotten. As soon as Emmet and Wilson began to box after the blackout, no sooner was the bell rung for the end of round one.

We were too far away from the ringside to hear Dad's instructions, but we could clearly view his falling tracksuit bottoms as he performed his ambidextrous activities of towel spinning and sponging down. Rounds two and three saw Emmet administer more punishment than is usually allowed in amateur boxing before the bout is stopped by the referee. It was quite obvious whose side the ref was actually on. And as that biased referee held the hands of Emmet and Wilson, with blood pouring from each of Craig Wilson's orifices, I considered the judges would not be able to be as prejudiced, because it was clear to a blind man who had won the bout.

The tuxedo-clad MC clambered into the ring. "The winner of the lightweight division of the 1989 British Amateur Boxing Association Championships, who will proceed to the finals at Wembley Stadium, London, is in the red corner from Shankill Boys' Club of Belfast, Craig Wilson."

Emmet's head dropped to his chest, his eyes closed themselves tight and his arms hung limp at his sides. It was a blow that couldn't be expertly dodged - the only blow that had managed to hit Emmet that evening, on target, with the full force of travesty behind it. It also appeared to have hit every spectator who had no connection with Craig Wilson; there was a stunned silence lingering in the hall. I felt sick. I felt sad.

By the time Patrick entered the ring he must have been physically and mentally exhausted. He had warmed up and psyched himself up three times for the bout but, as the bell was rung for round one and he proceeded to box his fugitive opponent, the tiredness was not apparent. He danced his waltz to perfection; one two three, one two. Perfectly executed punches were thrown down the invisible pipe at supersonic speed, to meet the face and body of his opponent; one two three, one two. He turned his opponent, tricking him with the Rory Ruse by side-stepping a punch which subsequently sent his opponent through the ropes. Every dextrous textbook punch and manoeuvre there was Pat managed to put them into action; one two three, one two. The only thing Pat hadn't achieved within the three three-minute rounds, was to knock his opponent out.

"By a unanimous decision, the winner of the 1989 featherweight semi-finals, who will proceed to the finals at Wembley Stadium." My heart pounded faster, there was no question Patrick had won, but the preceding decisions had been utterly confounding - these judges and officials could not be trusted. "In the red corner, representing Shankill Boys' club..." I didn't hear his name. I should have known that I wouldn't hear Patrick Emmet. The opponent was as stunned as Patrick - he hadn't won - and he knew it.

Everything was silent in my mind; the noise of cheering and booing was wiped out. I felt like I was on a waltzer ride at a fairground, spinning around and around; I couldn't stop and it seemed I couldn't control my anger. I didn't hear what anyone said to me, it was like I was in a disco with really loud music; mouths were moving but I couldn't hear a spoken word. I ran from Dominic and Emmet's side in the direction of the ring. A judge sat with his back to me. They had been the same judges throughout the evening. How could they do this?

I had witnessed what our boys had been through to train for these championships: the psychological torture as well as physical. Those judges hadn't watched our boys change their diets, watch their weight, forget a social life. Every ounce of sweat and determination had been wasted because these officials had decided that they wanted the home boys to win. Well, I just wasn't going to stand for it.

I couldn't see the face of the first judge I was to encounter, and I didn't really wish to. I didn't need to look into his eyes to hate him. I hated the wisps of greasy grey hair combed into the nape of his neck and the specks of dandruff which had scattered over the shoulders of his navy-blue blazer. The first judge received my shocking left jab into the bone at the top of his spine, followed by a right hook, which he didn't have a clue was coming. It side-swiped him off his brown-plastic chair, causing him to lie like a coward on the parquet wooden floor.

"There's a couple more punches for you that you didn't see thrown. Like you obviously missed every punch that was thrown right in front of your eyes tonight by *my* brothers and *my* friends." Everything remained silent in my head. My adrenaline was pumping into every extremity of my body. My eyes then focused on the next culprit - a second judge. The bright embroidered red hand protruded from his heavyset chest. Behind his goatee beard I saw a smirk which read, 'oh, and what are you going to do to me?'

With any punch I threw at this man the element of surprise was not going to be present. I had to think quick. I longed for retribution and elucidation. I made my way around the boxing ring, passing the red corner and the three wooden steps which led up to the ring. At the base of the steps sat the small wooden resting stool, which the boxers sat on in-between rounds. I picked it up. The smirk disappeared into the judge's goatee and he appeared to be stuck at his table. He didn't know whether to get up or stay where he was. He searched around him for aid - none came forth. I flipped the stool over and gripped the base of the short legs. My anger was at its pinnacle and everything seemed to be happening in slow motion. The judge's arms came up to cover his face, and I swiped.

"Why?" I squealed, hitting his shoulder with the thick wooden-seat area. I swiped again. "Why? Why did you rob them of their victories? Why?" Again I swiped and the injustice of it all gave me strength.

I heard a barely audible, whimpering cry as I continued to strike him with the stool; "We were told we couldn't let the Irish represent Britain in the Olympics."

Dropping the stool, I saw the final judge scampering away from his table at the opposite side of the ring, like a rat running to the sewer. I didn't have the heart to argue, to state that these were the British Amateur Boxing Association championships, that they were all representing Britain.

We had English accents, Irish names, English homes and Irish heritage - they had Irish accents with English names in Irish homes boasting an English heritage. It was all about symbols of segregation once again. Didn't this conflict have limitations, I thought? Where was the sportsmanship?

Then in the maze of my bewilderment and wrath the distinct tones of Dad's voice emanating from inside the boxing ring became audible: "Emmet, get her out of here, she's going to cause a riot. Yer've still got the keys to the minibus haven't yer? Take her for a drive, calm her down a bit."

I didn't hear Emmet's response as suddenly the roar of the crowd had become deafeningly discernible.

I deduced Emmet was adhering to Dad's instructions as he swiped me up in a fireman's-type lift and ran me through the screaming crowd, into the open foyer of The Europa Hotel. I viewed everything from a bouncing upside-down position. He didn't speak as we ran; I suspected he was totally enraged with me.

Emmet still hadn't put me down as we left the hotel. He ran across Glengall Street and into the Grand Opera House car park. We ran to the minibus which lay in the shadow of the majestic Victorian structure. Emmet opened the passenger door with myself still on his shoulder, then flopped me down on to the front seat, closed the door and made his way around to the driver's side.

He hadn't uttered a single word, which increased my irritation. I had only been sticking up for him and the other lads. He should have been grateful. I was seething as I stared out of the window at the red brick rear wall of the Opera House. I then decided I didn't really care what Emmet thought at all.

He reversed out of the packed car park as fast as the vehicle would allow. It sounded as though the engine was going to explode. He changed into first gear and had soon reached sufficient speed to go briefly into second and straight into third. There was no need to stop at the junction of Glengall Street and Great Victoria Road as no cars were coming; if there were, I don't think it would have made any difference to Emmet. He was about to do a right on to Howard Street when he realised it was going the opposite direction in the one-way system which was in operation around the city centre. He slammed his hand on the steering wheel and shouted: "I want to get as far away from this feckin' place as possible. By the way," he said, a little more composed, as he did a right on to Donegal Square, "well done, baby. You did great back there. If one of us lads'd done it, we'd have been arrested. I think they're all probably still in shock at a beautiful little thing like you being the one to sort 'em out!"

I realised I obviously did care for his opinion when relief swept through me as he uttered his overwhelming approval. My attention was then diverted as we drove past the rear of the City Hall building. I thought of the banner which flapped in the bigoted Belfast wind.

"Ulster says no," I began. "The judges say no; it seems the man from Delmonté is the only one who's saying yes," I stated, behind a smile full of indignant irony.

We zigzagged through the Belfast streets in silence, until we finally hit North Queen Street, the escape from a city of shattered dreams.

"Here we feckin' go," Emmet uttered, breaking the silence.

"What, what's wrong?"

"These lot, look." Emmet pointed to a set of headlights approaching us, which quickly multiplied into two sets, then three.

"What's going on, Emmet?"

"UDR, Orlagh. Basically, the last thing we need right now."

"What's their problem? Do you think they've been sent to get us because of what I just did?"

"I doubt it," he said with a slight smile. "But yer never know."

He brought the minibus to a complete halt. We could go no further. The three, what I could now clearly see were dark-green Land-Rovers, had totally blocked our path. As Emmet turned off the ignition one of the Land-Rovers proceeded around to block the rear of our vehicle. I couldn't comprehend what was taking place. Emmet was taking it all in his stride.

Numerous camouflaged bodies emerged from the Land-Rovers, armed with self-loading rifles. One stood at my side window pointing his rifle in my direction while another stood at the front offside wing, also pointing his rifle in my direction. I froze, worried that if I moved it might cause alarm and one of them would shoot me.

"What's your hurry?" the soldier at Emmet's window asked.

"I'm in no hurry," Emmet bluntly replied.

"Well, we've been told yer're." I suspected my assumption was correct - they had been sent by the Europa.

"Well, then, you've been misinformed."

"What's you're name, son?"

"Emmet O'Malley."

The soldier sniggered.

"Mmm, how'd you spell it?"

"Any way you please." Emmet sarcastically smiled.

"What're you doing out at this time of night?"

Moving for the first time I looked at my watch. It was eleven o'clock. What could he possibly mean - *at this time of night?*

"I didn't know we had to adhere to some unwritten curfew," Emmet coolly replied. He seemed at ease with the whole pointless procedure - unlike myself; I was now, after my reckless time check, back to impersonating a statue.

"What're you doing in this neighbourhood?"

"Driving out of it."

"Who do you know in the city?"

"Well, I don't know you, that's for sure," Emmet retorted.

"Why has this got English plates? What's a Fenian doing driving an English vehicle?"

"I didn't know there was an embargo on the Irish having English vehicles?"

"Well, there should be and there should be an embargo on your lot entering our country." Emmet merely smiled at the soldier's prejudiced comment. We were then instructed to get out of the vehicle and were directed with the long, black barrels of their rifles to a brightly painted brick wall at the side of the road. The soldiers began to search the minibus.

"Why were you so cheeky, Emm? They wouldn't be doing this if you'd answered their questions properly."

"Of course they would, Orlagh. With my name and my accent, if I didn't have the attitude they would suspect me even more. This isn't a one-off, Orle, it's a regular occurrence. They're only doing this to waste our time; they know only too well what we're about. It's a policed state."

I turned my attention to the painted wall we had been instructed to stand against. There was a green, white and orange flag, with a bird painted within the white section. Underneath the flag in huge, bold letters was; 'SAOIRSE'.

"What's does this stand for, Emm?" I pointed to the mural, not even attempting pronunciation of the word.

"It's pronounced, Seer-sha, and ironically it means..." With a melancholic smile his eyes left my gaze and focused on the soldier who was pointing his gun at us thirty feet from where we stood, and then to our minibus which was presently, without any explanation, being ransacked by five other soldiers. "It means... Freedom."

We attained *our* freedom after almost an hour of wasted time. Our kind departing words to guide us on our way were; "Go on, fuck-off back down the South where yers belong."

"Are we still going for a drive, Emm?" I asked, while freely glancing at my watch without the black eyes of a rifle glaring hollowly at me, to notice midnight was already upon us.

"Sure we are. I've got to get away from this place for a while and so do you. I thought I'd take you to the home of my childhood giant hero. The greatest giant on our planet."

"I don't think so, Emmet."

"You don't think so, what? You don't want to go?"

"No, not that. I don't think that your giant is the greatest giant on this planet. There's no way that Finn MacCool is in the same league as Freddie The Friendly Farting Giant." I laughed for the first time that evening.

"Well, we'll see about that, wee one. Anyway, who said anything about Finn MacCool?"

"It's obvious, we're heading north where Giant's Causeway is situated... the home of Finn MacCool."

"Is there anything you don't know?"

"Yeah, there is actually... When is all this bullshit which is wrapped up in this land going to end? All the bombs and bullets, all the hatred and segregation? When will sportsmanship matter, not religion or nationality? When will you be able to drive down the street and not be stopped by a bunch of armed soldiers? When will people disregard scornful symbols to live in peace? Like this lot, look," I stated, waving my opened palm at a Union Jack-clad village we had entered. Photographs of the Queen of England hung above front doors. Each house had a Union Jack flapping with allegiance from a flag pole in the garden. The kerb-stones were red, white and blue. The roundabouts were red, white and blue. Swaying from lamp-post to lamp-post were red, white and blue buntings. I had to come to Ireland to see such a patriotic English village. "When is Robert Emmet's epitaph finally going to be written? What's going to resolve this horrifying, enduring situation, Emmet?"

"Talk, Orlagh, talk... Every faction is to blame for this continual conflict: the British, the SDLP, the Unionists, the IRA. All of 'em. Some more than others of course, but that's what we've got to forget - who did what and where. We can't be blinded by history. We have to think about the future - not the past. We all have to get around a table and talk. That's the only way there will be a peaceful resolution."

chapter forty-eight

Emmet drove the minibus into an off-road lookout and lifted the gloomy cloak of contemplative silence we had been shrouded in. I hadn't wanted to interrupt his thoughts as we traversed the meandering country lanes of County Antrim. It wasn't very often he was so subdued, but realisation of the evening's events had obviously hit him harder than any punch his opponent had managed to throw. I wanted to comfort him, tell him everything was going to be great. I wished I had one of Dad's wonderful stories for making everything sound perfect; a reassuring 'everything happens for a reason' speech.

"Here we are then," he apathetically declared, with an opened palm, "the home of Finn MacCool."

What I suspected was a spectacular view two-hundred feet below us was in fact a mass of darkness. For the little my eyes could make out, the obscure expanse could have been a green-grass field, maybe a vast peat bog or even a continuous concrete-covered car park. But from the distinct melodic natural soundtrack of the ocean, my ears confirmed we were at the coast.

"Come on then, let's see what this giant of yours has done." I was attempting to raise Emmet's spirits a little and wanting to make the most of the hour's drive.

"We might as well now we're here."

As we closed the doors of the minibus a full moon glided

languidly from behind a cloud. It was as though God had turned on His lights just for us. I was expecting Emmet to grasp my hands, attempt to do the jive while performing a rendition of 'Moondance', prompting me to fill in the gaps; but he was unaware of the haunting presence of the moon. Instead he headed towards the entrance to the walkway which led down to Giant's Causeway.

DO NOT ENTER!
opening hours - 9.00-18.00
Under Protection Of The National Trust
World Heritage Site.

"Oh, Emmet, they're joking? We've come all this way and we can't even go and see it?"

"Why can't yer, Orlagh?" I thought I almost caught one of his crafty smiles in the bright moonlight.

"Well, it does say no entry, and there is barbed-wire on top of that gate, Emm."

"And...? Is that supposed to stop me? When has a sign, or barbed-wire for that matter, stopped me before? Yer should be used to that now, Orlagh. Would a sign and a bit of blunt metal stop yer da'?"

This was true. It was second nature for me to sneak into places, so I attentively followed Emmet, who scaled the gate with virile perfection, waiting the other side for me to imitate his agile, barbed-wire-eluding movement. I placed my hands in-between two sets of ominous-looking spikes, trying my hardest to look as though I was accomplishing the feat with ease (I still had my tomboy status to live up to) while trying to look modestly lady-like. I just hoped the legend of Finn MacCool was worth it. I managed to climb the horizontal slats of the wooden gate and succeeded in transferring my right leg over the top of the gate. I now stood with a leg either side of the barbed-wire.

"Give me your left hand, princess, swing your leg over'nd jump. You've no need to touch the wire again then."

I did as Emmet instructed. As he grabbed my hand, pain filled my whole body. I couldn't place where the pain originated. Was I unbeknown to myself caught in the barbed-wire? I couldn't ascertain the origin from my straddled position; so, gripping tighter to Emmet's hand, I leapt into the fresh sea air. The agony increased and there was soon no mystery about the source of it.

"Agghh! Ow!" I screeched, as I landed on the dusty path.

"What, what's wrong? Did the wire get ye?" Even in the moonlight I could see concern reflecting in Emmet's eyes; he knew I wouldn't usually complain over nothing.

"It's my hand. God knows how I've done it, but I'm sure it's broken."

He took my left hand in his and we could quite clearly see why I was in pain. I had a lump the size of a small egg covering the entire area of my knuckles.

"Yer don't know how yer've done it? Are ye serious? Think of that judge's head, that may jog your memory, yer nutter. Wiggle yer fingers." I did as I was instructed. The pain was bad, but I had almost full movement. "It doesn't look like it's broken. Not that I'm a doctor or anything, but I don't think you'd be able to move it so freely if it were. I know just what it needs."

Like a gentleman of aristocracy, not taking his eyes off me, he raised my hand to his lips and sensually kissed it, allowing his lips to linger over my swollen hand. It had the same effect as a magic motherly kiss which I'd received as a child when I'd grazed my knees or the palms of my hands, miraculously disposing of the discomfort instantaneously. But with Emmet my rapid recovery didn't occur because I wanted to jump back up and continue with playtime. I suspected it had more to do with my body not being able to cope with so many outstanding emotions all at the same time. It was the first time since we had been in Ireland he had shown any physical affection. I didn't like to badger him and attempt to catch secret kisses when all the lads were around. I left it all up to him to make the first move. I didn't want to annoy him and risk total alienation. I wished it wasn't like that, but I suppose I understood his predicament - it was a case of having to.

My mind was then diverted into thinking about being alone with Emmet. Not just alone in his car, or alone in the cinema, but totally isolated - in Ireland, on an ancient promontory surrounded by obscure shapes. It was just the two of us in the home of a giant.

"Wow! Look at this - it's totally amazing," I exclaimed, as we finally descended the twisting cliff path to view the fairytale land of hexagonal stepping stones which protruded out of the sea at varying heights. The thunder of the waves crashing into the stones added to the mystique. The spray which the waves produced wet the tops of the stones so they shimmered like stars in the bright moonlight, producing a mirror image of the night-time sky.

"How far does this go on, Emm?" I shouted, over the roar of the crashing waves.

"All the way to Staffa Island in the Hebrides, where Sibh, the love of Finn MacCool's life, resided. It's said he built the causeway so he could walk across to her. But as the years have passed the seas have buried the majority from our sight, so they have." He held out his hand for me to place mine in. I jumped over a couple of the hexagonal rocks to appear at Emmet's left side so my undamaged hand could sit undisturbed in his, as he pointed out features hidden within the formation of the rocks. "That's the Honeycomb, the Keystone, the Giant's Loom and right here's the Wishing Chair. The Wishing Chair was where Finn MacCool ate his feasts of fish, but it has magical powers too. If yer sit in it, yer can make a wish and Finn will grant it, so he will."

The Wishing Chair was made up from various rocks of all sizes and levels. Four hexagonal stones which sat side by side formed the seat area. The armrests were the tops of two of the six-sided-stones, and the backrest was shaped from numerous eight-foot-tall hexagonal basalt columns. I established myself in the centre of the seat area, and playfully, like a meditating guru, lifted my feet from the floor. On each hand I placed my index finger and thumb together to form a circle, then placed the tips of the circles on my temples. I closed my eyes and created a humming sound which was expelled from my nose as I made my wish to Finn MacCool.

"Now I'm totally convinced yer're a complete loony tune." Emmet laughed heartily for the first time since his robbery.

Without interrupting my 'homming' I broke into a slight smile and attempted to ignore him so I could continue on with my meditative wish. Although I was behaving as though it was all in jest, the actual wish I beseeched was the desire I hungered for habitually: a hunger which gnawed in the pit of my stomach, which ached in my throat, that eradicated my saliva and intercepted each of my thoughts. Presently I felt I was only experiencing a taste of the feast which lay before me. I had never had the full meal to nullify my hunger. Whether it was Finn MacCool, the Angels or Miraculous Saint Martha authorising my wish, I didn't care, I just desperately desired for it to be granted. I didn't want to be considered a glutton, but I didn't want to die of romantic malnutrition either.

With my legs beginning to ache from being suspended in mid-air and my throat beginning to get sore from excess 'homming' I decided to put the finishing touches to my wish; only there seemed to be so many fine details I could not omit. As I concluded the supplementary aspects of my desire, it was christened by a huge wave, which swept across the hexagonal rocks and ended its journey over the wishing chair. The remnants of the frothy salt water dripped down my face like tears, which were then absorbed by my clothes. Emmet had been standing out of harm's way and remained dry, except for real saline tears which trickled down his face from uncontrollable laughter.

"Come on, I know a great little place where yer can warm up, oh high and mighty wet-wish-master."

He took hold of my right hand, rubbed droplets of sea-water off and wrapped his warm fingers around it and led me over the hexagonal stones in the direction of where the cliff sprung as if by magic from the ocean. Shadows cast by the moon gave the cliff face a deep blackness, like we were approaching the unknown, but Emmet seemed to know exactly where we were heading.

"When the moon comes from behind those clouds, you'll be able to see the organ."

"A real one, Emm?"

"A real one if your name is Finn and you're a giant, yeah."

On cue, the swirling smoke clouds were blown away in the sea breeze, displaying the white haunting moon in its entire glory, giving life to the vision before us. It was just as Emmet had said - a giant's organ. A dozen or so sixty-foot precipitous basalt columns rose sheer from a black hole at the base of the cliff face; they were like the pipes of an immense organ.

"What's the black hole at the bottom, Emm? I still can't quite make out what it is."

"That's the organ cave, where Finn would sit and play his sweet music for his beautiful giantess, Sibh."

"But I thought you said she lived on Staffa Island in the Scottish Hebrides."

"Well taken in, princess. She did, but the music Finn played travelled through his cave in an under-water channel, where his sweet music would echo in Fingal's Cave which was the home he'd built for her on Staffa Island. Fingal's cave is constructed from thousands of these hexagonal columns which are here. Apparently, Fingal's Cave is one of the most beautiful caves in the world. It must be one of the most famous caves too. Mendelssohn composed his Hebrides Overture named Fingal's Cave after he was inspired by its magnificence.

Keats and Wordsworth wrote poems about it and Turner even painted it."

We entered Finn's Organ cave, which for ten feet was almost as bright as outside. The six-sided rocks were continuous along the floor and I could just make out the jagged edges of the hexagonal rocks on the ceiling of the cave chamber. It was as though Finn had haphazardly chopped his way through with his giant axe, desperate to reach his loved one. Echoing, eerie drips from the depths of the darkness alternated with the crashing waves outside. I imagined icicle-shaped stalactites and stalagmites growing with each haunting drip, drip, drip, adding to the splendour of Finn's Organ Cave.

"You're pretty clever for a Derry man, aren't yer? And behind that mask of masculinity I reckon you're a bit of a romantic at heart: classical music, poetry and art. Mmm, sounds very suspect to me." I poked his chest with my undamaged hand.

Seizing my wrist he pulled me into him, wrapping my arm around his waist. "I'll show you what a romantic I am, Miss Emmet."

And he playfully kissed me like a Twenties' movie star, supporting my weight at the base of my back and lowering me down to the cave floor, as if practising a tango corté. As we regained a standing position the kiss continued, long and hard. I could taste the slight metallic pungency on my tongue as it explored the inside of his grazed lips. All the disappointing memories of the evening's events evaporated into that kiss.

His hands rose and cupped my face. The small calluses on his otherwise soft hands made me tingle as he slid them down my face and allowed his fingertips to skim over my neck. Once again he placed his palms flat on my body. They travelled over my collar bone and slowly, firmly, on to my breasts. I took a sharp intake of breath as pins and needles rose from my feet, through my legs and exploded in my pelvic bone. He began to undo my damp blouse as his lips departed my mouth and began a journey of moist pecks across my cheek. As each peck terminated, the sound of the trapped air being released was just about audible over the sound of the roaring, white-tipped waves outside. His lips glided over the peach hair of my face, making it feel like each hair was standing to attention. As the final button of my blouse was opened his palms once again met with the skin of my torso. Pressing comfortably hard they moved in an upward motion, rambling over the contours of my breasts and beyond my collar-bone. His thumbs hooked underneath the collar of my blouse and continued their expedition over my shoulders, taking the blouse with them. I drew my arms to my side, so it could come off with ease. The sleeves turned inside-out as it left my body and dropped to the rocky ground. While his hands traversed the meandered curves of my waist, his teeth playfully nipped the skin of my neck. Stopping on the curve where my shoulder and neck met, he rubbed his smooth lips lingeringly, before erotically biting the taut muscle.

The passion rose higher than the cliff we were sheltered under and faster than the crashing waves of the Irish Sea. I was convinced the mighty goddess Aphrodite had once again sprung from her home in the foam of the waves and instructed her powers of passion to penetrate our spirits. We had removed every item of each other's clothes. I lay naked on the smooth hexagonal rocks of Finn MacCool's Organ cave, as the silhouette of Emmet's sculptured body kissed every inch of my body. His lips massaged my breasts and his cavorting tongue made my nipples rise like the stalagmites I imagined were in the darkness of the cave. The tip of his nose expelled a soft trail of breath as it traced its way past my navel, through my pelvis, where he teasingly bit the insides of my thighs. As his tongue tantalisingly tasted my escaping juices, every muscle in my body felt as though it were tense, as though Aphrodite had possessed my entire being; Wordsworh, Keats, Tennyson or Byron couldn't poetically express the sensation I was experiencing at that moment. I longed for Emmet to be part of me, to enter me, so we could become one. And when he did I thought I heard Mendelssohn's overture echoing from Fingal's Cave. Or maybe it was Finn MacCool sensually striking the chords on his organ, enticing Sibh through their underwater channel to unite with him. Or it could have been Aphrodite squealing melodically through the thunderous waves her joy at the consummation of our love. It could even have been a choir of my heavenly angels approving. Or perhaps it was a conglomeration of them all, aiding in the symphony of *my* ecstasy.

chapter forty-nine

I lay enclosed in Emmet's muscular defined arm, with my ear against his chest. With no words passing between us I listened to his heart beat fast, and then slow, to a leisurely hypnotic beat as all his energy evaporated into sleep. My bare body was covered in a film of miniature goose-bumps; from the slight dawn breeze entering the cave and from the rousing thoughts of the past few hours. I lay still so as not to disturb him. I wanted to stay there forever. I wanted to hear the rhapsodic beat of his heart perpetually. I wanted to watch the slight stubble sprout under his chin each and every night. But would it ever be as perfect again? Would things be different between us now? Had I succumbed to being another of his accomplishments? I hadn't resisted - I'd encouraged. Would he still regard me as his sweet princess?

Still, all the negative thoughts couldn't surmount the rapture I felt, couldn't obliterate the fact that my dreams had come true. Most of the wish I appealed for as I had sat homming in Finn MacCool's Wishing Chair had been granted. I had finally feasted on the scrumptious banquet, but hunger still loitered. I longed for the table to be laid again. Only time would tell if the second part of my wish was to be granted.

I slowly lifted my head from the pit of Emmet's arm, attempting not to disturb him from his sleep. His naked body lay still except for the expansion of his chest from his rhythmic breathing. Then, unexpectedly, his whole body moved. For some reason I panicked. I wasn't ready to face him in my nakedness. I felt vulnerable - embarrassed even. But he didn't wake, he rolled on to his side, placed his palms together as if in prayer and sheltered them in-between his warm thighs. I silently dressed myself and covered Emmet's torso with his opened shirt and his legs with his jacket. The scent of his aftershave escaped the confines of his clothes and filled the sea water-smelling cave with his own luscious aroma.

I returned to Finn's wishing chair. Taking my seat, I hugged my calves and balanced my chin on my knees. It was quite chilly but my heart felt as warm as the dawn sky appeared, which was a rippling sea of red and gold which reflected into the wide expanse of the open sea. The sea which a few hours ago crashed into the rocks of Giant's Causeway with intensity, but now calmly lapped to the shore, like a rippling garden pond. The Mighty Aphrodite had disappeared, adding my purity to the froth of her waves and had whisked it away to the depths of the ocean, never to be retrieved.

I'm sure I heard the calm water, which lapped on to the rocks, begin to murmur. I concentrated on the sound and sure enough I heard: "Tempus omnia revelat," the voice of the water whispered. "Time... whoosh... brings everything... Patience... whooosshh... and laughter... whooosshh." The whoosh of the waves translated into a repetitious "Wisest... whoosh... is she... whooooshhh... who knows... whooooshhh... what she does not know... whooooossshhh."

"So yer sneaked away and left me then?" Emmet startled me from the whispering water as he took a seat on the armrest of the wishing chair. Placing his palm under my hair he stroked the bare skin at the nape of my neck.

I didn't take my eyes off the oscillating, whispering water as I replied; "Sorry, I was just going to watch the sun rise. I'm not usually awake at this hour to witness it."

Emmet gazed out at the golden horizon. "I wonder what's waiting for us, Orlagh? For me and you, out there on that horizon. I do know something for sure though..."

"What's that then, Emm?" I now stared out to the horizon.

"That I managed to get the girl I love in the country I love." I turned to face him, shocked by his passionate phrase, and the blackbird which flew through his paradise sky-blue eyes took flight and landed with both feet on my heart. For a moment I thought the second part of my wish might just be granted. "And yer know what?" Before I could answer he continued. "They're both *big* trouble." I didn't want to spoil the initial part of his comment and ask what he meant by trouble, but I'm sure I felt that blackbird's claws penetrating deep into my heart. He kissed my forehead and said, "Come on, let's make a move. We should make it back before anyone notices we've been gone for the night."

We walked the winding cliff path to the minibus in silence. I couldn't find a suitable subject to talk about so thought it best if we said nothing at all. The only thoughts which entered my mind were those of our actions in the Organ Cave. When we finally reached the top and scaled the gate, taking care to be helped with my undamaged hand (the egg was still present, with an added shade of dark blue) I looked over what had been an obscure expanse when we had arrived and had now transformed in the dawn light to a magnificent view of thousands of miniature hexagonal fairytale stepping stones. I was certainly impressed by *all* aspects of the giant's land.

Emmet turned the ignition of the minibus. A thin film of condensation sat on the windows and on the radio 'Soul to Soul' aptly sang; *'Back to life. Back to reality. Back to the here and now-ow, yeah.'*

What was the reality?

Back to the one reality of facing losses which were a lot less triumphant than the one I had experienced.

chapter fifty

My jewel-encrusted locked box, full of priceless gems of the variety which had been instilled to sparkle with infinite knowledge, no longer bobbed on the surface of my subconscious, awaiting discovery of the lost key. It had traversed the rivers and tributaries of my mind and escaped into the estuary to enter the tranquil ocean of contentment. Along the way it had eroded the desire to reach my destiny... Well, I thought, I had already reached my destiny. I considered I had stumbled upon the warm paradise plains of heaven, where the pot of gold shimmered in the bright sun under the utopian rainbow of happiness; where I had been silently instructed to help myself to the treasures which lay before me. Treasure in the form of Emmet O'Malley.

Although initially I thought I had been reprimanded for reaping what I had harvested. I thought I had ruined everything with my greed. Since the occurrence at Giant's Causeway I had dressed my mind in black, placed a black net veil over the face of it and began to mourn the loss of my purity.

Not many words had passed between Emmet and myself as we travelled the Antrim roads back to Belfast. When rejoining all the rest of the lads, it had progressed from few words to little eye contact. There was a sense of awkwardness lodged right between us. When our eyes did meet, he would quickly look away as if they hadn't. Each time the blackbird's claws penetrated further into my heart.

As we all made our way back to England, I sat in the minibus watching the scenery go by. I was encapsulated within a sorrowful atmosphere, which lingered over each chair, down the entire aisle, in the overhead racks and in the breath of everyone's unusually sporadic speech. I chose to sit in the front with Dad, so to avoid all other conversation. My cover was safe as no one wanted to talk anyway. I too, like them, was preoccupied in thoughts of my own loss.

Patrick's guidance from preceding years resounded in my head: *"You know never to fall for any of those sweet-talkin' lines guys dream up, Orle? You have to wait. We all like the girls who are waiting; they're the ones to get!"* Should I have refused? Should I have said, 'No, Emmet, I'm waiting for the right man. The man I want to marry. The man I want to spend the rest of my days with.?' Well, he was that man, so that would have just been downright ridiculous.

Had I taken the JCB of lust and smashed down the wall of respect which had taken years to build, destroying any chance of an unblemished reconstruction? Half my mind thought so. The other half, which housed my intrinsic, *liberated* (not so adolescent) sensual urge, endeavoured to exonerate Emmet's subdued attitude, his lack of 'hey princess' or 'angel face' comments. It attempted justification of his averted, shameful eyes. The pessimistic side of my mind would have none of it. Wouldn't listen. Didn't care. There was only one explanation as far as it was concerned - I had been foolish, greedy and irrational.

There was a war going on between two factions of my mind. They would soon have to come to a compromise before the detonator was ignited and my mind exploded into absolute incomprehension. The ticking bomb was becoming unbearably loud. Comments being fired back and forth over the no-man's-land of reasoning could not be silenced. I thought the only thing I could do to hush the battle was sleep. I was as worn out as the grass under the seat of a child's swing. But even the *thought* of sleep caused controversy. The pessimistic part shrieked that frivolous hedonism was responsible for my tiredness. The idealistic entity retorted only with Epicurean adulation. It considered every conscious second was worth the heavy eyes, the tired muscles, even the exhausted mind.

But would it all be worth rejection?

The anti-bomb squad finally came in the form of a long, deep sleep, a sleep which disconnected the fuse and evaded a devastating detonation.

I awoke hours later on the approach to Birmingham. I had a few serene awakening seconds of uncomplicated thought until my memory reactivated itself and the battle commenced once again, when realisation hit me of what had occurred the previous evening. I cringed and thought to myself, 'Oh my God, what have I done?'.

Dad drove into the gym car park and made an announcement which was to sink my heart deeper into the pool of despondency.

"No training for a couple of weeks, lads. What'de ya think, eh? Give yerselves a well-deserved break. Have a rest, get over them terrible decisions and we'll come back to a nice fresh start, raring to go."

I couldn't cope with these mind wars for another two weeks. I had to get things into perspective. It was imperative to my sanity that I see Emmet, and training was always the perfect excuse, the best alibi - he couldn't avoid me and I couldn't avoid him. Maybe he would go out with Patrick or Dominic in the week, but there was a chance of missing him, or the probability of too many ears and eyes being present to make or say anything other than the usual friendly gestures. Dad's timing to give them a break couldn't have been worse.

A group of parents awaited our return and numerous conversations struck up, almost drowning the argument in my own head; decisions on who was giving whom a lift, talk of robberies, talk of black eyes. I even heard distant references to my own judge-beating story

Through all the talking relatives I caught Emmet's eye, but this time he didn't look away, he held my gaze. Uncontrollably I felt my lips turn into a smile. My eyes witnessed a mirror image on his face. Pure relief swept through my body. My nerves began to tingle as he made his way towards me.

"Hey, angel face, I thought you'd fallen out with me for a wee while there. Just in case I don't see yer before, I'll pick yer up on Sunday for the movies, if yer like?" If I like? *If I like?* The black veil was swiped off my head in double-quick time. My mourning period was over and rejoicing started. Maybe I should have a little more faith in my angelic guidance which was last whispered from the waters of the Irish sea - time *may just* bring everything!

I saw Emmet that Sunday and my *liberated* sensual urge had won the war and it basked in its glory, relished its freedom. The optimistic part of my mind had won its war too and celebrated like the thousands of people in the streets on VE Day. And so began the journey of my locked box full of infinite knowledge. It flowed with the rapid current of satisfaction, over the perilous white water, like an expert kayaker. When Emmet and I had a secret date - the further the box travelled. And when we talked of telling everyone about us - my parents, my brothers, his family, all the lads at the gym - my box full of angelic-bestowed knowledge finally ended its journey and entered the tranquil ocean of contentment; where it gradually started to sink. I really wasn't bothered about the treasures it preserved, the life-long advice it stored. All I cared about was - Emmet O'Malley.

CHAPTER fifty-one

A few months had passed since the occurrence of the losses in Ireland. The boys did return back to the gym and were more determined than ever to procure each and every title available. My own appearance at the gym lapsed, traded for nights staring at school textbooks, memorising laws of atomic and molecular physics or engrossed in the principles of electrodynamics, fluid dynamics, or thermodynamics, which, in my mind, were anything *but* dynamic. Unlike Archimedes I wasn't about to shriek '*EUREKA!*' In my eyes Maths equations and ratios were beginning to mutate into Egyptian hieroglyphics. Lineage of British royalty couldn't persuade my mind not to steer towards the signpost which directed the way to an Emmet O'Malley line of thought.

I cursed the timing of my exams in more ways than one. Firstly, Dad had taken Dominic and Patrick on a trip to Canada and America. They would be spending time with Teddy Bailey and his coconut creme pie, ketchup-free burgers and his nonsensical salutation of: '*hey, man boy man boy man, have you been to Chattanooga and a seen a biga da lika Rosa, with the biga da lika watermelons?*'.The primary reason for the trip was that a friendly bout had been arranged for Dom and Pat to box the winners of the American Golden Gloves Championships at their respective weights. Even if I'd begged, squealed or had a raging tantrum, an emphatic *no* would have reverberated in my proximity to a request of, 'Can I go?'

Secondly, if their trip hadn't fallen right smack bang in the middle of the main weeks of my exams, it would have given me more of a chance to see Emmet without secretly creeping around. As it was, I actually saw him less. Instead, like Galileo had, who I was re-reading up on, I sat gazing at the moon from the desk in my bedroom. Unlike Galileo I couldn't begin to think about the moon's surface irregularities; the only thing that sprung to my mind was Emmet as he sang '*Moondance*' and I filled in his gaps. I needed an Isaac Newton apple to fall on my head, to remind my mind there was such a thing as gravity, that it shouldn't be floating up there with the stars, but come back down to earth where it belonged.

Ironically Dad, Dom and Pat arrived back the day of my last exam, although this turned out to be a good thing, as that day was also Emmet's twenty-first birthday. Thus, a birthday, plus welcome home, plus fight-win celebration night-out had been arranged (not that they needed an excuse). When Patrick said there was room for one more in the car, added to that list of revelry reasons was a 'leaving school celebration' too. I was being allowed the honour of going on a lads' night-out. It wasn't just a usual night-out in town either. No, we were going to an open-air party in a farmer's field off the M25 motorway - the kind of open-air party which soon evolved into the youth cultural milestone of our time, the dance phenomenon known as - raves. I'd heard all the stories of these rave nights and couldn't wait to be involved at the start of something new. I wouldn't be jumping on the bandwagon of a preceding generation's craze, I would be up there on top of the wagon, geeing up the horses, leading them into the history books of youth culture.

I had listened in awe while Patrick and Dominic enthusiastically described the birth of the whole rave phenomenon. They gave me so many details I almost felt

I'd already been to one, but I couldn't wait to experience it all first hand.

They explained how the rave scene was born when a few promoters from small London-based clubs had a brain-wave to stage open-air parties. With no planning permission granted, these parties were deemed illegal. It was through word of mouth and funky-styled flyers given out at certain clubs that 'would-be ravers' got to hear about these secret-location parties, which were to be held in fields adjacent to the M25. Thousands of cars packed into a convoy in the early hours of the morning of Friday or Saturday, on what would usually have been an empty M25, to follow an unknown allotted leader who apparently knew the secret location of the rave. A few false alarms usually occurred when thousands of people arrived in a mud sodden, rave-less field. The designated guide would then have to get on their huge mobile phone to listen once again to cryptic directions to the covert location.

Before those final bends to the correct location were turned, the high decibels of dance beats with whispers of lyrics pumped into the dark summer air could clearly be heard, played by DJ's such as Nicky Holloway, Paul Oakenfold or Carl Cox. Upon taking that final turn, the vision of a fantasy world laid out before you on the brow of a hill was astounding. There were carousels, Ferris wheels, bumper cars and neon lights flashing in a field of ten thousand or more secret revellers, who had eluded the police to release their inhibitions and indulge in the party until the sun rose, giving the entrepreneurial promotional organisers the concept to name these events such as - Sunrise, and as was often the case - Raindance. Spawned from Sunrise and Raindance, numerous promotional rave nights eventually set up country-wide, all with innovative concepts and creative names, such as Delirious, Amnesia, Eclipse, Spectrum, Quest, Starlight, Genesis, Pandemonium, Raw, Time Out and Biology. They sprang up in unconventional buildings, aircraft hangars or disused warehouses which Dominic maintained had been left to wrack and ruin as a result of Thatcher's destruction of the British manufacturing industry - but that's a whole other story.

Patrick reckoned that as a result of these 'raves' the intense football hooliganism of the Eighties came to an end almost overnight, as Aston Villa and Birmingham City, Manchester City and Manchester United, Arsenal and Tottenham, Millwall, Chelsea and West Ham all danced in harmony to the *chill*-ing, empathising effects of a £15 Ecstasy pill. It was the pacifier, the instiller of that *loved-up vibe*. The ecstasy masqueraded with such names (with an embossed stamp on top to differentiate) as Doves, Double Doves even Turtle Doves, plugging that love vibe once again. California Sunrise, Dolphins, Shamrocks, P and T's, Phase fours, Snowballs, Love Hearts and Purple Hearts, or even the strong New Yorkers. Ecstasy didn't merely appear as embossed little white pills either; there were red and black capsules known as Dennis The Menace, or yellow and red capsules recognised as Rhubarb and Custard. There were the energising flat speckled-brown tablets, dubbed Disco Biscuits or mini-*BigMac* shaped Disco Burgers. Exhilarating names - the key to a night of insouciance. There were the acid tabs too, known as trips - which took you on a journey into the land of hallucination. They were attached with almost as many diminutives: Batman, Jokers, Purple Homs, Pink Floyds, the ubiquitous Smiley Faces or the potent Welsh Dragons. Turning the landscape for the participant into a mightier, brighter, more fascinating place to be.

But, like Patrick, Dominic, Emmet and their gang never, you didn't have to partake in the drug taking to enjoy the mellow experience, the non-aggressive aforementioned *loved-up vibe*. There wasn't a pusher in every dark alcove coaxing you to buy their merchandise; it was there if you wanted it. The whole atmosphere was exhilarating, and the lack of sleep brought with it its own highs. As with the Mods and Rockers, or Punks and Teds there weren't any

422

conflicting groups of youths, only an antagonistic-evading-atmosphere. Class was transcended and replaced with a feeling of togetherness - united in dance... No wonder 1989 was being dubbed the first 'Summer Of Love'. No wonder I was excited at the thought of going to my first rave!

Both Dominic and Patrick were taking their cars for the journey down to Hertfordshire, or Buckinghamshire, we wouldn't really know which until we approached the M25 vicinity. I was allocated to Pat's car, and thankfully so was Emmet - the birthday boy - along with Mickey Duffy and Sean McCabe. As usual everyone (except Sean) met at our house. Mam and Dad had gone up to the Lake District to attend the wedding of Aunt Teresa's eldest daughter, Nuala. I had had the choice to go. My mind transformed into scales: a rave on one side and a family wedding in the Lake District on the other... It wasn't difficult to view which one outweighed the other.

Sean was to be picked up from his present girlfriend's house, located just outside the city in a small village in the countryside. So Dominic's car carried on ahead of us. We were to meet at McDonalds in St Albans.

We all looked more like we were heading to the gym rather than on a night out. The appropriate attire was anything sporty, colourful and large.

With American football, baseball and basketball garments being rare, I was the envy of everyone in my new, direct from the stadium, Toronto Blue Jay's jacket and matching baseball cap. I was a little apprehensive in wearing my cap, as they were so scarce, making me all the more noticeable. Although Patrick, my predominant stylist, insisted everyone would soon be wearing them and encouraged me to set the trend.

So, with my psychedelic hooded sweatshirt, lustrous silver Blue Jay's jacket, Armani jeans, green and purple Kickers, baseball cap and a fully fledged freedom-from-school elation, I was set to *rave* the night away.

Emmet and I had the back to ourselves, where we traded clandestine caresses, which, if our discussion on divulging our relationship came to fruition, would cease being so secret. Maybe tonight would be the night we would tell everyone?

"Orlagh, duck down so Sean's girl can't see you; we don't want her coming. She's been told it's a lads' night-out - which it is, we just can't begin to explain to her that you're one of the lads," Mickey instructed from the passenger seat as Sean joined Emmet and myself in the back.

Coleshill was a quaint chocolate-box village, with centuries-old dwellings lining the streets, along with numerous charming country pubs. It was one of those enchanting pubs we guessed the occupants of the car which was driving behind us had been captivated by, for what must have been quite some time. Maybe they had gone in for a quick drink straight from work, which most probably turned into a second, then a third and maybe a fourth. When the landlord suggested they leave the company car on the car park and take a taxi, they angrily refused and left - inebriated... It was the only reasonable explanation for their erratic behaviour.

Patrick was keeping to the thirty miles per hour speed limit as we drove through the single-lane-each-way town centre, when he spotted the red Mercedes for the first time.

"Look at these feckin' wankers behind," he stated, with his eyes darting back and forth from the road to the rear-view mirror.

The car was as close as it could possible get, almost appearing as if it were hooked on to Pat's tow bar. Pat increased his speed to forty, but they continued to tailgate, flashing their headlights as they did.

"Fuckin' pull over, Pat, and we'll give it to the fuckin' pricks," Mickey Duffy irately stated.

Emmet attempted to calm Mickey down: "Let 'em carry on for now, the eejits are obviously pissed. They're all suited-up, look. They're just a bunch of pen-pushin' pricks on a Friday night drink from the office and 've got a little Dutch courage."

"I'll give 'em Dutch courage, I'll get the biggest bunch of fuckin' tulips from Amsterdam and ram 'em right up their arses. Followed with a kick from the sharp end of a yella fuckin' clog," Mickey jovially replied.

My heart pounded hard and fast as it attempted to contend with the ecstatic adrenaline pumping around my body which sensed trouble was looming.

"I'm not gonna go any faster, they've enough room to overtake me now," Pat stated in annoyance, as the town centre ended and the hedge-lined country lane began. "They're givin' us the fingers now, look." Pat nodded into his rear-view mirror. Emmet, Mickey, Sean and myself turned around to be greeted with masturbation-mimicking hand signals.

"These guys are too much now, pull over, Pat," Sean instructed.

"No, no, just ignore 'em for now. Believe me, it'll wind 'em up even more. They'll think we're bottling it," Emmet advised everyone.

"The only thing I'll be bottling are their heads," Mickey retorted.

"Yeah, I know that, you know that, we all feckin' know that, except them morons in that car. So chill and save your anger until it goes off, cause it's almost inevitable that it will," Emmet replied.

We turned a sharp bend, mounted a humpback bridge and the Mercedes continued to ride our bumper. There was silence in the car. Was it the calm before the storm?

A T-junction was rapidly approaching. Patrick was going to have to come to a halt. We were all silently speculating whether the car behind was going to adhere to the rules of the road too.

As we were coming to a standstill Mickey rolled down the window.

"Leave it be Mick, like Emm said, they'll think we're

cowering. The element of surprise is one of yer best defences," Pat professed.

Because Mickey had opened the window, we could hear muffled chants coming from the occupants of the car behind, as they shook their fists with unprovoked rage; "Come on, pull over you little wankers. Come on. We're gonna batter ya, knock ya to Kingdom-fuckin'-come. You'll think twice about coming by our hood agen."

"Our hood? Where the fuck do they think they are? The fuckin' Bronx? The woolly-back country-bumpkin bollixes," Mickey uttered, through a clenched-tooth smile.

Emmet decided it was time to liven things up a little. "Watch this, they'll think we're total imbeciles," he said.

Turning around to face the four male occupants of the Mercedes, Emmet crossed his eyes, stuck out his tongue, placed his thumbs above his ears, spread his fingers wide apart, and wiggled them back and forth like a child teasing.

The child-like atmosphere in Pat's car rapidly metamorphosed into a hostile war zone when they drove their car into the back of Pat's. All of us jolted forward. Pat's car emptied as fast as if they had been informed it was imminently going to explode. I was left alone to witness the battle.

The Mercedes emptied a little slower. I think this had something to do with their size. They were not small and nimble like Pat, Emm, Sean and Mickey, but, tall, fat and wide.

The driver was first to emerge, with a shaven head and tattoos peeping from under his rolled-up shirt-sleeves. He was that tall he just seemed to continue to emerge from the car.

"Who're ya pulling faces at, ya little ponces? I'm gonna rip off your heads," the driver proclaimed. He made his way to the no-man's-land in front of his car and behind Pat's, where Pat was presently dancing around in his boxing stance with his guard up. Clad in his white and green Boston Celtics tracksuit, Pat could well have been going to the gym.

"You'll do what, you fat prick. You'll do fuckin' *what?*"

426

Pat confidently retorted, gesturing him on. Emmet was in-between them, as if he were a referee in the boxing ring, ready to shout 'BOX' for the commencement of the bout. The driver attempted to push past Emmet, who looked a midget in comparison to this Goliath of a man. I was praying that *David* would emerge in the spirit of one of my lads. The driver's right hand lay on Emmet's chest and pushed him aside, leaving Pat wide open for his attack. His hooked-nose-profile was now Emmet's view - or more to the point - Emmet's target. As the colossal driver lunged forward to take a pitiful swing at Patrick's head, Emmet released the stone from the sling and delivered two shocking right hooks into his moving chin: *'The shock treatment it's one of yer best defences.'* Shocked he probably would have been, if he wasn't concentrating on trying to remain conscious.

As he was making his descent to the tarmacked road, he seized Emmet's shirt for stability. Emmet's £130.00 Fiorucci shirt, which was being donned for the very first time. When Emmet witnessed the embossed buttons flying and heard the fabric of his shirt ripping, wrath ricocheted off every sinew of his being and was absorbed by the downed driver. No referee - no rules.

This was not the *raving* I had had in mind.

While Emmet tackled the driver, Patrick was contending with the first passenger to emerge who was also huge, but more fat that muscle. Pat was keeping him at bay, at the end of his long arms, with fast adamantine straight punches: left, right, left, right. The passenger resembled a drowning person, fighting the remorseless water for his life - to no triumphant avail. In his case it was thin air he was lashing out at as Pat danced divinely out of the way.

Even with the seriousness of the situation Pat was still the showman. I had to smile to myself as I witnessed a humorous cartoon-strip manoeuvre. It was like watching Popeye defeat Pluto after he'd consumed his spinach. Pat had obviously decided the tubby-thug, with his bloody nose, had taken enough punishment. Thus, with a comical twist Pat swivelled him around so he was facing the ground with his round backside in the air, which was to be met with an amusing kick, sending him head-first into the hedge. Then the expression on Pat's face abruptly mutated from one of satisfaction - to one of shock. What was he so surprised at, I thought?

My eyes darted from Emmet who was straddled over the recumbent conquered Goliath while rampageously head-butting him, to flyweight Sean. It appeared Sean had also vanquished his oversized opponent, who was presently attempting to emulate a car mechanic and had disappeared under the Mercedes. I suspected this had nothing to do with a sudden interest in the workings of the engine - more so the art of escape. Then my eyes finally focused on Mickey. A presently psychotic Mickey. The fourth and final passenger had made it from the back seat to the driving seat, where he had retrieved the yellow crook lock from under the chair and was about to exit the car - weapon in hand. He was stopped in his tracks by Mickey, who ran up and slammed the door full force on his arm. The crook lock fell to the floor with an echoing metallic bang, mixed with the squeals of the would-be attacker. But none of the above scenes provoked Patrick's dumbfounded disposition.

I couldn't quite comprehend what Patrick was doing, or more to the point, *why* he was doing it. Neither did I hear his departing words as he started jogging off down the country lane in his Boston Celtics tracksuit and Adidas shell-toes as though he was an athlete on an evening run. His mass of spiralled curls were springing to the rhythm of his sprint.

When I saw the flashing blue light glide across my skin, his departure became perfectly understandable.

As the officers approached the site of the fracas, Emmet froze in his straddled head-butting position. Sean ceased to attempt to pull the opponent by his protruding legs from under the vehicle, and Mickey released the rim on the roof of the Mercedes which had enabled him to pull his body closer to the door; thus, squeeze the arm of the would be assailant with enhanced force.

"We're mates, Officer. Aren't we?" Emmet prompted the semi-conscious Goliath who lay bleeding beneath him.

"I'm not your fuckin' mate, ya little wanker. Arrest him, Officer, arrest him."

Some people never learn, I thought. I also pondered the location of my brother, which prompted thoughts of how I was now going to escape this scene, since the police had handcuffed Emmet, Mickey and Sean, along with the four conquered browbeaters. They awaited a second police car to cart them off to the station. I remained an unobserved entity.

"Please re-lease meeee let meeee gooooo, for I-eeeeee don't love you annnyeeeee-more," Mickey began to sing.

My anxiety increased when I witnessed the boys being loaded into the police car and erupted when Emmet shouted over: "Don't worry about us, princess, just take the car back home. We'll see yer later."

Take the car back home? *Take the car back home?* And just how did he expect me to carry out this chore? Sure, I knew the rudimentary fundamentals of driving, but drive - *alone, unsupervised*, in Pat's new car on a route I was unfamiliar with? Was he serious? Was this actually really happening? As I sat abandoned on the side of an isolated country lane, I realised it was most definitely transpiring. I was expecting Patrick to jump from behind the hedge, take the controls and transport us home... That was just wishful thinking.

Eventually I summoned the courage to commence my agonising jaunt. I turned the key and listened to the engine purr over. The 'rumm, rumm, rumm, rumm, rumm,' of the engine was beginning to sound like 'run, run, run, run, run.' But I didn't - I did the A, B, C - accelerator, brake, clutch. I pressed my foot on the clutch, pushed the gear stick into first, removed my foot from the clutch - and hopped forward like a kangaroo. I slammed my foot on the brake, bumped my head on the windscreen... and stalled. I simultaneously regained my composure, cursed my brother, and due to the bump on the head, put on my seat-belt. I then made a second attempt at what appeared was going to be a long journey home.

I talked myself through; "Clutch down, into first, foot *slooooow-leee* off the clutch." I miraculously didn't mimic a marsupial, but headed slowly towards the T-junction. The engine raged noisily, begging for a gear change, which I considered pointless in view of the fact that I was about to do a three-point turn.

The three-point turn turned into a fifteen, maybe twenty-(plus four stallings)-point turn. But I got there in the end, the car bound for the town centre. The chocolate-box town centre which I had visited on so many occasions I couldn't begin to remember an amount. But which, when driving through - alone, driving-licence-less; actually, driving-licence-prohibited-due-to under-age-ness-less, still cursing my brother along with the occupants of the Mercedes, I realised I didn't know the way home. I knew it was a left - but *where* the left actually occurred did not wish to enter my conscious memory.

Although it felt like a lifetime, it was just over an hour since the police had carted away the lads and my brother had mutated into Sebastian Coe.

After driving up and down the high street too many times to recall I finally spotted the army and navy outlet store and realised that was where I should turn left. Being familiar with the road once again, my mind focused on a song emanating from the speakers. I smiled to myself at the absurdity of the lyrics in relation to my predicament.

"Everybody's freeeee to feel good, feel good. Everybody's freeeeeee to feel good - brother and sister together we'll make it through, oh, yeah."

Oh, no, in my situation! Brother was attempting to break some cross-country running world record, while sister was breaking the law. Certainly *not* making it through, and as for everybody being free - well! I began to wonder if Emmet, Sean and Mickey had attained their freedom and were at this very moment coming to my salvation, or waiting with bated breath for my safe arrival.

"*Some day a spirit will take you and guide you there, Oh-hh, ye-ah, ohhhh to feel good. Everybody's freeeeee, to feel good.*"

I was praying for that spirit. A celestial spirit to take me and guide me to my home; because one round-about-island with no significant distinguishing markings looked like another in the countryside. I was not feeling good, merely lost.

"*I know you've been hurting, but I've been waiting to be there for you. And I'll be there just helping you out whenever I cannnn, oh, yeah...*"

Hurting, that's what my stomach began to do when the same blue lights which had startled Patrick earlier flashed in my rear-view mirror. I definitely needed *helping out* of this situation. My heart beat louder and faster than I considered humanly viable, while my body vibrated like a battery-operated toy in a Duracell advertisement, as I watched the black-clad policeman in my wing mirror gradually increase in size. '**Danger! Objects may appear further away**' was written along the bottom of the mirror. I wished this object would appear further away, because it wasn't long before it arrived, smiling and knocking at my window.

"Can you turn your engine off, miss? And yer radio too." My brother's engine I wanted to say, and his radio too. The brother who departed thinking only of himself. I did as I was told, minus the supplementary information.

"Do you know why we stopped yer, miss?" I couldn't begin to think of an answer. I could only visualise iron bars, concrete cells, a solitary toilet in the corner and lumpy gruel in metallic bowls. "Don't look so worried, we haven't arrested yer yet. Yer haven't stolen the car, have yer?" I was mortified, until I looked up to witness him chuckling. That was also the point when his comment penetrated into my brain, where it was absorbed and construed. Not the comment itself, but the accent with which it was uttered - an Irish one. I'll use this to my advantage, I thought.

I put on my best Irish accent and stated: "No, no, erm, uurrr not at all. I was just ermm, urrr, droppin' off me aunt who was over from home, ye know from Ireland. Yes, I was droppin' her at the airport. It's me first trip there alone and I got a little lost."

"Righto, so that answers my second question. We stopped yer because you'd driven around that island back there about eight times. We thought yer might be a little drunk. But I can see now a good Irish gal like you wouldn't be breakin' the law like that now, would yer?"

"No, *nooo*, Officer. I, erm don't, urrr drink." I didn't add because I was - as with my driving - under age.

"That's grand to hear. So where're yer off to? I can point yer in the right direction."

"That's it?" I regretted saying that as soon as the declaration departed my mouth.

"Well, it is unless you want to give me a reason to arrest yer! Now come on, where to?" he asked, laughing more than you expect a policeman to.

"Ermm, right, Hodge Hill, erm please."

"Just keep going straight over all the islands, then you'll come to the Collector Road..."

"Oh, I know from there, thank you," I interrupted, desperate to escape.

"Off yer go then, and keep that music down. You'll be able to concentrate on yer driving a little more then."

Someday a spirit will take you and guide you there... They appear in so many guises, I thought, as I pulled away perfectly leaving the jam-sandwich police car behind me.

As I was driving, yes, I couldn't quite believe it myself - driving, and quite competently too; past the overgrown common land of Summerfield Road on the approach to my home, I estimated that it had taken me almost two hours to accomplish a twenty-minute journey. Patrick must surely be home by now. It would have taken him less time to run than it had for me to drive. I suspected he would be consumed with concern for my safety, overwrought with guilt for leaving me behind as he ran into the sunset.

I was quite proud of myself as I manoeuvred into our driveway, past the brick-built pillars, with the concrete moulded lions atop. Pat wasn't hysterically pivoting on the doorstep drooling with guilt as I had anticipated. I then felt a pang of guilt strike me as a thought invaded my mind of him being hunted down by police with sniffing, salivating dogs nuzzling beneath the undergrowth of the countryside.

The porch door was unlocked, informing me someone was home. I turned the key to be greeted by another surprise in the long chain of the evening's shocking incidents. There was Mickey Duffy, sitting quite comfortably on the couch, feet on the pouffe, concentrating on catching soggy biscuits on his tongue before they could disintegrate into his fresh tea.

"Hi ya, Orle," he remarked nonchalantly. He had not taken his eyes off the psychedelic patterns coruscating behind a dancing Lady Miss Kier, as she sang *Groove Is In The Heart* on MTV.

Hi ya, Orle? Not, 'Oh my God, Orlagh, sweetheart, we thought you were dead. We were just about to phone the police we were so worried.' Consternation was beginning to crush my proud disposition.

"What'd you mean *Mickey*, hi ya? Were you not worried about me?"

"How could I be worried about you, O? We knew you'd make it, no probs. D'ya wanna cuppa?"

"No, *Mickey*, I don't. What happened with you lot? And where're the rest of 'em?"

"Oh, funny story, Orlagh. Feckin' funny."

"I'm glad you had a good time." I shook my head, appalled at his apathy.

"Well, as you know, we were taken to the station, right?

Them four pricks are mouthing off all the way there, while us lot sat like scared kids. We get to the station and they mix us up in two cells. Them wankers, can you believe, were beggin' the police to be separated from us, said they were scared that we were going to beat 'em up agen. The police must've looked at them big bruisers and then at us like, and remember 'cause Pat had done a runner there were only three of us and four of them, and thought - what the hell is going on here?

"Anyway, cutting a very long story very short, they gave us all the Breathalyser, proving that they were totally pissed and we were as sober as the proverbial judge. They were all charged with breach of the peace. The driver got a drink-driving charge too. And we were released! So, we all get a taxi back here to find Pat, the jammy bastard, had talked some slag from Coleshill into bringing him home, and now he's bangin' her upstairs."

So much for my thoughts of a fretting brother ready to bestow a hero's welcome upon me; or thoughts of him being hunted down by a pack of vicious dogs. It turned out he was the one that had been nuzzling - nuzzling in the undergrowth of some slut's nether regions as I evaded police, broke the law and single-handedly saved the day.

Emmet would be worried - and proud, I knew he would. This would be a great opening to tell the others about us, I thought. 'Yeah, she's the best, right? Driving all that way on her own...' I could hear him saying. 'And, she's my girl!'

"So, where's Emm and Sean?"

"Sean's waitin' to go next on the slag, but I'm gonna jump in 'cause he's on the phone in the other room. She's mad for it. You just wouldn't believe it, Orlagh. She offered it to Pat, not the other way round. Feckin' scrubber."

I shook my head in shock. I wasn't stunned by the fact that a girl had voluntarily given my brother a lift home and subsequently slept with him... and imminently his friends too - but that he couldn't care less about my agonising two-hour jaunt.

434

"And Emm, where's he?" I cautiously quizzed, petrified with the expectancy of the group of words which I dreaded would come forth, along with biscuit crumbs from Mickey's mouth.

"He's upstairs."

"What!? With the slut?" I (a little too zealously) enquired.

"Narr, I don't think so. He said something about sickening sloppy seconds. That sounds like him now."

At that Mickey jumped up from his seated position, placed his cup, which had the remnants of mushy biscuits strewn around the interior, on to the tray and proceeded towards the staircase; while at the same time Sean opened the front-room door. I could just about view the figure which reached the bottom step on the descent as Mickey reached it on the ascent. It wasn't Emmet as we had anticipated, but quite obviously the slut - who Mickey proceeded to kiss. As I approached the scene you could hear the saliva slopping as their mouths opened and closed.

"Ach, Mickey, don't do that."

It was Emmet. My heart momentarily leapt with excitement as my ears absorbed the mesmerising tone of his voice. A shiver began to climb the steps of my spine with the excitement of imminently viewing his face. But I was blissfully unaware. I was like a wildebeest nonchalantly lapping up the water from a crocodile-infested lake in the Serengeti, unaware of the lethal bite that would rise from the water and slaughter my conception of contentment.

Mickey temporarily ceased his sloppy snog; "Why's that, O'Malley?"

"'Cause she's just sucked me ccc... erm, errr, ermmm..."

Before he finished his predictable sentence I had slipped into his view. Mickey released the waist of the girl and dropped his head. Sean fidgeted behind me. Patrick bit his lower lip as he stood a step behind Emmet on the staircase. It was as if they all knew, as though they sensed my

435

anguish, felt my pain as I looked into Emmet's paradise sky-blue eyes with its blackbird now darting around disorientated... But soon enough the blackbird retrieved its bearings and flew in the direction of my heart, landing, with both its clawed feet on target. It took away my breath. The luminous yellow beak then proceeded to peck its way through the perimeter of my heart, desperately attempting to annihilate my soul.

CHAPTER fifty-two

Emmet,

I'm so upset I can't even bring myself to write 'dear' before your name. I've toyed with the idea of writing this letter, starting one to discard it a few lines later, to begin another and another, without being able to complete them. But, if I'm to retain an iota of my dignity, I have to fight with my mind to choose the right words to place down on this paper so I can at least attempt to get my message across to you in a way in which you will be able to understand the anguish and torment which I experienced after the incident the other night; and which I have felt every minute of each long day since.

If we hadn't talked so recently about telling everyone about our relationship, maybe the pain wouldn't be as intense, perhaps a little easier to bear. Or maybe it would, who's to know? But we did talk about it, which as silly as it sounds, led me to believe that you cared about me enough for there only to be 'me'.

To say I was devastated when I heard those words coming out of your mouth... would be an understatement.

I feel that I've never put you under pressure. I've let you make all the decisions regarding us; when I'm allowed to see you, or when I'm not. I knew about all the other girls you also 'saw' in the past, but I surmised it wasn't as serious on your part then. I really thought that had all stopped, Emm. You led me to believe it had.

So, Emmet, I have another decision regarding our relationship for you to make. Which I hope isn't as hard for you to make as is it for me to put into words and ask. I'm just so sorry that I have to ask you to even make this decision, but I need to, so that, as I said, I can at least retain some of my self-respect...

It's either all or nothing. If I can't have you one hundred percent with everyone knowing about us, then I don't want you at all. Not even your friendship, which I value more than anything, making it the hardest aspect to deal with. But after what we've experienced together I don't think I could converse with you on a friendly basis alone. In the back of my mind I'm sure I would still want you to kiss me, to hold me...

The ball is entirely in your court now, and I await your decision.

The only thing of any relevance left for me to say is: I love you, and whatever your decision... I always will.

Orlagh.

When I finally placed the Queen's crowned head on the corner of the envelope my hands trembled, and as I walked towards the red-enamelled postbox my legs quivered. I tried to talk myself out of placing the envelope in the dark slot. I positioned my forehead on the cold cast-iron and endeavoured to convince myself how stupid I was being, giving him an ultimatum... it was absurd. I was totally over-reacting, I thought. What if he went the way that I didn't want him to go? How would I feel then? A lot worse than I did now, I assumed. But how would I feel if I let the whole humiliating incident pass without complaint? How would he perceive me then? A pushover, a mug, a sucker? If I didn't say anything, he could continue to hurt me over and again. I just wasn't prepared to become his *welcome* doormat; to have his work boots scraping the mud from their soles, trampling over me whenever he felt the urge.

My hand entered the cool air within the postbox, but

emerged seconds later still clammily gripping the envelope, so much so that tiny creases appeared around his address. It went in and out. More pondering. Further reasoning. Eventually I released my grip and I heard the 'crruushhhh' as it landed softly on the mound of correspondence already in the box.

My initial instinct when it left my hand was - panic, and the instincts which followed didn't alter much. I deliberated setting up camp beneath the red box, awaiting the first collection of the day at six o'clock. I would plead relentlessly with the postman that he allow me to sift for my letter through the jumbled mail before he loaded it into his hessian sack. I then thought, how would I prove it was *my* letter? It had Emmet O'Malley's name and address on - it belonged to him now. As I had stated in the letter itself, the ball was now in his court. I was yearning for him to return an uncomplicated ball, one which would sail slowly through a blue sky, giving me time to position myself so I could return an equally easy ball to him; continuing a perfect rally, enabling the score to remain - *love all*.

As the ensuing days passed without word I considered I had served a catastrophic unreturnable ball... an ace, which really wasn't *ace* at all. I distraughtly determined I had definitely taken the wrong road and had ventured down the avenue of despair.

Having no school to attend and my job at the bank not commencing for another month, my days were consumed with contemplating the ultimatum letter. I cringed when I thought of the words I had actually audaciously written down. I was living in hope and agitated anticipation that he would imminently contact me with the great news. Each time the bell in the telephone jumped into action, simultaneously my heart did too, making its way to the back of my throat as I listened for my name to be called: 'Orlagh, it's Emmet' I wanted to hear, but I didn't and my heart would sink back to its melancholic position awaiting the next call or knock at the door.

439

"I really can't work you out, Orlagh. When you were at school I couldn't keep you in the house. Now you've left, you're moping around, lookin' like you've the world laying upon your shoulders. You should be making the most of this time before you start work, because you won't know what's hit you when you do start. Why don't you go to Siobhan's? Or get yourself off to that gym with your father. Do something, for God's sake," Mammy instructed.

I couldn't bring myself to go to the gym. I couldn't risk seeing Emmet without him making contact first. I was too embarrassed: *If I can't have you one hundred percent, then I don't want you at all, not even your friendship*... I had definitely ruined my life. I decided just to wallow in my own self-pity.

Out of the blue, a couple of weeks after the posting of the letter, I felt I had drifted so deep into the despairing desert of damnation that I considered I would never emerge. I was feeling I would be permanently destitute with the sand grains of euphoria flying around my head in a tornado of torment, when I received a visit from a surprising elusive guest.

It was the knocking which first seized my attention. Then I heard the laugh, that thunderous, vile laugh which could easily have been mistaken for an Australian aboriginal blowing on a didgeridoo. Then my eyes focused and through the night-time darkness I perceived the golden key swinging like a pendulum. I hadn't had the displeasure of this guest's presence for quite some time.

"Tick-tock, tick-tock, tick-tock," the shadow-like appearance teased, behind its despicable laugh.

"Who are you?" I screamed. "What do you want?"

"You... I want you, so we can discover together. *Lets* discover together. Come with me... come with me... Everything will be clarified if you come with me... come with me. All that wander are not lost. But all that wander have something to discover. Discover with me... Come with me..." The shadow swung the golden key with one hand, while holding out the other so I could place it in my hand.

"But who are you? WHO ARE YOU?" I shrieked, in a petrified trance while wrapped in my patchwork quilt.

"It's Pat, Orlagh. Calm down, it's Pat." Patrick wrapped his arms around my shivering body. "No one can get you now, it's okay."

"But he's still here, Pat. Can't you see? Look, please say you can see him. Pleeeaaase." I pointed to the shadow which slowly ebbed into the floral pattern of my wallpaper.

"It's okay, babe. It's okay now." Pat reassuringly kissed my forehead and I then realised he could never begin to understand.

It was the morning after the first of the renewed visits that my mind began to think about the key - the key which opened the box. That locked box full of infinite knowledge which the angels had bestowed upon me, which I had contentedly forgotten about while I basked in the triumph of getting Emmet romantically. But while that box was bobbing down the tributaries of my mind, making its way to the tranquil ocean of contentment, where I willingly let it sink; not once had I given a thought to thank my angels and God for placing me in the position that I was in.

I always found it so easy to beseech for my desires to be granted: 'please let me have this', 'please make this occurrence happen', 'please do this', 'please do that' - but I never gave a single sign of appreciation in exchange. Maybe that was the answer. I began to consider that I was being punished for dismissing the teachings of the angels. For taking for granted the honour of being a *Chosen One* and ignoring all the infinite knowledge which was locked away in that box. Punished for not being the least bit interested in prising it open and using that vast wisdom to my advantage.

If there ever was a time when I needed spiritual guidance, it was now. My whole days were literally being ambushed with thoughts of Emmet. So, I decided it was time to go back to church. I had been missing Mass on a regular basis. I excused it with the presence of my exams, but that was just a convenient justification. I'd merely been apathetic towards worship. Lazy in expressing gratitude. I hoped re-attending Mass and prayer would take my mind off Emmet for a while, as well as aiding me in getting him back.

Mammy was ecstatic when I informed her on the first Sunday morning after my freshly conceived sanctifying supposition that I was accompanying her to Mass once again - without her even suggesting it.

Why ever I believed that going to church might take my mind off Emmet I really couldn't begin to comprehend. For as soon as I entered the grandeur of the gothic church and saw the statues of the saints and Jesus on his cross hanging majestically above the altar, and primarily when my eyes focused on the red-carpeted aisle, I promptly realised I could never forget about him there either. My mind instantaneously placed itself into auto-pilot and transported itself off to my wedding day which I had always organised in my mind as I stared at the aisle - dreaming of meeting Emmet at the altar. And when I listened to the priest read out the responsorial psalm, I realised there definitely wasn't a chance of my forgetting about him.

"O God, you are my God, for you I long; for you my soul is thirsting. My body pines for you like a dry, weary land without water," the priest declared at the altar.

For Emmet I longed and pined; it was all so relative to my feelings for him.

"For you my soul is thirsting, O Lord my God," I, along with the whole congregation, responded.

"So I gaze on you in the sanctuary to see your strength and your glory. For your love is better than life, my lips will speak your praise."

"For you my soul is thirsting, O Lord my Emmet," I responded, almost unaware of to whom I was pledging worship.

"So I will bless you all my life, in your name I will lift up my hands. My soul shall be filled as with a banquet, my mouth shall praise you with joy."

"For you my soul is thirsting, O Emmet, my Emmet."

"What did you say?" Mammy whispered.

"The response, why what's the problem?" I asked, feigning knowledge of what had unintentionally emanated, a little too loud, from my mouth. She shook her head with pursed lips, as the priest concluded the final verse.

"For you have been my help; in the shadow of your wings I rejoice. My soul clings to you; your right hand holds me fast."

Although Mammy's head didn't move, I felt her eyes upon me as I recited the response. "For you my soul is thirsting, *O Lord* my *God*," I proclaimed, concentrating hard on not replacing the Almighty's name with Emmet's.

I continued to pray hard and fast. I even considered a Novena to Saint Martha; like Mammy used to say, I needed light at the end of *my* dark tunnel. But my entreaty wouldn't come to fruition until the end of nine unbroken weeks and I couldn't perceive waiting that long for that ball in Emmet's court to be returned.

God was certainly biding his time in helping me out. I didn't see any fruits originate from my praying labours - not even tiny little buds began to grow, ready to spurt into full bloom.

It was now a month since Emmet's birthday - four whole weeks since that fateful night and I still hadn't spoken to him or laid eyes upon him. I must have painted his portrait in my mind at least a thousand times. It was the longest period since I had first met him all those years ago in Dad's boxing gym; when I was actually black - and a boy - that I had gone without seeing or speaking to him. I didn't want to question Patrick or Dominic as I used to; I didn't want them to suspect anything, and I didn't want them to mention to Emmet in passing that I had been making enquiries about his welfare.

443

Siobhan had been great. She attempted to take my mind off him by doing her usual funny child-like tricks. They were amusing for the moment, when she'd wet herself in absolute hysterics, but my mind would soon revert back to my dilemma. It was usually me in the consoling, advising position, when one of her many relationships would end. The roles were now reversed - she was the one trowelling on the lumps of cement which fused the pieces of my heart back together.

I had ventured around to Siobhan's house on that fateful night, after Emmet's vocal cords had vibrated, resulting in the uttering of those hurtful words. I had to go to her when the walls, floor and ceiling of the hallway began to close in on me, as though I was suffering from claustrophobia. I had made some lame excuse to Pat, Emmet, Mickey and Sean that I needed to go and see Siobhan as she had just witnessed me driving Pat's car on my journey home from Coleshill, and she wanted to know why. None of the lads made any attempt to talk me into sticking around; I think they were all relieved I was vacating the embarrassing atmosphere. They all either suspected Emmet and I were having a relationship, or they just knew that I was totally infatuated with him. Emmet didn't say another word after his hurtful statement; he merely stared at the floor.

I didn't even know whether Siobhan would be in or not - I didn't really care, I just needed to get out of the house, away from the hurt and humiliation. As I walked around to her house, the tears poured from my eyes. I was telling myself I was being silly. This wasn't me. I was strong, I could get through anything. It was another hurdle I should just fly over. Another brick in my towering wall. Another stitch on the tapestry of my life. Orlagh Emmet is strong. Orlagh Emmet doesn't cry over boys. I knew them inside-out, upside-down. I knew how their minds worked and the antics which they got up to. But all those hours spent in the gym, at the boxing shows and acting as though I was one of the lads had not prepared me in the slightest for how deflated I felt. Luckily Siobhan was in, and she held me in her arms allowing my tears to absorb into her cotton blouse and assured me everything was going to work out. She also chose some names for Emmet I didn't realise were existent in her vocabulary.

In the ensuing weeks she organised activities in an attempt to keep my mind occupied. I declined almost all of her suggestions. I would rather just pity myself while eating mounds of chocolate or devouring a packet of digestive biscuits after dipping them into hot coffee, while listening to Atlantic Starr's *Secret Lovers*. She then came up with another Emmet-forgetting incentive - one that I couldn't dismiss. One which would prove somewhat fatal.

"It's all arranged, Orle. I've told Andy we're going in his car. It's too late to drop out now. He'll go crazy if we do, 'cause he could have filled his car up with his mates. He promised me that he'd make room. Anyway, it's your last weekend before you start work and you've got to snap out of this sooner or later."

I reluctantly agreed to join her and Andy, her undying-love-of-the-moment, and his friends, to attend a rave in Coventry which was being hosted for the very first time - called *Amnesia*. It wasn't the rave itself which caused the problem; that part of the whole experience was astounding. Thousands of people clad in their floppy hats, dungarees and hooded tops which showed prints of yellow smiley faces, matching those transfers on the popular acid tab, vibrated their bodies in smooth rhythm to the dance beats spun by Sasha, Danny Rampling and Keith Suckling. Half of them swayed mini luminous-green light-sabres, while a chant of, 'Acieeeed, Acieeeed' blended in with the murmuring lyrics being transported from the rotating vinyl to the gigantic speakers. The MC recited his own controversially disturbing mantras about Ecstasy, like: 'D. O. V. E. S... *Doves*; they won't do you no harm... They won't do you no harm.' I wasn't about to investigate if he was correct. Whatever frame of mind I had been in, I had no interest in the E's or trips. Although, after the rave had finished, when I was in the makeshift car park, I wished I could have been in my own mesmerising world, hallucinating my very own outcome to the devastating occurrence which was to follow.

I was walking alongside Andy's friend through the car park as we searched the rows of vehicles for Andy's. The grassy ground had turned into strips of mud with the imprint of Dunlop car tyres and human feet embedded into it. As the mud squelched into the deep grooves on the soles of my purple and green Kickers, I was thinking of what a great time I had had at my very first *rave* experience. Siobhan had been right; it had taken my mind off certain issues which hadn't really invaded my mind all night. I then heard a familiar voice calling;

"Hey, Orlagh, over here." It was Mickey Duffy screaming out of a rolled-down car window a few rows away. A car window which was attached to a vehicle instantly recognisable as... Emmet's. I hesitated in approaching them. I could make out that the car was full. That meant Emmet was in there. I was apprehensive. My body began to tremble slightly and numerous scenes of reconciliation flooded my mind, drowning my astute line of thinking.

"Don't ignore me. What're you being so coy about? Is that your boyfriend or somethin'? Are ya not gonna introduce us, Orle?"

"He's not my boyfriend at all, Mickey. He's Siobhan's boyfriend's friend." I made sure I was loud enough for Emmet to hear from where I suspected he was sitting in the driving seat. While at the same time I was debating whether to go over or not.

"Mmmm, likely story. Don't worry, we won't harass him," I heard Sean McCabe shout from somewhere in the darkness. I thought I had better go over, I would usually jump at the chance of being with them and they would certainly notice if I didn't.

"He's not my boyfriend, and if he was, you lot'd be the last people I'd introduce him to. What're you all doing here anyway?" I asked, as I finally made my way nervously to the window, directing my question at them all. I made a quick inspection of the car where I ascertained that both my brothers were in the vehicle. Dominic was in the front and Patrick in the back along side Sean and Mickey; and Emmet certainly was in the driving seat - metaphorically as well as literally. The ball was still entirely in his court and I was wondering whether this would be the definitive returning moment. I directed my attention to Mickey who was closest, but out of the corner of my eye I checked if Emmet had turned around like Dominic had to face me as I leaned in the back window. He hadn't, and my happy frame of mind was rapidly diminishing.

"What're *you* doing here is more to the point, *missy*. You didn't tell us you were coming here," Dominic facetiously interrogated, with a hint of seriousness resonant in his tone. I didn't have a chance to answer.

"Anyway, give me a kiss 'cause I'm the birthday boy," Mickey insisted, grabbing my cheeks and pulling my head into the car.

"Your birthday's not 'til Monday, Mickey." I pretended to resist. It was futile, Mickey landed a sloppy kiss on my lips.

"And I want one too," Sean said, pulling me further into the car, donating an array of moist-lipped kisses all over my face. In usual circumstances I would have fought them off and been as cheeky back, but I felt as though they were doing it in front of an audience of strangers. I felt awkward in front of Emmet. He still hadn't acknowledged me and, although the boys were keeping me occupied, I was so very aware of it. I was awaiting: 'Leave her alone boys, she's my girl, so she is.' But no, he hadn't even turned around.

"Orlagh! Come on, Andy's waiting. Hi guys, by the way. Come on, Orle, we've gotta go," Siobhan screeched over from Andy's car.

"Go on, you're boyfriend's waitin'," Mickey teased. I didn't even endeavour to clarify.

"See you later then, everyone." I avoided individual names. They all shrieked their farewells - except Emmet. It was as though time had slowed down. Mickey's voice, as he continued to ramble, was almost inaudible when Emmet turned his head to face me. Was he waiting for me to say something? He looked sad. His eyes were a stormy grey, not the usual paradise sky blue - but that blackbird was still there, and when he turned his head away without uttering a word to me the blackbird had taken flight once again, and the harsh pecking at my heart commenced. I wanted to annihilate that blackbird like a shooter does a clay pigeon. I wanted it not to affect me, not to be able to land itself quite contentedly on my heart and feed on my torment.

"Did he talk to you?" Siobhan asked, as I dispiritedly arrived at Andy's car.

"No, he could only just about bring himself to look at me." I fought back the tears.

"The bastard."

"Mmmm, that's what I thought." And those were the final words I uttered on the way home. I laid my forehead against the cold, moist glass, not bothered about the bumps it was enduring as the car made its journey back to Birmingham, and I pretended to sleep. There wasn't a chance of real sleep because my mind was a circus with my thoughts doing death-defying somersaults over the black hole of bewilderment. There was no net to catch me and I was coming closer and closer to falling.

Why didn't he acknowledge me? I'd been to church, I'd thanked. Why didn't God or my angels incite him to talk to me? I then contrived a whole list of excuses why it might be: I considered it was my clothes which were bad luck. I had worn the same Toronto Blue Jay's jacket, baseball cap, Armani jeans and hooded sweatshirt the night I was supposed to go to the M25 rave - the night Emmet went with the girl. Or maybe it was just the association with

448

dance parties which was bad luck. Then I contemplated that maybe Emmet thought that Andy's friend really was my boyfriend and was hurt himself. There were a thousand more pitiful excuses to go with those; because that's all I eventually decided they were... pitiful.

After I had arrived home, quietly, so as to not wake Mam and Dad, I consoled myself in a box of Cadbury's chocolate fingers. As I stared at the moving pictures on the portable television in the kitchen, not absorbing the programme, it was then I came up with the exact reason why he hadn't spoken to me.

When I had completed all the biscuits, I crept up the stairs, tight to the wall, avoiding any of the creaking floor boards and made my way to the bathroom. I then proceeded to wash off my make-up. When completing this I stared in the mirror above the sink to discover eight little white dots present in my birthmark, by my hair-line. I thought some make-up had stubbornly stood its ground after vigorous scrubbing. This only heightened my infuriation. I attempted washing a second time - scrubbing harder. Taking another glance in the mirror, I was confronted with the sight of the unremovable white dots. Through my consternation I realised they were in the exact position where the test patch for the Pulse-Dye Laser had been carried out six months previously. Those eight diminutive dots should have instilled immense joy, but they didn't, because I had come to the damning conclusion why Emmet no longer wanted me. Why he felt compelled to sleep with other girls. Why he no longer wanted our relationship to continue with everyone knowing... It was plain and simple. I didn't know why it had taken me so long to come to the conclusion. It was because - I was *fat*.

chapter fifty-three

I was almost seventeen years old, five feet, five inches tall and I weighed eight stone or one hundred and twelve pounds, even fifty one kilos; whichever way it was expressed it still sounded too much. When I looked into the mirror and recited, 'Mirror, mirror on the wall, who's the fattest of them all?' It squealed back, 'YOU! ORLAGH EMMET. YOU!'.

On the night I had arrived home from the rave called *Amnesia*, wishing I could temporarily have been suffering from *amnesia*, so I didn't have to endure the agonising scenes of Emmet's dismissive look repetitively playing over and over in my mind. The look which depicted the return ball which I had left in his court, which was smashed over the net to land full force in my stomach, expelling ever ounce of wind from my body. On the night I had decided to console myself by gorging on a box of Cadbury's chocolate fingers was the night I first realised Emmet didn't have any interest in me because I was fat and because of this I decided to wager a huge war on food. It was the start of something I wished I could have turned back on, because like a fly in a spider's web, I was well and truly captured. It was on that disastrous night that I first stuck my fingers down my throat and fought the enemy... the felonious food.

'Do you think you'll ever starve, baby doll?' 'I doubt if you'll ever suffer with anorexia!' 'Is that a baby elephant running up those stairs?' I had heard those comments all my life, when I had experienced a good relationship with food. When I had allowed it to travel through the entire digestive system unhindered. When any comment relating to my weight flew by unnoticed. But now I had commenced this battle, each innocent jibe hurt; each one was construed in its very own way.

I blamed it on my exams. I had had to stop attending the gym, to sit and revise over meaningless rubbish, while layer upon layer of fat attached itself to my bones. I couldn't give up my food; I enjoyed it too much. At first it was so much easier to play finger puppets with my own head. My stomach would gargle the dialogue and the audience was the fetid remnants of food in the toilet bowl.

It had started off with those chocolate fingers, then progressed to my breakfast, lunch and finally dinner. A voice in my mind was shouting out, drowning all other rational thoughts. It screamed: 'You're fat. You're obese. You're disgusting. If you had any self-respect, you'd get yourself off to that bathroom and rid yourself of that demonic food.'

I would enter my bedroom, put on music and turn the volume up loud enough for it to engulf the sound of my imminent actions. Proceeding to the bathroom, I would turn the key on the silver lock and lean my body against the cold tiles to psyche myself up. Adding more noise for distraction, careful to keep my disgusting habit secret, I would turn on the powerful shower, causing the clean, unused water to waste away as it trickled down the plug-hole; like the cells of my mind wasting away into a drain of despair as I stuck two, three or four fingers or if the food was obstinate in staying where it belonged, even my whole hand in my mouth and down the orifice which was my throat. I knew every nook and cranny of a part of my body I was not meant to fondle: the rough texture at the front of my tongue, further back the cluster of tiny goosebumps, my dangling pharynx, or the smooth flesh of my cheeks.

451

Then it went one step further - I began to binge. I would eat everything in sight. I began to identify food with how easily it could be regurgitated; chocolate was easy, digestive biscuits were smooth, cornflakes were compliant, liquorice proved difficult as did Eccles cakes and malt loaf. They lay heavy on my stomach - defiant of making a curtain call. I learnt the strategic amount of time between eating and vomiting. I discovered that whatever I ate last, it didn't necessarily come back first. I decided that the more I ate, the easier it was to vomit, the more eager it was to depart my body.

But there was so much hypocrisy involved in the whole process and in my thinking about it...

I binged on anything I could lay my hands on. I would even walk to the shop to purchase copious amounts of chocolate, which would be followed by a trip to the fish and chip shop, where I would obtain a family-size bag of grease-sodden chips. Secretly I would gorge on them while concealed in the over-grown grass of the common land. I would then return home, turn the music on loud, lock myself in the bathroom, run the water in the shower and bend over the toilet bowl for so long, enabling my body to recover between bouts of self-inflicted vomiting, I became proficient at making anagrams from Armitage Shanks. I wouldn't leave until the last trace of food - the dreaded evil food - was retched into the toilet water. Until an array of multi-coloured stars would flash before my eyes, causing disorientated dizziness. Until my stomach rumbled, begging for nourishment. When my stomach began to beg for food I would momentarily feel fresh, free of demons, empty of food, and most importantly - thin. The hypocrisy, the ridiculous stupidity was that I would return to the kitchen - hungry. I would eat an apple, something 'non-fattening'. Then that voice in my mind would take over, informing me I had broken the rules *again*, that I might as well eat something fattening, worthy of retching, as it wasn't worth being sick for just an apple. And all over again it would begin: the bingeing, the regurgitating, so much so that I actually began to hate food.

I soon began to show signs of this destructive disorder: miniature red veins in the whites of my eyes appeared, continual soar throat, spitting blood, mouth ulcers, mood swings. I knew what I was doing wasn't normal, that what I was doing was wrong. Every time my fingers entered my mouth I promised myself - it was the last time. Every end of the week I would proclaim to myself: 'I'm not doing this as of tomorrow.'

That tomorrow wouldn't raise its sorrowful head.

Thankfully no one noticed, and I wasn't about to tell anyone. I couldn't disclose this disturbing secret to anyone, not even Siobhan. I couldn't let anyone think I was so weak as to engage myself in this horrible eating disorder, to not have the will-power to overcome this devil that had blurred my vision so much so that every time I glanced in the mirror I was repulsed by the fat reflection which stared back at me. My birthmark was a secondary concern; in fact everything was. I had acquired a total disinterest in life really, except when it came to Emmet. If I lost half a stone, maybe even a stone, then he'd want me - I was sure...

chapter fifty-four

If there is such a thing as a right time to start a new chapter in one's life, to end one era and begin another, then this certainly wasn't the right time in my life to embark on a chapter titled 'Work'. Along with the bulimia, work suffocated me too, smothering me in a blanket of office small talk.

"I hate it, Siobhan. The only worthwhile aspect is the money, and I don't really want it to be like that. I know I don't want to be there forever but I would like a bit of satisfaction out of the work I'm doing. I'm definitely not gaining any satisfaction from sorting thousands of cheques into their respective banks, or sending cheques back to customers 'refer to drawer please re-present'."

"Yeah, I hate my job as well, Orlagh. I'm thinkin' about leavin' the office and trainin' to be a nurse. But it must be good for you being around all that money."

"Handling thousands of pounds was a novelty at first, but it doesn't belong to me, does it? So, it just became more paper with numerical symbols to file into bundles of thousands or five hundreds. What really pisses me off is no one has any interest in anything I have to say, they just think I'm some little kid. They can't understand why I don't drink or smoke or get involved in their bullshit beer and skittles nights, or their after-work meaningless meetings which they try to make into dumb social events. None of them like sport, or books, or music, or clubs and I wouldn't even dream of asking any of them if they'd been to a rave. It'd disgust them. All they seem to live for is to work, watch *Coronation Street* and go on their nights out together. Life doesn't exist outside of their little banking bubble."

"I thought I had it bad, Orlagh, but they're not as bad as that who I'm with. At least they have a laugh. What're you gonna do?"

"You know what, Shiv, I really don't know. I thought I was going to come up with something after a while, but my desire to dream is rapidly diminishing. All I'm bothered about is where we're going to rave at the weekend."

"You've only been there just over a month, Orlagh, things'll get better, I'm sure. I'll cheer you up tomorrow and send you some more faxes."

"You know the highlight of my working day is receiving a fax of your photocopied shockingly squashed face!"

"I almost wet myself when I'm sending them through the fax and think of your bank manager seeing them. Anyway, where're we going this weekend?"

"I don't know, we could go to the Hacienda in Manchester again. That was wicked a few weeks ago, right?"

"Yeah, it was. I'll do whatever, I'll leave it up to you."

"I can't wait to pass my driving test, then we can go to a few places in a weekend, like Manchester on Friday and Liverpool on Saturday. We could even drive home rather than staying in those tacky B & B's and being woken up at nine o'clock for a greasy breakfast we don't even eat."

"Oh my God, I forgot, your test is tomorrow, right? I can't believe you got a test on your birthday."

"Well, it's the first day I can take it, so that's what I'm doing. You know what? I'd better go 'cause Dad's taking me out on my last lesson in a little while and I have to eat first."

Although I still hadn't reached seventeen, Dad had been teaching me to drive of an evening. Mammy had attempted to take me out, but she merely screamed, panicked, held on to the door for dear life and made me totally uncomfortable. Whereas Dad was the complete opposite: 'Put you're foot down, baby doll, and you'll make it through them lights," he'd instruct, as we approached traffic lights on amber.

My meals had to be strategically planned around my driving lessons. I had to eat not long before I went out on my lesson, which would usually last an hour or so before Dad went off to the gym. Consequently it would leave the perfect time lapse, so when we returned I would be ready to act out my repulsive penchant for regurgitating all the food - without a hindrance.

Because there was a major turning point about to occur in my life (that was, if I passed), and because a whole new year of my life was about to begin I had decided once again that it was the perfect opportunity for it to be the last time to play finger puppets with my own head. So, I binged. I might as well, I thought... it's my very last time. I ate a little bit of all the kinds of food which I promised myself I definitely wouldn't touch when I turned seventeen, had passed my driving test and wasn't retching: biscuits, chocolate, cheese, buttery toast.

"You might as well've had yourself a nice dinner as opposed to eating all that rubbish," Mammy commented, as I was spreading lashings of yellow butter into each corner of my hot toast.

"Leave her be," Dad remarked. "As long as she's eatin' somethin'. We wouldn't want her going anorexic now would we?" Dominic, Patrick and Dad thought the idea of myself being anorexic was hilarious. I'll show them, I thought. When I lose my stone they'll be laughing on the other side of their faces. "When you've finished that, baby doll, we'll make a move and get you on the road one last time before you take the test. But for now we'll be going on with testin' if any of yers can beat the quiz master tonight."

Dinner-table pursuit continued but, along with everything else, except my obsessions with body fat and Emmet, I had no interest in it. The last few weeks had seen me give up on my quest to attain as much knowledge as possible. I thought, 'what's the use?' Emmet obviously wasn't interested in my wisdom. He'd proved that on the night he went with the dumb bimbo, who I suspected wouldn't know the difference between Pol Pot and a piss pot, and she'd probably think the Khmer Rouge was the latest colour for blusher. The only information I had been interested in absorbing recently were the details of the Highway Code.

"As we're in automobile mode, tell me, who devised the first motor car? In what year was it? And, where did the family of the inventor in question originate?" Although I knew Henry Ford, whose parents were Irish immigrants, completed the first automobile in 1896, I couldn't be bothered to respond. I was too busy debating whether to have malt loaf or a moist, sugar-coated jammy donut. The continual ringing of the door bell prevented me from concluding my detrimental decision. Conversation ceased as we awaited conformation as to who was at the door.

"To what do we owe the honour of this Thursday evening visit, Mr Sweeney?"

The distinct Belfast tones of Tommy Two Saints travelled into the kitchen. "Come ooonnnn, Grania, darlin', do I need an excuse to visit the vision of beauty which stands before me?"

"Can yer view me from the hallway then, yer smooth talker you?" Dad jovially voiced.

"Hey, hey, hey guys, what's going on?" he asked, entering the kitchen with his skinny arms wide open, as though he were embracing all our spirits. His presence was so intense there was certainly no ignoring him. "Yers are not going out, are yer? The gym isn't open tonight, is it?"

"No, Two Saints, it's not, but I'm taking Orlagh out one last time before she takes her driving test tomorrow."

"Ach, Jeysus, Orlagh, yer haven't got this big eejit to teach yer to drive, have yer? Please tell me yer haven't." Two Saints continually made the sign of the cross, screwing up his already wrinkled face so it completely resembled a war-time washboard. "And anyway, yer not seventeen already, are yer?"

"I'm afraid he has taught me, Tommy, although I've had a couple of lessons with an instructor we know who was prepared to take me before I turn seventeen, which is actually tomorrow. I got a cancellation with the DVLA for tomorrow afternoon. I want to be on the road as soon as possible."

"Well hopes be to God you don't drive like yer father. The Horace's hot-dog stand story is a perfect example of his atrocious driving. Have yers heard the Horace's hot-dog stand story?"

"Yeah, sure she has - they all have. Not again.... not tonight. Please, not tonight," Dad jokingly implored. I actually couldn't recall the Horace's hot-dog stand story, and I wasn't really anxious to hear it either. I had to get out on my last lesson, so I could get back in time to comfortably make my date with the toilet basin. I had the unpleasant procedure precisely timed. But as Two Saints began to narrate the hot-dog tale, the chances of me making my regurgitating rendezvous in time were rapidly diminishing. I was going to be left with all the disgusting evil food inside of me which was intent on fulfilling its formidable mission of deforming my body. Although it didn't stop me from devouring both the jammy donut and the buttered malt loaf as we all listened to Two Saints' tale.

"Let's take it back to 1965, and that eejit over there." Two Saints pointed at Dad from where he stood, acting out, as well as spinning his yarn. "He hadn't long been back from Canada. I'd cashed in his ticket to go back over there and had received that notorious dig on me chin, which of course paved the way for you lot to make it into the world - 'cause if I hadn't cashed in that ticket he would've gone back to Canada and never returned."

"Would yer get on with it, yer romancer, sure, they know all that," Dad intervened.

"I know, I know, but I'm setting the scene for 'em.

Anyway, as I was sayin', yer father was just back from Canada and was driving a Ford V8 Pilot, like a Bonnie and Clyde gangster car. Well, the eejit had, how can I put it? he'd created a couple of bumps in the few months he'd had it, so he'd been slobberin' on that he wanted another, so he was. Well, it turned out our friend, Wiggy Walters, had an uncle who had one, and this uncle of his was prepared to sell it, at the right price like.

"Yer've never seen a car in such immaculate condition in yer life. It was as though it had just been driven out of the showroom when Wiggy Walters brought it around to yer da' for a test drive. His old uncle was trustin' I can tell ya. He'd never met yer da' and he was prepared to let a stranger drive his pride and joy. Trustin' or senile, one or the other anyway. It was about twenty years old at the time and had been looked after as though it had belonged to the Queen of England herself. Royal blue it was, with not a scratch in sight. It had red-leather seats and a chrome column gear change, which ye could see yer face in. There was loads of shining chrome all over: the huge bumpers, the radiator grill, the shielding on the big frog-eyed headlights. Yers get the picture, right? The car was a dream.

"There I was over at Rory's place waitin' for him to finish pamperin' himself so we could head out, when Wiggy Walters turns up with our Bernie's Finnian. You know, Emmet's Uncle Finnian."

There was no need to explain who Finnian was, we had known him all our lives, longer than we had known Emmet; he was married to Two Saints' sister and was my godfather after all.

"Talkin' of Emmet, where is that one? He's as much a fixture at that table as you lot. Where is he, Orlagh?" I knew there had to be some deceptive reason for the Finnian explanation.

"Why ask me, he's their friend," I replied, just a little too defensively, pointing at Dominic and Patrick, who were both sucking in their lips as though suppressing smiles. Mammy was standing behind me. I had a funny feeling, like the one you get when you are sure someone is staring at you when you can't actually see them, that she was waving her arms around in a signal to Two Saints.

"Oooo, touchy subject is it?" He raised his eyebrows and flipped his bottom lip over to exhibit the glistening fleshy interior.

"No, not at all. Why should it be? Carry on, Two Saints, I'm *dying* to know what Horace's hot dogs have to do with driving," I replied facetiously, desperately attempting to change the subject. Did he know about Emmet's and my relationship? (or what *had been* our relationship)? Did they all know? Could it really be that obvious to everyone that I was infatuated with him?

"So, when Finnian and Wiggy turned up, we decided to combine the night-out with test-driving the V8. Big mistake; especially when we headed to Digbeth to Sid's Scrumpy Saloon and went on that rough cider he used to ferment himself. After a few lethal pints of the rough stuff we started on a tour, from one pub to the next, testin' not the car, but different drinks! Black 'nd tans, with rum and black chasers, some old Jack D's."

"Okay, okay, you've set the scene, we were pissed," Dad interjected, laughing. "Just get on with it."

"We didn't want to leave at closin' time, so the bouncers got heavy and the punches, the glasses and the bottles flew. We smashed the place up before runnin' straight out the door and jumpin' into the V8. Like four gangsters we were."

"Four eejits more like," Mammy remarked.

"Anyway, we weren't happy with the amount of alcohol we'd managed to consume - we wanted more. But the only place we could think of that'd be open at that hour was The Wolfe Tone Private Members' Club. The only way ye could gain entry was to gamble. It was a notorious rip-off joint - illegal gamblin'. If yer did manage to win, which wasn't likely, as they had it all fixed, they'd keep yer in there until yer lost it all again, enticing yer with food and drink. But The Wolfe Tone was near the city centre and we'd ventured out to Moseley. We needed petrol to make it 'cause we were running on vapour.

"Rory pulls into the only all-night petrol station in the city and Finnian tells the attendant to fill it up. The guy couldn't believe his luck. To fill a car up like that cost a week's wage, around fifteen pound, which none of us had on us of course. As the ald guy shook the last drops of petrol out the nozzle, Rory there put the car in gear. As he placed the nozzle back in the pump yer da' put his foot down and skidded away. The attendant was almost tryin' to grab the back bumper of the car as he attempted to catch us. That gangster-lookin' car had an effect on us I can tell yer; we really thought we were Bonnie and Clyde."

"Yeah, and you were definitely the Bonnie character," Dad added.

"We get to The Wolfe Tone and parks the car directly outside the front door like we were important. It was a good ploy too, as when we knocked on the door the peroxide-headed ald bag who slid back the iron-barred hatch, like on a prison-cell door, could see we'd come in style. 'We wanna gamble, on the cards,' we told her. She must've been rubbin' her hands together behind that door, thinkin', 'I've got four suckers here with money te burn.'

"She takes us upstairs to the big room with the professional card tables and its own little bar. It was empty. 'I'll go 'nd get yers some players and a dealer,' she said, leavin' us alone as she headed off on her little mission to set us up good 'nd proper. Finnian heads straight for the bar and grabs himself a bottle of whisky and Wiggy follows him and steals the rum, placin' 'em in the inside pockets of their big crombies."

Although I adored Two Saints' animated story telling, tonight I was frustrated. I wanted to get out, so I could get back in time to retch. Food seemed to be ruling my life.

"After they'd stolen the liquor, we headed to the downstairs bar, which was packed solid, and told the

461

peroxide-head that we'd just have a quick drink while we were waitin' for players. She was happy with that as it was givin' her more time to organise the set-up. So, don't we bump into some girls we know who knew of a party that was goin' on in the Jewellery Quarter. We must've been in the bar about ten minutes, havin' downed the first drink, when the peroxide-head, a couple of heavies and the owner were makin' their way over to us. She said we had to go upstairs now, the players were ready. Rory, in his intoxicated wisdom told them to fuck their gamblin', their club and themselves and made his way out've the club, with us lot, the three girls and the heavies behind him.

"The heavies tried to get heavy outside and Rory knocks the one spark out and Wiggy, the eejit, smashed the bottle of rum over the other one's head. We all piled into the car. Finnian decided to drive, Wiggy was the passenger, Rory lay across all the girls in the back and I'd jumped in the boot. The next thing we knew a copper had run over the road, must've witnessed all the commotion and had come to arrest us. If he'd 've got hold of us we'd have been banged up for sure. Because apart from the fight he'd witnessed himself; the driver was pissed, the car was totally overloaded with passengers, we'd just done a runner from a petrol station not an hour before and smashed up the bar in Moseley. All done by a group of guys in a V8 Pilot.

"The copper appears at Finnian's window and demands we all get out've the car. Without warning Finnian, the eejit, threw a right into the cop's face and lay him out cold, and we once again wheel-spun away in the V8. Rory was most definitely seein' what the car could do, especially 'cause right behind us there was a cop car in tow. Finnian shot through all the stop signs and traffic lights and the police still followed. Down a huge hill we went, which had a wild bend halfway, which was the place where Finnian lost control. He drove straight through a coppice of trees, came out the other side and smashed straight into the rear of another parked and thankfully vacant car. I'd been knocked

462

from pillar to post in the boot. The girls were all in shock in the back, squealing at the top of their lungs they were. Poor things had been havin' a grand quiet night before we'd arrived. Rory had rolled off their laps on impact and was lyin' half concussed under the front seats.

"The cops soon arrive on the scene, so Wiggy and Finnian simultaneously jump out've the car, but the coppers are quick on their trail. The cops must've thought only the girls were left in the car as they instructed them to stay right where they were. They couldn't see Rory on the floor and they couldn't see me in the boot, so they goes in pursuit of the other two, leaving us unguarded. Rory sobered himself up, sharpish like. He hobbled out've the car, let me out've the boot and told the girls to shut up as he tried to start the car. But the car that was runnin' like a dream at the beginnin' of the night wouldn't start. So Rory, the genius that he is, grabbed the steel turnin' rod, made his way to the front of the car and put the two foot long crank into the hole in the caved-in radiator grill, just above the once straight, but now smashed chrome bumper. I could see Rory turning the crank, with no response from the engine, and I could also see in the wing mirror the police on their way back. He turned the crank again and again and - nothing. I was beginning to visualise prison when the engine spluttered into action. Rory jumped in the driver's seat and because he was so pissed, instead of headin' out the city centre on the nice big tree-lined roads, he drove straight back into town. Jesus, it was like the wacky races, through all those little streets, with the cops not far behind. By mistake he ventured up a one-way street the wrong way, and wasn't there a Citroen approachin' from the correct direction? Ach, there certainly was and we were about to meet head on. The Citroen attempted to swerve out've the way, but unfortunately didn't swerve far enough, 'cause Rory side swiped him and took the side off the car. The last we saw of it, it was spinnin' around in circles.

"So, what's this got to do with hot dogs?" I politely attempted to speed up the story.

"Oh, Orlagh, sweetheart, I'm about to come to that. Rory there was in a state of shock as well as panic, escapin' the police and now the Citroen, and he was totally disorientated as to where he was. His disorientation made him forget that at the end of the one-way street which we were presently speedin' up the wrong way there was a triangular mini-island in the middle of it, which housed a set of public toilets, surrounded by green cast-iron railings.

"He took that island at about thirty miles an hour, with full lock on the wheel. But we could have been going in slow motion, 'cause everythin' was so vivid and clear, like the shocked expression on Horace the hot-dog man's face on the opposite corner, as he was about to squirt mustard on top of one of his famous hot dogs. So famous in fact that he had a queue of thirty-odd eager customers waitin' to purchase his culinary delights. The queue rapidly scattered when they witnessed the mammoth, smashed-up V8 lose control and veer towards 'em, which then collided directly into Horace's hot-dog stand.

"The chrome-covered barrow on wheels, with its enormous umbrella, shot up into the night-time sky like a rocket headin' into outer-space. Luckily Horace had moved out've the way, his white scientist-like coat flapped behind him as he did! Thanks be to God the only casualties were the wieners, the onions, the mustard, the buns and of course the hot-dog stand and umbrella which rained down on top of the obliterated car.

"The last me and Rory saw of that car the radiator grill was attemptin' to sit in the driver's seat, and the once non-scratched royal-blue driver's side was a mixture of raw metal and bright yellow paint which had been transferred from the Citroen. Steam was billowing out of what had once been the engine and Horace's hot-dog stand was embedded into the roof."

"So, did you get arrested then?" I asked, momentarily forgetting about my full stomach.

"No, noooo," Dad replied. "We did a runner. We left the girls in the car and instructed 'em to tell the cops that we'd just met and they didn't have a clue who we were. Two Saints and meself ran into the sunset. Well, the moonlight."

"Oh, you must've heard this story before then, Patrick? And picked up a few tips!" I sarcastically declared. He smiled and winked in response.

"What's that then?" Mammy probed.

"Nothing, just Pat and a Sebastian Coe impression he does. So, what happened to Finnian, Wiggy and the girls?" I attempted to change the subject before Mammy could make any more enquiries.

"Oh, them two got away; but Finnian had broken his ankle jumpin' off a twelve-foot wall, and Wiggy almost had his neck broke by his uncle when he went back and told him the car had been stolen. That was the easiest way for him and us to get out of it! 'Cause obviously yer da' didn't want the car after that night. Well, even if he'd wanted it, he couldn't, it was written off!

"And the girls, they were grand. They cracked on to the cops that they'd just been picked up by us in The Wolfe Tone. The police hounded 'em for months. Sure, they were that honourable I ended up marryin' one of 'em. If she could be trusted to keep her gob shut, then she was worthy of being me wife! And do yer know somethin'? In twenty-odd years of marriage, sure, she's never made me a hot dog!"

"Wow, Annie was one of the girls? That's great... Dad, we better be going now."

"Ach, I've more drivin' stories to tell yers."

"Another time, Two Saints, another time," Dad thankfully replied.

Too many references to hot dogs had directed my mind to think of all the junk I had eaten, which was at that very moment on its deadly mission of being broken down and converted into fat.

I was tormented. I just couldn't go on like this - could I?

CHAPTER fifty-five

I'd rolled on my hill start. My perfect three-point turn was comparable to the twenty-point-turn which I had performed on my first public-road driving experience in Coleshill. I'd kangaroo-ed, stalled and veered too close to parked cars. I was like an inadequate learner driver, not the competent driver I had been for the last couple of months. Dad put it down to pre-test nerves. I put it down to the Shylockesque voice in my mind, demanding I hurry home and relinquish my pound of flesh. I was endeavouring to establish what my debt to this tormentor actually was and when my Portia would come along and assist me.

I was desperate to enter the bathroom on my return. I sprinted directly upstairs to discover it locked.

"Who's in there?" I frantically banged my closed fist upon the white-glossed door.

"Dominic. Why, what's the problem?"

"What're you doing?"

"Well, Orlagh, I thought about having a party, then I thought, no, I'll have a wee nap while I'm in here... What'd you think I'm doing, ye eejit?"

"Don't be sarcastic, Dom. How long will you be?"

"Orlagh, I'm having a shower. You spend your life in here lately. You can't be that desperate, you're not going out."

"But I need a wee," I lied.

"Well, then go downstairs. I'll be twenty minutes or so."

I couldn't go downstairs; it was in such close proximity to everyone else. With no music or shower-noise distraction, it was way too risky. I'd just have to wait, but another twenty minutes; my shameful task was going to prove so much more difficult. Why did Tommy Two Saints have to come tonight of all nights? Even the story which had delayed my routine was about the thing which was presently troubling my mind, well, I suppose my life - food... What else? I was beginning to really detest the neurotic I was gradually turning in to. Why had I allowed this disorder to grasp me so tightly within its crushing grip and insidiously demolish my once vibrant life and energy? I couldn't begin to answer, but what I did know was that I so desperately wanted it to set me free and for the spirit of life to occupy my being once more.

I eventually got to the bathroom almost an hour after my return. Patrick, to my consternation, had sneaked in on Dominic's departure.

I suspected, I was performing a pointless procedure as I commenced the ritual to rid my body of the ominous adversary which I had voluntarily allowed to pass enemy lines. My head once again became the puppet and the show began. The stinking audience which sat in the toilet basin was small. But I still implored them to come in their droves. My body swayed in waves of self-induced retching. I had sunk to the deepest depths of my own desperation. I couldn't accept that the food had travelled its correct path unhindered, thus, still I continued. Sweat dripped from my forehead and saliva dripped from my right hand heading in the direction of my elbow. In front of my eyes a blackness appeared, which changed to a curtain of red. I was straining every muscle in my body. I hated this... but it was my last time. It really was the last time... I was determined to complete my task.

Then, one by one the tiny stars appeared: left and right, in the centre, above, below - they were everywhere. Usually

467

they would fade within a few seconds, but more and more stars appeared, twinkling like a fairytale landscape... The scene could not have been more conflicting.

I stood up straight to recover, but I merely felt dizzy. I staggered back to be saved by the cold tiled wall, which I slowly slid down to end in a seated position, with my bent knees placed just below my chin. The stars appeared to become brighter. The tighter I closed my eyes in an attempt to make them disappear, the brighter they became, so I opened them - wide. I pulled the skin under my eyes down and my lids up. Then, out of the hundreds of stars which flashed before my eyes, one grew brighter and larger, until it encompassed the rest and in front of my eyes I had a glistening yellow light. Out of that yellow light a diaphanous figure appeared. Although transparent, the appearance was strangely wholesome and real. It stood as tall as I did with huge wings flapping noisily from its back, which were equal to its body in size. On each passing second and wing flap its transparency was splashed with an array of colour, like a blank canvas being painted on by an expert artist.

"Now, I must say that *was* a novel appearance. My job becomes more interesting by the day," the apparition declared, while brushing down her wings with her hands, and shaking her legs as though she was an athlete on the starting block about to commence a race, making sure every muscle was ready to perform.

"I'm not falling for your rubbish again. You don't exist. You're not really there," I declared, closing my eyes and shaking my head, trying to rid my mind of this figure which stood before me. But, as my eyes reopened, the figure sat cross-legged on the corner of the bath with a self-satisfied smile plastered on her perfect, beatific face.

"Oh, cynical now? I remember when you were soooo optimistic. This certainly is serious. They were right, you do need sorting out. Anyway, if I'm not real, then why are you talking to me?" she replied, in a blasé fashion.

I couldn't answer that, but I continued to dispute. "If you existed, you wouldn't have let me go through these last couple of months. You wouldn't have let me sink to these depths of despair."

"God wanted you to work your own way out."

"I'm beginning to think God doesn't exist either, if he did he'd pop down from wherever he is and see me. If he existed, he'd make sure he was seen. I've never seen him. Why can't I see him?"

"Oh, come on, Orlagh, you know better than that. You know he sends his messengers. And don't try the, 'if I can't see it, it doesn't exist' line with me." I'd never encountered an angel as direct before. She continued; "You've never viewed your thoughts, but they exist. You can't see your dreams, but they exist... don't they?"

"I suppose, but I've given up dreaming, what's the use? I've begged him to help me with the Emmet situation, and he hasn't. He's sat back in his big old chair in the sky and smugly watched me go out of my mind."

"He's not a genie, Orlagh. You can't just rub a lamp to make Him appear ready to grant you your every wish and respond to your every whim. He's set out guide-lines. As we've informed you before, time brings everything. Patience and laughter, that's the key.. patience and laughter. I haven't seen much laughter from you of late.

"Anyway, God didn't just observe you and watch you suffer. You are a Chosen One, receiving unique concessions and thus, you were called to Him; not by a lowly archangel like me, but by the highest order of angel... *the seraphim*. Although you keep ignoring their invitation. So, I've been sent to your aid today because you seem to have no trouble with my kind. It appears you are not strong or wise enough yet to accept the seraphim's Godly-invitation."

"No one has invited me anywhere. What're you talking about?"

"All I can say is, because the seraphim are the closest

beings to God, they appear to humans in a formidable-looking way... it's their disguise to get past the real demons. It is only the wise and righteous who can differentiate between the seraphim and the demons."

"Seraphim, what are you talking about? Why are you here? To talk to me in riddles and rhymes, I presume. Puzzles and pointless poems which I can't comprehend."

"We can't tell you everything, Orlagh; you have to work things out for yourself. You'll understand when you want to; subconsciously you have before. We're just the signposts to guide you in the right direction on the journey to discover your destiny. We can't buy your tickets and place you on the vehicle which will lead you there. That would be too easy."

"Are you going to guide me to the ticket office which specialises in trips to the land of laughter? How can I laugh when all I think about is sticking my fingers down my throat?"

"This, my child," she remarked, with concern burrowed deep within the contours of her angelic beauty, pointing to the contents of my stomach which lay in the toilet bowl, before she pressed the flush handle down slowly. "This was what I was coming to. Orlagh, why are you doing this? Surely you have been through enough not to let something as superficial as your own misconception of your appearance get you down. Don't be a prisoner of your own image. Favour is deceitful, and beauty is vain; but a woman that feareth the Lord, she shall be praised. Give her of the fruit of her hands; and let her own works praise her in the gates... I shouldn't, but I will translate this one message for you, so you can understand, because you *must* understand... It is simple... The woman who is wise - she is the one to praise."

"Maybe so, but is it such a bad thing to want to look good?"

"No, no. But it mustn't be the most important issue in your life and you must go about it the right way."

"And what's that?"

470

"Oh, we both know you know the answer to that; you've practically been brought up in a gym around a healthy lifestyle. Orlagh, life is about sacrifice. God sacrificed his son. Jesus sacrificed himself for the people. A good mother sacrifices everything for her child. You must sacrifice the excess eating for a healthy life. You can't go on sticking your fingers down your throat. How are you supposed to do the job we ask of you when your mind is full of thoughts of food and then an urgency to vomit?

"You must also ascertain the correct interpretation of *good*. Remember... beauty is in the eye of the beholder, therefore you have to work out which beholder it is you are trying to look *good* for - for they may not agree with your own conception of *good*! *Good* for some is *bad* for others."

"Okay, I understand that. But what's this job of mine you talk about?"

"That's what I was getting to. Enough chit chat, we must get down to the important issues I've been sent here to relay to you. I only have so much time on earth, so I must proceed with my main assignment."

"Is this where all the riddles begin?"

The angel ignored my impudence and began with the words that would hopefully change my present pessimistic state of mind.

"Happy is the woman that findeth wisdom, and the woman that getteth understanding. For the merchandise of wisdom is better than the merchandise of silver, and the gain thereof than fine gold. Wisdom is more precious than rubies; and all the things thou can desire are *not* to be compared unto it. Wisdom is a tree of life to them that lay hold upon it; and happy is every one that retaineth wisdom. The Lord by wisdom hath founded the earth; by understanding hath he established the heavens. Orlagh, my child, let them not depart from thine eyes; keep sound wisdom and discretion. The holy and enlightened mind that knows all things have worth and knows no outcast humankind, may *serve* and *save*

471

the earth. A wise woman is strong; yes, a woman of knowledge increaseth strength.

"I must also reiterate the message I previously translated for you... the woman who is wise, she is the one to praise... Surely, Orlagh, these, as you put it... *riddles*, are not so hard to understand, are they?"

"You want me to be wise? And what am I to do with my wisdom?"

"That you will discover when you have attained it."

"How am I to go about becoming, *oh so wise?*"

"That, Orlagh, is for you to work out. As I've already said, I can only guide you to the ticket office which will sell you admission for the journey: not merely for laughter, but for an inspiring odyssey which will enable you to discover your destiny." Her wings once again commenced to flap noisily and on each blustery flutter her colour began to fade. "But, before I depart, I must instruct you about the first signpost... It is imperative you pass it. If you successfully pass, you'll be on the right road. If you do not, then you will be embarking on a fruitless mission, like a dog chasing its tail. Basically, you *must* comprehend the following message to continue on the road to destiny discovery."

I awaited this most important signpost which would guide me on my life-changing journey...

"Wisest is she who knows what she does not know," she uttered, as she pressed the silver flush handle on the toilet and dived into the clean water which spiralled around the perimeter of the basin. As the water disappeared; so too did she...

So much for the final life-changing instruction - the all-important signpost. I had heard this so many times I suppose I should try harder to discover its meaning.

chapter fifty-six

There were a thousand bewildering thoughts swirling around my mind, like the angel had disappeared while swirling around the toilet basin. It had taken me some time to pull myself together, remove myself from the seated position on the bathroom floor and place myself in the shower; which I took as cold as my body could endure in order to revitalise my mind and bring me back to my senses. Not back to the state of mind I had been in directly before the angel's apparition, but to when my mind contained clear, concise thoughts.

Was she my Portia? Had I been saved? As I lay on my patchwork quilt staring at the ceiling, I considered the possibility that maybe I had. I felt the tectonic plates in my mind had slid against each other. The stress on my fault-line had finally been released, destroying the whole crop of the seeds of despair which had been planted in every available crevice in my brain.

I felt I had been liberated from a room I had been wandering around for a couple of months. I had entered that room to collect an item, but I had forgotten what that item actually was. I had then become trapped and had not bothered to retrace my footsteps for the purpose of jogging my memory, to discover what it actually was I had entered for. But the angelic apparition had given my memory that nudge. I realised I hadn't searched every nook and cranny of my subconscious. I hadn't bothered trying to look in that locked box full of infinite knowledge; it had to be thrown in front of my eyes once again, where clues trickled out.

It was with that angelic nudge and those clues that I then began to attempt to understand the directions the angel had given me. The first and, as the angel had said, most significant signpost, which had been relayed to me so many times I had happily dismissed it, was the one I had to pass first: *Wisest is she who knows what she does not know*. I had always considered this to be a paradox. However many times I said it, each word of the statement contradicted itself. My interpretation of this repeated instruction was that if you knew what you didn't know - then you knew it. It was a pointless proverb: an annoying angelic adage. Although, as I lay seriously contemplating all my angelic teachings, my mist of confusion began to lift and the correct interpretation of this saying, which had eluded me for so long, shone through so bright it was blindingly obvious.

"I understand... Come back," I whispered as loud as I possibly could, hoping the angel who had disappeared down the toilet would reappear. "I finally understand it! I hope you can hear me. I hope you'll come back and tell me if I'm right. I'm just going to go ahead and explain; I know you're listening somewhere. *Wisest is she who knows what she does not know*... Well, what do I know? Not just think I know, but categorically know...? I realise that I don't really know much at all. Nothing that's worthy of counting or boasting about... *That's it*, isn't it? That's the simple explanation of this riddle. That's the clarification of my confusion. I know that I really know *nothing*, but I also know that I want to know as much as possible about every subject imaginable. I can go on pretending I know lots of things, not listen to anyone, be a know-all going around with my own delusional interpretation of being wise; when really what I do know is insignificant in comparison to what there is to learn. Please tell me that's it. You

474

wanted me to realise that if I admit I don't know everything, then I will try to discover what I don't know. Am I right?" The realisation of this simple instruction made my heart race and caused my mind to go into overdrive. I was one step closer to knowing what my job was. One step closer to discovering my destiny.

The bedroom window was closed, but the curtains moved as though a strong breeze was pushing them. "Are you there? Have you come to tell me what my job is?" Nothing appeared.

I then began to contemplate whether I could attain all the knowledge I desired while working in a bank in Birmingham - I doubted it. I presumed I could learn a certain amount from books, but I wanted to experience the university Dad had attended... I needed to obtain knowledge in the university of the world. I didn't just want to do a part-time course either; I wanted to complete the entire course. I desired to meet fascinating people, just as Dad had on his travels. I wanted to drive across America in a pink Cadillac and maybe look up biga da lika Rosa with the biga da lika da watermelons in Chattanooga. I needed to revisit the city of the angels, where I had conversed for the very first time with my angels. Maybe while there I would encounter another significant signpost. I wished to visit Doctor Sudki's Egyptian pyramids. I wanted to travel to Luxor and experience its scorching sun before entering the coolness of Tutankharmen's tomb, where I could view the limestone walls which had been covered with paintings of Cleopatra-looking ladies. I wanted to experience Angelica's Africa too and hear the tribal languages which she said rolled off tongues like sweet music. To trace her track to India where the Calcutta humidity clings to the bodies of the sick in Mother Teresa's leper colony. I wanted to smell the spices she said were piled along the sides of the dusty roads. To continue on to Australia and view the white sails of the Sydney Opera House and feel the fresh sea breeze blowing into the harbour from the Tasman Sea. I wanted to see Che's

Argentina, Fidel's Cuba. I wanted to find Father Maguire, wherever his missionary work had taken him. I wanted to visit Sean Kennedy in his new American home and check that he wasn't consuming too many Buds too quick.

As we would circumnavigate the globe in a game of dinner-table pursuit, I wanted to do it in person; to feel the spirit of the people, learn their politics and embrace cultures. I wanted to follow in the fairytale footsteps of Freddie The Friendly Farting Giant and create my very own fairytale life.

I continued to speak to the fluttering curtains. "I know what I'm going to do in an attempt to attain as much knowledge as possible, I've worked it out - I'm going on a wisdom-seeking journey around the world. I'm not going to let that dreaded banking bubble suck me into its mundane monotony because my desire to dream has returned. Thank you for making me realise. This is what you've been guiding me towards every day of my life, isn't it? Through every message you angels have ever given me. You obviously wanted me to seek wisdom. Oh, I understand now. *Wisest is she who knows what she does not know.* You couldn't just make me do it. I had to realise for myself that I was ignorant. How has this taken me so long to understand? The sooner I become wise, the sooner I will discover what job I have been chosen by God to do. Am I right? But there are still things I can't quite comprehend: You said that God didn't just observe me and watch me suffer. You said I'm a Chosen One, receiving unique concessions and that I was called to Him by the highest order of angel... the seraphim. I don't understand; no angel has invited me anywhere."

Suddenly the angel's added comment was pushed to the forefront of my mind.

'Because the seraphim are the closest beings to God they appear to humans in a formidable-looking way. It is their disguise past the real demons; but it is only the wise and righteous who can differentiate between the seraphim and the demons.'

476

"Is the seraphim the shadow-like thing that appears in the night begging me to discover with it? Swinging its key and laughing its haunting laugh? Please tell me. Should I go with it to see? But what if I've misunderstood? What if it is, as I've always thought - a demon..?"

No answers came from my curtains or from angels in opaque balls. A bumblebee didn't buzz through my mind with an angel on its back showering me with solutions. There was no laughing leprechaun angel at the ready with clarity. There were no chicken-leg-eating chubby cherubs to answer my questions. I jumped out of bed, opened my bottom drawer of happy memories and shook my childhood nightdresses. No angel appeared from dust particles to answer my questions either. I suppose I would merely have to wait for wisdom to open my eyes.

I was awake most of the night contemplating my freshly deciphered divine instruction, when I stumbled upon another important revelation. I realised I had been foolishly mistaken when I had concluded that I knew nothing of any relevance. There was something I knew which weighed so heavy in the balancing scales of my happiness that presently it psychologically affected every day of my life. I knew, not just thought I knew, but unequivocally knew - that I loved Emmet, and needed him in my life. If I couldn't have him romantically - as I undoubtedly desired - I would settle for his friendship.

It was imperative I discover a creditable excuse to go and visit Emmet. Maybe I could talk him into accompanying me on my wisdom-seeking pilgrimage. It's not very often people meet their soulmate, but I had met mine... I was convinced I had. I missed him drastically. As they say; absence makes the heart grow fonder. But, there again, I didn't really go along with idiotic sayings, because if I did, I would then have to agree with 'familiarity breeds contempt' and I couldn't foresee a time when I would feel contempt for over-exposure to Emmet O'Malley.

chapter fifty-seven

I had no problem getting out of bed on the morning after the night I had deciphered my angelic instructions. I started the day by eating a nourishing healthy breakfast: not overly buttered toast and biscuits, but musili and orange juice. It wasn't just the fact that I was eating healthily either, but that I was eating without the thought lingering in the back of my mind, gnawing away at my brain cells every time I swallowed, of imminently going to the bathroom to make myself sick. I was determined that the red needle on the scales was not going to rule my life. That needle was such a thin line, but it had held so much significance in my existence: literally the thin line between love and hate, between a good and a bad day. A high on the scales meant a low in my day, or a low on the swirling dial meant a high. Not any more, because I was bursting with optimism. Now my ideas were the only things which were gaining weight and they were getting big, fat and satisfying. You see, I had come up with a great excuse to visit Emmet... That was if my day went as planned.

As Dad entered the kitchen, he immediately burst into song and simultaneously pulled me out of the farm-house chair and commenced a jive around the kitchen cabinets. "She was just seven-*teen*, you know what I *mean*, the way she looked was way beyond compare.

Ohhhhh, how could I dance with another, *owwww*, when I *saawww* my Orlaghhhh staaaan-ding there. Bop bop. Bop bop."

"Okay, enough dancing, Dad."

"But it's not everyday my baby girl's seventeen." And once again he broke into song, as I sat down and attempted to finish my breakfast, while opening the pile of cards and presents laid out on the table.

"You might've noticed," Mammy voiced as she entered the room yawning, " that there isn't a present off us in that little pile."

"No I didn't actually, although there sounds like a *but* coming."

"Yes, there is... *But*, you're going to receive it later on this afternoon."

"Okay, thanks." I wasn't interested in the late-arriving gift. I had more important issues on my mind. "Errmmm, if I pass today can I borrow the car or van for an hour or so tonight?" I requested, as quickly as the words could escape my mouth.

"We'll see," they both said concurrently, with smirks they thought I couldn't detect almost breaking through; which made me consider whether they were just being condescending, or whether they had another agenda.

"You look very relaxed this morning, especially considering you've got your test in a couple of hours."

"Well, Mammy, if I pass I pass, if I don't I suppose there's always a next time."

"Well said, baby doll. That's the attitude you need," Dad added, then grabbed Mammy to jive with around the cabinets. Her dressing gown flew behind her as she gave in to the early morning bop.

I laughed as I watched them and thought how very lucky I really was. I once again was beginning to appreciate the important things in life.

The truth was, I desperately wanted to pass. There couldn't be a *next time* because I had plans to remember another

479

important factor in my life. That was the excuse I needed - that was my key. I had it all planned out in my mind. That was why I needed the car, or the van. I intended to drive to Emmet's house alone and show him the accomplishment I had achieved. I thought my birthday would be a perfect time to give in. On which terms? His, of course. I had decided I couldn't be without his friendship any longer... I only hoped he felt the same way.

My driving test adjudicator - the would-be wish granter - was a skinny man in an over-sized, tattered tweed jacket that had worn suede patches on the elbows. What little hair he had was thick with grease, but he had grown it long enough to brush over his shining scalp. Under the bitten fingernails he tapped with impatience on the ply-wood clipboard was a film of grime. But in his scuffed, unpolished shoes he walked with an air of pompousness.

I was convinced he hated me immediately, especially when he contemptuously informed Dad, who was waiting with me until the examiner arrived, that it wasn't a family outing and that he should leave instantly.

I could see my master plan going in the same direction the angel had the previous evening - yes, down the toilet; and when I spotted Dad in the rear-view mirror driving behind me halfway through the test, waving and sticking up his thumb, I considered the flush had been pressed down hard and my hopes of driving to Emmet's to show him my achievement sat stinking in the sewer of unaccomplished dreams.

For the remainder of the test I was petrified to look in the rear-view mirror, just in case the examiner followed my gaze and viewed Dad's sparkling blue eyes and mischievous smile reflecting back at him.

"Pull over in front of that blue Mini-Metro." The examiner pointed to the blue Metro which I knew I had driven too close to as I obeyed his command. This would probably be the deciding factor for him to fail me, I considered.

When I viewed Dad's Ford Escort manoeuvring into the small space in front of the Metro and behind the examining vehicle, and witnessed the examiner looking into his own rear-view mirror with a look of confusion on his face - probably wondering why a motorist preferred to squeeze into that cramped gap when the rest of the road remained free - I strangely felt no apprehension that he would discover it was Dad. Because I assumed my failing fate had already been decided. Thus, I unenthusiatically answered the Highway Code questions he asked, while he continually looked from his picture cards to his mirror, with Dad's face reflecting back.

He completed the Highway Code questions sooner than I anticipated. While he rustled his paperwork and placed his picture cards in the glovebox, I watched Dad in the oblong rear-view mirror continuously rub his forehead with his fingertips, probably so his hand and forearm would hopefully conceal his identity, and I thought how his senseless stunt had put me off my driving and had spoilt the only relevant excuse I had for visiting Emmet today.

The examiner then startled me out of my contemplation. "Do you consider you made any mistakes during the test?"

"Well, I know I definitely drove too close to that Metro."

"Anything else?"

"Errrmm, nothing that springs to mind, sorry," I declared, with an impassive shoulder shrug.

"There was something significant; you didn't use your rear-view mirror enough." I knew it, Dad had gone way too far this time. The examiner then continued with what I considered to be the failing speech. "But apart from that and the mistake which you acknowledged, everything was in compliance with my strict testing regulations, and I'm pleased to inform you that you've passed."

I was arrested by the emotion of euphoria. My arms had been seized behind my back and the handcuffs locked. I

481

was paralysed by the power of pleasure; that was until I reached over to the examiner and hugged his musty-smelling torso. I sensed his embarrassment and hastily resumed my driving-seat position.

While the examiner filled in the requisite forms on his ply-wood clipboard, I attempted to signal Dad - to no triumphant avail, due to the continual irritation he appeared to have on his forehead which resulted in his eyes being obscured. So my mind wandered to the auspicious application of my driving-to-Emmet plan. There was one final hurdle to overcome... getting a vehicle.

With his clammy hand the examiner bid me a formal goodbye. I contemplated another hug, until recollection of his unwelcoming malodour registered in my brain. I proceeded to Dad's car and as I opened the passenger door I caught a final view of the examiner slowly shaking his head, probably due to the realisation as to who had been tailing him for most of the test.

Feigning anger I slumped into the car seat and irately stated, "Dad, what were you thinking, following me on my driving test? You put me right off."

"Yer didn't look put off, princess. You drove better than most of the people on the road. He didn't fail yer now, did he?" The sun which glistened over the turquoise tropical-sea blue eyes slipped behind a cloud of anguish.

It was difficult pretending to be angry when I saw his despondent eyes and when I felt so much elation. I had planned on informing him that due to his foolishness I'd failed, but my vocal cords rejected my animosity and I screeched; "NO, I PASSED!"

After he had plastered my face with an array of moist kisses, we began the short journey from the testing centre to our home. I needed to ask Dad about obtaining one of their vehicles before we arrived home. I had more chance of influencing his decision than I did Mammy's.

"So, can I have the car tonight then, Dad?" I had scenes of driving to Emmet's house floating through my mind, and of seeing that blackbird flying through those paradise sky-blue eyes, which hopefully wouldn't peck away at my heart.

"No. I think you need a bit more experience before you have this on yer own."

"But, Dad..."

"No buts, Orlagh. I said *no!*"

Appeal denied. He was never that harsh, there was usually some room for negotiation, but apparently not in this instance. I had stumbled over that final hurdle, unable to drag myself to my feet and reach the ribbon stretched across the finishing line. We drove the rest of the way in perturbed silence. So much for my euphoria. So much for my master plan. There were too many flaws I just hadn't considered. It appeared my life was a continual roller-coaster of ups and downs.

We passed the concrete lions on their pillars as we entered the driveway, which stood as silent as Dad and myself. As I sat sulking, I was entirely unaware that the next manoeuvre in my roller-coaster life was about to occur. It wasn't merely a mediocre up or a down, but a giddy loop-the-loop of exhilaration.

In the centre of the driveway sat a red Austin Mini, with a gargantuan golden bow swamping its four sides.

"We thought ye could gain a little experience in this first. Happy birthday and congratulations, baby doll."

The three images of wads of cash on the rotating dials on the slot-machine of life had lined themselves up - and stopped... I'd hit the jackpot, with the prize of rapture flowing.

I hugged Dad. I jumped out of the car and hugged Mammy, who had emerged from the house upon our arrival.

"I take it you passed then?"

"I did. Thanks for this, Mammy... It's unreal."

"Well, we did it for the boys, although it was for their eighteenth, which this is also: a joint seventeenth and eighteenth present. It's taxed, M.O.T-ed and insured for the year too, then you're on your own."

With my wisdom-seeking world trip I planned to be well and truly 'on my own' by that time.

My plan of the day was back on track. I had dragged myself to my feet and was making my way to that finishing line. But by the time I could begin to institute the plan which I had at first believed was fantastic - I began having second thoughts. I'd had all afternoon to contemplate an embarrassing rejection. There were too many 'should or shouldn't I's' crashing around in my brain, when I decided - what the hell. What did I have to lose? A bit of self-respect in the eyes of Emmet? Well, if he did snub me, I wouldn't have to worry about what he thought anyway.

So, I got in my new car... *my very own car...* and began the journey to regain a part of my life I so desperately missed.

I competently drove out of the driveway, along Summerfield Road, past the over-grown grass on the common land, when I had to stop behind a convoy of traffic which was gridlocked while awaiting exit at the approaching T-junction. I then heard an urgent beeping from another vehicle's horn. It sounded dangerously close. The first thought to enter my nervous mind was - was I doing something wrong? I soon decided I wasn't; it must be directed at someone else. But the honking didn't cease.

When I ascertained the identity of the person responsible for the horn honking my heart almost leapt out from under my skin, while my healthy breakfast somersaulted its way closer to my mouth and every nerve in my body seemed to have been activated. My brain was a mixture of bewilderment and elation when my eyes took in the sight of Emmet frantically waving at me from a van I hadn't seen before. He was driving in the direction I had just come from. He pointed to the private, almost unused road which cut through the common land, and screeched out of his rolled down window: "PULL OVER."

How was I going to greet him? Should I tell him that I was in fact on my way to his house? Were my angels at work once again? I knew there was no such thing as a coincidence... everything happens for a reason. So what was the reason for this chance encounter? I was about to find out, as Emmet's green van pulled up behind my car. That was when I completely lost the function of thought; my mind had once again packed itself a wicker hamper, plastic cutlery, paper plates, its chequered cloth and had wandered off on a feast of a picnic.

I was feeling a mixture of emotions; agitation, excitement, embarrassment, and then one of overwhelming passion as I witnessed the contours of his toned muscles sensually moving under the fabric of his designer clothes as he slowly sauntered towards me. As I viewed his chiselled cheekbones and strong jawbone and of course those paradise sky-blue eyes, I began to tremble as if I was meeting him for the very first time. His face exhibited a look of concern, combined with an uncertain smile, which caused his terracotta lips to stretch and exhibit the perfection of his immaculate tombstone teeth, as he made his way towards where I was now leaning against the driver's door of my new car.

"What the hell's going on? Are yer on another emergency getaway mission or something?" he asked, with caring urgency, which created a torrid warmth in my stomach.

"No, nothing as exciting as that. I passed my test today."

"Ach, grand, that's wonderful news, so it is. Congratulations, angel face." How I'd missed his pet names spoken in his distinctive soft Irish tones. "So, where're you off to?"

Should I tell him? Trepidation hit me once again. I couldn't think of a suitable excuse. I was uncharacteristically flummoxed and lost for words, "Urrmm, to see, errr..."

"Come on, spit it out. Got yerself a new boyfriend have yer?" I sensed hurt and a little animosity reverberating in his question, or maybe that was just my own wishful thinking playing tricks with my ears.

"No, I haven't. I was well, going to, well... to see you actually."

"Oh, that's good, 'cause that's where I was off to as well ... Not to see me like... to see you. Yer didn't think I'd forget, did ye? Happy birthday, princess." Now I was convinced my ears were playing the most mammoth of magical pranks. "Is it that much of a surprise that me remembering yer birthday leaves yer speechless?"

"I suppose it is a surprise, yeah. Were you, urmm, really on your way to see me? Does this mean, you know, erm, urrr?" I had so many awkward questions to ask, ones which in Emmet's eyes might render me absurd. I didn't know whether I was jumping to ridiculous conclusions, so everything I said transformed into one big jumble of hesitant urr's and erm's. "But, erm, what about what I said in my stupid letter? You know about, erm. You know, urr, if I can't have you one hundred percent?" I eventually asked, after begging the words to flow forth. I was cringing and almost dying inside, wanting to cover my face with shame at the thought of what I had just asked. While at the same time I also felt exorbitant amounts of euphoria mixed with hysteria; curious as to what his reply might be.

"It wasn't a stupid letter at all, Orlagh. It shows you stand by what you believe is right. But it's just taken me a little time to understand that. To come to me senses like - way too much time. I've really missed you, angel."

I stood open-mouthed at the foot of that slot-machine of life, like an old lady with her paper cup of quarters in a Las Vegas casino. Because, for the second time in one day the jackpot had lined itself up and landed in my path and I was catching copious amounts of the quarters of happiness, adding up to a million dollars of delight.

Emmet didn't allow me to reply; he just continued with his speech. "Everything you said in yer letter was right. I was taking you for granted and I was an eejit. Where else would I find someone like you? One of the lads, but a strong-willed beautiful lady with it? I would love yer to have me one-hundred percent, but things aren't going to be as plain sailing as that, Orlagh. Yer see, there are going to be a few major changes occurring in me own life that may well complicate things." I knew things were going too well. "You see, I was thinking about going back to Ireland." The final quarter rolled and the echoing metallic sound reverberated in my brain. Should I be happy with my win, or sad at how much it added up to? He continued: "But then I decided there was too much to do in life to settle down in one place. I'm not going to fulfil my dreams in Derry, or Birmingham for that matter. I want to look back in fifty years and be able to regret things that I *have* done, not what I haven't. I don't want to talk about going to all these amazing places in the world and never get around to it. There's so much out there to learn and experience, so I've decided on a trip around the world." He then gripped my waist with his strong hands, lifted me up and sat me on the bonnet of my new car and concluded, "And if you play your cards right, Miss Emmet, you may just be able to come along with me."

Play my cards right? I wasn't merely going to play - I was going to win. I intended to attain the royal flush in poker, to reach twenty-one with two cards in blackjack and be the first to rid myself of cards in rummy. I would count cards, cheat, basically be the ultimate card shark, ensnaring the prize in my strong jagged jaws, unprepared to release it.

I thought how astounding it was that he had at the same time as myself made an identical decision to go on a world trip. I had been nudged into this line of thinking by the angels... had he?

"You didn't get a visit last night by any chance, did you?" I asked, not giving away too much. If he had been visited by the angels he would certainly know what I was talking about.

"What're yer babbling about, Orle? I'm glad to see yer still talking in riddles. So, what were you coming to see me for anyway?" His cheeky smile made his dimples deep and enticing.

"Oh, about the same reason you were coming to see me."

"See what I mean... more riddles," he stated, while softly placing mini moist pecks across my entire face.

Little did he know that after I had ascertained the precise nature of our relationship, I too was going to inform him of *my* planned wisdom-seeking trip. I didn't want to confuse matters now, so I went along with his riddle interpretation and produced a playful smile followed by a mysterious wink.

"And do you know what else I've noticed about you, Orlagh Emmet?"

"Go on tell me, I'm in suspenders here," I bantered back, as though we hadn't been apart for two months.

"You're looking way too skinny. So, let's go and feed yer up and go for a big slap-up birthday meal, get yer lookin' like yer old self again."

I assumed I had just ascertained *my* beholder's interpretation of *good*.

"Oh, and do you know what else, Orle?"

What now? Had he forgotten some unwelcome piece of information which would obliterate my rapidly ripening plans? "What?" I asked, a little anxious.

"In eighteen-o-three we sailed out to sea," he began to sing. My melancholy lifted and I awaited my gap-filling job. "Out from the sweet town of..."

"Derry," I bellowed, with gap-filling joy!

"For Australia bound, if we didn't all drown, the marks of our shackles we carried. In our rusty iron chains we sighed for our weans, our good wives we left in...."

"Sorrow."

"As the mainsails unfurled our curses we hurled, on the English and thoughts of..."

"Tomorrow."

"Ohhhh, oh, oh, oh, oh, ohhhhhh, I wish I was back home in Derrrrryyyy. Ohhhh, oh, oh, oh, oh, ohhhhh, I wish I was back home in..."

Instead of filling in the desired gap, I asked, "Do you, Emmet?"

"Do I what?"

"Wish you were back home in Derry?"

"Orlagh, I only wish I may be wherever you are. Whether it be Derry, Birmingham or Timbuktu."

I went crashing through the finishing line of rhapsody in record time with the ribbon wrapped around me as I commenced my joyous lap of honour.

chapter fifty-eight

What a difference a day makes. In the space of twenty-four little hours the course my life had been taking was completely diverted. I had speedily swerved off the avenue of despair to perform a life-metamorphosing three-sixty manoeuvre. The screeching tyres were sweet music and the burning rubber aromatic pleasure. I then positioned myself to speed down the highway of happiness, breaking the speed limit, heading in the direction of destiny discovery. I'd successfully passed the first signpost, picked up my desired passenger and was looking forward to the next angelic symbol.

I jumped high on life's spring diving board, plummeting head first into my old routine with ease; the boxing gym, raving, Sunday cinema; only this time there was a major difference with my dive - I considered I had created a substantial splash, due to the added weight of Emmet O'Malley. Although none of the spectators seemed to observe the added white spray splashing in all directions. Maybe it was because they had always witnessed it? I don't know what I had been expecting when Emmet and I made our relationship known: a fanfare? fireworks?... Something, *anything*. I think Emmet did too. I don't know who the two of us thought we had been fooling; quite obviously it was just ourselves. The lack of trumpets, bugles, and gunpowder was replaced with sarcastic or suppressed smiles and silent *I-knew-it* facial expressions.

I didn't just dive into the old routine either - I performed new tricks along the way. Dressing like an eighteenth-century maid, wearing a starched, white-lace cap and apron, I somersaulted into silver-service waitressing six evenings a week - at Abbey Hall of all places, with its princess turrets, mist off the moat and memories of lingering first kisses with Emmet on a cold December evening; which I would re-enact each night after I had finished work, when Emmet and I would meet and continue with as much of a social life as was possible, while working all the possible hours we could. On a couple of evenings a month, Emmet and the rest of the Birmingham Irish boxers would join me at Abbey Hall when the boxing shows were held, put on for the righto-boyo, finger twiddling men's clubs. I would be working the banquet, the boys working the ring.

On the first evening I worked a boxing show I heard the tuxedo toffs on my table placing bets on boys I knew didn't have a chance of winning. When I offered them valuable inside information I was faced with glares of disdain, which I interpreted as, 'don't disturb us, woman, just get back to the kitchen where you belong.' That was until all my pugilistic predictions proved correct and they had squandered all their money on lost causes. The next month they came searching for me, offering me a percentage of their win for my expert inside knowledge on the boxers. I negotiated commission and soon had a lucrative little side-line running.

I also worked weekends in Mammy's sister's bar, where the clientele were, well - Irish: Irish who knew Grandpa. Irish who knew Dad. Irish who knew Emmet, Dominic and Patrick. Off-the-boat Irish. Forty years-settled Irish. First, second and third generation Irish. Half Irish. Quarter Irish. Even the, not-a-trace-of-Irish but when in Aunt Shona's bar transfigured into fully fledged ancestors of the Emerald Isle. Thus, being a young Emmet behind the bar (too young to be there actually, but

Shona wasn't concerned about that) my tip jar was filled as fast as the pint glasses.

Being at work all the time didn't mean I wasn't having fun. On a Saturday and Sunday afternoon Shona employed Dave The Rave, an Irish folk singer who sang all the songs I knew and ones I didn't. I soon got to know them all after I'd heard them every weekend for ten months. I joined in the singing while pouring creamy smooth pints of Guinness. The ritual of the week, when all conversations ceased and every voice in the pub transformed to song, was when Francis pumped the bellows of his ancient accordion, releasing the opening chords, and Dave The Rave's hoary head bobbed from side to side with the beat of the music, as he uttered the first line of everyone's favourite song;

"There was a girl from I-er-land in 1964."

Everyone in the pub joined in;

She was all alone and lonely
like she's never been before.
She met a man from Pakistan,
They were married just like that.
And then when I came along, they christened
*   meeeee...*
Pakistani Pat.

When the chorus arrived, the volume increased:

Fair-dy well it is killin'
Fair-dy well for a while.
Proud I am of Pakistan,
And of the Emerald Isle.
I was born in Birmingham,
Now there's nothing wrong with that.
Until you tell 'em that your name, isssss...
Pakistani Pat.

Me father he's a Muslim,
And mother, she's RC
I've got Mohammed for me breakfast,
And Saint Patrick for me tea.
Father loves chapatti, me mother Irish stew.
If it wasn't for the fish and chips,
I don't know what I'd do.

Fair-dy well it is killin'
Fair-dy well for a while.
Proud I am of Pakistan,
And of the Emerald Isle.
I was born in Birmingham,
Now there's nothing wrong with that.
Until you tell 'em that your name, isssss...
Pakistani Pat.

Not a day or week goes by,
When he dreams of a plan.
Of how he'd make a fortune
And return to Pakistan.
Mother said, we'll let him go,
We won't stand in-between,
'Cos I know she'd love to pack her bags,
And head for Skibereen.

The final chorus was repeated over and again and each week no one tired of hearing it - myself included.

It was a far cry from the seriousness and sobriety of the bank, where I plodded along in the humdrum atmosphere. I couldn't change being there for the moment. I needed the money, so I merely modified my perception of the place. I told myself every day when I woke up to put on my suit that it would all be worth it, that it wouldn't be long until I would be leaving.

I had to work all the hours possible. I did if we were sticking to our plan. It wasn't as if the angels had come along and said, 'Here you go, Orlagh. Here you are, Emmet. Here's a few thousand pounds to start you off on a life-changing journey around the world. Go and enjoy yourselves.'

"I can't believe my baby doll's leavin' me to go around the world with that eejit of a man, Emmet O'Malley. Do yer think we should let her go, Grania?"

"Well, Rory, I think it's a bit late for that. They've just picked up the tickets and she handed her notice in at the bank today, didn't yer, Orlagh? Tell yer da' what that moron of a bank manager said."

"I gave him the two weeks' notice, Dad, and he was in total and utter shock. He said in his pompous accent, 'You do know you're making the biggest mistake of your life leaving a promising career in the bank to gallivant around the world like a hippie. I always knew that you were a total loser. I can't understand why the bank employ people like you in the first place.'"

"Yer jokin'? And what did yer say to the eejit?"

"I said, 'You know what? You're totally demented. But I wish you all the luck in the world as you slog your guts out for the next thirty years of your pitiful life working for an establishment who regard you as a mere number; while I experience things you will only ever read about in your broadsheet Sunday supplements or watch on television.' Dad, I've never seen the pompous idiot looking so deflated; he left the office looking as though his world had come crashing down around him."

"That's me girl, that'll teach him. Listen, I'm tied up on that big job I've got and can't get away for your last treatment tomorrow."

"You never told me, Rory? You've never in her life missed one of her appointments. Why now?"

"I know, I'm sorry, but the job's too far behind. There's just no way I can leave the lads; things just won't get done, I know it. Orlagh doesn't mind, do yer, baby doll?"

"No, of course not."

"But I do. I can't go into that operating theatre with her, you know that. She can't go in on her own. What'll we do?"

"I'm sure Emmet will come, Mammy. Don't worry."

"Come where?"

"Jesus, talk about an eejit and one appears. How are yer, Emmet, son?"

"Why, were yer talkin' about yerself there, Rory? What're yer on about, Orlagh? Where do you want me to go?"

"To the hospital tomorrow for my laser treatment. Dad can't get there and Mammy's convinced I need someone in the operating theatre with me."

"Of course I'll go. Anything for my princess."

"Ach, Jesus, Rory, will you listen to the love birds. I wonder if you'll still feel like that when you're around each other every minute of everyday with no escape."

I was convinced we would.

chapter fifty-nine

I felt overwhelming contentment as I sat in the waiting room of the hospital, holding Emmet's hand, because another of my life-long dreams was being projected from the film reel in my mind on to the big screen of reality. A dream I had devised so long ago I could barely remember when. A simple dream of having a partner with me to hold my hand. And as I sat there, I looked at the reserved little girls awaiting their treatment and I wondered if they too were dreaming those same dreams I had. Even though I didn't know if they were or not, I felt a compelling passion to inspire them to chase all their dreams, to give them some of the precious guidance I had received over the years from my heavenly and earthly angels.

My thoughts then turned to Emmet himself, particularly to the issue of his notorious talkative disposition, or in this instance, lack of it. It became apparent that somewhere in-between my home and the hospital he had lost the function to talk. I couldn't bring up the issue of his lost tongue due to the fact that the waiting room was full of people with the same speechless condition. That wouldn't have been the reason why he was silent. Like Dad, Emmet didn't usually care if he was the only one talking. There was some other underlying issue occurring somewhere within Emmet's mind. I'd have to wait until we left to dig it up, clean off the dirt and address it.

"Orlagh Emmet, Doctor Delaney is ready for you now."

"Really? Already? That was quick," Emmet mumbled.

"No it wasn't quick, Emm, we've been here almost an hour. What's going on with you? You're losing your mind," I whispered as we made our way to the theatre.

Mammy took the chair outside the theatre door. In the silence you could almost hear her pain reactor purring like a mollycoddled cat.

"And how's my favourite patient doing?" Doctor Delaney greeted, with opened arms. His hair was a touch greyer and his skin a shade darker, both presumably due to his most recent life-saving mission in the depths of the Amazon rainforest.

"I bet you say that to all the girls, doctor," I jovially replied, as I lay down on the mint-green, tissue-covered bed. I introduced Emmet and answered the usual medical questions as Doctor Delaney scanned my file.

"What's this all about, Orlagh? On your record it tells me there is no need to book another appointment. Are you not happy with how wonderfully the treatment is progressing?"

"No, not at all, I'm delighted with the results. The test patch seems to have produced the best results so far, and all the consequent treatments appear to be working by the day. It's just that Emmet and I are going around the world for a while."

"Around the world, huh? All sounds very exotic. Tell me about it while I work. It might take your mind off the pain a little if you do that."

Emmet still hadn't spoken. It was an effort for him to thank Doctor Delaney when he was handed his goggles. It was so unlike him. I took one last look at him in his goggles which turned everything that Lucozade-cellophane shade of orange, before I placed on my own goggles, which sent me into the land of darkness. I could have done with viewing Emmet through his tan-enhancing goggles, because he desperately needed some

497

colour in his cheeks. Was he sick? Maybe that was his problem.

Emmet took my hand in his as Doctor Delaney commenced the treatment. The initial pulses caused the most pain. I didn't bother having any anaesthetic, because after so many punch-like pulses my face seemed to numb itself. I couldn't relay the itinerary of our trip until the numbing had occurred.

On each pulse my hand squeezed Emmet's, while my head sunk deep into the pillow as though that flash of light was a perfect right cross. It was peculiar for there to be silence in the theatre; by this time Dad had usually broken into a rendition of his chosen song.

Doctor Delaney perceived the point when I could tolerate the pain and encouraged me to divulge my destiny-discovery route. Through clenched teeth I began;

"We leave in three weeks, a few days after my eighteenth birthday. I won't bother giving you time scales in each place, because we don't really know ourselves yet. We're just going to play it day to day. The flights we have are flexible and we can change them along the way.

"Our first destination is New York City, from there we're going to make our way by land down to Florida, via all the most easterly states, then back up the east coast, trying not to retrace our route. We want to cover as many of the states as possible. We're going to head up to Toronto and stay with family friends for a while. From there we want to drive across America, incorporating the most interesting spots and then head up to my uncle who lives in Vancouver. We then plan on driving down the west coast of America and heading down Mexico-way. We hope to begin travelling through Central America from there, straight through to South America. I don't know which way we'll go, but we're going to attempt to circle the continent. We'll then have to buy a flight back up to the States, because the ticket we have wouldn't include South America. From Los Angeles we're flying to Hawaii, then

Tahiti, Fiji and the Cook Islands. Then to New Zealand and on to Australia. We shall need to replenish our savings by then and will find work for a little while before we fly into Asia, first stop Bali. We hope to travel through Indonesia, Malaysia, Thailand, Cambodia and Laos overland, before we fly from Bangkok to Hong Kong and once again go by land up to Beijing; where we have another flight booked to Delhi, and from there we plan on travelling around India."

"Oh my goodness!" Doctor Delaney exclaimed.

"I know, it's amazing, isn't it? In a way I can't wait until we've experienced everything."

I didn't obtain a response, and I could no longer feel the electrifying-like pulses of the laser. I felt a tugging on my hand before Emmet released it. I then heard a metallic crash. Although I couldn't see, I had a sneaking suspicion a commotion was occurring.

"Get an ice pack, quickly," Doctor Delaney shouted. Was something going wrong with my treatment?

I quickly pulled off my goggles. I experienced a sensation of disorientation from sitting up so fast, from resuming sudden sight and from the visualisation of the scene which was playing before my eyes. There lay Emmet on the floor, his head on the ample thighs of the kneeling nurse. The second nurse soon appeared in full flight, an ice pack in hand and Mammy hysterically in tow.

"Oh my God, what's happened? Orlagh, darling, are you okay?" As she entered the theatre and she too witnessed the scene, her hysteria metamorphosed into mystification. "Emmet?!"

Emmet couldn't answer her, because his blackbirds had taken full flight, migrating momentarily to the land I had been in before I had removed my goggles, presumably flying around disorientated, desperate to find an escape from the land of darkness.

The nurse slapped Emmet's face as Doctor Delaney took his pulse. It wasn't long before his eyes began to flicker.

He got to his feet, awash with embarrassment and uttered: "Do yer mind if I wait outside with yer ma'?"

"Of course not. I won't be long."

I assumed Emmet had been equipped with the identical pain-reacting engine as Mammy.

"You were somewhere in India, Orlagh!" Doctor Delaney humorously stated, as *I* once again became his patient.

"I reckon Emmet was too, running around in the Black Hole of Calcutta!"

"So, come on, is it home after India?"

"No, although Delhi to Kathmandu is the last flight on our ticket, except back to England. But there's still so much to see. We want to safari through Africa and then there's Europe too. But that's such a long way off, I'm sure it'll develop as time goes by."

"And how long do you plan on being away?"

"Oh, well we haven't really got a time scale, but at least a couple of years."

"I can foresee it being a little longer than that."

"Don't say that to my mammy, doctor. She's having palpitations at the thought of us going away for a year. My dad reckons we'll only last six months."

As I came to the end of the trip, Doctor Delaney came to the end of my treatment.

"No disrespect intended, but I think I can safely say Mr Emmet's mistaken. I can see you're set on some sort of mission which'll last a lot longer than six months. Oh, and by the way, make sure to look me up if you're in the Amazon basin at the same time as myself. We could do with a few volunteers."

"That's a deal, doctor. It will be my pay-back. I owe you so much. Thank you for everything."

"Your confidence is thanks enough, Orlagh. People like you make my job so worthwhile. Go on and see how *your* patient is doing."

I left the theatre to view the unusual sight of Emmet and Mammy sitting in silence.

"How are you, Emm?"

"Don't worry about me, you're the patient!"

I could see he was fine. Anxiety alleviated, I sarcastically stated: "Over a hundred boxing matches and you've never been down - I knew I'd be able to floor you eventually."

"Orlagh, princess, you floor me every day with your overwhelming beauty."

Mammy tut-tut-tutted her way into a smile.

"Seriously, what happened in there, Emm?"

"Well, I wasn't lookin' forward to the whole thing in the first place. I didn't like the thought of seein' you in pain. Then when the doctor started the whole procedure, you were squeezin' me hand dead tight. I was watchin' your poor wee cheek go as black as coal and it all made me go dizzy. As each little black bruise appeared I got dizzier and dizzier, and then the next thing I knew I was wakin' up with nurses and doctors around me; and you with a big grin on your face. I don't know how yer da' has watched yer go through that, and worse, for so long."

"But he doesn't really watch... not like you were. While he's holding my hand or tickling my feet, he's talking to the doctor, or singing a stupid song, diverting the attention from what's going on away from me and himself."

"Talkin' of yer da', don't tell the eejit, 'cause he'll milk it and I'll never live it down."

"I'll try not to," I replied, with raised eyebrows and a smile.

epilogue

The enormity of what we were embarking on didn't hit me until the final weekend before we were due to leave on our wisdom-seeking trip. Preoccupation with organising our expedition had manoeuvred my mind from being cornered by apprehension. Realisation slowly began to creep in when I was surrounded by the majority of people who had made an impact on my life. They surrounded me at a party to celebrate my coming of age, and to rejoice with us in the departure from our ordinary everyday existence.

I silently stood alone and viewed an array of people who in their own ways had added bricks to my towering wall. I watched as Mickey Duffy, in front of the DJ's flashing disco lights, dropped his trousers and yet again exhibited his posterior to all, with the rest of my beloved boxing brotherhood encouraging him. I moved on to the bewildered expression on Doctor Sudki's wrinkled face as he discovered pickled onions and a pork pie in the pockets of his sheepskin coat, and then to the childlike delight on the face of Jack-the-Fat-Dublin-timekeeper. I witnessed Siobhan sobbing on the shoulder of a man named Michael, who I for once agreed, 'was definitely the one'. I smiled as I heard Nanna Bridie talking to Angelica and Dad;

"I've done a bit of travellin' in me time." Nanna began. "She must've inherited this travellin' bug from me."

"No, Ma, she's goin' travellin' for fun and knowledge

and to broaden her horizons; not as an excuse to do a runner from her family."

"Ooo, sorry I spoke."

I expected I'd miss them all. Every last one of them... Even Nanna and her relentless rudeness.

It wasn't until I stood on the linoleum floor, in the enormous amplitude of the airport, that the realisation of our departure hit me - with dynamic intensity. It was the sight of Mammy's trembling jaw and the petrified look on her face, as though she would never see me again. When she dug her quivering fingernails into my forearms and told me she loved me more than life itself was when I fully comprehended I was actually fleeing her secure, loving nest. Dominic softly pulled her away and consolingly stroked her chestnut curls as she sobbed into his chest. Dad silently stepped forward and enclosed me within his powerful arms. He placed a lingering kiss on the crown of my head and squeezed me really tight, as though I was still his little girl. His silence said as much as Mammy's tears.

"Go and add some more bricks to that wall of yours, my golden princess," he whispered into my curls, before he walked away and gave solace to my weeping mother.

Dominic, Patrick, Emmet and myself all linked arms and held each other close.

"Look after her, Emm," they said in unison.

"We'll be looking after each other, hey, Orle?"

I was leaving my divine family - the one love of my life - to go off with the other.

"I'll make you all so proud," I shouted, as Emmet and I proceeded to the departure gate.

I sat on the Boeing 747 bound for New York City. The Big Apple being the first fruit to be picked from the tree of knowledge. After those goodbyes I was desperate to taste that apple, suck in the wisdom juice, lick my lips and savour the flavour.

While Emmet watched the hostess perform the emergency procedure, I gazed into his wide eyes and saw the blackbird fluttering in a sky more perfect than the one we were flying through. On the blackbird's wings flew the vivid images of my unborn children. Then, quite unexpectedly with a blink of his eye, that image of my unborn children had transformed into a tiny cherub which instantaneously departed his being, glided past my eyes, through the partly condensed window and joined a mass of angels who were all gliding gracefully through the skies, watching over me as we embarked on our wondrous, wisdom-seeking odyssey...

The End

There will be a sequel to Kissed By The Angels......

SEND YOUR FEEDBACK
AND REVIEWS TO:

Reviews@Kissedbytheangelsnovel.com

gLossary
of words and phrases and their derivation

Bogtrotter: an offensive term for an Irish person from the country, (backward)

Bollocks, bollix: hot ashes, used to express contempt or disagreement, or as an exclamation of annoyance (Gaelic: botharín, live ashes)

Celt: a native of any of the modern nations or regions in which Celtic languages are (or were until recently) spoken; a person of Irish, Scottish, Manx, Welsh or Cornish decent

Coddle: an Irish soup-like dish consisting mainly of potatoes and meat

Country bumpkin: an unsophisticated or socially awkward person from the countryside

Craic (krak): fun, also witty conversation (Gaelic)

Culchie: used as a derogatory term for an Irish country person, backward. An alteration of Kiltimagh (Irish Coillte Mach or culcheumnaich), the name of a town in County Mayo, Ireland

Earwig (ear-wigging): to overhear or eavesdrop (British slang)

Eejit: idiot (Irish)

Free Stater: a member of the Irish Free State (Republic of Ireland)

Orangeman: Protestant bigot, follower of King William of Orange

Orthodox: a right handed boxer who leads with his left hand

Redemptorist: an order of missionary priests in the Roman Catholic Church, founded by Saint Alphonsus Ligouri

Roadwork: athletic exercise or training involving running on roads

Slag: stony waste matter separated from metals during the smelting of refining ore. Used as a curse – a derogatory term for a promiscuous woman (equivalent U.S. term Slut)

Slapper: a derogatory term for a promiscuous or vulgar woman (British slang)

Southpaw: a left handed boxer who leads with the right hand

Stone: a British unit of weight equal to 14lb (6.35kg)